A
GREAT
AND
TERRIBLE
BEAUTY

A GREAT AND TERRIBLE BEAUTY

Libba Bray

SIMON AND SCHUSTER

SIMON AND SCHUSTER

First published in Great Britain in 2005 by Simon & Schuster UK Ltd.
A CBS COMPANY

This paperback edition first published in 2006

Originally published in the USA by Delacorte Press, an imprint
of Random House Children's Books, New York 2003.

Text copyright © 2003 Martha E. Bray
Jacket photograph copyright © 2003 by Michael Frost

3 5 7 9 10 8 6 4

Simon & Schuster UK Ltd
Africa House
64-78 Kingsway
London WC2B 6AH

A CIP catalogue record for this book is available from the British Library

ISBN-13: 978-0-6898-7535-9

Printed and bound in Great Britain by Cox & Wyman Ltd, Reading, Berks

www.simonsays.co.uk

For Barry and Josh

ACKNOWLEDGMENTS

This book couldn't have been written without the sage advice and welcome help of many people. I owe a huge debt of gratitude to the following:

The Trinity of Fabulousness: my agent, Barry Goldblatt; my editor, Wendy Loggia; and my publisher, Beverly Horowitz.

Emily Jacobs, for her invaluable input; and Barbara Perris, copy editor extraordinaire.

The tireless staffs of the British Library and the London Transport Museum, especially Suzanne Raynor.

Professor Sally Mitchell, Temple University, who gave me some great leads in my research, for which I am very much indebted. For anyone interested in the Victorian age, I strongly recommend her books, *The New Girl* and *Daily Life in Victorian England*.

The Victorian Web, Brown University.

The supportive writing communities of YAWriter and Manhattan Writers Coalition.

The generous, big-hearted Schrobsdorff family: Mary Ann, for the wonderful resources and actual Victorian clothes for study; Ingalisa, for the terrific author photo; and the ever-great Susanna, for cheering, baby-sitting, and correcting my terrible French.

Françoise Bui, for correcting even more of my terrible French.

Franny Billingsley, who read the first draft and gave me ten pages of in-depth insight.

Angela Johnson, for telling me to write the book I needed to write.

Laurie Allee, for helping me find the heart of it.

My friends and family, who cheered me on and excused me from returning phone calls, checking the expiration on the milk, and getting birthday cards in the mail on time because (sigh) "she's writing that book."

And especially Josh, for being so patient when Mommy had to finish "just one last thing."

There she weaves by night and day
A magic web with colours gay.
She has heard a whisper say,
A curse is on her if she stay
To look down to Camelot.
She knows not what the curse may be,
And so she weaveth steadily,
And little other care hath she,
The Lady of Shalott.

And moving through a mirror clear
That hangs before her all the year,
Shadows of the world appear.
There she sees the highway near
Winding down to Camelot . . .

       • • •

But in her web she still delights
To weave the mirror's magic sights,
For often through the silent nights
A funeral, with plumes and lights
And music, went to Camelot;
Or when the Moon was overhead,
Came two young lovers lately wed.
"I am half sick of shadows," said
The Lady of Shalott.

       • • •

And down the river's dim expanse
Like some bold seer in a trance,
Seeing all his own mischance—
With a glassy countenance
Did she look to Camelot.
And at the closing of the day
She loosed the chain, and down she lay;
The broad stream bore her far away,
The Lady of Shalott.

—from "The Lady of Shalott" by Alfred, Lord Tennyson

CHAPTER ONE

JUNE 21, 1895
Bombay, India

"PLEASE TELL ME THAT'S NOT GOING TO BE PART OF MY birthday dinner this evening."

I am staring into the hissing face of a cobra. A surprisingly pink tongue slithers in and out of a cruel mouth while an Indian man whose eyes are the blue of blindness inclines his head towards my mother and explains in Hindi that cobras make very good eating.

My mother reaches out a white-gloved finger to stroke the snake's back. "What do you think, Gemma? Now that you're sixteen, will you be dining on cobra?"

The slithery thing makes me shudder. "I think not, thank you."

The old, blind Indian man smiles toothlessly and brings the cobra closer. It's enough to send me reeling back where I bump into a wooden stand filled with little statues of Indian deities. One of the statues, a woman who is all arms with a face bent on terror, falls to the ground. Kali, the destroyer. Lately, Mother has accused me of keeping her as my unofficial patron saint. Lately, Mother and I haven't been getting on very well. She claims it's because I've reached an impossible age. I state emphatically to anyone who will listen that it's all because she refuses to take me to London.

"I hear in London, you don't have to defang your meals first," I say. We're moving past the cobra man and into the throng of people crowding every inch of Bombay's frenzied marketplace. Mother doesn't answer but waves away an organ-grinder and his monkey. It's unbearably hot. Beneath my cotton dress and crinolines, sweat streaks down my body. The flies – my most ardent admirers – dart about my face. I swat at one of the little winged beasts, but it escapes and I can almost swear I hear it mocking me. My misery is reaching epidemic proportions.

Overhead, the clouds are thick and dark, giving warning that this is monsoon season, when floods of rain could fall from the sky in a matter of minutes. In the dusty bazaar the turbaned men chatter and squawk and bargain, lifting brightly coloured silks towards us with brown, sunbaked hands. Everywhere there are carts lined with straw baskets offering every sort of ware and edible – thin, coppery vases; wooden boxes carved into intricate flower designs; and mangos ripening in the heat.

"How much farther to Mrs Talbot's new house? Couldn't

we please take a carriage?" I ask with what I hope is a notice-able annoyance.

"It's a nice day for a walk. And I'll thank you to keep a civil tone."

My annoyance has indeed been noted.

Sarita, our long-suffering housekeeper, offers pomegranates in her leathery hand. "Memsahib, these are very nice. Perhaps we will take them to your father, yes?"

If I were a good daughter, I'd bring some to my father, watch his blue eyes twinkle as he slices open the rich, red fruit, then eats the tiny seeds with a silver spoon just like a proper British gentleman.

"He'll only stain his white suit," I grumble. My mother starts to say something to me, thinks better of it, sighs – as usual. We used to go everywhere together, my mother and I – visiting ancient temples, exploring local customs, watching Hindu festivals, staying up late to see the streets bloom with candlelight. Now, she barely takes me on social calls. It's as if I'm a leper without a colony.

"He *will* stain his suit. He always does," I mumble in my defence, though no one is paying me a bit of attention except for the organ-grinder and his monkey. They're fol-lowing my every step, hoping to amuse me for money. The high lace collar of my dress is soaked with perspiration. I long for the cool, lush green of England, which I've only read about in my grandmother's letters. Letters filled with gossip about tea dances and balls and who has scandalised whom half a world away, while I am stranded in boring, dusty India watching an organ-grinder's monkey do a juggling trick with dates, the same trick he's been performing for a year.

"Look at the monkey, memsahib. How adorable he is!" Sarita says this as if I were still three and clinging to the bottoms of her sari skirts. No one seems to understand that I am fully sixteen and want, no, *need* to be in London, where I can be close to the museums and the balls and men who are older than six and younger than sixty.

"Sarita, that monkey is a trained thief who will be begging for your wages in a moment," I say with a sigh. As if on cue, the furry urchin scrambles up and sits on my shoulder with his palm outstretched. "How would you like to end up in a birthday stew?" I tell him through clenched teeth. The monkey hisses. Mother grimaces at my ill manners and drops a coin in its owner's cup. The monkey grins triumphantly and leaps across my head before running away.

A vendor holds out a carved mask with snarling teeth and elephant ears. Without a word, Mother places it over her face. "Find me if you can," she says. It's a game she's played with me since I could walk – a bit of hide-and-seek meant to make me smile. A child's game.

"I see only my mother," I say, bored. "Same teeth. Same ears."

Mother gives the mask back to the vendor. I've hit her vanity, her weak point.

"And I see that turning sixteen is not very becoming to my daughter," she says.

"Yes, I am sixteen. *Sixteen.* An age at which most decent girls have been sent for schooling in London." I give the word *decent* an extra push, hoping to appeal to some maternal sense of shame and propriety.

"This looks a bit on the green side, I think." She's peering intently at a mango. Her fruit inspection is all-consuming.

"No one tried to keep Tom imprisoned in Bombay," I say, invoking my brother's name as a last resort. "He's had four whole years there! And now he's starting at university."

"It's different for men."

"It's not fair. I'll never have a season. I'll end up a spinster with hundreds of cats who all drink milk from china bowls." I'm whining. It's unattractive, but I find I'm powerless to stop.

"I see," Mother says, finally. "Would you like to be paraded around the ballrooms of London society like some prize horse there to have its breeding capabilities evaluated? Would you still think London was so charming when you were the subject of cruel gossip for the slightest infraction of the rules? London's not as idyllic as your grandmother's letters make it out to be."

"I wouldn't know. I've never seen it."

"Gemma . . ." Mother's tone is all warning even as her smile is constant for the Indians. Mustn't let them think we British ladies are so petty as to indulge in arguments on the streets. We only discuss the weather, and when the weather is bad, we pretend not to notice.

Sarita chuckles nervously. "How is it that memsahib is now a young lady? It seems only yesterday you were in the nursery. Oh, look, dates! Your favourite." She breaks into a gap-toothed smile that makes every deeply etched wrinkle in her face come alive. It's hot and I suddenly want to scream, to run away from everything and everyone I've ever known.

"Those dates are probably rotting on the inside. Just like India."

"Gemma, that will be quite enough." Mother fixes me with her glass-green eyes. Penetrating and wise, people call them. I have the same large, upturned green eyes. The Indians say they are unsettling, disturbing. Like being watched by a ghost. Sarita smiles down at her feet, keeps her hands busy adjusting her brown sari. I feel a tinge of guilt for saying such a nasty thing about her home. Our home, though I don't really feel at home anywhere these days.

"Memsahib, you do not want to go to London. It is grey and cold and there is no ghee for bread. You wouldn't like it."

A train screams into the depot down near the glittering bay. Bombay. Good bay, it means, though I can't think of anything good about it right now. A dark plume of smoke from the train stretches up, touching the heavy clouds. Mother watches it rise.

"Yes, cold and grey." She places a hand on her throat, fingers the necklace hanging there, a small silver medallion of an all-seeing eye atop a crescent moon. A gift from a villager, Mother said. Her good-luck charm. I've never seen her without it.

Sarita puts a hand on Mother's arm. "Time to go, memsahib."

Mother pulls her gaze away from the train, drops her

hand from her necklace. "Yes. Come. We'll have a lovely time at Mrs Talbot's. I'm sure she'll have lovely cakes just for your birthday – "

A man in a white turban and thick black travelling cloak stumbles into her from behind, bumping her hard.

"A thousand pardons, honourable lady." He smiles, offers a deep bow to excuse his rudeness. When he does, he reveals a young man behind him wearing the same sort of strange cloak. For a moment, the young man and I lock eyes. He isn't much older than I am, probably seventeen if a day, with brown skin, a full mouth, and the longest eyelashes I have ever seen. I know I'm not supposed to find Indian men attractive, but I don't see many young men and I find I'm blushing in spite of myself. He breaks our gaze and cranes his neck to see over the hordes.

"You should be more careful," Sarita barks at the older man, threatening him with a blow from her arm. "You better not be a thief or you will be punished."

"No, no, memsahib, only I am terribly clumsy." He drops his smile and with it the cheerful simpleton routine. He whispers low to my mother in perfectly accented English. "Circe is near."

It makes no sense to me, just the ramblings of a very clever thief said to distract us. I start to say as much to my mother but the look of sheer panic on her face stops me cold. Her eyes are wild as she whips around and scans the crowded streets like she's looking for a lost child.

"What is it? What's the matter?" I ask.

The men are suddenly gone. They've disappeared into the

moving crowd, leaving only their footprints in the dust. "What did that man say to you?"

My mother's voice is edged in steel. "It's nothing. He was obviously deranged. The streets are not safe these days." I have never heard my mother sound this way. So hard. So afraid. "Gemma, I think it's best if I go to Mrs Talbot's alone."

"But – but what about the cake?" It's a ridiculous thing to say, but it's my birthday and while I don't want to spend it in Mrs Talbot's sitting room, I certainly don't want to waste the day alone at home, all because some black-cloaked madman and his cohort have spooked my mother.

Mother pulls her shawl tightly about her shoulders. "We'll have cake later. . ."

"But you promised –"

"Yes, well, that was before . . ." She trails off.

"Before what?"

"Before you vexed me so! Really, Gemma, you are in no humour for a visit today. Sarita will see you back."

"I'm in a fine humour," I protest, sounding anything but.

"No, you are not!" Mother's green eyes find mine. There is something there I've never seen before. A vast and terrifying anger that stops my breath. Quick as it comes on her, it's gone and she is Mother again. "You're overtired and need some rest. Tonight, we'll celebrate and I'll let you drink some champagne."

I'll let you drink some champagne. It's not a promise – it's an excuse to get rid of me. There was a time when we did everything together, and now, we can't even walk through the bazaar without sniping at each other. I am an embarrassment and a disappointment. A daughter she does not want to take anywhere, not London or even the home of an old crone who makes weak tea.

The train's whistle shrieks again, making her jump.

"Here, I'll let you wear my necklace, hmmm? Go on, wear it. I know you've always admired it."

I stand, mute, allowing her to adorn me in a necklace I have indeed always wanted, but now it weighs me down, a shiny, hateful thing. A bribe. Mother gives another quick glance to the dusty marketplace before letting her green eyes settle on mine.

"There. You look . . . all grown up." She presses her gloved hand to my cheek, holds it there as if to memorise it with her fingers. "I'll see you at home."

I don't want anyone to notice the tears that are pooling in my eyes, so I try to think of the wickedest thing I can say and then it's on my lips as I bolt from the marketplace.

"I don't care if you come home at all."

CHAPTER TWO

I'M RUNNING AWAY THROUGH THRONGS OF VENDORS and beggar children and foul-smelling camels, narrowly missing two men carrying saris that hang from a piece of rope attached to two poles at either end. I dart off down a narrow side street, following the twisting, turning alleys till I have to stop and catch my breath. Hot tears spill down my cheeks. I let myself cry now that there is no one around to see me.

God save me from a woman's tears, for I've no strength against them. That's what my father would say if he were here now. My father with his twinkling eyes and bushy moustache, his booming laugh when I please him and far-off gaze – as if I don't exist – when I've been less than a lady. I can't imagine he'll be terribly happy when he hears how I've behaved. Saying nasty things and storming off isn't the sort of behaviour that's likely to win a girl's case for going to London. My stomach aches at the thought of it all. What was I thinking?

There's nothing to do but swallow my pride, make my way back and apologise. If I can find my way back. Nothing looks at all familiar to me. Two old men sit cross-legged on the ground, smoking small, brown cigarettes. They watch me as I pass. I realise that I am alone in the city for the first time. No chaperone. No entourage. A lady unescorted. It's very scandalous of me. My heart beats faster and I quicken my pace.

The air has grown very still. A storm isn't far off. In the distance, I can hear frantic activity in the marketplace, last-minute bargains being struck before everything is closed down for the afternoon shower. I follow the sound and end up where I started. The old men smile at me, an English girl lost and alone on Bombay's streets. I could ask them for directions back to the marketplace, though my Hindi isn't nearly as good as Father's and for all I know *Where is the marketplace* may come out as *I covet your neighbour's fine cow.* Still, it's worth a try.

"Pardon me," I ask the elder man, the one with a white beard. "I seem to be lost. Could you tell me which way to the marketplace?"

The man's smile fades, replaced by a look of fear. He's speaking to the other man in sharp bursts of a dialect I don't understand. Faces peek from windows and doorways, straining to see what's bringing the trouble. The old man stands, points to me, to the necklace. He doesn't like it? *Something* about me has alarmed him. He shoos me away, goes inside and shuts the door in my face. It's refreshing to know that it's not just my mother and Sarita who find me intolerable.

The faces at the windows remain, watching me. There's the first drop of rain. The wet seeps into my dress, a spreading stain. The sky could break open at any moment. I've got to get back. No telling what Mother will do if she ends up drenched and I'm the cause. Why did I act like such a petulant brat? She'll never take me to London now. I'll spend the rest of my days in an Austrian convent surrounded by women with moustaches, my eyes gone bad from making intricate lace designs for other girls' trousseaus. I could curse my bad temper, but it won't get me back. *Choose a direction, Gemma, any direction – just go.* I take the path to the right. The unfamiliar street leads to another and another, and just as I come around a curve, I see him coming. The boy from the marketplace.

Don't panic, Gemma. Just move slowly away before he sees you.

I take two hurried steps back. My heel catches on a slippery stone, sending me sliding into the street. When I right myself, he's staring at me with a look I can not decipher. For a second, neither of us moves. We are as still as the air around us, which is either promising rain or threatening a storm.

A sudden fear takes root, spreads through me with cold speed, given wings by conversations I've overheard in my father's study – tales over brandy and cigars about the fate of an unescorted woman, overpowered by bad men, her life ruined forever. But these are only bits of conversation. This is a real man coming towards me, closing the distance between us in powerful strides.

He means to catch me, but I won't let him. Heart pounding, I pull up my skirts, ready to run. I try to take a step and my legs go shaky as a calf's. The ground shimmers and pitches beneath me.

What is happening?

Move. Must move, but I can't. A strange tingle starts in my fingers, travels up my arms, into my chest. My whole body trembles. A terrible pressure squeezes the breath from me, weighs me down to my knees. Panic blooms in my mouth like weeds. I want to scream. No words will come. No sound. He reaches me as I fall to the ground. Want to tell him to help me. Focus on his face, his full lips, perfect as a bow. His thick dark curls fall across his eyes, deep, brown, foot-long-lashes eyes. Alarmed eyes.

Help me.

The words stick fast inside me. I'm no longer afraid of losing my virtue; I know I must be dying. Try to get my mouth to tell him this but there is nothing but a choking sound in my throat. A strong smell of rose and spice overpowers me as the horizon slips away, my eyelids fluttering, fighting to stay awake. It's his lips that part, move, speak.

His voice that says, "It's happening."

The pressure increases till I feel I will burst and then I'm under, a swirling tunnel of blinding colour and light pulling me down like an undertow. I fall forever. Images race by. I'm falling past the ten-year-old me playing with Julia, the rag doll I lost on a picnic a year later; I'm six, letting Sarita wash my face for dinner. Time spins backwards and I am three, two, a baby, and then something pale and foreign, a creature no bigger than a tadpole and just as fragile. The strong tide grabs me hard again, pulling me through a veil of blackness, till I see the twisting street in India again. I am a visitor, walking in a living dream, no sound except for the thumping of my heart, my breath going in and out, the swish of my own blood coursing through my veins. On the rooftops above me, the organ-grinder's monkey scampers quickly, baring teeth. I try to speak but find I can't. He hops onto another roof. A shop where dried herbs hang from the eaves and a small moon-and-eye symbol – the same as on my mother's necklace – is affixed to the door. A woman comes quickly up the sloping street. A woman with red-gold hair, a blue dress, white gloves. My mother. What is my mother doing here? She should be at Mrs Talbot's house, drinking tea and discussing fabric.

My name floats from her lips. *Gemma. Gemma.* She's come looking for me. The Indian man in the turban is just behind her. She doesn't hear him. I call out to her, my mouth making no sound. With one hand, she pushes open the shop's door and enters. I follow her in, the pounding of my heart growing louder and faster. She must know the man is behind her. She must hear his breath now. But she only looks forward.

The man pulls a dagger from inside his cloak, but still she doesn't turn. I feel as if I'll be sick. I want to stop her, pull her away. Every step forward is like pushing against the air, lifting my legs an agony of slow movement. The man stops, listening. His eyes widen. *He's afraid.*

There's something coiled, waiting in the shadows at the back of the shop. It's as if the dark has begun to *move*. How can it be moving? But it is, with a cold, slithering sound that makes my skin crawl. A dark shape spreads out from its hiding spot. It grows till it reaches all around. The blackness in the centre of the thing is swirling and the sound . . . the most ghastly cries and moans come from inside it.

The man rushes forward, and the thing moves over him. *It devours him.* Now it looms over my mother and speaks to her in a slick hiss.

"Come to us, pretty one. We've been waiting . . ."

My scream implodes inside me. Mother looks back, sees the dagger lying there, grabs it. The thing howls in outrage. She's going to fight it. She's going to be all right. A single tear escapes down her cheek as she closes her desperate eyes, says my name soft as a prayer, *Gemma.* In one swift motion, she raises the dagger and plunges it into herself.

No!

A strong tide yanks me from the shop. I'm back on the streets of Bombay, as if I'd never been gone, screaming wildly while the young Indian man pins my flailing arms at my side.

"What did you see? Tell me!"

I kick and hit, twisting in his grip. Is there anyone around who can help me? What is happening? *Mother!* My mind fights for control, logic, reason, and finds it. My mother is having tea at Mrs Talbot's house. I'll go there and prove it. She will be angry and send me home with Sarita and there'll be no champagne later and no London but it won't matter. She'll be alive and well and cross and I'll be ecstatic to be punished by her.

He's still yelling at me. "Did you see my brother?"

"Let me go!" I kick at him with my legs, which have found their strength again. I've hit him in the tenderest of places. He crumples to the ground and I take off blindly down the street and around the next corner, fear pushing me forward. A small crowd is gathering in front of a shop. A shop where dried herbs hang from the roof.

No. This is all some hideous dream. I will wake up in my own bed and hear Father's loud, gravelly voice telling one of his long-winded jokes, Mother's soft laughter filling in after.

My legs cramp and tighten, go wobbly as I reach the crowd and make my way through it. The organ-grinder's tiny monkey scampers to the ground and tilts his head left and right, eyeing the body there with curiosity. The few people in front of me clear away. My mind takes it in by degrees. A shoe upturned, the heel broken. A hand splayed, fingers going stiff. Contents of a handbag strewn in the dirt. Bare neck peeking out from the bodice of a blue gown. Those famous green eyes open and unseeing. Mother's mouth parted slightly, as if she had been trying to speak when she died.

Gemma.

A deep red pool of blood widens and flows beneath her lifeless body. It seeps into the dusty cracks in the earth, reminding me of the pictures I've seen of Kali, the dark goddess, who spills blood and crushes bone. Kali the destroyer. My patron saint. I close my eyes, willing it all to go away.

This is not happening. This is not happening. This is not happening.

But when I open my eyes, she's still there, staring back at me, accusing. *I don't care if you come home at all.* It was the last thing I'd said to her. Before I ran away. Before she came after me. Before I saw her die in a vision. A heavy numbness weighs down my arms and legs. I crumple to the ground, where my mother's blood touches the hem of my best dress, forever staining it. And then the scream I've been holding back comes pouring out of me hard and fast as a night train just as the sky opens wide and a fierce rain pours down, drowning out every sound.

London, England. Two months later.

CHAPTER
THREE

"VICTORIA! THIS IS VICTORIA STATION!"

A burly, blue-uniformed conductor moves through on his way to the back of our train, announcing that I've arrived in London at last. We're slowing to a stop. Great billowing clouds of steam sail past the window, making everything outside seem like a dream.

In the seat across from me, my brother, Tom, is waking, straightening his black waistcoat, checking for anything that isn't perfect. In the four years we've been apart, he has grown very tall and a little broader in the chest, but he's still thin with a flop of fair hair that droops fashionably into his blue eyes and makes him seem younger than twenty. "Try not to look so dour, Gemma. It's not as if you're being sent to the stocks. Spence is a very good school with a reputation for turning out charming young ladies."

A very good school. Charming young ladies. It is, word for word, what my grandmother said after we'd spent two weeks at Pleasant House, her home in the English countryside.

She'd taken a long, appraising look at me, with my freckled skin and unruly mane of red hair, my sullen face, and decided that a proper finishing school was what was needed if I was ever to make a decent marriage. "It's a wonder you weren't sent home years ago," she clucked. "Everyone knows the climate in India isn't good for the blood. I'm sure this is what your mother would want."

I'd had to bite my tongue to keep from asking how she could possibly know what my mother would want. My mother had wanted me to stay in India. I had wanted to come to London, and now that I'm here, I couldn't be more miserable.

For three hours, as the train made its way past green, hilly pastures, and the rain slapped wearily at the train's windows, Tom had slept. But I could see only behind me, whence I'd come. The hot plains of India. The police asking questions: Had I seen anyone? Did my mother have enemies? What was I doing alone on the streets? And what about the man who'd spoken to her in the marketplace – a merchant named Amar? Did I know him? Were he and my mother (and here they looked embarrassed and shuffled their feet while finding a word that wouldn't seem too indelicate) "acquainted"?

How could I tell them what I'd seen? I didn't know whether to believe it myself.

Outside the train's windows, England is still in bloom. But the jostling of the passenger car reminds me of the ship that carried us from India over rough seas. The coastline of England taking shape before me like a warning. My mother buried deep in the cold, unforgiving ground of England. My father staring glassy-eyed at the headstone – *Virginia Doyle, beloved wife and mother* – peering through it as if he could change what had happened through will alone. And when he couldn't, he retired to his study and the laudanum bottle that had become his constant companion. Sometimes I'd find him, asleep in his chair, the dogs at his feet, the brown bottle close at hand, his breath strong and medicinally sweet. Once a large man, he'd grown thinner, whittled down by grief and opium. And I could only stand by, helpless and mute, the cause of it all. The keeper of a secret so terrible it made me afraid to speak, scared that it would pour out of me like kerosene, burning everyone.

"You're brooding again," Tom says, casting a suspicious look my way.

"Sorry." *Yes, I'm sorry, so sorry for everything.*

Tom exhales long and hard, his voice travelling swiftly under the exhalation. "Don't be sorry. Just stop."

"Yes, sorry," I say again without thinking. I touch the outline of my mother's amulet. It hangs around my neck now, a remembrance of my mother and my guilt, hidden beneath the stiff black crepe mourning dress I will wear for six months.

Through the thinning haze outside our window, I can see porters hustling alongside the train, keeping pace, ready to place wooden steps beside the open doors for our descent to the platform. At last our train comes to a stop in a hiss and sigh of steam.

Tom stands and stretches. "Come on, then. Let's go, before all the porters are taken."

⁂

Victoria Station takes my breath away with its busyness. Hordes of people mill about the platform. Down at the far end of the train, the third-class passengers climb off in a thick tumble of arms and legs. Porters hurry to carry luggage and parcels for the first-class passengers. Newsboys hold the day's papers in the air as far as their arms will stretch, screeching the most enticing headlines. Flower girls wander about, wearing smiles as hard and worn as the wooden trays that hang from their delicate necks. I'm nearly upended by a man buzzing past, his umbrella parked beneath his arm.

"Pardon me," I mutter, deeply annoyed. He takes no note of me. When I glance to the far end of the platform, I catch sight of something odd. A black travelling cloak that sets my heart beating faster. My mouth goes dry. It's impossible that he could be here. And yet, I'm sure it's him disappearing behind a kiosk. I try to get closer, but it's terribly crowded.

"What are you doing?" Tom asks as I strain against the tide of the crowd.

"Just looking," I say, hoping he can't read the fear in my voice. A man rounds the corner of the kiosk, carrying a bundle of newspapers on his shoulder. His coat, thin and black and several sizes too big, hangs on him like a loose cape. I nearly laugh with relief. *You see, Gemma? You're imagining things. Leave it alone.*

"Well, if you're going to look around, see if you can find us a porter. I don't know where the devil they've all got to so fast."

A scrawny newsboy happens by and offers to fetch us a hansom cab for twopence. He struggles to carry the trunk filled with my few worldly belongings: a handful of dresses, my mother's social diary, a red sari, a white carved elephant from India, and my father's treasured cricket bat, a reminder of him in happier days.

～～～～

Tom helps me into the carriage and the driver pulls away from the great, sprawling lady that is Victoria Station, clip-clopping towards the heart of London. The air is gloomy, alive with the smoke from the gaslights that line London's streets. The foggy greyness makes it seem like dusk, though it's only four o'clock in the afternoon. Anything could creep up behind you on such shadowy streets. I don't know why I think of this, but I do, and I immediately push the thought away.

The needle-thin spires of Parliament peek up over the dusky outlines of chimneys. In the streets, several sweat-drenched men dig deep trenches in the cobblestones.

"What are they doing?"

"Putting in lines for electric lights," Tom answers, coughing into a white handkerchief with his initials stitched on a corner in a distinguished black script. "Soon, this choking gaslight will be a thing of the past."

On the streets, vendors hawk their wares from carts, each

with his own distinctive cry – *knives sharpened, fish to buy, get your apples – apples here!* Milkmaids deliver the last of the day's milk. In a strange way, it all reminds me of India. There are tempting storefronts offering everything one can imagine – tea, linens, china, and beautiful dresses copied from the best fashions of Paris. A sign hanging from a second-storey window announces that there are offices to let, inquire within. Bicycles whiz past the many hansom cabs on the streets. I brace myself in case the horse spooks to see them, but the mare pulling us seems completely uninterested. She's seen it all before, even if I haven't.

An omnibus crowded with passengers sails past us, drawn by a team of magnificent horses. A cluster of ladies sits perched in the seats above the omnibus, their parasols open to shield them from the elements. A long strip of wood advertising Pears' soap ingeniously hides their ankles from view, for modesty's sake. It's an extraordinary sight and I can't help wishing we could just keep riding through London's streets, breathing in the dust of history that I've only seen in photographs. Men in dark suits and bowler hats step out of offices, marching confidently home after a day's work. I can see the white dome of St. Paul's Cathedral rising above the sooty rooftops. A posted bill promises a production of *Macbeth* starring the American actress Lily Trimble. She's ravishing, with her auburn hair loose and wild, a red gown cut daringly low on her bosom. I wonder if the girls at Spence will be as lovely and sophisticated.

"Lily Trimble is quite beautiful, isn't she?" I say by way of trying to make pleasant small talk with Tom, a seemingly impossible task.

"An actress," Tom sneers. "What sort of way is that for a woman to live, without a solid home, husband, children? Running about like she's her own lord and master. She'll certainly never be accepted in society as a proper lady."

And that's what comes of small talk.

Part of me wants to give Tom a swift kick for his arrogance. I'm afraid to say that another part of me is dying to know what men look for in a woman. My brother might be pompous, but he knows certain things that could prove useful to me.

"I see," I say in an offhand way as if I want to know what makes a nice garden. I am controlled. Courteous. Ladylike. "And what does make a proper lady?"

He looks as if he should have a pipe in his mouth as he says, "A man wants a woman who will make life easy for him. She should be attractive, well groomed, knowledgeable in music, painting, and running a house, but above all, she should keep his name above scandal and never call attention to herself."

He must be joking. Give him a minute, and he'll laugh, say it was just a lark, but his smug smile stays firmly in place. I am not about to take this insult in stride. "Mother was Father's equal," I say coolly. "He didn't expect her to walk behind him like some pining imbecile."

Tom's smile falls away. "Exactly. And look where it's got us." It's quiet again. Outside the cab's windows, London rolls by and Tom turns his head towards it. For the first time, I can see his pain, see it in the way he runs his fingers through his hair, over and over, and I understand what it costs him to hide it all. But I don't know how to build a bridge across this awkward silence, so we ride on, watching everything, seeing little, saying nothing.

"Gemma . . ." Tom's voice breaks and he stops for a moment. He's fighting whatever it is that's boiling up inside him. "That day with Mother . . . why the devil did you run away? What were you thinking?"

My voice is a whisper. "I don't know." For the truth, it's very little comfort.

"The illogic of women."

"Yes," I say, not because I agree but because I want to give him something, anything. I say it because I want him to forgive me. And perhaps then I could begin to forgive myself. Perhaps.

"Did you know that" – his jaw clenches on the word – "*man* they found murdered with her?"

"No," I whisper.

"Sarita said you were hysterical when she and the police found you. Going on about some Indian boy and a vision of a . . . a thing of some sort." He pauses, rubs his palms over the knees of his trousers. He's still not looking at me.

My hands shake in my lap. *I could tell him. I could tell him what I've kept locked tight inside.* Right now, with that lock of hair falling in his eyes, he's the brother I've missed, the one who once brought me stones from the sea, told me they were rajah's jewels. I want to tell him that I'm afraid I'm going mad by degrees and that nothing seems entirely real to me anymore. I want to tell him about the vision, have him pat me on the head in that irritating way and dismiss it with a perfectly logical doctor's explanation. I want to ask him if it's possible that a girl can be born unlovable, or does she just become that way? I want to tell him everything and have him understand.

Tom clears his throat. "What I mean to say is, did something happen to you? Did he . . . are you quite all right?"

My words pull each other back down into a deep, dark silence. "You want to know if I'm still chaste."

"If you want to put it so plainly, yes."

Now I see that it was ridiculous of me to think he wanted to know what really happened. He's only concerned that I haven't shamed the family somehow. "Yes, I am, as you put it, quite all right." I could laugh, it's such a lie – I am most certainly not all right. But it works as I know it will. That's what living in their world is – a big lie. An illusion where everyone looks the other way and pretends that nothing unpleasant exists at all, no goblins of the dark, no ghosts of the soul.

Tom straightens his shoulders, relieved. "Right. Well, then." The human moment has passed and he is all control again. "Gemma, Mother's murder is a blight on this family. It would be scandalous if the true facts were known." He stares at me. "Mother died of cholera," he says emphatically, as if even he believes the lie now. "I know you disagree, but as your brother, I'm telling you that the less said, the better. It's for your own protection."

He's all fact and no feeling. It will serve him well as a doctor someday. I know that what he's telling me is true, but I can't help hating him for it. "Are you sure it's my protection you're worried about?"

His jaw tightens again. "I'll overlook that last comment. If you won't think of me, of yourself, then think of Father. He's not well, Gemma. You can see that. The circumstances of Mother's death have undone him." He fiddles with the cuffs on his shirt. "You may as well know that Father got into some very bad habits in India. Sharing the hookah with the Indians might have made him a popular businessman, one of them in their eyes, but it didn't help his constitution much. He's always been fond of his pleasures. His escapes."

Father sometimes came home late and spent from his day. I remembered Mother and the servants helping him to bed on more than one occasion. Still, it hurts to hear this. I hate Tom for telling me. "Then why do you keep getting him the laudanum?"

"There's nothing wrong with laudanum. It's medicinal," he sniffs.

"In moderation . . ."

"Father's no addict. Not Father," he says, as if he means to convince a jury. "He'll be fine now that he's back in England. Just remember what I've told you. Can you at least promise me that much? Please?"

"Yes, fine," I say, feeling dead inside. They don't know what they're in for at Spence, getting me, a ghost of a girl who'll nod and smile and take her tea but who isn't really here.

The driver calls down to us. "Sir, we'll be needin' to pass through the East, if you want to draw the curtains."

"What does he mean?" I ask.

"We have to go through the East End. Whitechapel? Oh, for heaven's sake, the *slums*, Gemma," he says, loosening the curtains on the sides of his windows to block out the poverty and filth.

"I've seen slums in India," I say, leaving my curtains in place. The carriage bumps its way along the cobblestones through grimy, narrow streets. Dozens of dirty, thin children clamber about, staring at us in our fine carriage. My heart sinks to see their bony, soot-smeared faces. Several women huddle together under a gaslight, sewing. It makes sense for them to use the city's light and not waste their own precious candles for this thankless work. The smell in the streets – a mix of refuse, horse droppings, urine, and despair – is truly awful, and I'm afraid I might gag. Loud music and yelling spill out onto the street from a tavern. A drunken couple tumbles out after. The woman has hair the colour of a sunset and a harsh, painted face. They're arguing with our driver, holding us here.

"What's the matter now?" Tom raps against the hood of the carriage to spur the driver on. But the lady is really giving the driver what for. We might be here all night. The drunken man leers at me, winks, makes an extremely rude gesture involving his index fingers.

Disgusted, I turn away and look down an empty alley. Tom's leaning out his window. I hear him, condescending and impatient, trying to reason with the couple in the street.

But something's gone wrong. His voice grows muffled, like sounds heard through a shell held to the ear. And then all I can hear is my blood quickening, thumping hard against my veins. A tremendous pressure seizes me, knocking the air from my lungs.

It's happening again.

I want to cry out to Tom, but I can't, and then I'm under, falling through that tunnel of colour and light again as the alley bends and flickers. And just as quickly, I'm floating out of the carriage, stepping lightly into the darkened alley with its shimmering edges. There's a small girl of eight or so sitting in the straw-covered dirt, playing with a rag of a doll. Her face is dirty, but otherwise, she seems out of place here, in her pink hair ribbon and starched white pinafore that's a size too big for her. She sings a snippet of song, something I recognise faintly as being an old English folk tune. When I approach she looks up.

"Isn't my dolly lovely?"

"You can see me?" I ask.

She nods and goes back to combing her filthy fingers through the doll's hair. "She's looking for you."

"Who?"

"Mary."

"Mary? Mary who?"

"She sent me to find you. But we have to be careful. It's looking for you, too."

The air shifts, bringing a damp chill with it. I'm shaking uncontrollably. "Who are you?"

Behind the little girl, I sense movement in the murky

dark. I blink to clear my eyes but it's no trick – *the shadows are moving*. Quick as liquid silver the dark rises and takes its hideous shape, the gleaming bone of its skeletal face, the hollow, black holes where eyes should be. The hair a tangle of snakes. The mouth opens and the rasping moan escapes. *"Come to us, my pretty, pretty . . ."*

"Run." The word is a choked whisper on my tongue. The thing is growing, slithering ever closer. The howls and moans inside it making every cell in my body go ice-cold. A scream inches its way up my throat. If I let it out, I'll never stop.

Heart pounding hard against my ribs, I say again, stronger, "Run!"

The thing hesitates, pulls back. It sniffs at the air, as if tracking a scent. The little girl turns her flat brown eyes to me. "Too late," she says, just as the creature turns its unseeing eyes towards me. The decaying lips spread apart, revealing teeth like spikes. Dear God, the thing is grinning at me. It opens wide that horrible mouth and screeches – a sound that loosens my tongue at last.

"No!" In an instant I'm back inside the carriage and leaning out the window, yelling at the couple. "Get out of the bloody way – now!" I shout, snapping at the horse's rump with my shawl. The mare whinnies and lurches, sending the couple rushing for the safety of the tavern.

The driver steadies the horse as Tom pulls me down into my seat. "Gemma! Whatever has possessed you?"

"I . . ." In the alley, I look for the thing and don't find it. It's just an alley, with dull light and several dirty children trying to steal a hat from a smaller boy, their laughter bouncing off stables and crumbling hovels. The scene passes behind us into the night.

"I say, Gemma, are you all right?" Tom is truly concerned.

I'm going mad, Tom. Help me.

"I was simply in a hurry." The sound coming out of my mouth is a cross between a laugh and a howl, like the sound a madwoman would make.

Tom eyes me as if I'm some rare disease he's helpless to treat. "For pity's sake! Get hold of yourself. And please try to watch your language at Spence. I don't want to have to collect you only hours after I've deposited you there."

"Yes, Tom," I say as the carriage jostles back to life on the cobblestones, leading us away from London and shadows.

CHAPTER
FOUR

"THERE'S THE SCHOOL NOW, SIR," THE DRIVER SHOUTS.

We've been riding for an hour across rolling hills dotted with trees. The sun has set, the sky settling into that hazy blue of twilight. When I look out my window, I can't see anything but a canopy of branches overhead, and through the lacework of leaves, there's the moon, ripe as a melon. I'm starting to think that our driver must be imagining things, too, but we crest a hill and Spence comes into glorious view.

I had expected some sweet little cottage estate, the kind written about in halfpenny papers where rosy-cheeked young girls play lawn tennis on tidy green fields. There is nothing cosy about Spence. The place is enormous, a madman's forgotten castle with great, fat turrets and thin, pointy spires. It would take a girl a year just to visit every room inside, no doubt.

"Whoa!" The driver stops short. There's someone in the road.

"Who goes there?" A woman comes around to my side of

the carriage and peers in. An old Gypsy woman. A richly embroidered scarf is wrapped tightly about her head and her jewellery is pure gold, but otherwise, she is dishevelled.

"What now?" Tom sighs.

I poke my head out. When the moonlight catches my face, the Gypsy woman's face softens. "Oh, but it's you. You've come back to me."

"I'm sorry, madam. You must have mistaken me for someone else."

"Oh, but where is Carolina? Where is she? Did you take her?" She starts to moan softly.

"Come on now, missus, let us by," the driver calls. "There's a good lady."

With a snap of the reins, the carriage jostles forward again as the old woman calls after us.

"Mother Elena sees everything. She knows your heart! She knows!"

"Good lord, they've got their own hermit," Tom sneers. "How very fashionable."

Tom may laugh but I can't wait to get out of the carriage and the dark.

⌁⌁⌁⌁

The horse draws us under the stone archway and through gates that open onto lovely grounds. I can just make out a wonderful green field, perfect for playing lawn tennis or croquet, and what looks like lush, overgrown gardens. A little farther out lies a grove of great trees, thick as a forest. Beyond the trees sits a chapel perched on a hill. The whole picture looks as if it's been standing this way for centuries, untouched.

The carriage bounces up the hill that leads to Spence's front doors. I arch my neck out the window to take in the full, massive scope of the building. There's something jutting up from the roof. It's hard to make it out in the fading light. The moon shifts from under a bank of clouds and I see them clearly: gargoyles. Moonlight ripples over the roof, illuminating bits and pieces – a sliver of sharp tooth, a leering mouth, snarling eyes.

Welcome to finishing school, Gemma. Learn to embroider, serve tea, curtsy. Oh, and by the way, you might be demolished in the night by a hideous winged creature from the roof.

The carriage jangles to a stop. My trunk is placed on the great stone steps outside the large wooden doors. Tom raps with the great brass knocker, which is roughly the size of my head. While we wait, he can't resist giving his last bit of brotherly advice.

"Now, it is very important that you conduct yourself in a manner befitting your station while at Spence. It's fine to be kind to the lesser girls, but remember that they are not your equals."

Station. Lesser girls. Not your equals. It's a laugh, really. After all, I'm the unnatural one responsible for her mother's murder, the one who sees visions. I pretend to freshen my hat in the brass reflection of the knocker. Any sense of foreboding I feel will probably disappear the minute the door opens and some kindly housekeeper takes me in with a warm embrace and an open smile.

Right. Give the door another good, solid bang to show I'm a good, solid girl, the kind every eerie boarding school would love to claim as its own. The heavy oak doors open, revealing a craggy-faced, thick-waisted bulwark of a house-keeper with all the warmth of Wales in January. She glares at me, wiping her hands on her starched white apron.

"You must be Miss Doyle. We expected you a half hour ago. You've kept the headmistress waiting. Come on. Follow me."

<hr />

The housekeeper bids us wait for a moment in a large, poorly lit parlour filled with dusty books and withering ferns. There is a fire going. It spits and hisses as it devours the dry wood. Laughter floats in through the open double doors and in a moment, I see several younger girls in white pinafores shuffling through the hall. One peeks in, sees me, and goes on as if I'm nothing more than a piece of furniture. But in a moment she's back with some of the others. They swoon over Tom, who preens for them, bowing, which sets them to blushing and giggling.

God help us all.

I'm afraid I may have to take the fireplace poker to my brother to silence this spectacle. Fortunately, I'm spared from any murderous impulses. The humourless house-keeper is back. It's time for Tom and me to make our good-byes, which consist mainly of the two of us staring at the carpet.

"Well, then. I believe I'll see you next month on Assembly Day with the other families."

"Yes, I suppose so."

"Make us proud, Gemma," he says at last. No sentimental reassurances – *I love you; it's all going to be just fine, you'll see.* He smiles once again for the adoring crowd of girls still hiding in the hallway, and then he's gone. I am alone.

"This way, miss, if you please," the housekeeper says. I follow her out to a huge, open foyer where an incredible double staircase sits. The stairs branch off both left and right. A bit of breeze from an open window shakes the crystals of a chandelier above me. It's dazzling. Gobs of exquisite crystals strung along metal crafted into elaborate snakes.

"Watch yer step, miss," the housekeeper advises. "Stairs is steep."

The stairs rope up and around for what seems like miles. Over the banister, I can see the black-and-white marble tiles making diamond patterns on the floor far below. A painting of a silver-haired woman in a dress that would have been the height of fashion some twenty years ago greets us at the top of the stairs.

"That's Missus Spence," the housekeeper informs me.

"Oh," I say. "Lovely." The portrait is enormous – it's like having the eye of God watch over you.

We move on, down a long corridor to a set of thick double doors. The housekeeper knocks with her meaty fist, waits. A voice answers from the other side of the doors,

"Come in," and I'm ushered into a room with dark green wallpaper in a peacock feather pattern. A somewhat heavy-set woman with piles of brown hair going grey sits at a large desk, a pair of wire-rimmed spectacles on her nose.

"That will be all, Brigid," she says, dismissing the warm and embracing housekeeper. The headmistress goes back to finishing her correspondence, while I stand on the Persian rug, pretending I'm absolutely fascinated by a figurine of a little German maid carrying buckets of milk on her shoulders. What I really want to do is turn around and bolt for the door.

So sorry, my mistake. I believe I was supposed to report to another boarding school, run by human beings who might offer a girl some tea or at least a chair. A mantel clock ticks off the seconds, the rhythm lulling me into a tiredness I've been fighting.

Finally, the headmistress puts down her pen. She points to a chair on the other side of the desk. "Sit."

There is no "please". No "would you be so kind". All in all, I'm feeling as welcome as a dose of cod-liver oil. The beast attempts a beatific look that could be mistaken for a bout of painful wind.

"I am Mrs Nightwing, headmistress of Spence Academy. I trust you had a pleasant journey, Miss Doyle?"

"Oh, yes, thank you."

Tick-tock. Tick-tock. Tick-tock.

"Brigid saw you in comfortably?"

"Yes, thank you."

Tick, tick, tick, tock.

"I don't usually admit new girls at such an advanced age.

I find it is harder for them to grow accustomed to the Spence way of life." There's one black mark against me already. "But under the circumstances, I feel it our Christian duty to make an exception. I am sorry for your loss."

I say nothing and fix my gaze on the silly little German milkmaid. She's smiling and rosy-cheeked, most likely on her way back to a small village where her mother is waiting for her and there are no dark shadows lurking.

When I don't respond, Mrs Nightwing continues. "I understand that custom dictates a mourning period for at least a year. But I find that such persistent reminders are not healthy. It keeps us centred on the dead and not the living. I recognise that this is unconventional." She gives me a long look over the top of her glasses to see if I will object. I don't. "It is important that you get on here and be on equal footing with the other girls. After all, some of them have been with us for years, far longer than they've been with their own families. Spence is rather like a family, one with affection and honour, rules and consequences." She emphasises this last word. "Therefore, you will wear the same uniform everyone else wears. I trust this will be acceptable to you?"

"Yes," I say. And though I feel a bit guilty about abandoning my mourning weeds so soon, in truth I'm grateful for the chance to look like everybody else. It will help me to remain unnoticed, I hope.

"Splendid. Now, you will be in the first class with six young ladies also of your age. Breakfast is served promptly at nine o'clock. You will have instruction in French with

Mademoiselle LeFarge, drawing with Miss Moore, music with Mr Grunewald. I shall direct your lessons in deportment. Prayers are said at six o'clock each evening in the chapel. In fact" – she glances at the mantel clock – "we shall be leaving for the chapel very shortly. Dinner follows at seven. There is free time in the great hall afterwards, with all girls in bed by ten." She attempts one of those confessional smiles, the sort usually seen in reverent portraits of Florence Nightingale. In my experience, such smiles mean that the real message – the one hidden by manners and good posture – will need to be translated.

"I think you shall be very happy here, Miss Doyle."

Translation: That is an order.

"Spence has turned out many wonderful young women who've gone on to make very good marriages."

We don't expect much more from you. Please don't embarrass us.

"Why, you might even be sitting here in my position someday."

If you turn out to be completely unmarriageable, and you don't end up in an Austrian convent making lace nightgowns.

Mrs Nightwing's smile wavers a bit. I know that she's waiting for me to say something charming, something that will convince her that she hasn't made a mistake in taking in a grief-stricken girl who seems completely unworthy of Spence's training. *Come on, Gemma. Throw her a bone – tell her how happy and proud you are to be part of the Spence family.* I only nod. Her smile disappears.

"While you're here, I can be a solid ally, if you follow

the rules. Or the sword that cuts you into shape if you do not. Do we understand each other?"

"Yes, Mrs Nightwing."

"Excellent. Let me show you around, and then you may dress for prayers."

❧❧❧❧

"Your room is here." We're on the third floor, making our way down a long hall with many doors. Photographic portraits of Spence's various classes hang on the walls – grainy faces even harder to see in the dim light of the few gas lamps. Finally we come to a room at the end on the left. Mrs Nightwing opens the door wide to reveal a cramped, musty-smelling room that could optimistically be described as cheerless and realistically be called drab. There's a water-stained desk, a chair, and a lamp. Iron beds hug the left and right walls. One bed looks lived in, with a neatly tucked quilt. The other, my bed, fits tight in a nook under a steep eave that could probably break my skull if I sit up too quickly. It's a dormer room, one that juts out over the side of the building like an afterthought – perfect for an afterthought of a girl, added to the roster at the last possible moment.

Mrs Nightwing rubs a finger over the top of the desk and frowns upon discovering dust there. "Of course, we do give preference to those girls who are returning to us this year," she says by way of apology for my new home. "But I think you'll find your room cheery and quite serviceable. There is a marvellous view from the window."

She's right. Standing in front of it, I can see the moonlit back lawn, the gardens, the chapel on the hill, and a great wall of trees.

"It is a lovely view," I say, trying to be both cheery and serviceable.

This appeases Mrs Nightwing, who smiles. "You'll share a room with Ann Bradshaw. Ann is most helpful. She is one of our scholarship students."

That's a nice way of saying "one of our charity cases", some poor girl packed off to school by a distant relative or given a scholarship by one of Spence's benefactors. Ann's quilt is tucked in straight and smooth as glass, and I wonder what her situation is, or whether we'll get on well enough for her to want to tell me.

The wardrobe is ajar. A uniform hangs there – a flared white skirt; a white blouse with lace insets along the bib and puffed sleeves tapering to fitted cuffs; white boots with hooks and laces; and a dark blue velvet cape with a hood.

"You may dress for prayers. I'll give you a moment." She closes the door, and I slip into the uniform, fastening the many small buttons. The skirt is too short but otherwise it is a comfortable fit.

Mrs Nightwing notices the gap at the bottom, frowns. "You're quite tall." Just what a girl wants to be reminded of. "We'll get Brigid to add a ruffle to the hem." She turns and I follow her out.

"Where do those doors lead?" I ask, pointing to the darkened wing on the opposite side of the landing where two heavy doors stand sentry, secured by a large lock. It's the kind of lock needed to keep people out. Or hold something in.

Mrs Nightwing's brows furrow, her lips go tight. "That is the East Wing. It was destroyed in a fire years ago. We don't use it anymore, so we've closed it off. Saves on heating. Come along."

She swings past me. I start after her, then glance back, my eyes falling to the bottom of those locked doors, where there's a one-inch crack of light. It may be the lateness of the day and the long journey, or the fact that I'm growing accustomed to seeing things, but I could swear that I see a shadow move along the floor behind the doors.

No. Begone.

I refuse to let the past find me here. I have to get hold of myself. So I close my eyes for just a second and make myself a promise.

There is nothing there. I am tired. I will open my eyes and see only a door.

When I look, there is nothing.

CHAPTER
FIVE

DOWN IN THE PARLOUR AGAIN, THERE ARE ROUGHLY fifty girls assembled, all in their velvet capes. Night rolls in, bathing the room in a purplish light. Murmuring voices, broken by the occasional giggle or laugh, echo off the low ceilings and fall around me like glass. A tolling church bell announces that it's time to leave the school and walk the half mile or so up the hill to the chapel.

I steal a quick look to see if I can find some girls my age. Huddled together at the front of the line are a handful of girls who look to be sixteen or seventeen. They stand, heads together in conference, laughing over some private joke. One of them is incredibly beautiful, with dark brown hair and an ivory face that could be from a cameo pin. She's possibly the loveliest girl I've ever seen. There are three others who all seem somewhat alike – well groomed, with aristocratic noses, each wearing an expensive comb or brooch to distinguish her and flaunt her position.

One girl catches my eye. She seems different from the others. Her white-blonde hair is arranged neatly in a bun, as young ladies must wear their hair, but even so, it seems a bit wild, as if the pins won't really hold it. Arched eyebrows frame small, grey eyes in a face so pale it's almost the colour of an opal. She's amused at something and she tosses her head back and laughs heartily, without trying to stifle it. Even though the dark-haired girl is perfect and lovely, it's the blonde who gets the attention of everyone in the room. She's clearly the leader.

Mrs Nightwing claps her hands and the murmuring dies out in ripples. "Girls, I'd like you to meet the newest student of Spence Academy. This is Gemma Doyle. Miss Doyle is joining us from Shropshire and will be in first class. She has spent most of her life in India, and I'm sure she would be happy to tell you stories of their many quaint customs and habits. I trust you'll show her a proper Spence welcome and acquaint her with the way things are done here at Spence."

I am dying a thousand cruel and unusual deaths as fifty pairs of eyes take me in, size me up like something that should be hanging over a fireplace in a gentleman's den. Any hopes I'd had of blending in and not being noticed have just been killed by Mrs Nightwing's little speech. The blonde girl cocks her head to one side, evaluating me. She stifles a yawn and goes back to gossiping with her friends. Perhaps I'll blend in after all.

Mrs Nightwing pulls her cape tight at her neck and points the way with an outstretched arm. "Let's go to prayers, girls."

The other girls file out the door as Mrs Nightwing barrels over to me with a girl in tow. "Miss Doyle, this is Ann Bradshaw, your new roommate. Miss Bradshaw is fifteen and also in first class. She will accompany you this evening to make sure you get along."

"How do you do?" she says, her dull, watery eyes revealing nothing. I think of her snug quilt and don't expect her to be a fun-loving sort.

"Pleased to meet you," I reply. We stand awkwardly for a second, neither one of us saying a word. Ann Bradshaw is a doughy, plain girl, which is doubly damning. A girl without money who was also pretty might stand a chance at bettering her station in life. Her nose runs. She dabs at it with a shabby lace handkerchief.

"Isn't it terrible to have a cold?" I say, trying to be cordial.

The blank stare doesn't change. "I don't have a cold."

Right. Glad I asked. We're off to a rousing start, Miss Bradshaw and I. No doubt we'll be like sisters by morning. If I could turn around and leave this instant, I would.

"The chapel is this way," she says, breaking the ice with that bit of scintillating conversation. "We're not supposed to be late to prayers."

⌁⌁⌁⌁

We walk at the back of the group, heading up the hill through the trees towards the stone-and-beam chapel. A low mist has come up. It settles over the grounds, giving the whole place an eerie quality. Up ahead, the girls' blue capes flutter in the night air before the thickening fog swallows everything but the echoes of their voices.

"Why did your family send you here?" Ann asks in a most off-putting manner.

"To civilise me, I suppose." I give a little laugh. *Look, see how jolly I am? Ha-ha.* Ann doesn't laugh.

"My father died when I was three. My mother had to work, but then she took sick and died. Her family didn't want to take me in but they didn't want to send me to the workhouse, either. So they sent me here to train as a governess."

It's astonishing, this honesty. She doesn't even flinch. I'm not quite sure how to respond. "Oh, I'm sorry," I say, when I find my voice again.

Those dull eyes take me in. "Are you really?"

"Well . . . yes. Why wouldn't I be?"

"Because people usually just say that to be rid of someone. They don't really mean it."

She's right, and I blush. It is something to say, and how many times did I have to endure people saying the same thing about my own situation? In the fog, I trip over a thick tree root sticking up from the trail and let loose with my father's favourite curse.

"Blast!"

Ann's head shoots up at this. No doubt she's the prudish sort who'll run off to Mrs Nightwing every time I glance cross-eyed at her.

"Forgive me, I don't know how I could have been so rude,"

I say, trying to undo the damage. I certainly don't want to be lectured my first day.

"Don't worry," Ann says, looking around for eavesdroppers. As we're at the back of the pack, there are none. "Things around here aren't quite as proper as Mrs Nightwing makes them out to be."

This is certainly intriguing news. "Really? What do you mean?"

"I really shouldn't say," she answers.

The peal of the bell drifts over the fog along with hushed voices. Other than that, it's very still. The fog is really something. "This would be a fine place for a midnight walk," I say, trying to seem jovial. I've heard that people like jovial girls. "Perhaps the werewolves will come out to play later."

"Except for vespers, we're not allowed to go out after dark," Ann answers, matter-of-factly.

So much for joviality. "Why not?"

"It's against the rules. I don't like it at night much." She pauses, wipes at her runny nose. "Sometimes, there are Gypsies in the woods."

I think of the old woman at my carriage earlier. "Yes, I believe I met one. Called herself Mother something..."

"Mother Elena?"

"Yes, that's it."

"She's stark raving mad. You want to steer clear of her. She might have a knife and stab you in your sleep," Ann says, breathlessly.

"She seemed harmless enough..."

"You never really know, do you?"

I don't know if it's the fog or the bells or Ann's creepiness but I'm walking a bit faster now. A girl who sees visions paired with one who's a walking tour guide of things that go bump in the night. Perhaps this is Spence's little way of matchmaking.

"You're in first class with me."

"Yes," I say. "Who are the others?"

She ticks off the names one by one. "And Felicity and Pippa." Ann stops, suddenly on edge.

"Felicity and Pippa. Those are lovely names," I say cheerfully. It's such an insipid comment that I should be shot for it, but I'm dying to know more about these two girls who are going to be in our class.

Ann lowers her voice. "They're not lovely. Not at all."

The bell finally stops ringing, leaving a strange, hollow hush in its absence. "No? Part girl, part wolf? Do they lick their butter knives?"

Ann not only doesn't find me amusing, but her eyes take on a cold, hard look. "Be careful around them. Don't trust – "

From behind us, a husky voice cuts her off. "Talking too much again, Ann?"

We whip around to see two faces emerging from the mist. The blonde and the beauty. They must have lagged behind and sneaked up on us. The smoky voice belongs to the blonde. "Don't you know that's a most unbecoming trait?"

Ann's jaw hangs open, but she doesn't answer.

The brunette laughs and whispers something in the

blonde's ear, which makes her launch into that full, ripe smile again. She points to me. "You're the new girl, aren't you?"

I don't like the way she says this. New girl. As if I might be some sort of insect that hasn't been given a classification yet. *Hideous corpus*, female. "Gemma Doyle," I say, trying not to flinch or look away first. It's a trick my father used when he haggled over a price. Now I'm haggling over something undefined but more important – my place in the pecking order at Spence.

There is a second's pause before she turns away from me and holds Ann with a chilly gaze. "Gossip is a very bad habit. We don't indulge bad habits here at Spence, Mademoiselle Scholarship," she says, giving the last two words a nasty emphasis. A reminder that Ann isn't of the same class and shouldn't expect the same treatment. "You have been warned."

"Nice to meet you, Miss Doily," she says, linking arms with the brunette, who bumps my shoulder hard as they pass us.

"Terribly sorry," she says, and bursts out laughing. If I were a man, I'd flatten her. But I'm not a man. I'm here to be a lady. No matter how much I loathe it already.

"Come on," Ann says in a shaky voice once they're gone. "It's time for prayers." I don't know if she means in general or strictly for herself.

⌇⌇⌇⌇

We scurry across the threshold of the quiet, cavernous chapel and take our seats, our footsteps echoing off the marble floors. Arched wood-beamed ceilings soar a good fifteen feet above us. Candelabras line the sides of the church, casting long shadows over the wooden pews. Stained-glass windows line the walls, colourful advertisements for God, pastoral scenes of angels doing angelic sorts of things – visiting villagers, telling them good news, petting sheep, cradling babies. There is the odd panel with a severed gorgon's head, an angel in armour standing next to it, brandishing a sword dripping blood. Can't say that I've heard that particular Bible story – or want to, really. It's a bit gruesome so I turn my attention to the altar where a vicar stands, tall and thin as a scarecrow.

The vicar, whose name is Reverend Waite, leads us in prayers that all begin with "O Lord" and end with our somehow not being worthy – sinners who have always been sinners and will forever more be sinners until we die. It isn't the most optimistic outlook I've ever heard. But we're encouraged to keep trying anyway.

I have to watch Ann and the others to see when to kneel, when to rise, and when to mouth along to the hymn. My family is vaguely Anglican, like everyone else, but the truth is that we rarely went to church in India. On Sundays, Mother took me for picnics under hot, cloudless skies. We'd sit on a blanket and listen to the wind whip across dry land, whistling to us.

"This is our church," she'd say, combing fingers through my hair.

My heart's a tight fist in my chest while my lips form words I don't feel. Mother told me that most of the English only prayed with heart and soul when they needed something from God. What I want most from God is to have my mother back. That isn't possible. If it were, I'd pray to anyone's god, night and day, to make it so.

The vicar sits and Mrs Nightwing stands. Ann moans slightly under her breath.

"Oh, no. She's going to make a speech," she whispers.

"Does she do this every vespers?" I ask.

"No," Ann says, giving me a sidelong glance. "She's doing it for your benefit."

Suddenly, I can feel every pair of eyes glaring at me. Well, this should get me off to a rousing start with everyone.

"Ladies of Spence Academy," Mrs Nightwing begins. "As you know, for twenty-four years, Spence has enjoyed a reputation as one of England's finest finishing schools. While we can and will teach you the necessary skills to become England's future wives and mothers, hostesses and bearers of the Empire's feminine traditions, it will be up to each of you to nurture and feed your souls, and to apply yourselves with grace, charm, and beauty. This is the Spence motto: Grace, charm, and beauty. Let us all rise and say it together."

There is a great rustling as fifty girls stand at attention and recite the pledge, chins tilted upwards towards the future. "Thank you. You may be seated. For those girls who have returned to us this year, you shall set the example for the others. For those who are new to us" – Mrs Nightwing scans the chapel till she finds me next to Ann – "we expect nothing less than your very best."

Thinking this is our dismissal, I rise from the pew. Ann pulls on my skirt.

"She's just begun," she whispers.

And, indeed, Mrs Nightwing astonishes me by prattling on about virtue, the well-mannered girl, suitable breakfast fruits, the unfortunate influence of Americans on British society, and her own fondly remembered school days. Time has no meaning. I feel as if I have been left in the desert to die and am waiting eagerly for the vultures to begin their work and end my misery.

Candle shadows stretch long over the walls, making our faces look haunted and hollow. The chapel is hardly a comforting site. It's ghostly. Certainly not someplace I'd want to be alone after dark. I'm shivering at the thought of it. At last, Mrs Nightwing finishes her long-winded address, which makes me utter my own silent prayer of gratitude. Reverend Waite reads a benediction and we're dismissed for dinner.

One of the older girls stands at the door. When we reach her, she sticks out her foot and sends Ann sprawling to the floor. Her eyes dart past us where they find Felicity and Pippa a few heads behind.

I give Ann my hand and help her to her feet. "Are you all right?"

"Fine," she says, giving the same straight-ahead stare that seems to be her only expression.

The girl steps around her. "You really should be more careful." The others stream past us, casting glances at us, giggling.

"Grace, charm, and beauty," Felicity says as she breezes past. I wonder what she would look like if someone were to cut off all her hair in her sleep. My first evening at prayers has not made me into a particularly charitable girl.

Outside, the mist has thickened into a grey soup that settles around our legs. Down the hill lies the hazy outline of the enormous school, broken by thin slivers of lights from the various windows. Only one wing remains completely dark. I figure it to be the East Wing, the one destroyed by the fire. It sits, curled and quiet as the gargoyles on the roof, as if waiting. For what, I don't know.

Movement. To my right. A black cloak running through the trees, disappearing into the mist. My legs have gone rubbery.

"Did you see that?" I ask, voice shaking.

"See what?"

"Out there. Somebody running about in a black cape."

"No. It's the fog. Makes you see things."

I know what I saw. Someone was waiting there, watching us.

"It's cold," Ann says. "Let's walk faster, shall we?"

She steps briskly ahead of me, letting the fog consume her till she's only a blue spot, a shadow of a girl, fading into nothing.

CHAPTER SIX

I'M BEING WATCHED. THE FEELING STAYS WITH ME during a tedious dinner of lamb and potatoes followed by pudding. Who would be watching me and why? That is, who else besides the girls of Spence, who eye me and whisper to each other, stopping only when Mrs Nightwing reprimands one girl for letting her fork droop.

When dinner is finished, we are allowed a free period in the great hall. This is the time we're given to be at ease – to read, laugh, socialise, or just sit about. The great hall is just that – enormous. A massive fireplace commands the centre of one wall. Six beautifully engraved marble columns form a circle in the middle of the room. Mythical creatures have been carved into each one – winged fairies, nymphs, and satyrs. Strange décor, to say the least.

At one end of the room, the younger girls sit playing with dolls. Some have gathered to read, some to embroider, and some to gossip. In the best possible corner, Pippa and Felicity are holding court with a few other girls. Felicity has cordoned off a sitting area and turned it into her own fiefdom complete with exotic scarves that make it seem like a sheik's tent. Whatever she's telling the others seems to have them hanging on her every word. I have no idea how thrilling it might be, since I've not been invited. Not that I want to be invited. Not much, anyway.

Ann is nowhere to be found. I can't very well stand in the centre of the room like an imbecile, so I find a quiet seat near the roaring fire and open my mother's diary. Though I haven't looked through it in a month or so, I'm in the mood to torture myself tonight. In the firelight, Mother's elegant handwriting dances on the page. It's surprising how just the sight of her words on paper makes tears sting at my eyes. So much about her has begun to fade away. I want to keep holding on. And so I read, flipping through page after page of notes about teas and visits to temples and housekeeping lists, until I come to this, her very last entry:

June 2nd — Gemma is cross with me again. She wants desperately to go to London. That will of iron is formidable, and I am quite exhausted by it all. What will her birthday bring? It is agonising to wait, and torture to have her loathe me so.

Sentences go blurry, words run together as the tears pool. I wish I could go back and change everything.

"What are you doing?" Ann asks, hovering over me.

I wipe at my wet cheeks with the back of my hand, keep my head down. "Nothing."

Ann takes a seat and pulls out some knitting from a basket. "I like to read, too. Have you ever read *The Perils of Lucy, A Girl's Own Story?*"

"No. I can't say that I have." I know the type of book she means – cheap, sentimental claptrap about put-upon girls triumphing over adversity without ever losing that sweet, kindhearted, feminine softness everyone seems to prize so highly. The kind of girls who would never cause their families to worry and suffer. Girls nothing like me. The bitterness is too much to contain.

"Oh, wait," I reply. "That's the one where the heroine is some poor, timid girl at boarding school who gets bullied by everyone for being such a sap. She reads to the blind or raises a lame brother or perhaps even a blind and lame brother. And in the end everyone discovers she's really a duchess or some such who goes off to live like a queen in Kent. All because she took her punishment with a smile and a sense of Christian charity. What poppycock!"

My breath keeps catching in my chest. I've been overheard by the embroider-and-gossip set, who giggle in shocked delight at my bad manners.

"It might happen," Ann says, softly.

"Honestly," I say, with a brittle laugh, as if it will excuse the harshness of my words. "Do you know any orphan girls who've been plucked from obscurity and made into duchesses?" *Get yourself under control, Gemma. You mustn't cry.*

Ann's voice takes on a new determination. "But it could happen. Couldn't it? An orphan girl, a girl no one expected much from, someone who'd been dumped in a school because her relatives thought of her as a burden, a girl the other girls laugh at for her lack of grace, charm, and beauty . . . that girl might show them all one day."

She stares into the fire, knitting ferociously, the needles clicking together, two sharp teeth in the wool. Too late I realised what I've done. I've struck at the very heart of Ann's hope, a hope that she could become someone else, someone with a life that doesn't involve spending the rest of her days as governess to some rich man's children, grooming them for a wonderful life and opportunities she'll never see.

"Yes," I say, my voice hoarse and quiet. "Yes, I suppose it could happen."

"Those girls, the ones who misjudged . . . Lucy. They'd all be very sorry one day, wouldn't they?"

"Yes, they would," I agree. I don't know what else to say and so we sit and watch the fire crackle and spit.

Peals of high laughter draw our attention to the far corner. Pippa emerges from the sheik's tent where the other girls still sit. She saunters over to the two of us and slips her arm through Ann's.

"Ann, darling, Felicity and I feel simply awful about the way we treated you earlier. It was terribly unchristian of us."

Ann's face is still slack, but she blushes and I know she's pleased, sure that this is the beginning of her new, wonderful life among the beautiful. The end of *The Perils of Ann*.

"Felicity's mother sent a box of chocolates. Would you like to join us?"

There is no invitation issued to me. It's a huge slight. Across the room the other girls are waiting to see how I'll take it. Ann glances at me guiltily and I know what her answer will be. She's going to sit and eat chocolates with the very girls who torment her. And now I know that Ann is as shallow as the rest of them. More than ever I wish I could go home, but there is no more home.

"Well . . . ," Ann says, looking down at her feet.

I should just let her wallow in her discomfort, force her to snub me, but I'm not about to let them get the best of me.

"You should go," I say, flashing a smile that would put the sun to shame. "I really must catch up on my reading."

Yes, after all, if I were to join you, I might enjoy myself, and wouldn't that be a shame? Please, don't spare me another thought.

Pippa is all smiles. "There's a sport. Come on, Ann." She waltzes Ann off to the far end of the room. With a forced yawn for the benefit of the girls watching me from the tent, I sit down and open my mother's social diary again, as if I couldn't care less about being ignored. I turn the pages as if I'm captivated, though I've already read each one. Who do they think they are to treat me like this? Turn another page and another. More giggles waft out from the tent. The chocolate's probably from Manchester. And those scarves are ridiculous. Felicity is about as bohemian as the Bank of England. My fingers land on something crackly and stiff inside the book, something I hadn't noticed before. An account from a sensational London newspaper, the sort the upper classes pretend not to notice. It's been folded over so many times that the ink has worn away in the creases and elsewhere, making it hard to read. I can just make out the gist of it, something about the "scandalous secrets of girls' boarding schools!"

It's tawdry, of course. And that's what makes it so fascinating. In lurid prose, the article details a school in Wales where a few girls went out walking "and were never heard from again!" "A virtuous rose of England snipped by the tragic dagger of suicide" at a finishing school in Scotland. A mention of a girl who went "mad as a hatter" after some mysterious involvement in a "diabolical occult ring". What's diabolical is that someone received money for this rubbish.

I'm about to put it away when I see something near the bottom about the fire at Spence twenty years ago. But it's too worn for me to read. It's just like my mother to save such a sordid article to add to her list of worries. No wonder she wouldn't send me to London. She was afraid I'd end up on the front page. Funny how the things I couldn't bear about her bring a pang to my chest now.

A shriek comes from Felicity's sanctuary.

"My ring! What have you done with my ring?" The scarves fly open. Ann backs out with the other girls bearing down on her, Felicity pointing a finger accusingly. "Where is it? Tell me this instant!"

"I d-d-don't have it. I d-d-didn't d-do anything." Ann stumbles over her words and suddenly I realise that part of her flatness, her control, must be an effort to keep from stuttering like this.

"You d-d-didn't? Why d-d-don't I believe you?" Felicity's face is mocking and hateful. "I invite you to sit with us and this is how you repay my kindness? By stealing the ring my father gave to me? I should have expected something like this from a girl like you."

We all know what "like you" means. *Low-class*. Common. Plain, poor, and hopeless. You are what you're born, always and forever. That's the understanding.

An imposing woman with a handsome face sweeps over to the girls. "What's going on?" she asks, stepping between Ann, who is cowering, and Felicity, who looks ready to roast Ann on a spit.

Pippa goes wide-eyed as an ingénue in a bad play. "Oh, Miss Moore! Ann has stolen Felicity's sapphire ring."

Felicity thrusts out her ringless finger as proof and attempts a mournful pout. "I had it earlier and noticed it was missing just after *she* came in."

It's hardly a convincing performance. The organ-grinder's monkey is a better confidence man, but there's no telling whether or not Miss Moore will be taken in by these two. After all, they have money and position and Ann has none. It's amazing how often you can be right as long as you have those two things working in your favour. I'm ready for Miss Moore to straighten her spine and humiliate Ann in front of everyone by forcing her to admit her shame – and calling her all manner of horrible names as well. There's a certain type of spinster lady who takes her amusement by torturing others under the guise of "setting a good example". But Miss Moore surprises me by not taking the bait.

"All right, then, let's have a look around on the floor. Perhaps it fell somewhere. Come on, everyone, let's help Miss Worthington find her ring, shall we?"

Ann stands looking down at her shoes, unable to move or speak, as if she expects to be found guilty. I know I should feel pity for her but I'm still a bit miffed over the way she abandoned me, and an uncharitable part of me thinks she deserves this for trusting them. The others move chairs and peer behind curtains in a halfhearted attempt to find the ring.

"It's not here," a girl with a pinched face announces in triumph moments later when the ring doesn't turn up.

Miss Moore lets out a long sigh, chews at her bottom lip for a moment. When she speaks, her voice is soft but firm. "Miss Bradshaw, did you take the ring? If you admit it, the penalty will be less severe."

Ann's face has gone splotchy. The stutter returns. "N-n-no, mum. I d-d-didn't t-take it."

"That's what happens when you let her class into a school like Spence. We'll all be victims of her jealousy," Felicity gloats. The other girls nod. Sheep. I'm stuck in a boarding school filled with sheep.

"That will be quite enough, Miss Worthington." Miss Moore raises an eyebrow. Felicity glares back at her, places a hand on her hip.

"That ring was given to me by my father for my sixteenth birthday. I'm sure he would be most unhappy to hear that it had come to be stolen and no one was doing anything about it."

Miss Moore turns to Ann, reaches out a hand. "I'm sorry, Miss Bradshaw, but I'm afraid I'll have to ask you to let me see inside your knitting basket."

Thoroughly miserable, Ann hands over the knitting basket, and suddenly I know exactly what's going on, what's going to happen next. It's a prank. A vicious, nasty prank. Miss Moore will find the ring in there. The incident will be noted in Ann's academic record. And what family would possibly hire a girl as a governess who'd been labelled a thief? The poor, stupid girl is just standing there, ready to accept her fate.

Miss Moore pulls a dazzling blue sapphire from the basket, sad disappointment registering quickly in her eyes before she remembers herself and makes her face a mask of restraint and propriety. "Well, Miss Bradshaw, what do you have to say for yourself?"

A mixture of deep wretchedness and resignation pulls Ann's head and shoulders low. Pippa's mouth broadens into a smile, Felicity's a smirk as they exchange quick glances. I can't help wondering if this is Ann's punishment for talking to me earlier on the way to chapel. Is it a warning to me to watch my step?

"We'd best go and see Mrs Nightwing." Miss Moore takes Ann by the hand to see her executioner. What I should do is go back to the fire and read my book. Every bit of reason in me says I should keep quiet, blend in, side with the winning team. Some days my reason is no match for my temper.

"Ann, darling," I say, copying Pippa's chummy tone from earlier. Everyone seems surprised to hear me speak, no one more surprised than I am at the moment. "Don't be modest. Tell Miss Moore the truth."

Ann's huge eyes search mine for meaning. "The t-t-truth?"

"Yes," I say, hoping I can make this up as I go along. "The truth – that Miss Worthington lost her ring tonight during vespers. You found it and put it in your knitting basket for safekeeping."

"Why didn't she return it right away, then?" Felicity steps forward, challenging me, her grey eyes inches from mine.

Tricky, tricky. *Make this good, Gem.* "She didn't want to embarrass you in front of everyone and make it obvious that you'd been careless with something so valuable, a gift from your father. So she was waiting for a private moment. You know how kindhearted Ann is." A little *Perils of Lucy*. A little smacking Felicity with her own petulant story about dear old Father. All in all, not bad.

Miss Moore appraises me. There's no telling whether she believes me or not. "Miss Bradshaw, is this true?"

Come on, Ann. Play along. Fight back.

Ann swallows hard, raises her chin to Miss Moore. "Y-y-yes. It is."

Good girl.

I'm feeling pretty pleased with myself until I lock eyes with Felicity, who is glaring at me with a mix of admiration and hatred. I've won this round, but I know that with girls like Felicity and Pippa there will always be a next time.

"I'm glad that's settled, Miss . . . ?" Miss Moore stares at me.

"Doyle. Gemma Doyle."

"Well, Miss Gemma Doyle, it would seem that we are in

your debt. I'm sure Miss Worthington would like to thank you both for retrieving her lost ring, wouldn't you?"

For the second time tonight, Miss Moore surprises me, and I'm almost certain I see a satisfied smile pulling at the corners of her proper British mouth.

"She could have come forward sooner and not frightened us all so," Felicity says by way of thank-you.

"Grace, charm, and beauty, Miss Worthington," Miss Moore admonishes, waving a finger disapprovingly.

Felicity looks like a girl whose lollipop has just landed in the dirt. But then she's all smiles again, the bitterness gone, pushed down deep.

"It would seem that I am in your debt, Gemma," Felicity says. She's goading me by being so informal with my name when I haven't given her leave to do so.

"Not at all, Felicity," I volley back.

"This ring was a gift from my father, Admiral Worthington. Perhaps you've heard of him?"

Half the English-speaking world has heard of Admiral Worthington — a naval hero, decorated by Queen Victoria herself. "No, I can't say that I have," I lie.

"He's very famous. He sends me all sorts of things from his travels. My mother runs a salon in Paris, and when Pippa and I are graduated, we're going to Paris, where Mama will have us outfitted by the finest couturiers in France. Perhaps we'll take you along as well."

It's not an invitation. It's a challenge. They want to know if I have the means to keep up with them. "Perhaps," I say. They don't invite Ann.

"It's going to be a wonderful season, though Pippa will probably get the lion's share of attention." Pippa beams at this. She's so lovely that scores of young men will prod their relatives to introduce them. "You and I will simply have to be good sports about it."

"And Ann," I say.

"Yes, and Ann, of course. Dear Ann." Felicity laughs, giving Ann a quick kiss on the cheek, which makes her blush again. It's as if all is forgotten.

The clock strikes ten and Mrs Nightwing makes an appearance at the doors. "Time for bed, ladies. I bid you all good night."

Girls shuffle out in twos and threes, arms linked, voices and spirits high. The excitement of the evening lives on in a contagion of whispers that trickle from girl to girl. We're going round and round in a maypole dance of stairs and more stairs, inching towards the maze of doors where our rooms lie.

I'm finally unable to hold back my irritation with Ann. "You're welcome, I'm sure."

"Why did you do it?" she asks. Is no one here capable of saying a simple "thank you"?

"Why didn't you defend yourself?"

She shrugs. "What's the point? There's no winning against them."

"There you are, Ann, darling." Pippa comes up and takes Ann by the arm, slowing her down so that Felicity can slip in beside me. Her voice in my ear is confession-quiet.

"I shall have to think of a way to repay you for finding my

ring tonight. We have a bit of a private club, Pippa, Cecily, Elizabeth, and I, but there might be room for you."

"Aren't I the lucky one? I'll rush right out and buy a new bonnet for the occasion."

Felicity's eyes narrow, but her mouth never loses its smile. "There are girls who would give their eyeteeth to be in your position."

"Fine. Then ask them."

"See here, I'm offering you a chance to get on at Spence. To be a part of something and have the other girls look up to you. You might do well to think about it."

"To be part of something the way you made Ann a part of something tonight?" I say. I look back at Ann, several steps below me now, her nose running again.

Felicity sees this. "It's not that we don't want Ann involved. It's just that her life isn't going to be like ours. You think you're being so kind to her when you know very well that you can't be friends with her on the outside. It's much crueller to make her think otherwise, to lead her on."

She's right. I don't trust her farther than I can run full-steam in a corset, but she is right. The truth is hard and unfair, but there it is.

"If I were interested in joining – which I'm not saying that I am – but if I were, what would I have to do?"

"Nothing yet," she says, her face breaking into the sort of smile that doesn't make me feel at ease. "Don't worry – we'll come to you." She lifts her skirts and runs up the stairs, shooting past the rest of us like a comet.

CHAPTER
SEVEN

IT'S THE SOUND THAT WAKES ME. MY EYELIDS FLUTTER
open, fighting off the remnants of dreams. I'm lying on my
right side, facing Ann's bed. The door and whatever may be
just inside it are down past my feet at the far end of the
room. To get a good look, I'd have to move, sit up, roll over,
and I'm not about to let on that I'm awake. It's a five-year-
old's logic: If I can't see it, it can't see me. No doubt plenty of
unfortunate people have wound up with their heads cut off
by assuming the very same thing.

All right, Gem, no use getting frightened. It's probably nothing. I
blink and let my eyes adjust to the dark. Fingers of moonlight reach through the crack in the long velvet drapes and
up the walls, nearly touching the low ceiling. Outside, a
branch scratches against the windowpane with a squeak. My
ears strain for some other noise, something in the room with
us. There's nothing else but the rhythm of Ann's steady
snoring. For a moment I think I must have dreamed it. And
there it is again. The creaking of floorboards under careful

steps that tells me this is not my imagination. I let my eyelids close to small slits so that I can pretend to be asleep but still see. No one takes my head without a fight. A figure looms closer. My tongue feels thick and dry in my mouth. The figure reaches out a hand and I'm up quickly, smashing my skull into the overhang just above my bed.

I hiss in pain, forgetting my visitor and placing a palm on my throbbing forehead.

A surprisingly small hand clamps over my mouth. "Do you want to wake the whole bloody school?" Felicity leans over me, the moonlight catching the planes of her face in such a way that she is all wide, hard angles and milky-white skin. She could be the face of the moon itself.

"What are you doing here?" I ask, my fingers rubbing across the goose egg–sized lump rising along my hairline.

"I told you we'd come for you."

"You didn't say it would be in the middle of the bloody night," I say, matching her tone. There's something about Felicity that makes me want to impress her, show her that I'm a match for her strength and she can't win me so easily.

"Come on. I want to show you something."

"What?"

She speaks to me slowly, as she would a child. "Follow me and I'll show you."

My head still hurts from the bang. Ann is snoring lightly, completely unaware that we're having this conversation.

"Come back in the morning," I say, flopping back against my pillow. I'm awake enough to know that whatever she wants to show me at this hour can't be good.

"I won't make this offer again. It's now or never."

Go back to sleep, Gem. This does not sound promising. It's my conscience talking. But my conscience doesn't have to spend the next two years making inane teatime chatter, bored to the point of catatonia. This is a challenge, and I've never said no to a challenge in my life.

"All right, then. I'm up," I say. Then, just to make sure I don't seem too soft, I add, "But this had better be good."

"Oh, it will. I promise you."

I find myself following Felicity out of my room, down the long corridor, past rooms of sleeping girls tucked away behind walls that house pictures of women from Spence's past, grim-faced ghosts in white dresses whose sombre mouths are tight in disapproval of this little escapade, but whose sad eyes all seem to say *go. Go while you can. Freedom is brief.*

When we get to the huge landing and the stairs leading down, I pause. "What about Mrs Nightwing?" I say, glancing up the enormous stairs that extend to a fourth floor I can't see in the dark.

"Don't worry about her. Once she's had her glass of sherry, she's down for the night." Felicity starts down.

"Wait!" I whisper as loudly as I can without waking anyone. Felicity stops, turns to me, that pale face taunting. Hips swaying, she inches back up to the stair just below me.

"If you want to spend your time here embroidering God Bless Our Home samplers and learning how to play lawn tennis in a corset and skirt, go back to bed. But if you want to have a bit of real fun, well . . ." And with that she trips lightly down the stairs and around the corner to the next set of stairs, where I can no longer see her.

~~~~

Pippa meets us in the great hall. The huge fireplaces have all gone dark, with a few embers still crackling and spitting but no real warmth or light left. She's been hiding behind a large fern. Now she pops out, eyes wide and agitated.

"What took you so long?"

"It's only been a few minutes," Felicity says.

"I don't like waiting down here. All those eyes on the columns. It's as if they're watching me."

In the dark, the marble sprites and nymphs take on a ghoulish quality. The room feels alive, taking note of our every move, counting every breath.

"Don't be such a ninny. Let's be brave girls, shall we? Where are the others?" As if on cue, two girls descend the stairs and join us. I'm introduced to Elizabeth, a tiny ratlike creature who offers an opinion only after everyone else has, and the pinch-faced Cecily, whose narrow upper lip curls when she takes in the sight of me. Martha, the tripper in the chapel, isn't among them, and I realise she's not part of the club; she only wishes she were. That's why she was willing to trip Ann – to curry favour with them.

"Ready?" Cecily sneers.

What have I got myself into? Why don't I simply say, *All right, girls, it's been lovely. Thanks ever so for the midnight gambol about the old palatial grounds. Wouldn't have wanted to miss the way the parlour flares to life at night with a wonderful, nightmarish glow, but I'll just be getting back to bed now.* Instead, I follow them outside onto the back lawn, where the full moon bleeds yellow behind a thin, high bank of clouds. The bloody fog is still there and it's frightfully cold. I'm dressed in only my nightgown. They're clever girls with their blue velvet capes on.

"Follow me." Felicity starts up the hill towards the chapel, the fog swallowing her whole in just a few steps. I fall in behind her and the others fall in behind me so that turning back is no longer an option. Suddenly I'm second-guessing my decision to follow the Mystery Sisters out onto the vast, foggy night all the way to the chapel doors.

"We have a tradition here at Spence," Felicity says. "A little initiation ceremony for new girls who might prove worthy of our inner circle."

"Can you really have an inner circle with only four people?" I ask, sounding braver than I feel. "Seems more like an inner square, doesn't it?"

"You're lucky to be here," Cecily snaps.

Yes, I feel incredibly lucky to be standing out here in the freezing cold in only my nightgown. Some people might call it remarkably stupid, but I'm feeling quite optimistic.

"So, what is this secret initiation?"

Elizabeth looks to Felicity for permission to talk. "You only need to take something from the chapel."

"As in steal something?" I ask, not liking where this is going one bit but feeling too far in to get out now.

"It's not stealing. After all, it will never leave Spence. It's just a way to prove that you are trustworthy," Felicity says.

I have a few seconds to think and even though the most reasonable answer is to say I'm not interested and go back to bed, I say instead, "What do you want me to take?"

The clouds thin into wisps. Buttery moonlight spreads out and down. Felicity's mouth opens, her tongue rubbing against her top teeth, feeling them. "The communion wine."

"Communion wine?" I repeat.

Pippa makes a coughing noise in her throat before dissolving into giggles and I can see this is an impromptu request, an extra bit of daring on Felicity's part.

Cecily looks aghast. "But Fee, that's sacrilege!"

"Yes, I'm not sure that's a good idea," I begin.

"Really? I think it's an excellent idea," Felicity snaps. The admiral's daughter doesn't like it when her crew disobeys. "What about you, Elizabeth? What do you think?"

Elizabeth the puppet looks between her two masters, Felicity and Cecily. "Oh, I, I suppose—"

Pippa breaks in. "I think it's a tip-top idea."

I could almost swear I hear the trees whispering *idiot*. What have I got myself into?

"Don't tell me you're afraid to go in there by yourself?" Felicity says.

That's exactly what I'm afraid of, but I can't very well say it. "What happens when Reverend Waite discovers the communion wine is missing? Won't he be suspicious?"

A contemptuous "ha" escapes from Felicity's mouth. "That drunkard will only suspect that he drank it himself. Besides, there are always Gypsy caravans around here this time of year. We can blame it on them if we have to."

I don't like this idea much. The chapel doors seem to have grown taller and more ominous since vespers. Despite my misgivings, I know I'm going in. "Where does he keep the wine?"

Pippa pushes me towards the doors. "Behind the altar. There's a small cubbyhole."

She slides the bolt back with all her strength. The doors creak open on the tomb-like darkness inside.

"You can't very well expect me to find it in the dark."

"Feel your way," Felicity says, pushing me inside.

I can't believe that I'm here inside a dark, gloomy chapel ready to commit complete sacrilege by stealing. Thou shalt not steal. I seem to recall that as being one of God's *I'd rather you didn't lest I have to smite you into ash* commandments. Nor do I think it will help my case that I'm stealing what the Church believes is the holy blood of Christ. It's not too late. I could still turn back and go to bed. I could, but I'd forever yield what power I have now to those girls.

Right. Get this over quickly, then. The light from the open door brightens up the vestibule, but the far end, where the altar and wine are, is in complete darkness. I start towards it and hear the door creaking closed, the light vanishing with the girls, the heavy thud of the wooden bolt being thrown on the outside of the door. They're locking me in. Without thinking, I throw myself shoulder first into the door, hoping for enough time to push it open. It doesn't give. And actually, it hurts quite badly.

Stupid, stupid, stupid, Gem. What did I expect? How could I have been taken in by that story about wanting me to be part of their private club? Ann's voice swims in my head – *what's the point? There's no winning against them.* I don't have time to feel sorry for myself. I've got to think.

There must be another way out of here. I only have to find it. All around me, the church seems to breathe with shadows. Mice scurry under pews, their claws scratching against the marble floor. My skin crawls at the thought. But the moon is strong. It falls through the stained-glass windows, bringing an angel to life, then the gorgon's head, its eyes burning yellow in the dark.

I'm up and feeling my way from pew to pew, hoping I don't run into furry rodents or worse. Every sound is magnified. The clicking of night crawlers. Creaking and groaning of wood in the wind. Silently, I berate myself for falling prey to such a nasty prank. *It's just a little initiation we have here at Spence – we like to torture each other. Beauty, grace, and charm my foot. It's a school for sadists with good tea-serving skills.*

Click-click. Creak.

Felicity's probably no more related to Admiral Worthington than I am.

Click-click. Creak.

I don't even want to go to Paris.

Click, creak. Cough.

A cough. I didn't cough. And if I didn't, then who did?

It takes just a second for this to sink down into my legs and now I'm stumble-running up the middle aisle as fast as I can manage. My foot finds the first step to the altar. I trip and land sprawled on the hard marble, the sharp edge biting into my leg. But I can hear footsteps running up behind me, so I'm on hands and knees, scrambling for what I see just behind the organ – a door, open just a crack. Feel the last step and I'm up on wobbly legs, running hard for the promise of what's on the other side of that door. Reach out a hand and . . .

There's something overhead. Dear God, I must be imagining things because something, someone, is flying over my head, landing with a thump in the space between the door and me. A hand clamps over my mouth, trapping my scream there. The other arm pulls me in, pins me tight.

It's instinct that makes me bite the hand on my mouth. I'm unceremoniously dumped to the floor. And then I'm up on my feet again, leaping for the door. A hand snakes around my ankle, bringing me down hard till I see pinpricks of light behind closed eyes. I try to crawl away but my knee and head hurt too badly.

"Stop. Please." The voice is young, male, and vaguely familiar.

A match flares in the darkness. My eyes follow the light as it fills the chamber of a lantern. The light spills out, catches the outline of broad shoulders, a black cloak, before rising to frame a face with large dark eyes fringed in a halo of lashes. I'm not imagining things. He's really here. I jump up but he's faster, blocking off all access to the door.

"I'll scream. I swear I will." My voice is no more than a scratching sound in the dark.

He's tensed and ready, for what I don't know, but it makes my heart hammer against my ribs. "No, you won't. How will you explain what you're doing here with me in the middle of the night without proper clothes, Miss Doyle?"

Instinctively, I put my arms around my body, trying to hide the shape of me beneath my thin white gown. He knows me, knows my name. My pulse throbs in my ears. How long would it take for my scream to reach someone? Is there anyone out there to hear me?

I step behind the altar, putting it between us. "Who are you?"

"You don't need to know who I am."

"You know my name. Why can't I know yours?"

He ponders this before answering with a curt reply. "Kartik."

"Kartik. Is that your real name?"

"I've given you a name. That's enough."

"What do you want?"

"Just to talk to you."

Keep thinking, Gemma. Keep him talking. "You've been following me. At the train station today. And earlier at vespers."

He nods. "I stowed away on the *Mary Elizabeth* in Bombay. Rough passage. I know the English are terribly sentimental about the sea, but I can live without it." The lantern casts his shadow up and across the wall like a winged thing, hovering. He's still guarding the door. Neither of us moves.

"Why? Why come all this way?"

"As I told you, I need to talk to you." He takes a step

forward. I shrink back and he stops. "It's about that day and your mother."

"What do you know about my mother?" My voice startles a bird hiding in the rafters. Panicked, it flaps to another beam in a flurry of frantic wings.

"I know that she didn't die of cholera, for one thing."

I force a deep breath. "If you're hoping to blackmail my family . . ."

"Nothing of the sort." Another step forward.

Against the cool marble of the altar, my hands tremble, unsure whether they'll have to put up a fight. "Go on."

"You saw it happen, didn't you?"

"No." The lie turns my breath shallow and fast.

"You're lying."

"N-no . . . I . . ."

Fast as a snake, he's up on the altar, crouched before me, the lantern inches from my face. He could easily burn me or snap my neck. "For the last time, what did you see?"

My mouth has gone completely dry with the sort of fear that will say anything. "I . . . I saw her killed. I saw them both killed."

His jaw clenches tight. "Go on."

There's a sob riding hard on my ragged breath. I push it down. "I . . . I tried to call out to her, but she couldn't hear me. And then . . ."

"What?"

The weight in my chest is unbearable, making each word a struggle. "I don't know. It was as if the shadows started to move . . . I've never seen anything like it . . . some hideous creature." For some reason, it feels good to pour out to a complete stranger what I've been holding in from everyone else.

"Your mother took her own life, didn't she?"

"Yes," I whisper, astonished that he knows this.

"She was lucky."

"How dare you –"

"Trust me, she was lucky not to be taken by that thing. As for my brother, he was not so fortunate."

"What is it?"

"Nothing you can fight."

"I saw it again. On the carriage ride here. I had another … vision."

He's alarmed. I can see the fear in him, and now I'm sorry I've told him anything. In one move, he's off the altar and in front of me. "Listen to me well, Miss Doyle. You are not to speak about what you've seen to anyone. Do you understand?"

Moonlight pokes through the stained glass in weak slices. "Why not?"

"Because it will put you in danger."

"What was that thing I saw?"

"It was a warning. And if you don't want other, terrible things to happen, you will not bring on any more visions."

The night, the pranks, the fear and exhaustion – they all collide in a sneering laugh I can't seem to stop. "And how, pray tell, am I supposed to do that? It's not as if I asked for it in the first place."

"Close your mind to them and they'll stop soon enough."

"And if I can't?"

Without a sound, he reaches out quickly and clamps a hand around the delicate bones of my wrist, squeezing tightly. "You will." Down the centre aisle, a mouse makes a bold run for it, rushing across to the other side of the church, where it's only a scratching sound again. I'm bending under the pressure on my wrist. He lets go, a satisfied smirk on his face. I pull my arm close and rub at the sting on my skin.

"We'll be watching you, Miss Doyle."

There's a clattering sound at the chapel's heavy oak doors. I can hear Reverend Waite's drunken singing as he fumbles to lift the bolt, cursing as it falls back into place with a thud. I don't know whether to be thankful or terrified that he'll find me here. In the instant I turned to look, my tormentor has vanished. He's simply gone. The door is unguarded. I have a way out. And then I see it. The decanter of communion wine sitting full and ready in its cubbyhole.

The wooden bolt slides free. He's almost in. But tonight Reverend Waite will be denied his wine. It's cradled in my arm as I bound through the side door and stop at the top of a dark stairwell. What if he's waiting for me down those shadowy stairs?

Reverend Waite calls out, half-drunk. "Is anyone there?"

I'm down the stairwell and out behind the chapel as if I've been shot from a cannon. Not till I've stumbled my way down the hill and have the imposing bricks of Spence in sight do I stop for breath. A crow caws, making me jump. I feel eyes on me everywhere.

We'll be watching you.

What did he mean by that? Who is "we"? And why would anyone want to keep an eye on a girl who wasn't clever enough to outwit a quartet of boarding school pranksters? What does he know about my mother?

Just keep looking at the school, Gemma. You'll be all right. I keep my eyes on the rows of windows ahead. They bob up and down with each step. *You will not bring on any more visions.*

It's ridiculous. Galling, in fact. As if I have any control over them. As if I could just shut my eyes, like this, right now, and will myself into one. The sound of my breath slows, grows louder. My whole body has gone warm and relaxed, as if I'm floating in the most delicious bath of sweet rose water. At the smell of roses, I snap my eyes open.

The little girl from the alley stands in front of me, shimmering. She beckons me with her hand. "This way."

CHAPTER
EIGHT

"WHERE ARE WE GOING?"

She doesn't answer, just darts into a thicket of trees, her brightness leading the way in the night, like a flame under glass.

"Wait," I say. "Not so fast."

"We've got to hurry."

She flits ahead on the path. What am I doing? I've gone and done the one thing I've been asked not to do – bring on more visions. But how could I know that I could do it at will? We're in a clearing of some kind. There's a dark mound just before us. I'm terrified that these shadows will come alive and I'll hear that ghastly voice from the alley, but the little girl doesn't seem afraid. The mound is hollowed out inside, a sort of makeshift cave. She leads me down into the dank-smelling darkness. Her light fills the cave but even so, I can barely make out anything beyond a bit of rock, a spot of shiny moss.

"Behind that rock." Her hand, incandescent and tiny,

points to the near wall of the cave, where a large rock sits just at the base. "She says you've got to look behind it."

"Who is she?"

"Mary, of course."

"I've told you – I don't know any Mary." I'm arguing with a vision, a spirit. Next I know, I'll be calling myself the queen of Romania and wandering down the lane wearing my bed linens for a cape.

"She knows *you*, miss."

Mary. It's only the most common name for a girl in all of England. What if this is all a trick, a way of testing me? He said I was in danger. What if this otherworldly little girl is a malevolent spirit who means to do me harm? What if the bedtime stories used to keep children at heel – tales of ghosts and goblins and witches ready to trick you into giving up your soul – are true? And now I'm trapped here in a dark cave with some sinister force who only seems like a lost urchin?

I swallow hard but the lump in my throat stays. "Suppose I don't want to look."

"She says you must, miss. It's the only way to understand what's happening to you. To understand the power."

I have no idea what she's talking about. I only know I don't particularly fancy turning my back on her.

"Why don't you get it, then?"

She shakes her head. "She says you have to find it yourself. That's the way of the realms."

I'm tired and cold and in no mood for a mystery anymore.

"Please, I don't understand. Just tell me what this is all about!"

"You'd best hurry, miss." Those large brown eyes flit towards the mouth of the cave and back again, and I shudder to think of what she could be afraid of out there in the dark.

Whatever happens, I can't end up knowing less than I do right now. The rock is solid, but not unmovable. With effort, I push it away. There's a hole in the cave wall, about an arm's length deep. My heart is racing as my fingers feel their way inside the cold, hard rock. God only knows what's crawling around in there, and I have to bite my lip to stifle a scream. I'm in up to my shoulder when I feel something solid. It's stuck fast, and I have to pull hard to bring it into the light. It's a leather-bound diary. I open to the first page. A stream of dirt trickles free; the rest I brush away. An envelope has been tucked into the book's binding. The paper crackles in my fingers as I pull out one of the pages roaming loose inside.

What frightens you?

What makes the hair on your arms rise, your palms sweat, the breath catch in your chest like a wild thing caged?

Is it the dark? A fleeting memory of a bedtime story, ghosts and goblins and witches hiding in the shadows? Is it the way the wind picks up just before a storm, the hint of wet in the air that makes you want to scurry home to the safety of your fire?

Or is it something deeper, something much more frightening, a monster deep inside that you've glimpsed only in pieces, the vast unknown of your own soul where secrets gather with a terrible power, the dark inside?

If you will listen, I will tell you a story — one whose ghosts cannot be banished by the comfort of a roaring fire. I will tell you the story of how we found ourselves in a realm where dreams are formed, destiny is chosen, and magic is as real as your handprint in snow. I will tell you how we unlocked the Pandora's box of ourselves, tasted freedom, stained our souls with blood and choice, and unleashed a horror on the world that destroyed its dearest Order. These pages are a confession of all that has led to this cold, grey dawn. What will be now, I cannot say.

Is your heart beating faster?

Do the clouds seem to be gathering on the horizon?

Does the skin on your neck feel stretched tight, waiting for a kiss you both fear and need?

Will you be scared?

Will you know the truth?

Mary Dowd, April 7, 1871

Is this the Mary who thinks she knows me? I don't know any Mary Dowd. My head aches and I'm cold out here in just my nightgown.

"Tell Mary to leave me alone. I don't want this power she's giving me."

"She's not giving you the power, miss. Just showing you the way."

"Well, I don't want to follow! Do you understand, Mary

Dowd?" I'm shouting at the cave till my voice echoes in my ears. It's enough to pull me hard from the vision, until I'm alone in the cave, the diary in my hands.

❤❤❤

The life of Mary Dowd sits on my bed, taunting me. I could burn it. Take it back and bury it. But my curiosity is too strong for that. Alone in my bed, I light a candle, place it on the windowsill, and read as much as I can in that weak light. I discover that Mary Dowd is sixteen in 1871. She adores walks in the woods, misses her family, wishes her skin were fairer. Her dearest friend in the world is a girl named Sarah Rees-Toome who is the "most charming and virtuous girl in the world." They are like sisters, never apart. I find myself jealous of a girl I've never met. All in all, the first twenty pages of the diary are a thudding bore, and I can't understand why the little girl wanted me to have it. The threat of sleep makes my eyelids flutter and my head nod, so I place the diary at the back of my wardrobe behind Father's cricket bat. And then I'm off to sleep, banishing it from my mind.

When I dream, it's of my mother. She pulls my hair back gently in her hands, her warm fingers weaving through it like sunlight, making me drowsy and content. Her arms hold me close, but I slip out of her embrace into the ruin of an ancient temple. Snakes slither along deep green vines grown heavy over an altar. A storm blows in fast, thick ropes of clouds knotting up the sky. Mother's face looms, tight with fear. Lightning fast, she takes off her necklace, tosses it to me. It hangs in the air, making slow spirals, till it lands in my hands, the corner of the silvery eye cutting my palm. Blood seeps from the cut. When I look up, Mother is shouting to me over the storm. The howling wind makes it hard to hear. But I catch one word above all the others.

Run.

CHAPTER
NINE

WHEN I WAKE, IT'S AN ACTUAL BRIGHT BLUE MORNING
with real sun streaming through the window, making
windowpane patterns on the floor. Everything outside is
golden. No one asking me to steal anything. No young
cloaked men issuing cryptic warnings. No strange, glowing
little girls standing guard while I rummage about in dark
places. It's as if last night never even happened. I stretch my
arms overhead, trying to remember my strange dreams,
something about my mother, but it won't come back to me.
The diary's in the wardrobe, where I intend to let it gather
dust. Today, revenge is first in my mind.

"You're awake," Ann says. She's fully dressed, sitting on
her tidily made bed, watching me.

"Yes," I answer.

"Best get dressed if you want a hot breakfast. It's inedible
once it's cold." She pauses. Stares. "I cleaned away the mud
you tracked in."

A quick glance down and ah, there it is, my dirty foot

sticking out from the stiff white sheet. I quickly cover it up.

"Where did you go?"

I don't want to have this conversation. It's sunny out. There's bacon downstairs. My life is starting over today. I've just made it official. "Nowhere, really. I simply couldn't sleep," I lie, managing what I think passes for a radiant smile.

Ann watches as I pour water from a flowered pitcher into a bowl and scrub at my mud-caked feet and ankles. I step behind the dressing screen for modesty's sake and pull the white dress over my head, then sweep a brush through my Medusa curls and secure them in a tight coil at the base of my neck. The hairpin scrapes against my tender scalp on the way in, and I wish I could just wear my hair down as I did when I was a young girl.

There is the problem of the corset. There's no way that I can tighten the laces at my back by myself. And it would seem that there is no maid to help with our dressing. With a sigh, I turn to Ann.

"Would you mind terribly?"

She pulls hard on the laces, pushing the air out of my lungs till I think my ribs will break. "A bit looser, please," I squeak. She obliges, and I'm now only uncomfortable instead of crippled.

"Thank you," I say when we're finished.

"You've got a smudge on your neck." I do wish she would stop watching me. In the small hand mirror on my desk, I discover the spot, right below my chin. I lick my finger and wipe it off, hoping this offends Ann enough that she'll look away before I'm forced to do something really horrible – pick at my scabs, examine a blemish, search for nose hair – in order to gain a little privacy. I give myself one last glance in the mirror. The face staring back at me isn't beautiful but she isn't something that would frighten the horses, either. On this morning with the sun warming my cheeks, I've never looked more like my mother.

Ann clears her throat. "You really shouldn't wander around here alone."

I wasn't alone. She knows it, but I'm not eager to tell Ann about my humiliation at the hands of the others. She might think it bonds us together as misfits, and I'm an oddity of one, my strangeness too complicated to explain or share.

"Next time I can't sleep, I'll wake you," I say. "Goodness, what happened here?" The inside of Ann's wrist is a nightmare of thin, red scratches, like crosshatch stitching on a hem. It looks as if they've been gouged there by a needle or a pin. Quickly, she pulls her sleeves down past her wrists.

"N-n-nothing," she says. "It was an a-a-accid-d-ent."

What sort of accident could leave such a mark? It looks deliberate to me, but I say only, "Oh," and look away.

Ann walks towards the door. "I hope they have fresh strawberries today. They're good for the complexion. I read it in *The Perils of Lucy*." She stands on the threshold, rocking back and forth on her heels slightly. Her unnerving gaze falters a little. She examines her fingers as she says, "My complexion could use all the help it can get."

"Your complexion's fine." I pretend to fiddle with my collar.

She's not bought off so easily. "It's all right. I know I'm plain. Everyone says it." There's a hint of defiance in her eyes, as if she's daring me to say it isn't true. If I disagree, she'll know I'm lying. If I say nothing, she'll have her worst fears confirmed.

"Strawberries, you say? I'll have to try some."

The glazed calm is back. She was hoping for the lie from me, for one person to disagree and tell her she's beautiful. I've failed her.

"Suit yourself," she says, leaving me alone at last to wonder whether I'll ever make a single friend at Spence.

<hr>

There's just enough time to make the morning's first stop – a little offering of appreciation for Felicity's kindness last night – and then I'm off to breakfast, suddenly famished. As I'm late, I manage to avoid seeing Felicity, Pippa, and the others. Unfortunately, it means I cannot also avoid the now lukewarm eggs and porridge, which are every bit as bad as Ann predicted and then some. The porridge congeals on my spoon in cold, thick clumps.

"Told you so," she says, finishing the last of a piece of bacon that makes my mouth water.

<hr>

When we report to our first class, Mademoiselle LeFarge's French lesson, my luck runs out. Felicity's clique of girls is clumped together in their seats, waiting for me. They guard the back row of the small, cramped room so that I'm forced to walk the gauntlet past them to take a seat. *Right. Here goes.*

Felicity sticks out her dainty foot, stopping me in the narrow row between her wooden desk and Pippa's. "Sleep well?"

"Quite." I give it an extra cheeriness it doesn't deserve, to show how little I'm bothered by schoolgirl pranks in the night. The foot remains.

"However did you manage it? Getting out, I mean?" Cecily asks.

"I have hidden powers," I say, amusing myself with this rueful bit of information. Martha realises she's been left out of the night's foolery. She can't bring herself to say so. Instead, she tries to be part of them by mimicking me.

"I have hidden powers," she singsongs.

My cheeks go hot. "By the way, I did secure the object you requested."

Felicity is all attention. "Really? Where do you have it hidden?"

"Oh, I didn't think it wise to hide it. Might not be able to find it again," I say, cheerily. "It's sitting in plain view on your chair in the great hall. I do hope that was the best place for it."

Felicity's mouth flies open in horror. I give her foot a little shove with my leg and move up to a desk in the front row, feeling the heat of their gazes on my neck.

"What was that all about?" Ann asks, folding her hands neatly on her desk like a model pupil.

"Nothing worth mentioning," I say.

"They locked you in the church, didn't they?"

I lift the lid on my desk to block out Ann's face. "No, of course not. Don't be silly." But for the first time I see the hint of a smile – a real smile – tugging at the corners of her mouth.

"Will they never get tired of that one?" she mutters, shaking her head.

Before I can respond, Mademoiselle LeFarge, all two hundred pounds of her, sweeps into the room with a cheery "*Bonjour.*" She grabs a rag and rubs it vigorously across the already clean slate, prattling on in French the whole time, stopping to ask the occasional question, which, I'm panicked to discover, everyone has the answer to – in French. I haven't the faintest idea what's going on, French being a language I've always thought sounded vaguely like gargling.

Mademoiselle LeFarge stops at my desk, claps her hands together in discovery. "*Ah, une nouvelle fille! Comment vous appellez-vous?*" Her face hovers dangerously near mine so that I can see the space between her two front teeth and every pore on her wide nose.

"Beg your pardon?" I ask.

She wags a chubby finger. "*Non, non, non . . . en Français, s'il vous plaît. Maintenant, comment vous appellez-vous?*" She gives me that hopeful, wide smile again. Behind me, I hear snickering erupt from Felicity and Pippa. The first day of my new life and I'm stumped before I begin.

It feels like hours before Ann finally volunteers a helpful "*Elle s'appelle Gemma.*"

What is your name? All those strangled vowel sounds to ask one bloody stupid question? This is the silliest language on earth.

"*Ah, bon, Ann. Très bon.*" Felicity is still stifling her laughter. Mademoiselle LeFarge asks her a question. I pray she'll stumble through it like a cow, but her French is absolutely flawless. There is no justice in the world.

Each time Mademoiselle LeFarge asks me something, I stare straight ahead and say "Pardon?" a lot, as if being either deaf or polite will help me understand this impossible language. Her wide grin closes slowly into a scowl till she gives up altogether asking me anything, which is fine with me. When the gruelling hour is finally over, I have learned to stumble my way through the phrases "How charming" and "Yes, my strawberries are very juicy."

Mademoiselle lifts her arms and we all rise in unison, recite the goodbye. "*Au revoir, Mademoiselle LeFarge.*"

"*Au revoir, mes filles,*" she calls as we place books and inkwells inside our desks. "Gemma, could you stay for a moment, please?" Her English accent is bracing as cold water after all that flowy French. Mademoiselle LeFarge is no more Parisian than I am.

Felicity nearly trips in her mad rush to get out the door.

"Mademoiselle Felicity! There's no need to hurry."

"Pardon, Mademoiselle LeFarge." She glares at me. "I've just remembered that I need to retrieve something important before my next class."

When the room thins out to just the two of us, Mademoiselle LeFarge settles her bulk behind her desk.

The desk is clear except for a tintype of a handsome man in uniform. Probably a brother or other relative. After all, she is a mademoiselle, and older than twenty-five – a spinster with no hopes of marrying now, otherwise what would she be doing here, teaching girls as a last resort?

Mademoiselle LeFarge shakes her head. "Your French is in need of much work, Mademoiselle Gemma. Surely you know this. You will have to work very hard to stay in this class with the other girls your age. If I don't see improvement, I will be forced to demote you to the lower classes."

"Yes, mademoiselle."

"You can always ask the other girls for help, if need be. Felicity's French is quite good."

"Yes," I say, swallowing hard, knowing full well that I would rather eat nails than ask for Felicity's help.

~~~~~~

The rest of the day passes slowly and uneventfully. There are elocution lessons. Dancing and posture and Latin. There is music with Mr Grunewald, a tiny, stooped Austrian man with a weary voice and a look of defeat stamped across his sagging face, every sigh saying that teaching us to play and sing is one step below being tortured slowly to death. We're all competent, if uninspiring, with our music – except for Ann.

When she stands up to sing, a clear, sweet voice comes pouring out of her. It's lovely, if somewhat timid. With practice, and a little more feeling, she could be quite good, actually. It's a shame that she won't ever get the chance. She's here to be trained to be of service, nothing more. When the music is over, she keeps her head down till she finds her seat again, and I wonder how many times each day she dies a little.

"You have quite a nice voice," I whisper to her when she takes her seat.

"You're just saying that to be kind," she says, biting a fingernail. But a blush works its way into her full, ruddy cheeks, and I know that it means everything to her to sing her song, if just for a little while.

~~~~~

The week passes in a numbing routine. Prayers. Deportment. Posture. Morning and night, I enjoy the same social outcast's status as Ann. In the evenings, the two of us sit by the fire in the great hall, the stillness broken only by the laughter coming from Felicity and her acolytes as they pointedly ignore us. By week's end, I'm sure I've become invisible. But not to everyone.

There is one message from Kartik. The night after I discover the diary, I find an old letter from Father pinned to my bed with a small blade. The letter, rambling and sloppy, had hurt to read, and so I had stuffed it into my desk drawer, hidden away. Or so I thought. Seeing it on my bed, slashed, with the words *you have been warned* scrawled across Father's signature chills me to the bone. The threat is clear. The only way to keep myself and my family safe is for me to shutter my mind to the visions. But I find I can't close off my mind without closing off the rest of me. Fear has me retreating inside myself, detached from everything, as useless as the scorched East Wing upstairs.

✼✼✼✼✼

The only time I feel alive at all is during Miss Moore's drawing class. I had expected it to be tedious – little nature sketches of bunnies nuzzling happily in the English countryside – but Miss Moore surprises me again. She has chosen Lord Tennyson's famous poem, "The Lady of Shalott," as an inspiration for our work. It's about a woman who will die if she leaves the safety of her ivory tower. Even more surprising is that Miss Moore wants to know what we think about art. She means to have us talk and risk giving our opinions instead of making painstaking copies of cheery fruit. This throws the sheep into complete confusion.

"What can you tell me about this sketch of the Lady of Shalott?" Miss Moore asks, placing her canvas on an easel. In her picture, a woman stands at a tall window looking down on a knight in the woods. A mirror reflects the inside of the room.

It's quiet for a moment.

"Anyone?"

"It's charcoal," Ann answers.

"Yes, that would be hard to dispute, Miss Bradshaw. Anyone else?" Miss Moore casts about for a victim among the eight of us present. "Miss Temple? Miss Poole?" No one says a word. "Ah, Miss Worthington, you're rarely at a loss for words."

Felicity tilts her head, pretends to consider the sketch, but I can tell she already knows what she wants to say. "It's a lovely sketch, Miss Moore. Wonderful composition, with the balance of the mirror and the woman, who is rendered in the style of the pre-Raphaelite brotherhood, I believe." Felicity turns on her smile, ready to be congratulated. Her apple-polishing skills are the true art here.

Miss Moore nods. "An accurate if somewhat soulless assessment." Felicity's smile drops fast. Miss Moore continues. "But what do you think is going on in the picture? What does the artist want us to know about this woman? What does it make you feel when you look at it?"

What do you feel? I've never been asked that question once. None of us has. We aren't supposed to feel. We're British. The room is utterly silent.

"It's very nice," Elizabeth offers, in what I've come to realise is her no-opinion opinion. "Pretty."

"It makes you feel pretty?" Miss Moore asks.

"No. Yes. Should I feel pretty?"

"Miss Poole, I wouldn't presume to tell you how to respond to a piece of art."

"But paintings are either nice and pretty or they're rubbish. Isn't that so? Aren't we supposed to be learning to make pretty drawings?" Pippa pipes up.

"Not necessarily. Let's try another way. What is taking place in this sketch right now, Miss Cross?"

"She's looking out the window at Sir Lancelot?" Pippa phrases it as a question, as if she's not even sure of what she's seeing.

"Yes. Now, you're all familiar with Tennyson's poem. What happens to the Lady of Shalott?"

Martha speaks out, happy to get at least one thing right. "She leaves the castle and floats downstream in her boat."

"And?"

Martha's certainty leaves her. "And . . . she dies."

"Why?"

There's a bit of nervous laughter, but no one has an answer.

Finally, Ann's bland, cool voice cuts the silence. "Because she's cursed."

"No, she dies for love," Pippa says, sounding sure of herself for the first time. "She can't live without him. It's terribly romantic."

Miss Moore gives a wry smile. "Or romantically terrible."

Pippa is confused. "I think it's romantic."

"One could argue that it's romantic to die for love. Of course, then you're dead and unable to take that honeymoon trip to the Alps with all the other fashionable young couples, which is a shame."

"But she's doomed by a curse, isn't she?" Ann says. "It's not love. It's beyond her control. If she leaves the tower, she will die."

"And yet she doesn't die when she leaves the tower. She dies on the river. Interesting, isn't it? Does anyone else have any thoughts? Miss . . . Doyle?"

I'm startled to hear my own name. My mouth goes dry instantly. I furrow my brow and stare intently at the picture, waiting for an answer to announce itself. I can't think of a blessed thing to say.

"Please do not strain yourself, Miss Doyle. I won't have my girls going cross-eyed in the name of art."

There's a burst of tittering. I know I should be embarrassed, but mostly, I am relieved not to have to make up an answer I don't have. I retreat inside myself again.

Miss Moore walks around the room, past a long table holding partially painted canvases, tubs of oil paints, stacks of watercolours, and tin cups full of paintbrushes with bristles like straw. In the corner, there's a painting propped on an easel. It's a nature study of trees and lawn and a steeple, a scene we can see echoed through the bank of windows in front of us. "I think that the lady dies not because she leaves the tower for the outside world, but because she lets herself float through that world, pulled by the current after a dream."

It is quiet for a moment, nothing but the sound of feet shuffling under desks, Ann's nails drumming softly on the wood as if it were an imaginary piano.

"Do you mean she should have paddled?" Cecily asks.

Miss Moore laughs. "In a manner of speaking, yes."

Ann stops drumming. "But it wouldn't matter whether she paddled or not. She's cursed. No matter what she does, she'll die."

"And she'll die if she stays in the tower, too. Perhaps not for a long time, but she will die. We all will," Miss Moore says softly.

Ann can't let it go. "But she has no choice. She can't win.

They won't let her!" She leans forward in her seat, nearly out of it, and I understand, we all do, that she's no longer talking about the lady in the picture.

"Good heavens, Ann, it's just a silly poem," Felicity gibes, rolling her eyes. The acolytes catch on and add their own cruel whispers.

"Shhh, that's enough," Miss Moore admonishes. "Yes, Ann, it's only a poem. Only a picture."

Pippa is suddenly agitated. "But people can be cursed, can't they? They could have something, an affliction, that's beyond their control. Couldn't they?"

My breath catches in my throat. A tingle starts in my fingertips. *No. I won't be pulled under. Begone.*

"We all have our challenges to bear, Miss Cross. I suppose it's all in how we shoulder them," Miss Moore says gently.

"Do you believe in curses, Miss Moore?" Felicity asks. It seems a dare.

I am empty. A void. I feel nothing, nothing, nothing. Mary Dowd or whoever you are, please, please go away.

Miss Moore searches the wall behind us as if the answer might be hiding there among her pastel watercolour still lifes. Red, ripe apples. Succulent grapes. Light-dappled oranges. All of them slowly rotting in a bowl. "I believe . . ." She trails off. She seems lost. A breeze blows through the open windows, overturning a cup of brushes. The tingling in my fingers stops. I am safe for now. The breath I've been holding whooshes out in a rush.

Miss Moore rights the brushes. "I believe . . . that this week we shall take a walk through the woods and explore the old caves, where there are some truly astonishing primitive drawings. They can tell you far more about art than I can."

The class erupts in cheers. A chance to get out of the classroom is joyous news indeed, a sign that we have more privileges than the younger classes. But I've got a sense of unease, remembering my own trip to the caves and the diary of Mary Dowd still in the back of my wardobe.

"Well, it's far too beautiful a day to be stuck here in this classroom discussing doomed damsels in boats. You may start your free period early, and if anyone asks, you are merely observing the outside world for artistic inspiration. As for this," she says, scrutinising her sketch, "it needs something."

With a flourish, Miss Moore draws a neat mustache on the Lady of Shallot. "God is in the details," she says.

Except for Cecily, who strikes me more and more as a secret goody-goody, we're giggling over her boldness, happy to be naughty with her. Miss Moore's face comes to life with a smile, and my unease slips away.

<center>~~~~~</center>

When I rush full-speed into my room to retrieve Mary Dowd's diary, I run headlong into the back of Brigid, who is supervising the training of a new upstairs maid.

"I'm terribly sorry," I splutter with as much dignity as I can, considering that I'm flat on the floor with my skirts up to my knees. Running into the broad Brigid is a bit like flinging myself into the side of a ship. There's a ringing in my head and I fear I may go deaf from the crushing force of her.

"Sorry? Aye, and you should be," Brigid says, yanking me to my feet and straightening my hem to a modest level. The new maid turns away, but I can see her slender shoulders bobbing from her stifled laughter.

I start to thank Brigid for helping me to my feet, but she's only just begun her tirade.

"Carrying on in that way, galloping like a stallion about to meet the gelder's knife! Now, I ask you, is that any way for a proper lady to conduct 'erself? Hmm? Now wot would Missus Nightwing say if she was to see you makin' such a spectacle o' yerself?"

"I am sorry." I look down at my feet, hoping this passes for contrition.

Brigid makes a clucking sound. "I'm glad you're sorry, then. Wot's got you in such a rush, then, hmmm? Mind you tell old Brigid the truth. After twenty-some-odd years 'ere I've got keen eyes, I do."

"I forgot my book," I say, stepping quickly to my wardrobe. I grab my cape and slip the diary inside.

"All that runnin' about, nearly killin' folk for a book," Brigid grumbles, as if it were she and not me lying dazed on the floor a moment ago.

"Sorry to have troubled you. I'll just be off," I say, attempting to sail past her.

"'Old on a minute. Let's be sure you're presentable first." Brigid takes my chin and tilts my face towards the light to inspect it. Her cheeks go pale.

"Is something the matter?" I ask, wondering if I'm more seriously injured than I thought. Brigid's backside may be formidable, but I don't think I could've sustained a bleeding head wound from my battle with it.

Brigid drops my chin, backs away a bit, wiping her hands on her apron as if they're dirty. "Nuffin. Just . . . your eyes is very green. That's all. Go on, now. You'd best catch up wit' the others." And with that, she turns her attention to Molly, who is apparently using the feather duster in the wrong way, and I am free to go about my business.

CHAPTER
TEN

THE GIRLS ARE TAKING SOME FRESH AIR WHEN I COME
out to the great lawn. The sun has held all day, and now it's
a bright blue afternoon. Low clouds drift lazily across the
sky. Up on the hill, the chapel stands straight and tall. Out
on the green, the younger girls have wrapped a blindfold
around the eyes of a little brown-haired girl. They spin
her in circles, then scatter like marbles. She puts her arms
out unsteadily, wobbles across the lawn, calling out "Blind
man". They yell back "buff", and she feels her way towards
their high-pitched voices. Ann's sitting on a bench, reading her halfpenny paper. She spies me but I pretend I
don't see her. It's not very kind of me, but I want to be
alone.

The forest off to my right looks inviting, and I dart into
its cool shelter. The sunlight leaks through the leaves in
bits of warmth. I try to catch its sweetness in my fingers
but it drips through them to the earth. There's a stillness
here, broken only by the muffled calls of "buff" from the

girls' game. Mary Dowd's diary sits quietly inside my cape, her secrets weighing the pocket down against my thigh.

If I can discover what she wants me to know, perhaps I'll find a way to understand what is happening to me. I open to a new page and read.

December 31, 1870

Today is my sixteenth birthday. Sarah was quite saucy with me. "Now you will know how it is," she said. When I pressed her to tell me more, she refused me – I, who am like her very own sister! "I cannot tell you, my dearest, dearest friend. But you shall know soon enough. And it shall be as a door opening for you." I don't mind saying that I felt very cross with her. She is already sixteen and knows more than I, dear diary. But then she took both my hands in hers, and I cannot feel anything but fondness for her when she is so very kind with me.

What exactly is so glorious about being sixteen is beyond me. If I'd hoped Mary's diary would get more interesting or insightful, I was mistaken. But there's nothing else to do, so I find another passage.

January 7, 1871

Such frightful things are happening to me, dearest diary, that I am afraid to recount them here. I am afraid to speak of them all, even to Sarah. What will become of me?

There's a strange, knotting feeling in my stomach. What could be so terrible that she couldn't confide in her own diary? A breeze comes, bringing the sound of girls. *Blind man. Buff.* The next entry is dated February 12th. My heart beats faster as I read.

Dearest diary, such blessed relief at last! I am not mad, as I feared. No longer do my visions overtake me with their power, for I have begun to control them at last. Oh, diary, they are not frightful, but beautiful! Sarah promised it would be so for me, but I confess I was too afraid of their glory to let myself enter fully. I could only be pulled along against my will, fighting it. But today, oh, it was glorious indeed! When I felt the fever coming on me, I asked it to come. I choose this, I said, and stuck my courage fast. I did not feel a great pressure pushing in on me. This time, it was no more than a gentle shudder, and there it was — a beautiful door of light. Oh, diary, I walked through it into a realm of such beauty, a garden with a singing river and flowers that fall from trees like the softest rain. There, what you imagine can be yours. I ran, fast as a deer, my legs powerful and strong, and I was filled with a joy I cannot describe. It seemed I was there for hours, but when I came through the door again, it was as if I'd never left. I found myself again in my room, where Sarah was waiting to embrace me. "Darling Mary, you've done it! Tomorrow, we shall join hands and become one with our sisters. Then we shall know all the mysteries of the realms."

I'm trembling. Mary and Sarah both had visions. I am not alone. Somewhere out there are two girls — two women — who might be able to help me. Is this what she wants me to know? A door of light. I've never seen such a thing — or a garden. There's been nothing beautiful at all. What if my visions aren't like theirs at all? Kartik told me they would put me in danger, and everything I've experienced seems to prove him right. Kartik, who could be watching me right now, here in these woods. But what if he's wrong? What if he's lying?

⌁⌁⌁⌁⌁

It's too much for my head to hold right now. I tuck the book away again and thread in and out between enormous trees, letting my fingers trail over rough bumps on ancient bark. The ground is littered with acorn shells, dead leaves, twigs, forest life.

I reach a clearing and there in front of me is a small, glass-smooth lake. A boathouse stands sentry on the far side. A battered blue rowing boat with only one oar is anchored to a tree stump. It slides out and back with the breeze, wrinkling the surface slightly. There's no one around to see me, so I loose the boat from its mooring and climb in. The sun's a warm kiss on my face as my head rests against the bow. I'm thinking of Mary Dowd and her beautiful visions of a door of light, a fantastical garden. If I could control my visions, I'd want most to see my mother's face.

"I'd choose her," I whisper, blinking back tears. *Might as well cry, Gem.* With my arm across my face, I sob quietly, till I'm spent and my eyes scratch when I blink. The rhythmic lapping of the water against the side of the boat makes me go limp, and soon I'm under sleep's spell.

Dreams come. Running barefoot over forest floor in the night fog, my breath coming out in short white wisps. It's a

• 110 •

deer I'm chasing, its milky brown flesh peeking through trees like the taunts of a will-o'-the-wisp. But I'm getting closer. My legs picking up speed till I'm nearly flying, hands reaching out for the deer's flank. Fingers graze the fur and it's no longer a deer but my mother's blue dress. It's my mother, my mother here in this place, the grain of her dress real on my fingers. She breaks into a smile.

"Find me if you can," she says, and runs off.

Part of her hem catches on a tree branch but she tears free. I grab the scrap of fabric, tuck it into my bodice, and chase her through misty woods to an ancient ruin of a temple, its floor scattered with the petals of lilies. I'm afraid I've lost her, but she beckons to me from the path. Through the mist I chase her, till we're in the musty halls of Spence, up and around the endless stairs, down the hallway on the third floor where five class pictures hang in a row. Follow her laugh up the final flight of stairs till I'm standing, alone, at the top, in front of the closed doors to the East Wing. The air is whispering a lullaby to me . . . *Come to us, come to us, come to us.* Push open the door with the palm of my hand. It's no longer a scorched ruin. The room is alive with light, golden walls and gleaming floors. My mother is gone. Instead, I see the little girl huddled over her doll.

Her eyes are large and unblinking. "They promised me my dolly."

I want to say *Sorry, I don't understand,* but the walls melt away. We're in a land of barren trees, snow, and ice, of harsh winter. Darkness moves on the horizon. A man's face looms. I know him. Amar, Kartik's brother. He's cold and lost, running from something I can't see. And then the dark speaks to me.

"*So close . . .*"

I come to with a snap and for a moment, with the sun glinting off the water in sharp peaks, I'm not sure where I am. I do know that my heart is hammering away in my chest. The dream seems more real than the water licking at my fingers. And my mother. She was close enough to hold me. Why did she run? Where was she taking me?

My thoughts are interrupted by the sound of low, girlish laughter coming from behind the boathouse. I'm not alone. The laugh comes again and I recognise it as Felicity's. Everything collides in me. Longing for my mother, who slips away from me even in dreams. The layers of mystery in Mary's diary. The shiny-slick hatred I feel for Felicity and Pippa, and all those who flit through life without a care. They've picked the wrong day, the wrong girl for cruel pranks. I'll show them cruel. I could snap their slender necks like twigs.

Careful. I'm a monster. Better run for safety. Fly away on your little deer hooves.

I'm out of the rowing boat quiet as feathers falling on snow, creeping around the other side of the boathouse, sticking close to the cover of bushes. It's not me who's going to get a fright today. Not on your life. The giggling has softened into murmuring and something else. There's a deeper voice. Male. The Torture Twins are not alone. All the better. I'll surprise the lot of them, let them know I won't be their willing fool ever again.

I take two steps closer and jump out in time to see Felicity locked in an embrace with a Gypsy. She sees me and lets out a bloodcurdling scream. I scream. She screams again. And now we're both panting while the white-shirted Gypsy takes in the skittish sight of us, startled bemusement showing in his gold-flecked eyes and in the arch of his thick, dark eyebrows.

"What . . . what are you doing here?" Felicity gasps.

"I might ask you the same question," I say, nodding towards her companion. To be found alone with a man is shocking – a reason for a quick and necessary wedding. But to be found with a Gypsy! If I were to tell, Felicity would be ruined for life. If I were to tell.

"I am Ithal," he says in a thick Romanian accent.

"Don't tell her anything," Felicity snaps, still trembling.

Mrs Nightwing's strident voice cuts through the forest, moving towards us. "Girls! Girls!"

Sheer panic passes over Felicity's grey eyes. "Dear God, she can't find us."

A dozen voices call out our names. They're getting closer.

Ithal moves to hold Felicity. "*Bater*. Let them find us. I am not liking this hiding."

She pushes him away, her voice harsh. "Stop it! Are you mad? I can't be found with you. You've got to go back."

"Come with me." He takes her hand and tries to lead her away but she resists.

"Don't you understand? I can't go with you." Felicity turns to me. "You have to help me."

"Is this a request from the girl who locked me in the chapel last week?" I say, folding my arms across my chest.

Ithal tries to slip an arm around her waist, but she pulls free.

"I didn't mean anything by it. It was just a laugh, that's all." When she sees that I'm not amused, she tries a different tack. "Please, Gemma. I'll give you whatever you want. My pen set. My gloves. My sapphire ring!"

She moves to take it off her finger but I stay her hand. As delicious as it would be to watch Felicity squirm under Mrs Nightwing's interrogation, it's better to know that she'll owe her escape to my charity. That should be punishment enough for her.

"You'll be in my debt," I say.

"Understood."

I shove her towards the lake.

"What are you doing?"

"Saving you," I say, and push her in. While she splutters and shrieks in the cold lake water, I point Ithal in the other direction, towards the woods. "Go now if you ever want to see her again!"

"I will not run like a coward." He plants his feet stubbornly, adopting what he must think is an heroic pose. He's just begging for a pigeon to fly by and relieve itself.

"Do you really think you'd ever see any of her inheritance? She'd be cut off without a penny. If you weren't slapped in leg irons and hanged in Newgate first," I say, invoking the name of London's most notorious prison. His face blanches but he's still standing his ground. Male pride. If I can't get him out of here, we're done for.

Kartik appears from behind a tree, startling me. Except

for his black cloak, he's dressed just like a Gypsy – handkerchief about his neck, colourful waistcoat, trousers stuffed into high boots. In halting Romanian, he speaks to Ithal. I don't know what he's said but the Gypsy leaves quietly with him. On the path, Kartik glances back and our eyes meet. For some reason, I find myself nodding in a silent thank-you. He acknowledges my nod with a curt one of his own and the two of them move quickly towards the safety of the Gypsy camp.

"Here, take my hand." I pull the furious Felicity from the lake. She's missed it all in her struggle.

"What did you do that for!" She's soaked, her cheeks blossoming with rage.

Mrs Nightwing has found us. "What's going on here? What was all that screaming about?"

"Oh, Mrs Nightwing! Felicity and I decided to take the boat out on the lake and she fell in quite by accident. It was terribly foolish of us and we're dreadfully sorry to have frightened everyone." I'm speaking faster than I ever have in my life. Felicity is actually stunned into silence except for a well-timed sneeze, which immediately causes Mrs Nightwing to fuss and fret in her own irritable way.

"Miss Doyle, put your cape around Miss Worthington before she catches her death. We shall all go back to the school. This is not a suitable place for young ladies. There are sometimes Gypsies in these woods. I shudder to think what might have happened."

Felicity and I cannot stop staring at our feet. To my surprise, she nudges me in the ribs with her elbow. "Yes," she says, without cracking a smile. "That's a sobering thought indeed, Mrs Nightwing. I'm sure we're both grateful for your good advice."

"Yes, well, see that you're careful in the future," Mrs Nightwing harrumphs, preening a bit under Felicity's skillful manipulation. "All right, girls, back to the school. There's still daylight and work to be done."

Mrs Nightwing rallies the girls and starts them back on the path. I throw my cape over Felicity's shoulders.

"That was a bit melodramatic, wasn't it? 'We're both grateful for your good advice'?" I don't want her to think she can put anything over on me.

"It worked, didn't it? If you tell them what they want to hear, they don't bother to try to see," she says.

Pippa comes running over to us, breathless. "Good heavens, what really happened? You must tell me before I die of curiosity!"

Ann is a sudden shadow at my side. She says nothing, just follows along with sure, plodding steps.

"It's just as Gemma said," Felicity lies. "I fell in the water and she pulled me out."

Pippa's face falls. "That's it?"

"Yes, that is all."

"There's nothing more?"

"Isn't it enough that I nearly drowned today?" Felicity huffs. She's so good I could swear she almost believes it herself. Now I know that she's never confessed about her Gypsy beau to Pippa, her closest friend. Felicity and I have a secret, one she's not sharing with anyone else. Pippa senses that we're not telling the whole truth. Her eyes take on that suspicious, wounded look girls get when they know they've fallen off the top rung of friendship and someone else has passed them, but they don't know when or how the change took place.

She leans in close to Felicity. "What were you doing with *her?*"

"I do believe that one headmistress is enough, Pippa," Felicity scoffs. "Really, your imagination is so brilliant you should put it to use as a novelist someday. Gemma, walk with me."

She loops her arm through mine and we pass Pippa, who can do nothing to save face now but make a show of snubbing Ann to run off and talk with the other girls.

"Sometimes she is such a child," Felicity says when we're a few steps behind them all.

"I thought you were the best of friends."

"I adore Pippa. Really. But she's very sheltered. There are things I could never tell her. Like Ithal. But you understand. I can tell that you do. I think we're going to be great friends, Gemma."

"Would we still be great friends if I didn't hold a secret over your head?" I ask.

"Don't friends always share secrets?"

Would I ever share my secrets with any of these girls? Or would they run in horror to know the truth about me? Up ahead, Miss Moore shepherds the younger girls through the trees and out onto the great lawn. She watches us with a curious expression, as if we're windows into the past. Ghosts.

"Come along, girls," she calls. "Don't dawdle."

"Dawdle? I can barely breathe from trudging up this hill at a gallop!" Felicity sniffs.

"How long has Miss Moore taught at Spence?" I ask.

"She arrived this past summer. She's a breath of fresh air in this staid old place, I can tell you that. Oh, what's this?" Felicity says.

"What's what?" I ask.

"This remnant in your bodice. Bit torn. Ugh, and muddy. If you need a proper handkerchief, you only have to ask. I've got scads of them." She puts the scrap in my open palm. It's blue silk, torn and soiled around the edges, as if it might have been ripped by a branch. My legs shake so that I have to lean against the first tree I see.

Felicity looks puzzled. "What's the matter?"

"Nothing," I say, my voice whispery tight.

"It's as if you've seen a ghost."

I might have.

The muddy blue silk is a promise in my hands. My mother was here. *I'd choose her.* It's what I said before I fell asleep. Somehow, I've changed things. I've brought her back with this strange power of mine. For the first time, I want to know everything about it. If Kartik won't tell me, I'll find out on my own. I'll hunt down Mary Dowd and get her to tell me what I need to know. They can't stop me.

Felicity gives my hand a pull. "Don't be so slow."

"I'm coming," I say, quickening my pace till I'm clear of the trees and into the warm sun again.

CHAPTER
ELEVEN

AFTER DINNER, I PRETEND I'VE GOT A HEADACHE AND
Mrs Nightwing sends me straight to bed with a hot-water
bottle. It means passing up an invitation to Felicity's suddenly open sanctuary in the great hall – thanks to my new-
found status as the keeper of her secrets – but there's only
one thought in my mind: there has to be a way to control my
visions rather than have them control me.

I'm in the hallway when a small thump stops me. Shadows
flit across the floor and wall. Someone is in my room. Heart
racing, spine flat against the wall, I creep towards my room
and peek in. Kartik is at my desk, no doubt leaving me
another cryptic warning. Right. Not this time. Fast as I can, I
streak to the open window where he's come in and latch it
tight. He whips around, ready for a fight.

"There's only one way out now," I say, breathless.

His eyes narrow. "Step aside."

"Not until you answer a few questions."

I've blocked off his only means of escape. If I make a

sound, scream, he'll be caught. For the moment, he's trapped. He folds his arms across his chest and glares, waiting for me to talk.

"What are you doing in my room?"

"Nothing," he says, crumpling the paper in his fist tightly enough for me to hear it.

"Leaving another message?"

He shrugs. We're going nowhere fast.

"Why did you help me today in the woods?"

"You needed it."

My temper flares. "I most certainly did not."

He scoffs, and it makes him look less menacing. He's all of seventeen again. "As you wish."

"My plan worked, didn't it?"

The arms unfold. His eyes widen. "Your plan worked because I talked Ithal into leaving. What do you think would have happened if I hadn't?"

The truth is that I don't know. I can't think of anything to say.

"Right. I'll tell you. That stubborn Gypsy would have stayed and your little friend who likes to play with fire would have been very badly burned – expelled, ruined socially, whispered about for the rest of her life." He mimics the high, prim voice of a society matron. "'Oh, did you hear about her? Oh, my dear, yes, caught in the woods with a heathen.' Tell your friend to stick to her own kind and stop toying with Ithal."

"She's not my friend," I say.

He arches an eyebrow. "Who *are* your friends, then?"

I open my mouth but nothing comes out.

He smirks. "May I go now?"

"Not yet." It's bold of me when I don't feel bold at all. But I need more information from him. "Who is the 'we' that you mentioned? Why are they afraid of my visions?"

"I don't have to tell you anything."

I hate him, standing in my room as if he owns it and me, issuing warnings and insults, sharing nothing. "Shall I tell you what happens if I scream bloody murder right this minute and you're caught as a thief?" It's the wrong thing to say. Lightning fast, he's got me pinned against the wall, his arm to my throat.

"Do you think you can stop me? I am Rakshana. Our brotherhood has existed for centuries, stretching to the time of the Knights Templar, Arthur, and Charlemagne. We are the guardians of the realms now, and we have no intention of giving it back. The time of the old ways is past. We won't let you bring it back."

The pressure of his arm makes me feel dizzy. "I – I don't understand."

"You could change everything. Enter the realms. That's why they want you." He loosens his hold, lets me go.

My eyes water. I rub at my throat. "Who? Who wants me?"

"The Order." He spits out the name. "Circe."

Circe. That was the name Kartik's brother told my mother in the marketplace.

"I don't understand all these names. Who are the Rakshana, the Order, Circe—"

He cuts me off. "You only need to know what I tell you, and that is to stop these visions before they lead you into danger."

"What if I told you my mother came to me today in a vision?"

"I don't believe you," Kartik says, but his face drains of colour.

"She left me this." I pull out the fabric I've kept tucked near my heart. He stares at it. "I saw your brother there, too."

"You saw Amar?"

"Yes. He was in some sort of frozen wasteland—"

His voice is quiet but harsh. "Stop it."

"Do you know that place? Is that where my mother is?"

"I said stop it!"

"But what if they're trying to reach me through these visions? Why else would she leave me this?" I hold out the blue silk.

"This proves nothing!" he says, holding my arms tightly. "Listen to me: that was not my brother or your mother you saw, understand? It was just an illusion. You must put it out of your mind."

Put it out of my mind? It's the only thing I'm living for. "I think she was trying to tell me something."

He shakes his head. "It's not real."

"How do you know that?"

His words are sharp and deliberate. "Because this is what Circe and the Order do – they'll use any trickery they have to get what they want. Your mother and my brother are dead. They killed them to get to you. Remember that the next time you are tempted by those visions, Miss Doyle." There's pity in his eyes. It's harder to bear than his hatred. "The realms must stay closed, Miss Doyle. For all our sakes."

I'm responsible for their deaths. He's all but said it out loud. He won't help me. There's no use trying. The muffled drone of girls drifts up from below. They'll be coming up any moment. But there's one thing more I need to know.

"What about Mary Dowd?" I say, waiting to see what he knows about her.

"Who is Mary Dowd?" he says, distracted by the soft thud of feet on stairs. He doesn't know. Whoever he works for, they don't trust him with everything.

"My friend. You did ask me if I had any friends, didn't you?"

"So I did." There are footsteps on the landing. He pushes me aside and like a cat, he's over the sill and out through the window. I can see the knotted rope he's secured to the wall through a loop in a small railing. It's nestled into a thick patch of ivy, making it hard to see if you're not looking for it. Clever, but not infallible. And neither is he.

Closing the window behind him, I put my mouth up to the windowpane, watch my breath fog it over with each quiet word. "You may give the Rakshana a message for me, Kartik the messenger. That was my mother in the woods today. And I'm going to find her whether you help me or not."

CHAPTER
TWELVE

THE NEXT AFTERNOON IS BLUSTERY AND GREY, BUT MISS
Moore still makes good on her promise to take us to the
caves. It's a solid hike through the trees, beyond the boathouse and the lake, and along a deep ravine. Ann trips on
the slope's crumbling wall and nearly tumbles into it.

"Careful," Miss Moore says. "This ravine's a bit tricky.
Seems to come out of nowhere and then you're falling and
breaking your neck."

We cross the ravine, walking over a small bridge into a
spot where the trees open to form a small circular clearing. I
catch my breath. It's the same spot where the little girl took
me, where I found Mary Dowd's diary. The caves are in
front of us, tucked beneath a ledge overgrown with vines
that tickle our arms as we thread our way through them into
the velvety blackness. Miss Moore lights the lanterns we've
brought and the cave walls dance in the sudden brightness.
Generations of rain have smoothed the stone to such a high
sheen in some places that I catch a fractured glimpse of

myself on its uneven surface – an eye, a mouth, another eye, a composite of ill-fitting pieces.

"Here we are." Miss Moore's deep, melodic voice bounces against the craggy bumps and smooth planes of the cave. "The pictographs are just over here, on this wall."

She follows her light into a large, open area. We all bring our lanterns and the drawings come to startling life, a treasure revealed.

"Rather crude, aren't they?" Ann says, examining a rough outline of a serpent. I think instantly of her tidy quilt with no wrinkles, no loose ends.

"They're primitive, Ann. The people in these caves were drawing with whatever was available to them – sharp rocks, makeshift knives, a bit of clay paint or dye. Sometimes even blood."

"How revolting!" It's Pippa, of course. Even in the dark, I can practically feel her pert little nose wrinkling in distaste.

Felicity laughs and takes on the tone of a fashionable lady. "Darling, the Bryn-Joneses have just done the most marvellous thing in their parlour with human blood. We simply must have ours done straightaway!"

"I think it's disgusting," Pippa says, though I suspect she's more put out by Felicity and me sharing a joke than any mention of blood.

"Blood was used for a sacred drawing, to pay tribute to a goddess whose influence was being sought. Here." Miss Moore points to a faint red etching of what looks like a bow and arrow. "This is one for Diana, the Roman goddess of the moon and the hunt. She was a protector of girls. Of chastity."

At this, Felicity gives me a sharp nudge in the ribs. We all cough and shuffle our feet to hide our embarrassment. Miss Moore soldiers on.

"The quite remarkable thing about this cave is that there are depictions of all sorts of goddesses here. It isn't just the Pagan or Roman but the Norse, the Germanic, the Celtic. Most likely, this was a place known to travellers who heard they could practice their magic in safety here."

"Magic?" Elizabeth asks. "They were witches?"

"Not as we've come to think of witches. They would have been mystics and healers, women who worked with herbs and delivered babies. But it would have made them suspect. Women who have power are always feared," she says sadly. I wonder how Miss Moore came to be here, teaching us how to draw pretty pictures instead of living out in the world. She's not unattractive. Her face is warm, her smile quick, and her figure slim. The brooch at her neck has several rubies in it, which suggests that she's not without means.

"I think they are extraordinary," Felicity says, moving her lantern closer to the wall. Her fingers trail over a rough silhouette of what appears to be a crow woman flanked by two other women who've been partially rubbed away by time.

"Ugh, that's rather nasty," Cecily says. Shadows flicker across her face, and for a moment, I can imagine what she'll look like as an old woman – sort of pinched and thin with a large nose.

Miss Moore peers at the drawing. "That particular lady is probably related to the Morrigan."

"The what?" Pippa asks, batting her lashes and smiling in a way that will undoubtedly make men promise the earth.

"The Morrigan. An ancient Celtic goddess of war and death. She was greatly feared. Some said she could be seen washing the clothes of those who were about to die in battle, and afterwards, she flew across the battlefields, taking the skulls of the dead with her in her fury."

Cecily shudders. "Why would anyone want to worship her?"

"Don't you have any warrior spirit, Miss Temple?" Miss Moore asks.

Cecily is aghast. "I certainly hope not. How . . . unattractive."

"What makes it so?"

"Well." Cecily is clearly uncomfortable. "It's like . . . being a man, isn't it? A woman should never show anything so unseemly."

"But without that spark of anger, without destruction, there can be no rebirth. The Morrigan was also associated with strength, independence, and fertility. She was the keeper of the soul till it could be regenerated. Or so they say."

"Who are these women here?" Ann points a pudgy finger at the worn drawings.

"The Morrigan was a threefold goddess, often seen as a beautiful maiden, the great mother, and the bloodthirsty crone. She could change shape at will. Quite fascinating, really."

Felicity regards Miss Moore coolly. "How did you come to know so much about goddesses and such, Miss Moore?"

Miss Moore leans her face in towards Felicity's till they're separated by only a breath or two. I think Felicity is really going to be raked over the coals for being so cheeky. Miss Moore speaks slowly, deliberately. "I know because I read." She pulls back and stands, hands on hips, offering us a challenge. "May I suggest that you all read? And often. Believe me, it's nice to have something to talk about other than the weather and the Queen's health. Your mind is not a cage. It's a garden. And it requires cultivating. Now, I think we've had enough of mythology. Let's do some sketching, shall we?"

Dutifully, we take out our sketching pads and slender reeds of charcoal. Already Pippa is complaining that the cave is too hot for sketching. The truth is that she can't draw. Not a whit. Everything she attempts ends up looking like a clump of gloomy rocks, and she's not a good sport about it. Ann is tackling her project with her usual perfectionism, making small, careful strokes on the page. My charcoal flies across the pad, and when I'm finished, I've captured the smudgy likeness of the hunt goddess, spear in hand, a deer running ahead of her. It seems bare, so I add a few symbols of my own. Soon, the bottom of the page is filled with the moon-and-eye symbol of my mother's necklace.

"Very interesting, Miss Doyle." Miss Moore peers over my shoulder. "You've drawn the crescent eye."

"There's a name for this?"

"Oh, yes. It's a very famous symbol. A bit like the Freemasons' pyramid."

Ann speaks up. "It's like that strange necklace you wear."

The girls stare at me, suspicious. I could kick Ann and her big mouth. Miss Moore arches an eyebrow. "You have this symbol on a necklace?"

With effort, I pull the amulet out from its hiding place under my high collar. "It was my mother's. It was given to her by a village woman a long time ago."

Miss Moore stoops down to examine it. She rubs a thumb over the hammered metal of the moon. "Yes, that's it, all right."

"What is it, exactly?" I say, tucking it back inside my bodice.

Miss Moore stands, adjusts her hat on her head. "Legend has it that the crescent eye was the symbol of the Order."

"The what?" Cecily says, making a face.

"You've never heard of the Order?" Miss Moore says, as if this should be as familiar to us as basic arithmetic.

"Do tell us, Miss Moore!" Pippa's over in a flash. She'd do anything to get out of drawing.

"Ah, the Order. Now, there's an interesting story. If I can remember my folklore correctly, they were a powerful group of sorceresses who'd been around since the dawn of time. Supposedly they had access to a mystical world beyond this one, a place of many realms where they could work their magic."

Kartik mentioned realms. So did Mary Dowd's diary. My skin has gone cold, and I'm desperate to know more.

"What sort of magic?" I hear myself asking.

"The greatest of them all – the power of illusion."

"That doesn't seem terribly special to me," Cecily scoffs.

Elizabeth folds her arms. It's obvious they don't have much use for Miss Moore.

"Really, Miss Temple? That comb in your hair – it is the latest fashion, isn't it?"

Cecily is flattered. "Why, yes, it is."

"And does that make you fashionable? Or does it merely create the illusion that you are?"

"I'm sure I don't know what you mean." Cecily's eyes blaze.

"I'm sure you don't," Miss Moore says. Her wry smile is back.

"Could they do anything else?" I ask.

"Oh, yes. These women could help spirits cross over into the afterlife. They had the power of prophecy and clairvoyance. The veil between the supernatural world and this one was a very thin one for them. They could see and feel things that others couldn't."

My mouth is dry as sawdust. "Visions?"

"You're awfully interested," Elizabeth taunts. Felicity yanks a lock of her hair and she yelps, then quietens.

"How did they get to that other world?" It's Felicity's voice now, asking the question I want the answer to. Cold shivers run down my arms.

"Oh, my, I see I've started a little fire." Miss Moore laughs. "Didn't you have any sadistic nannies who told you these tales to keep you quiet and well behaved at night? Heavens, what's to become of the Empire if governesses have lost their touch for scaring the wits out of their girls?"

"Please tell us, Miss Moore," Pippa begs, shooting a glance at Felicity.

"According to the legends – and my own vicious nanny,

God rest her wicked soul – the sisters of the Order would hold hands and concentrate on a way in – a doorway, a portal of some kind."

A door of light.

"Did they need to do anything else to cross over? Did they have to say something, an incantation or some such?" I press. Behind me, Martha does her annoying mimicry, and if I weren't so absorbed, I'd find a way to take her down a peg.

Miss Moore laughs, shakes her head. "Gracious, I haven't the faintest idea! It's a myth. Like all of these symbols. A bit of story passed down through the generations. Or lost through them. Such legends tend to fade away in the face of industrialisation."

"Are you saying we should go back to the way it was?" Felicity asks.

"I'm saying nothing of the kind. One can never go back. One always has to move forward."

"Miss Moore?" I ask, unable to stop myself. "Why would someone have given my mother the crescent eye?"

Miss Moore ponders this. "I suppose someone must have thought she needed protection."

A horrible thought works its way inside me. "But suppose a person was without the necklace – without its protection. What would happen to her?"

Miss Moore shakes her head. "I hadn't considered you to be so impressionable, Miss Doyle." The girls snigger. My face goes hot. "These symbols are no more effective than a rabbit's foot. I shouldn't place too much stock in your amulet's protective powers, no matter how attractive a piece it may be."

I can't let it alone. "But what if—"

Miss Moore cuts me off. "If you wish to know more about ancient legends, ladies, there is a place that can help you. It's called a library. And I believe that Spence is in possession of one."

She pulls a pocket watch from her canvas bag of art supplies. I've never seen a woman carry a man's watch before, and it only deepens the mystery that is Miss Moore. "It's almost time to go back," she says, closing the watch with a decisive snap. "Now, how did we end up wandering about with ancient goddesses when we came to admire art? I want to do a bit of sketching near the mouth of the cave. You may join me when you've gathered your things."

Tucking the bag under her arm, she strides confidently towards the mouth, leaving us alone in the semidarkness. My fingers are trembling so badly that I can barely bundle my supplies together. I'm vaguely aware of the other girls. Their gossipy whispers fill the cave like the buzzing of flies.

"Well, this was certainly a waste of our time," Cecily mutters. "I'll wager Mrs Nightwing would be interested to know all about what Miss Moore is teaching us."

"She's a curious creature," Elizabeth agrees. "Strange."

"I found it all very interesting," Felicity says.

"My future husband won't," Cecily grouses. "He'll want to know that I can draw something pleasant to impress our guests. Not ruin his dinner with talk about bloodthirsty witches."

"At least it got us out of that dreary old school for the afternoon," Felicity reminds them.

Ann's pencils slip from her hands and fall to the ground, the noise of their fall echoing loudly. She drops clumsily to her knees, trying to gather them all.

"That face of Ann's must be a talisman against all men," Elizabeth whispers just loudly enough to be heard. The others laugh in the way girls do when they can't believe someone has been cruel enough to say what they really feel. Ann doesn't even look up.

Felicity loops her arm through mine, whispers low. "Don't look so grim. They're harmless, really."

I shake my arm free. "They are the hounds of hell. Could you call them off, please?"

Cecily giggles. "Careful, Felicity, she might use her evil eye against us."

Even Felicity can't keep from spluttering with laughter. I wish I could use my evil eye. Or at least my evil boot right smack against Cecily's backside.

Miss Moore leads us back into the daylight and through the woods by a different path, which takes us to a small dirt road. Across the low stone wall that borders the road, I can see a Gypsy caravan nestled in the trees beyond. Felicity is suddenly by my side, using the advantage of my height to hide her from view, in case Ithal is near.

"Ann, I think Miss Moore wants you," she says. Ann

obeys, huffing in her ungainly way towards our teacher. "Gemma, please don't be cross." Felicity peeks her head out, searching. "Do you see him?"

There's nothing out there but three wagons and a few horses. "No," I answer in a surly tone.

"Thank the gods." She links her arm through mine, oblivious to my bad temper. "That would have been awkward. Can you imagine?" She's trying to win me over with her charm. It is working. I smile in spite of myself and she shares one of those rare, ripe grins that seem to make the world a fun, inviting place.

"Listen, I've got a capital idea. Why don't we form our own order?"

I stop cold. "And do what?"

"Live."

Relieved, I start walking again. "We're already living."

"No. We're playing their predetermined little game. But what if we had a place where we played by no one's rules but our own?"

"And where, pray tell, would we do that?"

Felicity looks around. "Why not meet here at the caves?"

"You're joking," I say. "You are joking, aren't you?"

She shakes her head. "Just think of it: We'd make our own plans, wield our own influence, have a bit of fun while we can. We would own Spence."

"We'd be expelled, that's what."

"We're not going to get caught. We're far cleverer than that."

Up ahead, Cecily is prattling on to Elizabeth, who seems

very distressed that her boots are getting muddy. I throw Felicity a look.

"They're not so bad once you get to know them."

"I'm sure the piranha fish is nice to its family, too, but I don't want to get too close to it."

Ann looks back at me, slack-jawed. She's just discovered that Miss Moore didn't want her after all. No one does. That's the trouble. But perhaps there is a way to change that. "All right," I say. "I'm game, with one provision."

"Name it."

"You have to invite Ann."

Felicity can't decide whether to laugh or spit venom at me. "You can't be serious." When I don't answer, she says, "I won't do it."

"As I recall, you owe me a debt."

She gives me a smirk meant to dismiss the whole idea. "The other girls won't allow it. You know that, don't you?"

"That shall be your dilemma," I can't help adding with a smile. "Don't look so grim. They're harmless. Really."

Felicity narrows her eyes and marches off to catch Pippa, Elizabeth, and Cecily. In a moment, they're arguing, with Elizabeth and Cecily shaking their heads and Felicity huffing her displeasure. For her part, Pippa just seems glad to have Felicity's attention. In a moment, Felicity is back by my side, fuming.

"Well?"

"I told you – they won't allow her in. She's not of their class."

"Sorry to hear your little club is doomed before it starts," I say, feeling a bit smug.

"Did I say it was off? I know I can sway Pippa. Cecily's becoming too arrogant these days. I brought her along from nothing. If she and Elizabeth think they can make a go of it at this school without my influence, they are sadly mistaken."

I've underestimated Felicity's need for control. She'd rather be seen with Ann and me than admit defeat to her acolytes. She's an admiral's daughter, after all.

"When should we meet?"

"Tonight at midnight," Felicity says.

I'm fairly certain this will all lead to shame, misfortune, and at the very least, having to listen to Pippa go on to the point of queasiness about the romantic ideal of love, but at least they'll have to stop tormenting Ann for a bit.

At the bend in the road, Ithal is there. Felicity stops suddenly, like a horse spooked. She holds tight to my arm, refusing to look in his direction.

"Dear God," she gasps.

"He wouldn't dare to speak to you in the open, would he?" I whisper, while trying to ignore Felicity's fingernails dug deep into my arm.

Ithal stops to pluck a flower from the ground. Singing, he hops up onto the wall and presents it to Felicity as if I'm not standing between the two of them at all. The others stop and turn to see what the fuss is about. They gasp and titter, both shocked and delighted by the scene. Felicity keeps her head low and stares at the ground.

Miss Moore seems amused. "I believe you have an admirer, Felicity."

The girls look from Ithal to Felicity and back again, watching and waiting.

Ithal extends the flower to her. It's there in his fingers, red and fragrant. "Beauty for beauty," he says in his low growl of a voice.

I can hear Cecily whispering, "The nerve," under her breath. Felicity's face is a stone as she tosses the flower to the ground. "Miss Moore, can't we clean out these woods of all this riffraff? It's a blight." Her words are a slap. She raises her skirts delicately with her hands, steps on the flower, crushing it with her boot, and races ahead of the pack. The others fall in behind her.

I can't help feeling humiliated for Ithal. He stands at the wall and watches us go, and when we reach the turnoff for the school, he's still there with the mangled flower in his hand, far behind us, a small, dying star fading out of our constellation.

CHAPTER
THIRTEEN

WE SNEAK OUT JUST PAST MIDNIGHT, WEAVING through the woods by lantern light till we're deep inside the dark womb of the caves. Felicity lights candles she's stolen from a cupboard. Within minutes, the place is alight, the drawings dancing again on the rocky walls. In the eerie glow, the skulls of the Morrigan twist and bend like living things till I have to look away.

"Ugh, it's so damp in here," Pippa says, sitting gingerly on the cave floor. Felicity has managed to talk her into coming, and all she's done so far is complain about everything. "Did anyone think to bring food? I'm famished."

Her gaze falls on Ann, who has pulled an apple from her cape pocket. It sits in Ann's hand while she debates which will win, her hunger or her need to belong. After an excruciating minute she offers it to Pippa. "You could have my apple."

"I suppose it will have to do," Pippa says with a sigh. She reaches for it, but Felicity grabs first.

"Not yet. We have to do this properly. With a toast."

There's a gleam in Felicity's eye as she reaches into her shift and pulls out the bottle of communion wine. Pippa's squeals of delight fill the cavernous space. She throws her arms around Felicity. "Oh, Fee, you're brilliant!"

"Yes, I am rather, aren't I?"

I want to remind them that I'm the one who risked life, limb, soul, and explusion to get the wine, but I know it would be pointless and I'd just look sullen.

"What's that?" Ann says.

Felicity rolls her eyes. "Cod-liver oil. What do you think it is?"

The colour leaks from Ann's face. "It's not spirits, is it?"

Pippa clutches at her throat melodramatically. "Heavens, no!"

Ann is just realising what she's in for. She tries to make light of the situation by putting the joke on someone else. "Ladies don't drink spirits," she says, mimicking Mrs Nightwing's plummy tones. It's a dead-on imitation, and we all laugh. Thrilled, Ann repeats the joke again and again till it's gone from amusing to irritating.

"You may stop now," Felicity scolds. Ann retreats behind her mask again.

"Mrs Nightwing certainly never misses her sherry at night. Oh, they're all such hypocrites. Cheers," Pippa says, taking a generous, unladylike swig from the bottle.

She passes it to Ann, who wipes its mouth with her hand and hesitates.

"Go on, then, it won't bite you," Felicity says.

"I've never had drink before."

"Really? I'm shocked." Pippa giggles in mock astonishment, and I can't help wondering what it would be like to pour that bottle right over her perfect ringlets.

Ann tries to hand the bottle back, but Felicity is firm. "It's not a request. Drink or you're out of the club. You can make your way back to Spence by yourself."

Ann's eyes widen. The spoiled girls haven't any idea how agonising it is for Ann to break the rules. They can always charm their way out of a certain amount of trouble, but for Ann, an infraction could be her undoing.

"Let her alone, Felicity."

"You're the one who wanted her to come – not us," she says, letting the cruelty sink in. "No more favours. If she wants in, she has to drink. The same goes for you."

"Fine, then. Hand it over," I say. The bottle passes my way.

"And no spitting it back in," Felicity taunts.

Raised to my lips, the bottle smells sweet and harsh at the same time. The scent is all things powerful, magical, and forbidden. It burns going down, making me cough and splutter, as if someone has set a match to my lungs.

"Ah, the vine of life." Felicity breaks into a devilish grin, and they all laugh, even Ann. There's gratitude for you.

I can barely croak out, "What is this?" It's like no wine I've ever sipped from my parents' glasses, and I'm sure it's something the servants use to clean floors or mix varnish.

Felicity is more pleased than I've ever seen her. "Whiskey. You accidentally took Reverend Waite's private collection."

Tears sting at my eyes from the pungency, but at least

I'm breathing again. A surprising warmth floods my entire body, weighing me down in a delicious way. I like the feeling, but Felicity has already snatched the bottle away and sent it to Ann who takes her medicine like a good girl with just the slightest grimace at the taste. Once Felicity has her drink, we've all been initiated. Into what, I'm still not certain. The bottle goes around a few more times till we're all as loose-limbed as new calves. I'm floating inside my skin. I could go on floating like this for days. Right now, the real world with its heartbreak and disappointments is just a pulse against the protective membrane we've drunk ourselves into. It's somewhere outside us, waiting, but we are too giddy to bother with it. Watching the rocks glimmer, my new friends talking in soft murmurs, I wonder if this is what the days look and feel like for my father, wrapped tight inside his laudanum cocoon. No pain, only the distant beating of memory. The sadness of that is overwhelming, and I'm drowning in it.

"Gemma? Are you all right?" It's Felicity, sitting up and looking at me, confused, and I realise I'm crying.

"It's nothing," I say, wiping at my eyes with the back of a hand.

"Don't tell me you're going to be one of those maudlin drunks," she says, trying to joke, but it only makes the tears come faster.

"No more for you, then. Here, have something to eat." She puts the bottle behind a rock and hands me the still uneaten apple. "This party is getting very dull. Who's got a clever idea for us?"

"If this is a club, shouldn't we have a proper name?" Pippa's head lolls against a rock. Her eyes glisten from the drink.

"How about the Young Ladies of Spence?" Ann offers.

Felicity makes a face. "Makes us sound like spinsters with bad teeth."

I laugh a little too loudly, but I'm grateful that the tears have stopped, even if I'm still having trouble catching my breath.

"It was just my first thought," Ann snaps. The whiskey has given her fangs.

"Don't get prickly on us," Felicity shoots back. "Here, have another go."

Ann shakes her head, but the bottle is still there at the end of Felicity's hand, so she takes another tight-lipped swig.

Pippa claps her hands. "I know – let's call ourselves the Ladies of Shalott!"

"Does that mean we're all going to die?" I ask, starting to giggle uncontrollably. My head is a feather on the breeze.

Felicity joins my sniggering. "Gemma's right. Too moping by far."

We throw out names, laughing at the completely outrageous – Athena's Priestesses! Daughters of Persephone! – and groaning at the truly terrible – Love's Four Winds! Finally, we fall silent, leaning against the rocks, our heads touching softly. On the walls, the goddesses hunt and cavort, free from all restraints, these makers of their own rules, punishers of trespassers.

"Why not call ourselves the Order?" I say.

Felicity sits up so quickly I can still feel the warmth of her next to me, trailing behind her by seconds. "How absolutely perfect! Gemma, you are our genius." I'm a little embarrassed, so I twist the stem of the apple in my hand till it breaks with a snap. Felicity pulls my hand to her mouth and bites into the fruit cupped there. Her mouth is still sticky sweet from it as she kisses me full on the lips. I have to put my hand to them to stop the tingling, and a blush has flooded my entire body.

Felicity raises the apple and my arm into the air, both held tight in her pale fist. "Ladies, I give you the Order, reborn!"

"The Order, reborn!" we all echo, our voices bouncing around the cave in ripples of sound. Pippa actually embraces me. We're alive with our new secret, with the way we belong to each other and to something other than the dull passing of hours with nothing to look forward to besides our routines. It makes me feel even more powerful than the whiskey, and I want it to go on forever.

"Do you suppose there was really such an order of women?"

Felicity snorts. "Don't be daft, Pip. It's a fairy tale."

Pippa is hurt. "I only wondered, that's all."

I don't want the spell of our evening to be broken so fast. "What if it were true?" The slim leather-bound diary is in my hands and out in the open before I can really think about it.

"What's that?" Ann asks.

"The secret diary of Mary Dowd."

Ann is afraid she has missed something. "Who's Mary Dowd?"

I tell them what I know of Mary Dowd, her friend Sarah, and their participation in the Order. Felicity grabs the diary from me, and the pages turn faster and faster as they read, their mouths hanging open in astonishment.

"Have you found the part where she goes into the garden?" I ask.

"We're past that," Felicity says.

"Wait a minute! I haven't even read past that! Where've you got to?" I say, sounding like a whining child.

"March fifteenth. Here, I'll read aloud," Felicity says.

"*Sarah and I were quite naughty today and entered the realms again without the guidance of our sisters. At first, we feared we were lost as we found ourselves in a misty wood where many lost spirits, those poor, wandering, wretched souls, asked us for help, but there was naught we could do for them yet. Eugenia says—*"

"Eugenia! Do you think she means Mrs Spence?" Ann asks.

We all shush her, and Felicity continues.

"*Eugenia says they cannot cross over until their soul's work is done, whether on one plane or another, and only then can they take their rest. Some of these wanderers never find release, and they are corrupted, becoming dark spirits who can cause all manner of mischief. These are banished to the Winterlands, a realm of fire and ice and shadows. Only the strongest and wisest of our sisters is allowed there, for the dark ones of that realm can whisper a thousand longings to you. They will make you a slave for power if you do not know how to use and banish them as the elders do. To answer such*" *a fallen spirit, to bind it to you, could change the balance of the realms forever."*

Felicity stops. "Oh, honestly, this is the worst attempt at a gothic novel I've ever read. All we're missing are creaking castle floors and a heroine in danger of losing her virtue."

Pippa sits up, giggling. "Let's read on and find out if they do lose their virtue!"

"Today, we were once again in that garden of beauty where one's greatest wishes can be made real . . ."

"This is more like it," Felicity says. "Bound to be something carnal here."

"Heather, sweet-smelling, the colour of wine, swayed under an orange-gold sky. For hours, we lay in it, wanting for nothing, turning blades of grass into butterflies with just the touch of our fingers, whatever we imagined made real by our will and desire. The sisters showed us wondrous things we could do, ways of healing, incantations for beauty and love . . ."

"Ooooh, I want to know those!" Pippa shouts out. Felicity raises her voice, talking over her till she shuts up again.

". . . for cloaking ourselves from the sight of others, for bending the minds of men to the will of the Order, influencing their thoughts and dreams till their destinies shake out before them like a pattern in the night stars. It was all written upon the Oracle of the Runes. Just to touch our hands to those crystals was to be a conduit, with the universe flowing through hard and fast as a river. Indeed, we could only stay for mere seconds, such was its greatness. But when we came away from it, we were changed inside. 'You have been opened,' our sisters said . . ."

Pippa giggles. "Perhaps they did lose their virtue after all."

"Would you allow me to finish, please?" Felicity growls.

"*. . . and we felt it, too. We carried our small bit of magic inside us, across the veil into this world. Our first attempt came at dinner. Sarah gazed at her measly soup and bread, closed her eyes and pronounced it pheasant. And so it appeared to be, and tasted of it too, every bite. So good was it that Sarah smiled heartily afterwards and said, 'I want more.'*"

I'm so lost in thought that I don't realise Felicity has stopped reading. It's quiet except for the sound of water trickling down a wall. "Wherever did you find this?" She's looking at me as if I were a criminal.

Why, a ghostly urchin led me to it in the night. Doesn't that ever happen to you?

"The library," I lie.

"And did you really think it was an actual account of the witching hour at Spence?" Felicity is looking at me in a bemused way.

"No, of course not," I lie. "I was only having a bit of fun with you."

"Oooh, the witching hour of the Order. Is that just before vespers or right after music?" Pippa is giggling so hard, she snorts like a horse. It is most unattractive, and I am just horrible enough to take great pleasure in this fact.

"Very clever – you're quite a wit," I say, trying to sound good-humoured when I feel surly and humiliated.

Felicity holds the diary aloft in mock seriousness. "I have been opened, my sisters. From now on, this shall be our sacred tome. Let us begin every meeting with a reading from this compelling" – she glances my way – "and absolutely true diary."

This sends Pippa howling. "I think that's a splendid idea!" She slurs the word so that it comes out *splendlid*.

"Wait a moment, that's mine," I say, reaching for the diary, but Felicity pockets it.

"I thought you said it came from the library," Ann says.

"Ha! Well done, Ann." Pippa smiles at her and I'm already regretting the beginning of their friendship. My lie has stuck me here, without the book and a way to understand what's happening to me, what my visions may mean. But there's no getting hold of it without telling them the whole truth, and I'm not ready to do that. Not until I understand it myself.

Ann passes the bottle to me again but I wave it away.

"*Je ne voudrais pas le whiskey*," I slur in my terrible French-English.

"We've got to help you with your French, Gemma, before LeFarge bumps you down in the ranks," Felicity says.

"How do *you* know so much about French?" I ask, irritated.

"For your information, Miss Doyle, my mother happens to run a very famous salon in Paris." She gives *salon* the French pronunciation. "All the best writers in Europe have been entertained by my mother."

"Your mother is French?" I ask. My thoughts are a bit foggy from the whiskey. Everything makes me want to giggle.

"No. She's English. Descended from the Yorks. She lives in Paris."

Why would she live in Paris instead of here, where her husband would return after his duty to Her Majesty had been completed? "Don't your parents live together?"

Felicity glares at me. "My father is away at sea most of the time. My mother is a beautiful woman. Why shouldn't she have the companionship of friends in Paris?"

I don't know what I've said wrong. I start to apologise but Pippa runs right over me.

"I wish my mother ran a salon. Or did anything interesting. All she seems to do is drive me mad with her criticism. 'Pippa – mustn't slouch. You'll never get a husband that way.' 'Pippa, we must keep up appearances at all times.' 'Pippa, what you think of yourself isn't nearly as important as what others say of you.' And there's her latest protégé – the clumsy, charmless Mr Bumble."

"Who is Mr Bumble?" I ask.

"Pippa's paramour," Felicity says, drawing out the word.

"He is *not* my paramour!" Pippa screeches.

"No, but he wants to be. Why else would he keep paying his visits?"

"He must be fifty if he's a day!"

"And very rich or your mother wouldn't be throwing him at you."

"Mother lives for money." Pippa sighs. "She doesn't like the way Father gambles. She's afraid he's going to lose all our money. That's why she's so desperate to marry me off to a wealthy man."

"She'll probably find you someone with a clubfoot and twelve children, all older than you are." Felicity laughs.

Pippa shudders. "You should see some of the men she's paraded in front of me. One was four feet tall!"

"You can't be serious!" I say.

"Well, he might have been five feet." Pippa laughs and it's contagious, sending us all into hysterical fits. "Another time, she introduced me to a man who kept pinching my bottom when we were dancing. Can you imagine? 'Oh, lovely waltz.' Pinch, pinch. 'Shall we have some punch?' Pinch, pinch. I was bruised for a week."

Our shrieks are animal sounds, loose and rambunctious. They die down to coughing and murmurs, and Pippa says, "Ann, Gemma. You don't have to worry about such things as impossible mothers trying to control your every waking moment. How lucky you are."

All the breath leaves my lungs. Felicity kicks Pippa hard in the shin.

"Well, that wasn't very nice, was it?" Pippa makes a show of rubbing her leg.

"Don't be so touchy," Felicity says snidely, but when she catches my eyes, there's a hint of kindness there and I understand she's done it for me, and I wonder for the first time if we really might be friends.

"How revolting!" Ann has been flipping through the diary. She's got some sort of illustration in her hands, which she tosses away as if it might burn her.

"What is it?" Pippa rushes over, her curiosity stronger than her pride. We lean in close. It's a drawing of a woman with grapes in her hair coupling with a man in animal skins, a mask with horns adorning his head. The caption reads, *The Rites of Spring by Sarah Rees-Toome.*

We all gasp and call it disgusting while trying to get a better look.

"Methinks he's already sprung," I say, giggling in a high voice I don't even recognise as my own.

"What are they doing?" Ann asks, turning quickly away.

"She's lying back and thinking of England!" Pippa shrieks, invoking the phrase that every English mother tells her daughter about carnal acts. We're not supposed to enjoy it. We're just supposed to put our mind on making babies for the future of the Empire and to please our husbands. For some reason, it's Kartik's face that swims inside my eyes. Those heavily fringed orbs of his coming closer, making my lips part. A strange warmth starts in my belly and seeps under every edge of me.

"Ann, don't tell me you don't know what men and women do when they're together. Shall I show you?" Felicity slithers off the rock and drags herself along the ground with her hands, leaning close to Ann, who recoils, her back against the cave wall.

"No, thank you," she whispers.

Felicity holds her gaze for a moment, then licks Ann's cheek in one long stroke. Horrified, Ann wipes at herself. Felicity only laughs and falls back against a low rock, stretching her arms over her head. Her full breasts strain at the bodice of her gown. She stares at a point beyond our heads. "I'm going to have many men." She says this matter-of-factly, as if commenting on the weather, but she has to know she's being scandalous.

Pippa doesn't know whether to gasp or giggle so she does both. "Felicity, that's shocking!"

Felicity smells blood. She's on the scent of our discomfort and won't let go. "I am. Hordes of men! Members of Parliament and stable boys. Moors and Irishmen. Disgraced dukes! Kings!"

Pippa has her hands over her ears. "No!" she screams. "Don't tell me any more!" But she's laughing, too. She loves Felicity's brazenness.

Felicity is up, dancing, throwing herself around like a whirling dervish. "I'm going to have presidents and captains of industry! Actors and Gypsies! Poets and artists and men who will die just to touch the hem of my dress!"

"You forgot princes!" Ann shouts, giving a small, guilty smile.

"Princes!" Felicity shouts with glee. She takes Ann's hands, dances her around in circles, Felicity's blonde hair whipping at the air.

Pippa is up, joining the circle. "And troubadours!"

"And troubadours who sing about the sapphires of my eyes!"

I'm joining them, caught up in the swirl of it all. "Don't forget jugglers and acrobats and admirals!"

Felicity stops. Her voice is cold. "No. No admirals."

"I'm sorry, Felicity. I didn't mean anything by it," I say, straightening my dress while Pippa and Ann stare awkwardly at their feet. The silence is raw electricity between us all –

one touch, one wrong word and we'll burn up. The bottle is in Felicity's hand. She takes a long, hard draw on it, doubles over from the force of the whiskey and rakes the back of her pale hand across her lips, dark with drink.

"Let's have a ritual, shall we?"

"Wh-wh-what sort of r-r-ritual?" Ann doesn't realise that she's taken a few steps away from us, towards the yawning mouth of the cave.

"I know – we could make up an oath!" Pippa is rather pleased with herself.

"It needs to be more binding than that," Felicity says, her eyes faraway. "Promises can be forgotten. Let's do a blood ritual. We need something sharp." Her eyes fall even with my amulet, which is hanging free. "That would do nicely, I think."

Instinctively, my hand goes to it. "What are you going to do?"

Felicity exhales, rolling her eyes dramatically. "I'm going to eviscerate you and leave your organs on a pike in the yard as a warning to those who wear large jewellery."

"It was my mother's," I say. Everyone is looking at me, waiting. Finally, I bow to the silent pressure and hand over the necklace.

"*Merci.*" Felicity curtsies. With one quick motion she brings down the edge of the moon and slices into the pad of her finger. Blood bubbles up instantly.

"Here," she says, streaking her blood across both of my cheeks. "We'll mark one another. Form a pact."

She passes the necklace to Pippa, who makes a face. "I

can't believe you want me to do this. It's so animalistic. I hate the sight of blood."

"Fine. I'll do it for you, then. Shut your eyes." Felicity breaks Pippa's skin and Pippa screams as if she's been mortally wounded. "Good heavens, you're still breathing, aren't you? Don't be such a ninny." Using Pippa's fingers, she streaks the blood over Ann's ruddy cheeks. In return, Ann wipes her bloody fingers on Pippa's porcelain skin.

"Please hurry. I'm going to be sick. I can feel it," Pippa whimpers.

Finally, it's my turn. The sharp point of the moon hovers over my finger. I'm remembering a snippet of a dream – a storm, I think, and my mother screaming, my hand gaping open, wounded.

"Go on, then," Felicity urges. "Don't tell me I'll have to do you, too."

"No," I say, and plunge the point into my finger. Pain shoots up my arm, forcing a hiss from my lips. The small crack bleeds quickly. My finger stings as I drag it softly over Felicity's china-white cheekbones.

"There," she says, looking around at us, newly christened in the candlelight. "Put your hands out." She sticks out her hand and we lay our palms over hers. "We swear loyalty to each other, to keep secret the rites of our Order, to taste freedom and let no one betray us. No one." She looks at me when she says this. "This is our sanctuary. And as long as we're here, we will speak only truth. Swear it."

"We swear."

Felicity moves a candle into the centre. "Let each girl tell her heart's desire over this candle and make it so."

Pippa takes the candle and says solemnly, "To find true love."

"This is silly," Ann says, trying to pass the candle to Felicity, who refuses it.

"Your heart's desire, Ann," she says.

Ann won't look at any of us when she says, "To be beautiful."

Felicity's grip on the candle is strong, her voice determined. "I wish to be too powerful to ignore."

Suddenly, the candle is in my hand, hot wax trickling over the sides and searing my skin before cooling into a waxy clump on my wrist. What is my heart's desire? They want the truth, but the most truthful answer I can give is that I don't know my own heart any better than I know theirs.

"To understand myself."

This seems to satisfy, for Felicity intones, "O great goddesses on these walls, grant us our heart's desires." A breeze blows through the mouth of the cave, snuffing out the candle, making us all gasp.

"I think they heard us," I whisper.

Pippa puts her hands to her mouth. "It's a sign."

Felicity passes the bottle one last time and we drink. "It seems the goddesses have answered us. To our new life. Drink up. The first meeting of the Order has come to a close. Let's get back while our candles hold."

CHAPTER
FOURTEEN

I AM POSITIVELY DEAD DURING MADEMOISELLE LeFarge's French class the next morning. The aftereffects of whiskey are the devil himself. There isn't a moment when my head doesn't pound, and breakfast – dry toast with marmalade – sits precariously on the sea of my stomach.

I will never, ever drink whiskey again. From now on, it's strictly sherry.

Pippa looks as washed out as I do. Ann seems fine – though I suspect she pretended to drink more than she did, a lesson I might heed next time. Except for the half-moon shadows under her eyes, Felicity doesn't seem any worse for the long evening.

Elizabeth takes in the rumpled sight of me and scowls. "Whatever is the matter with her?" she says, trying to cosy up to Felicity and Pippa again. I wonder if they'll take the bait, if last night's friendship will be forgotten and Ann and I will find ourselves on the outside looking in once more.

"I'm afraid we cannot divulge any of the secrets of our Order," Felicity says, giving me a furtive glance.

Elizabeth sulks and whispers to Martha, who nods. Cecily is not giving up easily, though.

"Fee, don't be cross," she says, oozing sweetness. "I've got new writing papers from the stationer's. Shall we write letters home tonight in your sitting area?"

"I'm afraid I'm otherwise engaged," Felicity answers, crisp as can be.

"So that's how it is, then?" Cecily purses her thin lips. She would make the perfect vicar's wife, with that deadly combination of self-righteousness mixed with an unforgiving streak. I'd enjoy her comeuppance a bit more if I weren't feeling so completely wretched. A belch escapes me, much to everyone's horror, but I feel much better.

Martha waves a hand in front of her nose. "You smell like a distillery."

Cecily's head is up at this. She and Felicity lock eyes – Felicity looking grim as a small, unfriendly smile pulls at the corners of Cecily's lips. Mademoiselle LeFarge barges into the room, spouting French phrases that make my poor head spin. She assigns us fifteen sentences to translate into our books. Cecily folds her hands on her desk.

"Mademoiselle LeFarge—"

"*En Français!*"

"Forgive me, Mademoiselle, but I believe Miss Doyle isn't feeling well." She gives Felicity a victorious look as Mademoiselle calls me to her desk for closer scrutiny.

"You do seem a bit peaked, Miss Doyle." She sniffs the air

and speaks to me in a low, stern voice. "Miss Doyle, have you been drinking spirits?"

Behind me, the scratch of pen on paper slows to a crawl. I don't know what's more palpable – the whiskey leaking from my pores or the smell of panic in the room.

"No, Mademoiselle. Too much marmalade at breakfast," I say with a half-smile. "It's my weakness."

She sniffs again, as if trying to convince herself that her nose has failed her. "Well, you may be seated."

Shakily, I take my chair, looking up only briefly to see Felicity grinning from ear to ear. Cecily looks as if she could happily choke me in my sleep. Discreetly, Felicity passes me a note. *I thought you were done for.*

I scribble back, *I did, too. I feel like the devil himself. How is your head?* Pippa sees the surreptitious handing off of folded paper. She cranes her neck to see what's being written and whether it could possibly be about her. Felicity shields the content of the note with the wall of her hand. Reluctantly, Pippa goes back to her lessons but not without first glaring at me with those violet eyes.

Swiftly, Felicity passes the note again just before Mademoiselle LeFarge looks up. "What's going on back there?"

"Nothing," Felicity and I say together, proving beyond a doubt that something is indeed going on.

"I shall not be repeating today's lesson, so I sincerely hope that you are not taking frivolously the matter of writing it all down."

"*Oui, Mademoiselle*," Felicity says, all French charm and smiles.

When Mademoiselle's head goes down again, I open the note Felicity has passed me. *We'll meet again tonight after midnight. Loyalty to the Order!*

Inwardly, I groan at the thought of another sleepless night. My bed, with its warm woolen blanket, is more inviting than tea with a duke. But I already know I'll be weaving my way through the woods tonight, eager to hear more of the diary's secrets.

Pippa is passing her own note to Felicity when I glance over. It's hard to admit it to myself, but I desperately want to know what's in that note. Something hard and mean flits across the surface of Felicity's face but it's replaced just as quickly with a closemouthed smile. Surprisingly, she doesn't respond to Pippa but passes the note to me, much to Pippa's horror. This time, Mademoiselle LeFarge is up and moving down the aisle between our desks, so there's nothing to do but slip the note between the pages of my book and wait until later to read it. When the hour is over, Mademoiselle LeFarge calls me to her desk once again. Felicity gives me a warning look on the way out. I shoot her my own look, which says, *What do you expect me to do?* Knowing that I still have her note burning a hole in my French book, Pippa wears an expression somewhere between fear and nausea. She starts to say something to me, but Ann closes the door, leaving me alone with Mademoiselle LeFarge and my own fast-beating heart.

"Miss Doyle," she says, peering up at me warily, "are you quite sure the odour on your breath is from marmalade and not some other substance?"

"Yes, Mademoiselle," I say, trying to expel as little breath as possible.

She suspects I'm lying but she can't prove it. Disappointment weighs her down to a sigh. I seem to have that effect on people. "Too much marmalade is bad for the figure, you know."

"Yes, Mademoiselle. I'll remember that." That Mademoiselle LeFarge, she of the wide girth, thinks she is in any position to comment on figures is astounding, but I'm only hoping to escape with my head intact.

"Yes, well, see that you do. Men don't care for plump women," she says. Her candour has us both looking away. "Well, some men don't." Instinctively, she brushes a finger across the tintype of the young man in uniform.

"Is he a relation?" I ask, trying to be courteous. It's no longer the whiskey that's turning my stomach but my own guilt. Honestly, I like Mademoiselle LeFarge, and I hate deceiving her.

"My fiancé. Reginald." She says his name with great pride, but also a hint of longing that makes me blush.

"He looks . . . very . . ." I realise I have no idea what to say about this man. I've never met him. He's only a bad photograph. But I've already started. "Trustworthy," I pronounce with difficulty.

This seems to please Mademoiselle LeFarge. "He does have a kind face, doesn't he?"

"Most definitely," I say.

"Best not hold you here. You don't want to be late for

Mr Grunewald. Remember – be sparing with the marmalade."

"Yes, I'll do that. Thank you," I say, and stumble out the door. I am lower than a crustacean. I don't even deserve to have a teacher like Mademoiselle LeFarge. And even so, I know I'm going to be out in the caves tonight, disappointing her in ways I hope she never discovers.

Pippa's note peeks out of the edges of my French book. Slowly, I open it. Her perfect round script is cruel and mocking.

Let's meet at the boathouse this afternoon. My mother sent new gloves, and I shall let you wear them. For pity's sake, don't invite her. If she tried to put her big ox hands inside, the gloves would be thoroughly ruined.

For the first time all day, I'm afraid I really will vomit, though it has nothing to do with the whiskey and everything to do with how deeply I hate them at this moment – Pippa, for writing the note, and Felicity for giving it to me.

ᕷᕷᕷᕷ

As it turns out, Pippa won't be going to the boathouse after all. The great hall is abuzz with the news – Mr Bumble is here. Every girl at Spence, from six to sixteen, is crowded around Brigid, who is delivering the latest gossip to us in breathless fashion. She goes on and on about what a fine, respectable man he is, how beautiful Pippa looks, and what a grand match they are. I don't believe I've ever seen Brigid so animated. Who could have guessed that the old sourpuss was a secret romantic?

"Yes, but what does he look like?" Martha wants to know.

"Is he handsome? Tall? Does he have all his teeth?" Cecily presses.

"Aye," Brigid says, knowingly. She's relishing this – being the oracle for a bit. "Handsome and respectable," she says again, in case we missed this salient quality the first time. "Oh, wot a luv'ly match our Miss Pippa has made. Let this be a lesson to you – if you take to heart all that Mrs Nightwing and the others – including yours truly – impart, you could be where Miss Pippa's headed. To the altar in a rich man's carriage."

It seems the wrong time to mention that if Mrs Nightwing and the others, including Brigid, were so knowledgeable they might be altar-bound themselves. I can see by the dewy-eyed rapture on the girls' faces that they are taking Brigid's words to be gospel truth.

"Where are they now?" Felicity presses.

"Well." Brigid leans in close. "I 'eard Mrs Nightwing say they'd be touring the gardens, but—"

Felicity turns to the girls. "We could see the gardens from the window on the second-floor landing!"

Amid Brigid's protests, there is a mad stampede up the stairs to the window. We older girls elbow our way past the younger girls, their petulant "no fair!"s no match for our sheer power and force. Within seconds, we've secured our position at the window and the others mash in behind us, straining for a view.

Out in the gardens, Mrs Nightwing chaperones Pippa and Mr Bumble along the path that weaves through the rows of roses and hyacinths. Through the open window, we have an unobstructed view of them standing awkwardly apart. Pippa is burying her face in a nosegay of red flowers that he must have brought her. She looks bored out of her mind. Mrs Nightwing is prattling on about the different flora on the path.

"Could you make room for the rest of us, please?" a chubby girl demands, hands on hips.

"Shove off," Felicity growls, deliberately using bad language to intimidate her.

"I'm going to tell Mrs Nightwing!" the girl squawks.

"Do it and see what happens. Now shush – we're trying to hear!"

Bodies squirm and press, but at least there's no more whingeing. It's so odd to see Pippa and Mr Bumble together. Despite Brigid's glowing report, he is, in fact, a fat, bushy-whiskered man, who is quite a bit older than Pippa. He looks off over Mrs Nightwing's head as if he's above it all. As far as I can tell, there is nothing special about him.

Some of the younger girls have managed to crawl beneath us. They're struggling up between our bodies and the window like weeds towards the window's light. We push against them, and they push back. We're all on top of each other, trying to get a better look and to listen.

"Lucky Pip," Cecily says. "She could marry a suitable chap

and not even have to go through a season, having every man and his mother size her up for marriage."

"I don't think Pip would agree with you," Felicity says. "I don't think that's what she wants at all."

"Well, it's not as if we can do what we want, is it?" Elizabeth says simply.

No one has anything to say to that. The breeze shifts towards us, carrying Mrs Nightwing's voice with it. She says something about roses being the flower of true love. And then they're around a tall hedge, hidden from sight.

CHAPTER
FIFTEEN

"CAN YOU BELIEVE THAT HE BROUGHT ME RED carnations? Do you know what that means in the language of flowers? Admiration! 'I admire you.' That will certainly win a girl's heart." Pippa is tearing the carnations apart one by one and sprinkling the colourful carnage over the cave floor.

"I think carnations are rather nice," Ann says.

"I'm only seventeen! My season has barely begun. I intend to enjoy it, not be married off to the first poxy old barrister with money." Pippa rips away the rest of the carnation in her hand, revealing a naked, nubby stalk.

I haven't said a word. I'm still smarting from that nasty letter this afternoon and the fact that Felicity is wearing one of Pippa's new gloves while Pippa wears the other, like badges of their friendship.

"Why is she in such a hurry to see you married?" Ann asks.

"She doesn't want anyone to know . . ." Pippa stops, stricken.

"Doesn't want anyone to know what?" I ask.

"What they're getting before it's too late." She tosses the flower stem to the ground.

I have no idea what she means. Pippa is beautiful. And her family may be merchant class but they are well-to-do and respectable. Other than being vain, obnoxious, and subject to romantic delusions, she's all right.

"What do you do when you're with a suitor?" Ann asks. She makes little xs in the dirt with a beheaded carnation.

Pippa sighs. "Oh, it's generally the same. You have to fawn over them. After they bore you to tears with some story about a legal case they argued, you have to lower your eyes and say something like 'My, I had no idea the law could be so fascinating, Mr Bumble. But when you put it that way, why, it's just like reading a novel!'"

We fall over laughing. "No! You didn't say that!" Felicity howls.

Pippa is losing her mopey air. "Oh, yes, I did! And how do you like this one." She bats her lashes and adopts a sweet, shy demeanour. "Well, perhaps I could manage just one chocolate..."

This has me laughing in spite of myself. We all know Pippa is a secret glutton.

"One chocolate?" Felicity screams. "My God, if he could see you put away an entire tray of toffees he'd be appalled! When you get married, you'll have to hide them in your boudoir and stuff them down when he's not looking."

Pippa screeches and pretends to beat Felicity with the carnation stem. "You're wicked! I most certainly am not marrying Mr Bumble. Gracious, his name is Bumble! That's a curse right there!"

Felicity runs just out of the carnation's reach. "Oh, yes, you are going to marry him! He's called on you four times now. I'll bet your mother's planning the wedding even as we speak!"

Pippa's laugh dies. "You don't really think so, do you?"

"No," Felicity says quickly. "No, it was a bad joke, that's all."

"I want to marry my true love. I know it's silly, but I can't help it."

Pippa looks so small suddenly, sitting there among her strewn petals, that I've almost forgotten how angry I am. I've never been able to hold a grudge anyway.

Felicity tilts Pippa's chin upwards with a finger. "And you will. Now, let's call this meeting to order. Pip, why don't you administer the sacrament?"

She brings out the whiskey again. I groan inwardly. But when it comes my way, I take my poison and find it's not so bad if you take small sips. This time, I drink only till I feel warm and light, not beyond.

"We must have a reading from the diary of our sister, Mary Dowd. Gemma, will you do the honours this evening?" With a bow Felicity hands the diary to me. I clear my throat and begin:

"*March 21, 1871*

"*Today we stood among the Runes of the Oracle. Under Eugenia's guidance, we touched our fingers to them for an instant, receiving the* magic. The sensation was overpowering. It was as if we could feel each other's very thoughts, as if we were one and the same."

Felicity raises an eyebrow. "Sounds naughty. Mary and Sarah are probably Sapphists."

"What on earth is a Sapphist?" Pippa is already bored. She's twirling the ends of her black ringlets round her ungloved finger, trying to achieve a more perfect curl.

"Must I tell you everything?" Felicity scoffs.

I have no idea what a Sapphist is either, but I'm not about to ask now.

"From the Greek Sappho, a lady poet who enjoyed the love of other women."

Pippa stops twirling. "Whatever is the matter with that?"

Felicity lowers her head and gives Pippa a baleful look. "Sapphists prefer the love of women to men."

I understand fully now, as does Ann, I gather, by the way she nervously straightens her skirts with her hands, not meeting anyone's eyes. Pippa squints at Felicity as if she might read the meaning in her forehead, but slowly, a blush creeps up her neck into her cheeks and she's gasping. "Oh, my heavens, you can't honestly mean that . . . that they . . . like husband and wife . . . ?"

"Yes, exactly."

Pippa is stunned into silence. The red does not fade from her face and neck. I'm embarrassed too, but I don't want them to know it. "May I please continue?"

"The Gypsies came back today to make camp. When we saw the smoke from their fire, Sarah and I hurried to see Mother Elena."

"Mother Elena!" Ann gasps.

"That lunatic with the ragged head scarf?" Pippa wrinkles her nose in distaste.

"Shhh! Go on," Felicity says.

"She welcomed us warmly with herb tea and tales of her travels. We gave sweets to Carolina, who devoured them. To Mother we gave five pence. And then she promised to read the cards for us, as she has before. But no sooner had Mother placed Sarah's cards in the familiar cross pattern than she stopped and shuffled them into a pile again. 'The cards have a bad temper today,' she said with a little smile, but in truth she seemed taken by a sense of foreboding. She asked to see my palm, snaking her sharp fingernail along the pathways of my hand. 'You are on a dark journey,' she said, dropping my hand like a hot stone. 'I cannot see the outcome.' Then, most abruptly, she asked us to leave as she needed to make her way through the camp to be sure things were well settled."

Ann is peering over my arm, trying to read ahead. I pull the book away and end up dropping it, scattering the pages.

"Bravo, my lady Grace!" Felicity applauds.

Ann helps me cluster the papers together in my arms. She can't stand having anything out of order. A patch of wrist is exposed. I can see the red cross-hatching of welts there, fresh and angry. This is no accident. She's doing it to herself.

She sees me looking and pulls hard at her sleeves, covering her secret.

"Come now," Felicity chides. "What more will the diary of Mary Dowd reveal to us tonight?"

I grab a page. "Here we go," I say. It's not the same page, but that hardly matters to them.

"April 1, 1871

"Sarah came to me in tears. 'Mary, Mary, I cannot find the door. The power is leaving me.'

"'You are overwrought, Sarah. That is all. Try again tomorrow.'

"'No, no,' she wailed. 'I have tried for hours now. I tell you it is gone.'

"My heart was gripped with an icy cold. 'Sarah, come. I'll help you find it.'

"She turned on me with such fury that I scarcely recognised her as my friend. 'Don't you understand? I must do it myself or it's not real. I cannot ride along on your powers, Mary.' She began to cry then. 'Oh, Mary, Mary, I cannot bear to think that I will never again touch the runes or feel their magic flowing through me. I cannot bear to think that I will be only ordinary Sarah from now on.'

"For the rest of the evening I could not rest or eat at all. Eugenia saw my misery and bade me sit with her in her own room. She says it is often that way — a girl's power flares, then fades. The power must be nurtured deep in the soul, else it's nothing more than grasping. Oh, diary, she confided that Sarah's power is such, fleeting and unanchored. She says that the realms make the decision about who shall rise in the Order and learn all the ancient mysteries and who must stay behind. Eugenia patted my hand and confessed that the power is great in me, but I am lost to think of going forward without my dearest friend and sister.

"When Sarah came to me late this evening, I felt as if I would do anything to make things as they were before, with us close as sisters again and the magic of the realms within our reach. I told her so.

"'Oh, Mary,' she cried. 'You've cheered me considerably. You know there is a way that we can be together always.'

"'What do you mean?'

"'I have a confession. I have visited the Winterlands. I have seen it.'

"I was shocked at this, it chilled me so. 'But, Sarah, that is a realm we are not to know yet. There are things we should not see without the guide of our elders here.'

"Sarah got such a hard look in her eyes. 'Don't you see? Our elders want us to know only what they can control. They fear us, Mary. That is why Eugenia is taking the power from me. I have spoken to a spirit that wanders there. She told me the truth.'

"Her words seemed true, but I was afraid still. 'Sarah, I'm afraid. To call up a dark spirit is to go against everything we've been taught.'

"Sarah clasped my hands. 'It's only to bring us the power we need. We will bind the spirit to us, make it do our bidding. Don't worry so, Mary. We will be its masters, not the other way around, and once the Order sees what we can do, what power we hold by ourselves, they'll have to let me stay. We'll be together forever.'

"This next part I shuddered to speak aloud. 'What will it require?'

"Sarah stroked my cheek lovingly. 'A small sacrifice, nothing *more. A grass snake or a sparrow, perhaps. She will tell us. Sleep now, Mary. And tomorrow, we shall make our plans.'*

"Oh, diary, my heart feels much misgiving about this endeavour. But what can I do? Sarah is my dearest friend in all the world. I cannot go on without her. And perhaps she is right. Perhaps, if we keep our hearts strong and pure, we can bend the creature to our will, using it only for the best intentions."

Pippa is nearly breathless. "Well, there's a fine place to leave off."

"Yes, the plot thickens," Felicity says. "In fact, it may be congealing."

Everyone shares a giggle except me. The passage has left me uneasy. Or it could be the heat. It's unseasonably warm for September. The air inside the caves is sticky, and I've begun to sweat beneath my corset.

"Do you suppose Mother Elena could tell us our futures?" Ann muses.

I can't help it. At the thought of Gypsies, my eyes find Felicity's. She gives me a piercing glare as if I'm betraying her with this quick look.

"I'm not sure that Mother Elena could tell us the day of the week," Felicity says.

❧❧❧❧

"I have the most marvellous idea," Pippa trills, and suddenly, I know we're in for it. "Let's see if we can make our own magic."

"I'm game," Felicity says. "Who else wants to commune with the other world?"

Pippa sits on Felicity's right, their gloved hands intertwined. Ann plops down next to Pippa. The hair on the back of my neck stands up.

"I don't think this is a good idea," I begin, realising at once that it sounds cowardly.

"Are you afraid we'll turn you into a frog?" Felicity pats the ground beside her. There's no getting around it. I'm going to have to join the circle. Reluctantly, I take my seat and join hands with Ann and Felicity.

Pippa has the giggles again. "What do we say to get started?"

"We'll go around in a circle and each add something," Felicity instructs. "I'll start. O great spirits of the Order. We are your daughters. Speak to us now. Tell us your secrets."

"Come to us, O daughters of Sappho." Pippa dissolves into laughter.

"We don't know that they're Sapphists," Felicity says, annoyed. "If we're going to do this, let's do it right."

Chastened, Pippa says softly, "Come to us now in this place."

"We beseech you," Ann adds.

It's quiet. They're waiting for me.

"All right," I say, sighing and rolling my eyes. "But I do this against my better judgment, and I'd best not hear these words come back to haunt me as private little jokes later."

I close my eyes and concentrate on Ann's heavy, congested breathing, willing my mind to stay blank. "Sarah Rees-

Toome and Mary Dowd. Wherever you are in this world, show yourselves. You are welcome here."

There's nothing but the sound of water trickling along the cave's walls. No spirits. No visions. I don't know whether to be relieved or a little disappointed in my lack of power.

I do not get the chance to ponder this dilemma for long. The air sparkles with random bursts of light. Suddenly, it's as if the cave is on fire, flames leaping up, so hot I can't catch my breath.

"No!" Using all my strength, I break the circle and find myself back in the cave while Pippa, Ann, and Felicity look at me, stunned.

"Gemma, what's the matter?" Ann asks, breathing hard.

I'm panting.

"Oh, my. I think someone got a wee bit frightened," Felicity says.

"I suppose that's it," I say, sinking to the floor. My arms feel heavy, but I'm relieved that nothing has happened.

"It's a curious thing, though," Pippa says. "But I could swear I felt a sort of tingling for a moment."

"So did I," Felicity says in wonder.

Ann nods. "And I."

They all look at me. My heart's beating so hard I fear it will leap from my chest. I force a calm I don't feel into my words. "I don't know what you're talking about."

Felicity puts the tip of her hair in her mouth, moistens it with her tongue. "You didn't feel anything at all?"

"Nothing." I'm trying hard not to shake.

"Well," she says, with a triumphant smile. "It would seem

that the rest of us have a bit of magic in us. Pity about you, Gemma."

It's very funny, this moment. They think I've got no aptitude for the supernatural. I would laugh, if I weren't so completely shaken.

"Heavens, Gemma," Pippa says, wrinkling her nose in distaste. "You're perspiring like a docks worker."

"That's because it's too bloody hot in here," I say, relieved to change the subject.

Felicity stands and offers me her hand. "Come on. Let's claim the night."

✶✶✶✶

We stumble out of the cave. Miles above us, the moon has started to wane, the edges bitten off, but we bask in its light anyway, howling like wolves. We join hands and run around in a circle, breathe the cold, mossy night air into lungs that can barely hold it all in. I feel better straightaway.

"It's terribly hot. I can scarcely breathe in this corset," Felicity says.

"Yes, I wish we could take a dip in the lake," Ann says.

"Why can't we?" Felicity muses. "Who will unlace me? Anyone?"

Pippa covers her mouth and gives a little giggle as if she's both horribly embarrassed by the idea and concerned about looking prudish. "We can't do that."

"Why not? There's no one to see us. And I want to breathe freely for a bit. Here, Gemma – give us a hand."

My fingers fumble with the laces and grommets but soon Felicity's thin shift and the soft skin beneath it are both exposed. She gleams in the moonlight, a sliver of bone. "Who wants a dip in the lake, then?"

"Wait!" Pippa stumbles after her. "What are you doing? Felicity – this is obscene!"

"How can my ankles and arms be obscene?" she calls back.

"But you're not supposed to show them. It isn't decent!"

Felicity's voice floats out to us. "Do what you will. I'm going in."

The water looks cool and inviting. With effort, I manage to liberate myself from the tight corset. My body expands in a thank-you.

"Not you, too?" Pippa says when I pass her.

The frigid water saps the heat from my body immediately, freezing the air in my lungs into hard lumps. When I finally catch my breath, it's to tell Pippa and Ann, hoarsely, "Come in. The water's perfect, as long as you don't need to breathe or feel your legs."

Pippa responds with a high-pitched shriek the minute she gets knee-deep.

"Shhh, keep your voice down. If Mrs Nightwing finds us, she'll punish us by forcing us to teach at Spence for the rest of our lives like that spinsterish, sour-faced crew she's got teaching us now," Felicity says.

Pippa tries to cover herself with her hands. Her modesty is showing. Right now, I wouldn't care if Prince Albert himself saw me. I only want to float here, suspended in time.

"If you're that modest, Pip, get under the water," Felicity says.

"It's so cold!" Pippa answers in that same high-pitched voice.

"Suit yourself, then," Felicity says, swimming out to the middle of the lake.

Ann stays on the bank, fully clothed. "I'll keep a watch out," she says.

The rest of us link our arms for warmth and let our feet lick at the sandy bottom. We're like a band of floating nomads.

"What do you suppose Mrs Nightwing would say if she could see us now in all our grace, charm, and beauty?" Pippa giggles.

"She'd probably fall over dead," Ann says.

"Ha!" Felicity says. "There's wishful thinking." She leans her head back, lets her hair float out on the water like a halo.

Pippa's head is up like a shot. "Did you hear that?"

"Hear what?" The lake water in my ears makes it hard to hear anything. But there it is. The woods echo with the sound of a tree branch snapping in two.

"There it is again! Did you hear it?"

"Criminy," Ann croaks.

"Our clothes!" Pippa scrambles out of the water on heavy legs and runs for her chemise just as Kartik steps out of the trees, carrying a makeshift cricket bat. I can't tell who is more shocked and surprised – Kartik or Pippa.

"Avert your eyes!" she says in near hysteria, trying desperately to cover herself with the bit of lace and cloth.

Too astonished to argue, Kartik does, but not before I've

seen the look in his eyes. Wonder and awe. As if he truly has seen a goddess made flesh. The visceral impact of her beauty is more powerful than any word or deed. The cloudiness of my mind clears long enough to record this.

"If this were ancient times, we would hunt you down and put out your eyes for what you've seen," Felicity snarls from the lake.

Kartik says nothing. As quickly as he came upon us, he's gone, running through the woods.

"Next time," Felicity says, moving to help Pippa, "we *will* put his eyes out."

⌁⌁⌁⌁

The room is dark, but I know she's awake. There's none of her snoring.

"Ann, are you awake?" She doesn't answer, but I'm not giving up. "I know you are, so you might as well respond." Silence. "I won't give up until you do." Outside, an owl announces that he is near.

"Why do you do that to yourself? Cut yourself the way you do?"

There's no answer for a good long minute, and I think that perhaps she has fallen asleep after all, but then it comes. Her voice, so soft I have to strain in the dark to hear it, to hear the faint cry she's holding back.

"I don't know. Sometimes, I feel nothing, and I'm so afraid. Afraid I'll stop feeling anything at all. I'll just slip away inside myself." There's a cough and a sniffling sound. "I just need to feel something."

The owl makes his call in the night again, waiting to see if anyone is at home.

"No more doing that," I say. "Promise me?"

More sniffles. "All right."

It feels as if I should do something here. Put my arm around her. Offer a hug. I don't know what to do that wouldn't horrify and embarrass us both.

"If you don't, I'll be forced to confiscate your needlepoint, and where would you be without the satisfaction of finishing your little Dutch girl and windmill in seven different colours of thread, hmmm?"

She gives a weak gurgle of a laugh, and I'm relieved.

"Gemma?" she says after a moment has passed.

"Hmmm?"

"You won't tell, will you?"

"No."

More secrets. How did I end up keeping so many? Satisfied, Ann shifts in her bed and the familiar snoring begins. I stare at a patch of wall, willing sleep to come, listening to the owl cry into a night that never answers.

CHAPTER
SIXTEEN

"I KNOW YOU DON'T BELIEVE ANYTHING HAPPENED last night, but I think we should try to contact the other world again," Felicity whispers to me. We're standing in the middle of the cavernous ballroom waiting for Mrs Nightwing to begin our dance instruction. Above us, four chandeliers drip crystals whose light cuts dazzling squares into the marble floors below.

"I don't think that's a very good idea," I say, choking back my panic.

"Why not? Are your feelings hurt that you didn't feel what the rest of us did?"

"Don't be ridiculous," I snort, a sound that seems to accompany my lies, which is most unfortunate. I'm on the road to becoming a snorting fool these days.

"What, then?"

"I happen to find it dull. That's all."

"Dull?" Felicity's mouth hangs open. "You call that dull? Dull is what we're going to experience in a moment."

Pippa is standing with Cecily and her crowd, desperately trying to get Felicity's attention. "Fee, come stand over here with us. Mrs Nightwing's about to pair us off."

Each time I start to like Pippa, she does something like this to make me despise her again. "It's so nice to be loved," I mutter under my breath.

Felicity looks over at the fashionable crowd and turns her back on them, rather obviously and deliberately. Pippa's face falls. I can't help gloating just a little bit.

"Ladies, may I have your attention, please?" Mrs Nightwing's voice booms across the room. "Today we are going to practice our waltzing. Remember: posture is paramount. You must pretend your spine is on a string pulled by God himself."

"Makes it sound as if we're God's puppets," Ann mumbles.

"We are, if you believe Reverend Waite and Mrs Nightwing," Felicity says with a wink.

"Is there something you wish to share with us all, Miss Worthington?"

"No, Mrs Nightwing. Forgive me."

Mrs Nightwing takes a moment, letting us squirm under her scrutiny. "Miss Worthington, you shall partner with Miss Bradshaw. Miss Temple with Miss Poole, and Miss Cross, you will please partner with Miss Doyle."

Of all the luck. Pippa lets out a petulant sigh and stands sullenly in front of me, throwing a glance to Felicity, who shrugs.

"Don't look to me. It's not my fault," I say.

"You lead. I want to be the woman," Pippa snaps.

"We shall take turns leading and being led. Everyone shall have a chance," Mrs Nightwing says wearily. "Now then, ladies. Arms held high. Do not let your elbows droop. Posture, always posture. Many a lady's chances of securing a good marriage prospect have rested on her perfect carriage."

"Especially if it's a private carriage attached to a good deal of money," Felicity jokes.

"Miss Worthington . . . ," Mrs Nightwing warns.

Felicity straightens like Cleopatra's Needle. Satisfied, the headmistress cranks the arm of the Victrola and drops the needle onto a phonograph disc. The measured bars of a waltz fill the room.

"And one, two, three, one, two, three. Feel the music! Miss Doyle! Watch your feet! Small, ladylike steps. You are a gazelle, not an elephant. Ladies, hold yourselves erect! You'll never find a husband looking down on the floor!"

"She's obviously never seen some of those men after a few brandies," Felicity whispers, waltzing by.

Mrs Nightwing claps sharply. "There is to be no talking. Men do not find chatty women attractive. Count the music aloud, please. One, two, three, one, two, three. And switch leads, one, two, three."

The switch confuses Elizabeth and Cecily, who both try to lead. They steer straight into Pippa and me. We collide into Ann and Felicity and the lot of us fall to the floor in a heap.

The music stops abruptly. "If you dance with so little grace, your season will be over before it begins. May I remind you, ladies, that this is not a game? The London season is very serious business. It is your chance to prove yourselves worthy of the duties that will be imposed upon you as wives and mothers. And more importantly, your conduct is a reflection upon the very soul of Spence." There's a knock at the door and Mrs Nightwing excuses herself, while we struggle to our feet. No one helps Ann. I offer her a hand up. She takes it shyly, not meeting my eyes, still embarrassed over last night's honesty.

"Spence has a soul?" I say, attempting a joke to put us at ease.

"It's not funny," Pippa says hotly. "Some of us want to better ourselves. I've heard you're silently graded from the moment you walk in the door of your first ball. I don't want to be gossiped about as *that girl who can't dance*."

"Do relax, Pippa," Felicity says, straightening her skirt. "You will do just fine. You're not going to be left a spinster. Surely Mr Bumble will see to that."

Pippa is aware that all eyes are on her. "I don't believe I said I would be marrying Mr Bumble, did I? After all, I might meet someone very special at a ball."

"Like a duke or a lord," Elizabeth says dreamily. "That's what I'd want."

"Exactly." Pippa gives Felicity a superior little smile.

Something hard glints in Felicity's eyes. "Dear Pip, you're not starting in on that fantasy again, are you?"

Pippa is holding fast to her debutante smile. "What fantasy?"

"The one currently floating through your head on gossamer wings. The one where your true love is a prince looking for his princess and you just happen to have the dress in your wardrobe, neatly pressed."

Pippa's trying hard to maintain her composure. "Well, a woman should always set her sights higher."

"That's high talk from a merchant's daughter." Felicity folds her arms across her chest. The air is alive. The room, charged.

Pippa's cheeks flush. "You're not exactly in the position to be giving advice, are you? With your family history?"

"What are you implying?" Felicity says with an icy coolness.

"I'm not implying anything. I'm stating a fact. For whatever else my parents may be, at least my mother isn't . . ." She stops cold.

"Isn't what?" Felicity growls.

"I think I hear Mrs Nightwing coming," Ann says nervously.

"Yes, could we please stop all this bickering?" Cecily says. She tries to pull Felicity away, with no luck.

Felicity moves closer to Pippa. "No, if Pippa has something to say about my character, I, for one, would like to hear it. At least your mother isn't a what?"

Pippa squares her shoulders. "At least my mother isn't a whore."

Felicity's slap echoes in the room like a gunshot. We jump at the sudden violence of it. Pippa's mouth is an O, her violet eyes tearing up from the sting.

"You take that back!" Felicity says through her teeth.

"I won't!" Pippa is crying. "You know it's true. Your mother is a courtesan and a consort. She left your father for an artist. She ran away to France to be with him."

"It isn't true!"

"It is! She ran away and left you behind."

Ann and I are both too stunned to move. Cecily and Elizabeth can barely keep the smiles off their faces. This is astonishing news, and I know later they'll be off to gossip about it. Felicity will never walk through Spence's halls again without hearing whispers behind her back. And it's all Pippa's fault.

Felicity gives a cruel laugh. "She'll send for me when I graduate. I'll go to Paris and have my portrait painted by a famous artist. And then you'll be sorry for doubting me."

"You still think she's going to send for you? How many times have you seen her since you've been here? I shall tell you – none."

Felicity's eyes shine with hate. "She will send for me."

"She couldn't even be bothered to send anything for your birthday."

"I hate you."

There is a chorus of embarrassed gasps from the goody-girls. To my surprise, Pippa goes soft and quiet. "It's not me you hate, Fee. It's not me."

Mrs Nightwing bustles in again. She reads the trouble in the room like a change in the weather. "What's going on here?"

"Nothing," we all say at once, moving away from each other, each one of us studying our own patch of floor.

"Then let's continue." She drops the arm on the phonograph. Felicity grabs for Ann's hand, and Pippa and I settle in. She's the man this time, slipping her arm around my waist, taking my left hand in her right. We waltz near the windows, putting space between us and Ann and Felicity.

"I've made an awful mess of things," Pippa says, miserably. "We used to get on so well. We did everything together. But that was before . . ." She trails off. We both know how the sentence ends: before you came along.

She's just gone and ruined Felicity and now she wants my sympathy in the bargain. "I'm sure you'll be thick as thieves again tomorrow, and this will all be forgotten," I say, twirling a bit harder than I need to.

"No. It's all different now. She asks you before she asks me. I've been replaced."

"You have not," I say, with a contemptuous half-laugh, because I'm a terrible liar when it really counts.

"Be careful she doesn't get bored with you next. It's a long way to fall."

Mrs Nightwing counts loudly over the music, correcting our steps, our posture, our every thought before we even have it. Pippa is moving me across the floor and I wonder if Kartik ever imagines what it would be like to hold her in his arms. Pippa has no idea of the effect she has on men, and I wish I could experience having that power just once. How I'd love to get away from here and be someone else for a while in a place where no one knows or expects certain things from me.

What happens next is not my fault. At least, I don't mean to do it. The need to run has somehow taken over. The familiar tingling is back, pulling me down deep before I can get control of it. But it's different this time. I'm not simply falling, I'm moving! I'm stepping across a shimmering threshold into a misty forest. Suspended there for a moment, between two worlds, I catch sight of Pippa's face. It's pale. Confused. Scared. And I realise she's coming too.

Dear God, what's happening? Where am I? How did she get here? I've got to stop it, can't let her fall with me.

I close my eyes and fight against the overwhelming tide of my vision with everything I've got. But it's not enough to keep me from seeing small flashes. Dark on the horizon. Splashing. And the sound of Pippa's strangled, watery scream.

We're back. I'm panting hard, still holding Pippa's hand in a death grip. Did she see anything? Does she know my secret now? She's not talking. Her eyes roll up into her head. The whites of them a fluttering of wings.

"Pippa?" My voice has enough panic in it to alert Mrs Nightwing. She runs towards us as Pippa's whole body stiffens. Her arm knocks me hard in the mouth as it flies back towards her chest. I can taste blood on my lip, all coppery hot. With a high keening sound, Pippa falls to the floor, her body writhing and jerking in what seems like agony.

Pippa is dying. What have I done to her?

Mrs Nightwing grabs Pippa's shoulders, pins her to the floor. "Ann, bring me a wooden spoon from the kitchen! Cecily, Elizabeth, fetch one of the teachers at once! Go – now!" To me she barks, "Hold her head still."

Pippa's head thrashes in my hands. *Pippa, I'm so very sorry. Please forgive me.*

"Help me turn her," Mrs Nightwing says. "She mustn't bite her tongue."

With effort, we turn her on her side. For a dainty creature, she is surprisingly solid. Brigid pushes into the ballroom and lets out with a cry.

Mrs Nightwing barks out orders like a decorated commander. "Brigid! Send for Dr. Thomas at once! Miss Moore, if you would, please." Brigid scurries out as Miss Moore rushes in, spoon in hand. She shoves it into Pippa's gurgling mouth as if she means to choke her with it.

"What are you doing?" I scream. "She can't breathe!" I wrestle with the spoon, trying to pull it out, but Miss Moore stays my hand.

"The spoon will keep her from biting off her tongue."

I want to believe her, but the way Pippa is thrashing on the floor, it's hard to imagine we can do anything to help. And then the violent tremors subside. She closes her eyes and goes still as death.

"Is she . . . ?" But I can't finish what I'm whispering. I don't want to know the answer.

Mrs Nightwing struggles to her feet. "Miss Moore, would you check on the progress with Dr. Thomas, please?"

Miss Moore nods and marches towards the open door,

admonishing the girls peering inside at us to get away. Mrs Nightwing places her shawl over Pippa. There on the floor, she looks exactly like a sleeping princess from a fairy tale.

I don't even realise I'm murmuring to her softly. "I'm sorry, Pippa, I'm sorry."

Mrs Nightwing regards me curiously. "I don't know what you're thinking, Miss Doyle, but this is not your doing. Pippa suffers from epilepsy. She has suffered a fit."

"Epilepsy?" Cecily repeats, making the word sound like *leprosy* or *syphilis*.

"Yes, Miss Temple. And now I must ask that you never repeat a word of this. It must be forgotten. If I should hear gossip about this, I shall give the girls responsible thirty conduct marks each and take away all privileges. Do I make myself clear?"

We nod silently.

"Is there anything we can do to help?" Ann asks.

Mrs Nightwing dabs at her brow with a handkerchief. "You could say a prayer."

⌇⌇⌇⌇

Dusk falls softly. Early shadows leak through the tall windows, robbing the rooms slowly of their colour. I have no appetite for dinner, nor do I join the others in Felicity's scarf-draped sanctuary. Instead, I find myself wandering till I'm just outside Pippa's room. I knock quietly. Miss Moore answers. Behind her, Pippa is lying on the bed, beautiful and still.

"How is she?"

"Sleeping," Miss Moore answers. "Come. No use standing in the hall." The door is opened wide. She lets me take the chair by the bed and pulls another over for herself. It's a small, kind gesture, and for some reason, it adds to my sadness. If she knew what I'd done to Pippa, what a liar I am, she wouldn't want to be so nice to me.

Pippa is breathing deeply, seemingly untroubled. I'm afraid to sleep myself. Afraid I'll see Pippa's terrified face as she toppled into my bloody stupid vision. The fear and guilt have me exhausted. Too tired to keep the tears back, I bury my face in my hands and weep, for Pippa, my mother, my father, everything.

Miss Moore's arm slips around my shoulders. "Shhh, don't worry. Pippa will be fine in a day or two."

I nod and cry harder.

"Somehow I think these tears aren't all for Pippa."

"I'm a horrid girl, Miss Moore. You don't know what I'm capable of."

"There now, what's this nonsense?" she murmurs.

"It's true. I'm not at all a good person. If it weren't for me, my mother would still be alive."

"Your mother died of cholera. That wasn't your doing."

The truth has been bottled up inside me for so long that it comes pouring out, spilling everywhere. "No, she didn't. She was murdered. I ran away from her and she came after me and was murdered. I killed her with my unkindness. It's all my fault, all of it." My sobs are great gasping hiccups. Miss

Moore still holds me in her sure arms, which remind me so much of my mother's right now, I can barely stand it. Eventually, I'm completely cried out, my face a swollen balloon. Miss Moore hands me her handkerchief, bids me blow my nose. I'm five again. No matter how much I think I've matured, I always end up back at five when I cry.

"Thank you," I say, trying to give back the white lace handkerchief.

"You hold on to it," she says diplomatically, eyeing the limp, disgusting thing in my hand. "Miss Doyle – Gemma – I want you to listen to me. You did not kill your mother. We are all unkind from time to time. We all do things we desperately wish we could undo. Those regrets just become part of who we are, along with everything else. To spend time trying to change that, well, it's like chasing clouds."

New tears trickle down my cheeks. Miss Moore brings the hand with the handkerchief in it to my face.

"Will she really be all right?" I say, looking at Pippa.

"Yes. Though I think it takes a toll on her to have to keep such a secret."

"Why does it have to be a secret?"

Miss Moore takes a moment to tuck Pippa's blanket under her chin. "If it were known, she would be unmarriageable. It is considered a flaw in the blood, like madness. No man would want a woman with such an affliction."

I remember Pippa's strange comment in the caves about being married before it was too late. Now I understand.

"It's so unfair."

"Yes, yes, it is, but that is the way of the world."

We sit for a moment watching Pippa breathe, watching the blankets rise and fall with a comforting rhythm.

"Miss Moore . . ." I stop.

"Here in private you may call me Hester."

"Hester," I say. The name feels forbidden on my tongue. "Those stories you told us about the Order. Do you suppose any of it could be true?"

"I suppose anything's possible."

"And if such a power existed, and you didn't know whether it was good or bad, would you explore it anyway?"

"You've given this a lot of thought."

"It's just musing, that's all," I say, looking at my feet.

"Things aren't good or bad in and of themselves. It's what we do with them that makes them so. At least, that's how I see it." She gives me a cryptic smile. "Now, what's all this about, really?"

"Nothing," I say, but my voice cracks on the word. "Just curious."

She smiles. "It may be best to keep what we spoke of in the caves amongst ourselves. Not everyone has such an open mind, and if word got around, I might not be able to take you girls anywhere but up to the art room for an afternoon of painting cheery bowls of fruit." She lifts a limp piece of hair from my still-damp face and secures it behind my ear. It's so tender, so much like my mother that I could cry all over again.

"I understand," I say at last.

Pippa's hand stirs for a moment. Her fingers grab at the air. She takes a deep, halting breath, then settles into sleep again.

"Do you suppose she'll remember what's happened to her when she wakes?" I'm not thinking about her seizure but what happened right before, when I pulled her under.

"I don't know," Miss Moore says.

My stomach growls.

"Did you have anything to eat this evening?"

I shake my head.

"Why don't you go downstairs with the other girls and have some tea? It will do you good."

"Yes, Miss Moore."

"Hester."

"Hester."

As I close the door, I finally do say a prayer – that Pippa will remember nothing.

<hr />

In the hall, the four class pictures greet me in all their sombre-faced glory. "Hello, ladies," I say to their empty, resigned eyes. "Try not to be so merry. It's quite disruptive."

A coating of dust has settled over those faces. With the pad of my finger, I clear it away in circles, revealing grainy faces. They stare into a future that's not giving up its secrets. Did they ever sneak into the dark woods under a new moon? Did they drink whiskey and hope for things they couldn't explain in words? Did they make friends and enemies, mourn their mothers, see and feel things they couldn't control?

Two of them did, this much I know. Sarah and Mary. Why haven't I ever thought to look for them on these walls before? They must be here. Quickly, I scan the dates scrawled at the bottom of each photograph: 1870, 1872, 1873, 1874 . . .

There is no class portrait for the year 1871.

〜〜〜〜〜

I find the others in the dining room. After our rough afternoon, Mrs Nightwing has taken pity on us and had Brigid tell the cook to prepare a second custard. Famished, I wolf down the sweet, creamy dessert as if I expect to die in my sleep.

"Good heavens," Mrs Nightwing admonishes. "This is not a day at the races, Miss Doyle, and you are not a Thoroughbred. Please eat more slowly."

"Yes, Mrs Nightwing," I say sheepishly between gulps.

"Now, what shall we discuss?" Mrs Nightwing says this like an indulgent grandmother wanting to know the names of our favourite dollies.

"Are we really going to attend Lady Wellstone's Spiritualist demonstration next week?" Martha asks.

"Yes, indeed. The invitation says that she will have an actual medium there – a Madame Romanoff."

"My mother attended a Spiritualism séance," Cecily says. "It is very fashionable. Even Queen Victoria herself is a devotee."

"My cousin Lucy, that is, Lady Thornton," Martha corrects herself, so that we may all be reminded of how well connected she is, "told me of a demonstration she attended where a glass vase levitated above the table as if someone were holding it!" She gives this last bit a hushed quality for proper dramatic effect.

Felicity rolls her eyes. "Why not simply go to the Gypsies for fortune-telling?"

"The Gypsies are filthy thieves who are after your money – or worse!" Martha says meaningfully.

Elizabeth leans towards her, on the chance there might be more sordid details to come. Mrs Nightwing puts her teacup down a bit hard and gives Martha a warning glance. "Miss Hawthorne, please remember yourself."

"I only meant that the Gypsies are nothing but fakes and criminals. Whilst Spiritualism is a real science practiced by the most well-meaning of souls."

"It's a passing fancy on its way out. Nothing more," Felicity says, yawning.

"I'm sure it will prove a most enjoyable evening," Mrs Nightwing says, restoring peace. "While I'm afraid I'm not enamoured of such poppycock, Lady Wellstone is indeed a woman of fine character and one of Spence's greatest bene-factresses, and I have no doubt that your outing with Mademoiselle LeFarge will prove ... beneficial in some way."

We sip our tea in silence for a moment. Most of the younger girls have drifted out in whispering, giggling clumps of threes and fours. I can hear the rising buzz of their voices from down the hall in the great room. Bored, Cecily and her entourage excuse themselves, making it impossible for the rest of us to leave Mrs Nightwing with-out seeming rude. It's just the four of us now in the empty dining room, with Brigid bustling about here and there.

"Mrs Nightwing." I stop, summoning up my courage. "It's a curious thing . . . in the hall, there's no class photograph from 1871."

"No, there is not," she answers in her usual clipped style.

"I was wondering why not." I try to sound innocent, but my heart is in my throat.

Mrs Nightwing doesn't look at me. "That was the year of the great fire in the East Wing. There was no photograph. Out of respect for the dead."

"For the dead?" I repeat.

"The two girls we lost in the fire." She looks at me as if I'm a simpleton.

We're all on pins and needles. A few floors above us, where heavy doors hide scorched, rotting floorboards, two girls died. A new chill passes through me.

"The two girls who died . . . what were their names?"

Mrs Nightwing is exasperated. She stirs her tea hard. "Must we discuss so unpleasant a topic after such a long and trying day?"

"I'm sorry," I say, unable to let the matter drop. "I simply wondered about their names."

Mrs Nightwing sighs. "Sarah and Mary," she says at last.

Felicity chokes on her last bite of custard. "I beg your pardon?"

Already, this news is sinking in. My body is heavy with it. With an air of extreme impatience, Mrs Nightwing repeats the names slowly, a bell tolling a warning.

"Sarah Rees-Toome and Mary Dowd."

THE ONLY TWO PEOPLE WHO MIGHT BE ABLE TO SHARE my secret and explain it to me have been dead and gone for twenty years, everything they know returned to the earth.

"How dreadful," Felicity says, shooting me a quick glance.

"Yes, quite," Mrs Nightwing snaps. "I believe we should move on to a more pleasant topic of conversation. I've just had the most delightful letter from one of our former girls, now Lady Buxton. She has returned from a trip to the East, where she was privileged to see the famed whirling dervishes. Her letter is a perfect demonstration of a clever note – one that entertains and does not tax the recipient with problems of a personal nature. Should anyone wish to see it, I shall keep it at the ready."

She sips her tea. We're losing ground fast. I look at Felicity, who looks at Ann, who looks back at me. Finally, Felicity sighs heavily, working up real tears.

"Miss Worthington, what on earth is the matter?"

"Oh, I'm sorry, Mrs Nightwing, but I can't help thinking

about those girls and the fire and how simply awful it must have been for you."

I am so astonished that I have to bury my fingernails in my palm to keep from laughing out loud. But Mrs Nightwing takes the bait completely.

"Yes, it was quite terrible," she says, sounding miles away. "I was a teacher here then. Mrs Spence was headmistress, God rest her soul. She died in that fire, trying to rescue the girls. All for naught, all for naught."

She seems tortured by it, and I'm feeling guilty for dragging her into it again. Brigid is standing next to me, clearing plates and listening.

Felicity rests her chin in her hands. "What were they like, Sarah and Mary?"

Mrs Nightwing considers for a moment. "Like all girls, I suppose. Mary was a reader. A quiet girl. She wanted to travel, to see Spain and Morocco, India. She was a particular favourite of Mrs Spence."

"And Sarah?" I ask.

Brigid's hand hovers over the plates as if she's forgotten her purpose for a moment. Quietly, she gathers the silver.

"Sarah was a bit of a free spirit. In hindsight, Mrs Spence might have done more to rein her in. They were fanciful girls, taken with stories of fairies and magic and whatnot."

I stare into my custard dish.

"How did the fire happen?" Cecily asks.

"It was a foolish accident. The girls took a candle to the East Wing. It was after they should have been in bed. We shall never know why they went. Probably one of their fanciful adventures." Mrs Nightwing sips from her cup for a moment, lost. "The candle caught on a drapery, I suppose, and spread quickly. Mrs Spence must have rushed in to help them, the door slammed shut behind her . . ." She trails off, staring into her tea as if it might help her. "I couldn't get it open, you see. It was as if something heavy was holding it fast. I suppose we should count ourselves very lucky. The entire school might have gone up in flames."

It's quiet except for the clatter of dishes in Brigid's hands.

Ann barges in. "Is it true that Sarah and Mary were involved with something supernatural?"

A dish crashes to the floor. Brigid is on hands and knees, sweeping the pieces into her apron. "Sorry, Missus Nightwing. I'll just get a broom."

Mrs Nightwing fixes Ann with a glare. "Wherever did you hear such a scurrilous rumour?"

I stir my tea with a concentration particular to nuns at prayer. Blast Ann and her stupidity.

"We read—" Ann is interrupted by my swift kick to her leg. "I-I c-c-can't rem-m-member."

"Nonsense! If someone has been telling you such tales, I should know at once . . ."

Felicity is on top of the game. "I am relieved to hear it isn't true and that Spence's reputation is above reproach. What a terrible accident." She glares at Ann when she says *accident*.

"I do not believe in the supernatural in the slightest," Mrs Nightwing sniffs, straightening her spine and pushing away from the table. "But I do believe in the power of young girls' minds to conjure all sorts of hobgoblins that have nothing to do with the occult and everything to do with very real mischief. So, I'll ask you again – has someone been filling your head with nonsense about magic and whatnot? Because I won't stand for it."

I'm sure she can hear the hammering of my heart across the table as we all swear our innocence on the topic. Mrs Nightwing stands.

"If I find out otherwise, I shall punish those responsible severely. Now, it's been a long day. Let's all say good night."

We promise to turn in when we've finished, and Mrs Nightwing retreats to make her nightly pronouncement in the great hall that it is time for bed.

<hr>

"Were you dropped on your head as a child?" Felicity snaps at Ann the moment Mrs Nightwing has left us.

"S-s-sorry," she stammers. "Why didn't you want her to know about the book?"

"And have her confiscate it? I think not." Felicity sneers.

Brigid bustles back in, wiping her hands on a dish towel.

"You seem on edge tonight, Brigid," Felicity says.

"Aye," she says, sweeping crumbs from the table. "Talking about those two is enough to give anyone the chills. I remember 'em, all right, and they wasn't the saints the missus makes 'em out to be."

If you want to know something about a household, ask the servants. That's what my father used to say. I offer Brigid a seat next to me. "You should rest for a moment, Brigid. It'll do you good."

"Don't mind if I do. Oooh, my feet."

"Tell us about them. The truth," Ann says.

A low whistling sound escapes from Brigid's mouth. "They was wicked girls. Especially that Sarah. Very cheeky she was. I was young then – not bad-lookin' m'self. Had plen'y of suitors who come for me on Sundays for the walk to church. Always went to church, rain or snow or shine, I did."

Brigid is unravelling. We could be here all night listening to tales of her piety.

"And the girls?" I prompt.

Brigid fixes me with a stare. "Getting to it, ain't I? As I was saying, I'd go to church on Sundays. But one Sunday, Missus Spence, who was the Good Lord's angel on m' right hand, Missus Spence asks me would I stay and look after young Sarah, who's feeling poorly. This would be about a week before the fire." She stops, coughs for effect. "It's hard to talk, m' throat bein' so dry."

Dutifully Ann brings her a cup of tea.

"Oh, that's a good girl. Now, I'm only tellin' you wot I know as a lesson. And it don't go no further than these four walls. Swear it."

We fall all over ourselves swearing, and Brigid picks up where she left off, happy to be holding court.

"Mind you, I wasn't happy about staying. M' regular suitor, Paulie, was to call for me and I had a new bonnet besides, but I knew m' duty. You'll learn that soon enough, Miss Ann, once you've secured a position."

Embarrassed, Ann looks away and I can't help feeling sorry for her.

"Oooh, this wants sugar . . . ," Brigid says, holding out her teacup like a queen. She's taking us for all we're worth but she has information we need so I'm back with the sugar bowl and we wait till she has stirred two lumps in. "I admit I wasn't feeling charitably towards Miss Sarah that day. But I go to bring her breakfast on a tray and find her not in bed where she should be but down on the floor, crouched low like an animal, talking to Mary. They was having harsh words. I hear Mary sayin', 'Oh, no, Sarah, we can't do that, we can't!' And Sarah says something about 'That's easy enough for you to say. You want to go off and leave me.' And Mary started in cryin' soft and Sarah wrapped her in her arms and kissed her bold as you please. Well I 'bout fell out right there, I can tell you. 'We'll be together, Mary. Always.' And then she said something else, I couldn't tell wot exactly, but something about 'sacrifice.' Sarah says, 'This is wot it wants, Mary, wot it demands. It's the only way.' And that's when Mary grabbed her and said, 'It's murder, Sarah.' That's wot she said: *murder*. Makes m' blood run cold all over again just thinkin' about it."

Ann is chewing on her fingernails. Felicity takes hold of my hand, and I can feel how her skin has gone cold. Brigid glances over her shoulder in the direction of the door to make sure we're alone.

"Well, I must've made a sound or something. Sarah was up quick as you please with murder in her eyes. Pushed me up against the wall, she did. Looked me in the face – cold eyes she had, eyes without a soul – she said, 'Snooping, Brigid?' I says, 'No, miss. Only brung you your tray like Missus said to do.' Because I was scared to m' bones, I don't mind saying. There was something not right going on."

We're all holding our breath, waiting. Brigid leans in towards us.

"She had one of them hex dollies – a ragged poppet like the kind them li'l Gypsy rats carry round – and she brings it to my face. She says, 'Brigid, do you know wot happens to snoops and traitors? They're punished.' And then she yanked a lock of hair clean out of my head and wrapped it round the poppet tight. 'Keep your mouth shut,' she warns me. 'Or next time . . .' Well, I never run so fast in all m' life. Stayed in the kitchen all day long, I did. And a few days later, them girls was dead, and I can't say as I was sorry 'bout it. Though it were a shame about poor Missus Spence."

Brigid makes the sign of the cross over herself quickly. "I knew they'd come to no good – the two o' them with their secrets and running off to visit that Mother Elena when the Gypsies came through." Brigid doesn't miss the nudge Ann gives my arm with her elbow. "Aye, I know all about trips to Mother Elena. Old Brigid weren't born last Sunday. Best stay away from her. She's not right in the head, always nattering on about somethin' or other. I hope you girls ain't getting mixed up in anything o' that sort."

She gives us a flinty stare. I practically drop the sugar bowl that's still in my hands.

"Of course not," Felicity says, putting the haughtiness

back in her voice. She's got what she wants from Brigid so there's not much point indulging her, as far as she's concerned.

"I should hope not. Don't want you to start putting on airs, taking fancy names like they did. Thought they was duchesses or some such, Sarah making me call her . . . wot was it now?" She stops, thinks, shakes it off. "Well, there's the steel trap o' the mind sprung open again. Was right on the tip o' m' tongue, too. But if I ever find the likes of you three doin' that Gypsy hocus-pocus, I'll haul you down to church by your ears and leave you there for a week. You see if I don't." She gulps the last of her tea down quickly. "Ah, now, who's enough of a luv to get her poor Brigid another cuppa?"

⌇⌇⌇⌇

After bringing Brigid more tea and promising to go straight to bed, we detour into the great hall. The other girls have all trundled off to bed. Two maids tend quietly to their duties in the large room, turning down the lamps till the white of their aprons is all we can see of them, and then they, too, are gone. The fires are fading to a glow. They flicker and smoke, casting shadows that seem to make the marble columns come alive.

"We've been reading the diary of a dead girl." Felicity shudders. "There's something terribly creepy about that."

"Do you suppose," Ann says, "that any of what Mary wrote could be true? The supernatural part?"

With a loud crack, the fireplace gives off a sudden spark, making us jump.

"We need to see Mother Elena," Felicity announces.

No. Absolutely not. Let's draw the curtains and stay in, warm and safe, away from the uncertain woods.

"Do you mean go to the Gypsy camp? Tonight? By ourselves?" Ann says. I can't tell whether she's panicked or thrilled by this prospect.

"Yes, tonight. You know how the Gypsies are – they never stay for long. By tomorrow, they could be gone for the winter. It has to be tonight."

"What about . . ." I almost say Ithal's name, but stop myself. Felicity's eyes are a warning.

"What about what?" Ann asks, puzzled.

"The men," I say, speaking deliberately to Felicity. "There are men in the camp. How will we make certain we're safe?"

"The men," Ann repeats solemnly. *Men.* How one small word could have so much current running through it . . .

Felicity matches my tone, sending me her coded message. "I'm sure we can handle the men. You know how those Gypsies make up all sorts of lies. We'll just laugh along with them."

"I don't think we should go," Ann says. "Not without an escort."

"Oh, I agree," Felicity mocks. "Why don't you go in right now and ask Brigid to accompany us on a midnight run to the Gypsies? I'm sure she'd be most obliging."

"I'm quite serious."

"Stay here, then!" Ann immediately bites at a ragged fingernail and Felicity puts an arm around her. "Look, there are three of us. We shall be each other's chaperones. And protectors if need be. Though I suspect any fears of being ravished are just wishful thinking on both your parts."

"Ann, I believe we've been insulted," I say, putting my arm around her too. There's an excitement in the air I can almost taste, a sense of purpose I've never felt before. And I want more of it. "Are you saying we're not ravish-worthy?"

Felicity grins so widely, her whole face comes to life. "Let's find out."

CHAPTER
EIGHTEEN

WE MUST WALK HALF A LEAGUE OVER BRAMBLES THAT scratch and cut our legs to get to the Gypsy camp. The nights are turning colder now. The damp air is raw. It hurts my lungs on the way in and it comes out of my mouth in short white puffs of mist. By the time we reach the edge of the camp, take in the tents and the campfire, the large, wooden wagons and the men playing boxy violins, my side aches from the effort. There are three large dogs sitting on the ground. How we'll get past them, I don't know.

"Now what?" Ann whispers between gulps for air.

The women are off in their own tents. A few children mill about. Five young men sit drinking around the fire, trading stories in a tongue we can't understand. One of the men tells a joke. His friends clap and laugh. The sound, low and guttural, creeps into my insides in a way that makes me feel like running for safety – or running till I'm caught. To face what, I'm uncertain. My mind doesn't reach that far. It's all enough to set my heart to hammering.

One of the men is Ithal. In the firelight, his strange gold eyes dance. I catch Felicity's eye, nod in his direction to show he's there.

Ann catches on, looks around, scared. "What is it?"

"A change of plans. We'll have to come back tomorrow, during the day."

Ann objects. "But you said . . ."

I turn to leave but my foot breaks a twig with a loud crack. The dogs bark wildly. Ithal is up with his dagger, alert as any feral thing is. Using their native tongue, he shushes his friends. Now they, too, are coiled, ready to strike.

"Bravo," Felicity snaps.

"Don't blame me. Take it up with the forest," I say through gritted teeth.

Ithal holds up a finger to his comrades. He calls out in English. "Who's there?"

"We're done for," Ann whispers, petrified.

"Not quite," Felicity says. She stands up straight and steps out from behind the tree while we try to pull her back down.

"What are you doing?" Ann says in a loud, panicked whisper.

Felicity ignores us. She walks out towards them, an apparition in white and blue velvet, her head held high as they stare in awe at her, the goddess. I don't yet know what power feels like. But this is surely what it looks like, and I think I'm beginning to understand why those ancient women had to hide in caves. Why our parents and teachers and suitors want us to behave properly and predictably. It's not that they want to protect us; it's that they fear us.

Ithal breaks into a lascivious grin. He bows to her. When he spies us hiding behind the tree as if it's our mother's apron, he whistles sweetly to us, but the wolfish grin is still there.

I want to run all the way back to Spence. But I can't leave Felicity here. And the men might come after me, into the deep cover of the woods. Taking Ann's clammy hand in mine, I walk tall into that towering circle of men as it closes around the three of us.

"I knew you could not stay away," Ithal says teasingly to Felicity.

"You knew nothing of the sort. As I recall, I left you standing on the other side of the wall the other day. That's where you'll always belong – on the other side of things." She's mocking him. It doesn't seem a wise course, but I've never found myself surrounded by virile Gypsy men in the middle of the night woods before. I'm in no position to advise or argue. I can only hold my breath and wait.

Ithal steps closer, toys with the cape's ribbon at the hollow of Felicity's throat. His voice is boisterous, laughing, but the smile doesn't travel to his eyes. They are wounded and angry. "I'm not on that side of the wall tonight."

"Please," Ann croaks. "We've only come to see Mother Elena."

"Mother is not here right now," one of the men says. He's not much older than a boy, really. Maybe fifteen, with a nose he hasn't grown into quite yet. If we have to make a run for it, he's the one I'm kicking first.

"I demand to see Mother Elena," Felicity says, cool and

sure. I'm the only one who can see how truly scared she is, and her fear frightens me more than the situation at hand.

How did we get into this mess? And how do we get out?

"What's going on?" Kartik strolls into the thick of things in his borrowed Gypsy disguise, his makeshift cricket bat in one hand. His eyes go wide when he sees me.

"Please, we need to see Mother Elena," I say, hoping I don't sound as terrified as I feel.

Ithal holds his hands up, exposing the thick calluses that crisscross his palms, a memento of a harsh life lived out-of-doors. "Ah . . . this *gadje* is yours. I apologise, friend."

Kartik scoffs. "She's not . . ." He stops himself. "Yes, she is mine." He grabs my hand and pulls me out of the circle. A chorus of whistles and cheers follow us. Another hand snakes around my free wrist. It's attached to the boy with the big nose I spied earlier.

"How do we know she's yours? She does not seem so willing," he teases. "Perhaps she will come with me instead."

Kartik hesitates, long enough for a small laugh of suspicion to ripple through the men. The other man's grip on my arm is strong and I can taste fear, cold and metallic, in my mouth. There's no time to be modest. Reason will not work here. Without warning, I kiss Kartik. His lips, pressed firmly against mine, are a surprise. They're warm, light as breath, firm as the give of a peach against my mouth. A scent like scorched cinnamon hangs in the air, but I'm not falling into any vision. It's his smell in me. A smell that makes my stomach drop through my feet. A smell that pushes all thought out of my head and replaces it with an overpowering hunger for more.

Kartik's tongue slips between my lips for a second, jarring me. I push away, gasping, my face gone bloodred. I can't look at anyone, especially not Felicity and Ann. What must they think of me now? What would they think if they knew how much I'd enjoyed it? What kind of girl am I to enjoy a kiss I've seized so boldly, without waiting to have it asked for and taken from me, the way I should?

A burly man at the back booms out laughing. "I see she is yours after all!"

"Yes," Kartik croaks. "I'll take them to Mother Elena to have their fortunes told. Get back to drinking. It's their money we need, not their trouble."

Kartik escorts us to Mother Elena's tent. Along the way, Felicity glances back, taking in the sight of Kartik beside me. Her eyes dart from me to him and back again. I make my face a stone, and finally, she turns away. Kartik opens the flap for Felicity and Ann but pulls me sharply aside. "Just what do you think you're doing here?"

"Having my fortune told," I say. It's a stupid thing to say but my lips are still warm from his kiss and I'm too embarrassed to come up with something clever. "I apologise for my conduct," I barely manage to say. "It was necessary under the circumstances. I hope you won't think me too forward."

He grabs an acorn from the ground, tosses it into the air and whacks at it with the cricket bat. The bat is so old and split it's largely ineffectual. His mouth is set in a tight line. "I'll never hear the end of it from them later."

The tingling in my stomach goes cold. "Sorry to have put

you out on my behalf," I say. He says nothing, and I'm so humiliated I wish I could disappear on the spot.

"Where's the other one of your little foursome? Hiding in the woods?"

It takes me a second to realise he means Pippa. I remember the way he looked at her in the woods. He obviously hasn't stopped thinking of her. It's the first real kindness he's shown, and it's surprising how much it stings.

"She's ill," I say, irritably.

"Nothing serious, I hope."

I don't know why I feel so wounded by Kartik's obvious infatuation with Pippa. There's no romance between us. There's nothing that tethers us but this dark secret neither of us wants. It's not Kartik's longing that hurts. It's my own. It's knowing that I'll never have what she has – a beauty so powerful it brings things to you. I fear I will always have to chase the things I want. I'll always have to wonder whether I'm truly wanted or whether I've just been settled for.

"Nothing serious," I say, swallowing hard. "May I go in now?" I move to lift the flap but his hand grips my wrist.

"Do not do this again," he warns, pushing me inside the tent while he walks off towards the forest to become the night's eyes, always watching me.

CHAPTER
NINETEEN

"THERE YOU ARE," FELICITY CALLS TO ME FROM A SMALL table where she and Ann are sitting with the old Gypsy. "Mother Elena was just telling us the most interesting story about Ann becoming a great beauty."

"She told me I'm going to have many admirers," Ann interrupts, excited.

Mother Elena crooks a finger. "Come closer, child. Mother Elena will tell you your fortune."

I make my way through a tent strewn with piles of books, colourful scarves, and bottles of herbs and tinctures of all kinds. A lantern hangs from a hook behind the old woman. The light is harsh and I can see how creased and brown her face is. Her ears are pierced, and she wears rings on every finger. She offers me a small basket with a few shillings in the bottom.

Felicity clears her throat, whispers. "Give her a few pence."

"But then I'll have nothing till my family's visit on Assembly Day," I whisper back.

"Give. Her. The pence," she says through smiling teeth.

With a heavy sigh, I drop my last few coppers into the basket. Mother Elena shakes it. Satisfied with their jingling sound, she empties the basket into her coin purse.

"Now, what will it be? The cards? The palm?"

"Mother Elena, I think our friend would be very interested in the story you were telling us – about the two girls from Spence?"

"Yes, yes, yes. But not with Carolina in the room. Carolina, fetch some water now." There's no one else in the room. I'm starting to feel uneasy. Mother Elena's hands pat her cards. She tilts her head as if she's listening to something she has forgotten – a bit of song or a voice from the past. And when she looks up at me, it's as if we're old friends reunited.

"Ah, Mary, what a nice surpise. What is it Mother Elena can do for you today? I've got lovely honey cakes, sweet as can be. Come now."

Her hands place imaginary cakes on an imaginary tray. We all exchange curious looks. Is it an act, or is the poor old thing really as mad as a hatter? She offers the pretend tray to me.

"Mary, dear, don't be shy. Have a sweet. You're wearing your hair differently. It suits you."

Felicity nods, urges me to play along.

"Thank you, Mother."

"Now, where is our lively Sarah today?"

"Our Sarah?" I falter.

Felicity jumps in. "She's off practicing the magic you taught her."

Mother frowns. "That I taught? Mother doesn't dabble in such things. Only the herbs and the charms for love and protection. You mean them."

"Them?" I repeat.

Mother whispers. "The women who come to the woods. Teaching you their craft. *The Order*. No good can come of it, Mary, you mark my words."

We're building a house of cards. One wrong question can send the whole tower tumbling before we reach the top.

"How do you know what sorts of things they teach us?" I ask.

The old woman taps the side of her head with a gnarled finger. "Mother knows. Mother sees. They see the future and the past. They shape it." She leans towards me. "They see the spirit world."

The whole room spins out of focus and comes back. Though the night is cold, sweat trickles down my neck, dampening my collar. "Do you mean the realms?"

Mother nods.

"Can you enter the realms, then, Mother?" I ask. The question reverberates in my ears. My mouth is dry.

"Oh, no. Only glimpse it. But you and Sarah have gone, Mary. My Carolina has told me you brought her sweet heather and myrtle from that garden." Mother's smile fades. "But there are other places. The Winterlands. Oh, Mary, I'm afraid of what lives there . . . afraid for Sarah and you . . ."

"Yes, what about Sarah . . . ," Felicity says.

Mother frowns again. "Sarah is a hungry one. She wants more than knowledge. She wants power, that one. We must keep her from the wrong path, Mary. Keep her from the Winterlands and the dark things that live there. I fear she will call them, bind one to her. And it will corrupt her mind."

She pats my hand. Her skin is dry and cracked against my knuckles. I feel I might faint. It's a struggle to get the next part out.

"What . . . dark things?"

"Wounded spirits of such rage and hate. They want to come back to this world. They will find your weakness and exploit it."

Felicity doesn't believe a word of this part. Behind Mother's back, she makes an ogre face. But I've seen the dark move and shriek.

"How could she call such a thing to her?" Despite the chill, I'm sweating and woozy.

"A sacrifice is what it wants, and then the power is hers," Mother whispers. "But she'll be forever bound to the dark."

"What sort of sacrifice?" I barely croak. Mother Elena's eyes glaze over. She's fighting something in her memory. I say it again, stronger. "What sort of sacrifice?"

"Don't get so carried away . . . *Mary*," Ann says quietly through gritted teeth.

Mother's faraway look has evaporated. She regards me with suspicion. "Who are you?"

Felicity tries to get her back. "It's your Mary, Mother Elena. Don't you remember?"

Mother whimpers, a frightened animal. "Where is Carolina with the water? Carolina, don't be naughty. Come to me."

"Mary can take you to her." Felicity jumps in.

"Stop it!" I shout.

"Mary, is it you come back to me after all this time?" Mother cups my face in her weathered hands.

"I'm Gemma," I say with difficulty. "Gemma, not Mary. I'm sorry, Mother."

Mother Elena withdraws her hands. Her scarf falls open, revealing the shine of the crescent eye around her weathered neck. She backs away. "You. You brought it on us."

The dogs bark at the rise in her voice.

"I think we had best leave," Ann warns.

"You destroyed us. Lost it all . . ."

Felicity tosses another shilling onto the table. "Thank you, Mother. You've been most helpful. The honey cakes were delicious."

"It was you!"

I cover my ears with my hands to hide the sound. The woods echo with it, the howl of a mother animal mourning its young, a tiny creature lost to a predator in the great cycle of things. It's the sound more than anything else that sets me running, past the Gypsy men, who are too drunk to come after us now, past the protesting Felicity and Ann I'm leaving behind. I'm deep into the woods when I stop. I cannot catch my breath and feel as if I will faint. The damned corset. With cold fingers I pull hard at the laces but can't undo them. In the end I'm on my knees sobbing with frustration. I feel his gaze before I actually see him. But there he is, watching – doing nothing but watching.

"Leave me alone!" I shout.

"Well, that's a fine way to treat us," Felicity says, huffing into view. Ann is just behind her, breathing heavily, too. "What the devil got into you back there?"

"I – I just got spooked," I say, trying to catch my own breath. Kartik is still there. I can feel him.

"Mother Elena may be mad, but she's harmless. Or perhaps she's not mad at all. Perhaps if you hadn't run off, her little performance would have ended and we could have had our fortunes told instead of wasting five pence for nothing."

"I'm s-sorry," I stammer. There's no one behind the tree anymore. He's gone.

"What an evening," Felicity mutters as she walks ahead, leaving me on my knees under the watchful eyes of the owls.

❧❧❧

In the dream, I'm running, my feet sinking into the cold, muddy earth with each step. When I stop, I'm at the mouth of Kartik's tent. He's asleep, blankets thrown back, bare chest exposed like a Roman sculpture. A line of dark hair snakes over a taut stomach. It disappears into the waistband of his trousers, into a world I do not know.

His face. His cheeks-nose-lips-eyes. Under the lids, his eyes move back and forth rapidly. Thick lashes rest against the tops of his cheekbones. The nose is strong and straight.

It slopes down to a perfect point at the top of his mouth, which is open just slightly to let his breath in and out.

I want to taste that mouth again. Wanting brings me down in a whoosh, feet planted, breathing shallow, head light. There's only the wanting. Bring my lips to his and it's like melting. Those black eyes flutter open, see me. The sculpture comes alive. Every muscle in his arms flexing as he pushes himself up, pulls me under, slides on top. The weight of him forces the air from my lungs like a bellows, but still it comes out as the lightest of sighs. And there's his mouth again on mine, a heat, a pressure, a promise of things to come, a promise I'm rising up to meet.

His fingertips are a whisper on my skin. A thumb inches towards my breast, traces circles over and around. Move my mouth to the salty skin of his neck. Feel my thighs moved apart by a knee. Something inside me falls away. It's as if I've stopped breathing for a moment. I'm hollowed out. Searching.

The warm fingers trail down, hesitate, then brush past a part of me I don't understand yet, a place I haven't let myself explore.

"Wait . . . ," I whisper.

He doesn't hear or won't listen. The fingers, strong and sure and not entirely unwanted, are back, the whole of his palm cupped against me. I want to run. I want to stay. I want both things at once. His mouth finds mine. I'm pinned to the earth by his choice. I could just float here, lose myself inside him and come out reborn as someone else. The thumb on my breast rubs my skin into a delicious rawness, as if I've never truly walked in my skin before. My whole body strains up to meet the pressure of him. His choice could be mine. He could swallow me up, if I just let go. *Let go. Let go. Let go.*

No.

My hands slide up against the slick skin of his chest and push him back. He falls away. His weight gone feels like a limb missing and the need to pull him back is nearly overpowering. There's a fine glisten of sweat on his brow as he blinks in his sleep-state, confused and groggy. He's asleep again, just as I found him. A dark angel just out of reach.

⚓⚓⚓⚓

It's a dream, only a dream. That's what I tell myself when I wake up, gasping, in my own bed in my own room with Ann snoring contentedly a few feet away.

It's only a dream.

But it felt so real. I put my fingers to my lips. They're not swollen with kissing. I'm still whole. Pure. A useful commodity. Kartik is miles away, lost in sleep that does not involve me. That part of me I haven't explored aches, though, and I have to lie on my side with my knees clamped together to stop it.

It's only a dream.

But most frightening of all is how much I wish it weren't.

CHAPTER TWENTY

DR. THOMAS HAS PRONOUNCED PIPPA FULLY RECOVERED, and as it's Sunday and church has been dispensed with, we have the afternoon to luxuriate as we wish. We're down by the water, casting the last petals of late-summer flowers onto the calm surface. Ann has stayed behind to practice her aria for Assembly Day – the day when our families will descend upon Spence and see what marvels of womanhood we're becoming.

I toss a handful of crumbling wildflowers. They sit on the lake like a blight before the breeze whips them out towards the deep middle. They settle, take on more and more water till they finally go under in silence. Across the lake, a few of the younger girls sit on a blanket, talking and eating plums, happy to ignore us as we ignore them.

Pippa is lying in the rowing boat. She can't remember anything before her seizure, for which I'm grateful. She's horribly embarrassed by her loss of control, by what she might have said or done.

"Did I make any vulgar noises?" she asks.

"No," I assure her.

"Not at all," Felicity adds.

Pippa's shoulders relax against the bow. Seconds later, a new worry has them knotted up again. "I didn't . . . soil myself, did I?" She can barely say this.

"No, no!" Felicity and I say in a tumble.

"It's shameful, isn't it? My affliction."

Felicity laces tiny flowers together into a crown. "It's no more shameful than having a mother who's a paid consort."

"I'm sorry, Felicity. I shouldn't have said that. Will you forgive me?"

"There's nothing to forgive. It's only truth."

"Truth," Pippa scoffs. "Mother says I can't ever let anyone know about my seizures. She says if I feel one coming on, I should say I have a headache and excuse myself." Her laugh is bitter. "She thinks I should be able to control it."

Her words pull me down like an anchor. I want so desperately to tell her I understand. To tell my secret. I clear my throat. The wind changes. It blows the petals back against my hair. I can feel the moment slipping away. It sinks under the surface of things, hidden from the light.

Pippa changes the subject. "On a cheerier note, Mother said that she and Father have a wonderful surprise for me. I do hope it's a new corset. The boning in this one practically impales me with each breath. Ye gods!"

"Perhaps you shouldn't eat so many toffees," Felicity says.

Pippa is too tired to be truly outraged. She offers a show of hurt. "I'm not fat! I'm not! My waist is a tidy sixteen and a half inches."

Pippa's waist is wasp-thin, as men are rumoured to prefer waists. Our corsets bind and bend us to this fashionable taste, even though it makes us short of breath and sometimes ill from the pressure. I haven't a clue how large or small my waist is. I'm not delicate in the slightest, and I have shoulders like a boy's. I find the whole conversation tedious.

"Is your mother coming this year, Fee?" Pippa asks.

"She's visiting friends. In Italy," Felicity says, finishing her crown. She places it on her head like a fairy queen's.

"What about your father?"

"I don't know. I hope so. I'd love for the three of you to meet him, and for him to see that I have actual flesh-and-blood friends." She gives a sad smile. "I think he was afraid I'd become one of those sullen girls who never get invited to anything. I was a bit that way after Mother . . ."

Left.

That's the word that hangs in the air, unspoken. It joins shame, secrets, fear, visions, and epilepsy. So many things unsaid weight the distance between us. The more we try to close the gap, the more its heaviness pushes us apart.

"How long has it been since you've seen him?" I ask.

"Three years."

"I'm certain he'll come this time, Fee," Pippa says. "And he'll be very proud to see what a lady you've become."

Felicity smiles and it's as if she's turned the sun on us

both. "Yes. Yes, I have, haven't I? I think he'll be pleased. If he comes."

"I'd loan you my new kid gloves but my mother expects to see them on my fingers as proof that we're somebody," Pippa sighs.

"What of your family?" Felicity turns her sharp eyes on me. "Are they coming? The mysterious Doyles?"

My father hasn't written in two weeks. I think of my grandmother's last letter:

Dearest Gemma,

I hope this letter finds you well. I've had a touch of neuralgia but you shouldn't worry as the doctor says it's merely the strain of caring for your father and will abate when you are home again and able to help shoulder the burden as a good daughter should. Your father seems to be comforted by the garden. He sits for long stretches on the old bench there. He's given to fits of staring and nodding off but otherwise is at peace.

Do not fret about us. I'm sure my shortness of breath is nothing at all. We shall see you in two weeks' time along with Tom, who sends his love and wishes to know if you've found him a suitable wife yet, though I feel certain he said this in jest.

Fondly,
Grandmama

I close my eyes and try to erase it all. "Yes, they're coming."

"You don't sound terribly excited about it."

I shrug. "I haven't given it much thought."

"Our mysterious Gemma," Felicity says, appraising me a

· 223 ·

bit too closely for comfort. "We'll find out what you're hiding from us yet."

Pippa joins in. "A crazy aunt in the attic, perhaps."

"Or a sexually depraved fiend who preys on young girls." Felicity waggles her eyebrows. Pippa screeches in mock horror but she's titillated by the very idea.

"You forgot the hunchback," I add with a false laugh. I'm widening the distance between us, sending them off to another shore.

"A sexually depraved hunchback!" Pippa squeals. She is most definitely recovered. We all laugh. The woods swallow our sounds in echoing gulps, but we've startled the younger girls across the lake. In their crisp white pinafores, they seem like misplaced loons dotting the landscape. They blink at us, then turn their heads and resume their chatter.

The September sky is uncertain. Grey and threatening one moment. A patchy, promising blue the next. Felicity lays her head back against the grassy bank. Her hair splays out and around the centre of her pale face like a mandala. "Do you suppose we'll have any fun at Lady Wellstone's Spiritualist meeting tonight?"

"My father says Spiritualism is nothing but quackery," Pippa says. She's rocking the rowing boat slightly with her bare foot. "What is it exactly again?"

"It's the belief that the spirits can speak to us from beyond through the use of a medium like Madame Romanoff," Felicity says.

We both sit straight up, thinking the same thing.

"Do you think . . ." she starts.

". . . that she could contact Sarah or Mary for us?" I finish. Why hasn't this thought occurred to me before?

"Brilliant!" Pippa's face clouds over. "But how will you get to her?"

She's right, of course. Madame Romanoff would never call on a pack of schoolgirls. We've got about as much chance of communing with the dead as we do of sitting in Parliament.

"I'll do the asking, if you'll help me get to Madame Romanoff," I say.

"Leave it all to me," Felicity says, grinning.

"If we leave it to you, we'll end up in the soup, I fear," Pippa giggles.

Felicity is up, quick as a hare. With nimble fingers she unties Pippa's boat and sends it out onto the lake with a shove. Pippa scrambles to grab the rope but it's too late. She's moving out, ripping open the surface of the water.

"Pull me back!"

"That wasn't a very nice thing to do," I say.

"She needs to remember her place," Felicity says by way of an answer. But she tosses an oar after her anyway. It falls short, bobs on the surface.

"Help me pull her back," I say. The loon girls are standing now, watching us in amusement. They enjoy seeing us behaving badly.

Felicity plops down onto the grass and laces a boot.

With a sigh, I call out to Pippa. "Can you reach it?"

She stretches her arm around the side of the boat for the oar just out of reach. She's not going to make it, but she stretches further to try. The boat tips precariously. Pippa falls in with a yelp and a splash. Felicity and the younger girls erupt in laughter. But I'm remembering the brief vision I had just before Pippa's seizure, remembering the chilling sounds of splashing and Pippa's strangled cry from somewhere under murky water.

"Pippa!" I scream, rushing into the heart-stopping cold of the lake. My hand finds a leg. I've got her, and I pull up with all my strength.

"Grab hold!" I sputter, kicking for shore with my arm around her waist.

She fights me. "Gemma, what are you doing? Let me go!" She breaks free. The water rises only to her shoulders. "I can walk from here, thank you," she says, with indignation, trying to ignore the giggles and finger-pointing on the other side of the lake.

I feel ridiculous. I distinctly remember an impression of Pippa struggling under the water during my vision. I suppose I could have been so panicked, I don't remember things clearly. At any rate, here we are, both safe and sound except for the dripping. And that's all that matters.

"I'm going to strangle you, Felicity," Pippa mutters as she balances unsteadily in the water. I throw my arms around her, relieved that she's all right, and nearly pull her under again.

"What are you doing?" she shrieks, slapping at me as if I were a spider.

"Sorry," I say. "Sorry."

"I'm surrounded by lunatics," she growls, crawling onto the grass. "Now, where's Felicity got to?"

The bank is empty. It's as if she's vanished. But then I see her disappearing into the woods, daisy crown perched on her head. She walks casually and easily away without so much as a backwards glance to see if we're all right.

CHAPTER TWENTY-ONE

THE HAND-LETTERED MARQUEE OUTSIDE THE ELEGANT town house in Grosvenor Square reads:

AN EVENING OF THEOSOPHY AND SPIRITUALISM WITH
MADAME ROMANOFF, GRAND SEER OF ST. PETERSBURG.
TO HER, ALL THINGS ARE KNOWN.
TO HER, ALL THINGS ARE REVEALED.
ONE NIGHT ONLY.

The London streets are an Impressionist painting of slick cobblestones, orangey streetlamps, well-manicured hedges, and clusters of black umbrellas. Puddles splatter the hem of my dress, weighing it down. We rush for the safety of the open doors, our delicate dress shoes tapping out careful steps on the slick cobblestones.

The audience shows its breeding. There are men in tuxedos and top hats. Women with their gems and opera gloves. We're all in our very best dresses. It feels strange and wonderful to be in silks and petticoats instead of our usual school uniforms. Cecily has taken the occasion to show off a new hat. It's far too old for her and makes her stand out in a glaring way, but as it's the height of fashion, she's determined to wear it. Mademoiselle LeFarge is in her Sunday best, a green silk dress with a high, ruffled collar, a green silk bonnet, and a pair of garnet drop earrings, and we make a fuss over her.

"You look simply perfect," Pippa says as we enter the imposing marble foyer, brushing past attentive butlers.

"Thank you, my dear. It's always important to look your best."

Cecily preens, certain she's been given a compliment.

We're ushered through heavy curtains to a conservatory that could easily hold two hundred people. Pippa is craning her neck, inspecting the audience.

"Do you see any attractive men here? Anyone under the age of forty?"

"Honestly," Felicity chides, "you'd only be interested in the afterlife if there were a chance to find a husband there."

Pippa pouts. "Mademoiselle LeFarge takes this seriously, and I haven't noticed you mocking her!"

Felicity rolls her eyes. "Mademoiselle LeFarge has taken us away from Spence and to one of London's most fashionable addresses. She could look for Henry the Eighth as far as I'm concerned. Let's not forget our mission."

Mademoiselle LeFarge slides her bulk into a red-cushioned chair and we file in behind her. People are beginning to get settled. Down in front is a stage with a table and two chairs. On top of the table sits a crystal ball.

"That crystal ball allows her to make contact with the spirits of the dead," Mademoiselle LeFarge whispers to us as she reads her programme. A gentleman behind us overhears our whisperings and bows his head to Mademoiselle LeFarge.

"I am compelled to tell you, my good lady, that this is all sleight of hand. Magician's trickery."

"Oh, no, sir, you are mistaken." Martha jumps in. "Mademoiselle LeFarge has seen Madame Romanoff speak in a trance state."

"You have?" Pippa asks, wide-eyed.

"I have heard about her gifts from a cousin who is very close to a dear friend of the sister-in-law of Lady Dorchester," Mademoiselle LeFarge asserts. "She is a truly remarkable medium."

The gentleman smiles. His smile is kind and warm, like Mademoiselle LeFarge. It's a pity she's engaged, for I like this nice man and think he'd make a very lovely husband.

"I'm afraid, dear lady, dear *mademoiselle*," he says, drawing out the word, "that you have been deceived. Spiritualism is no more a science than thievery. For that's all this is – very skilled dodgers stealing money from the bereaved for a little glint of hope. People see what they want to see when they need to."

My heart is squeezed tight in my chest. Is it possible that I see my mother, my visions, only because I want or need to? Could grief's hold be that strong? And yet, the scrap of cloth. I can only hope I'll know something for certain by night's end.

Mademoiselle LeFarge's mouth is a thin line. "You are mistaken, sir."

"I've upset you. My apologies. Inspector Kent of Scotland Yard." He hands her an embossed calling card, which she refuses to accept. Calmly, he places it back inside his breast pocket. "You've come, no doubt, to contact a loved one? A brother or dear departed cousin?" He's fishing but Mademoiselle LeFarge can't see that he's interested in more than her preoccupation with the occult.

"I am simply here as an observer of the science, and as a chaperone to my charges. And now, if you'll excuse us, it would seem the séance is about to begin."

Men rush along the sides of the room, dimming the lights to a hazy gas glow. They wear high-collared black shirts and sashes of deep red around their waists. A handsome woman in long, flowing robes of forest green takes the stage. Her eyes are rimmed with the blackest kohl and she wears a turban with a single peacock feather. Madame Romanoff.

She closes her eyes and lifts a hand over the audience as if feeling us. When she reaches the left side of the grand room, she opens her eyes and focuses on a heavyset man in the second row.

"You, sir. The spirits wish to commune with you. Please, come and have a seat with me," she says in a heavy Russian accent.

The man obliges and takes a seat at the table. Madame Romanoff gazes into the crystal ball and falls limp. In this state, she tells the man his fortune. "I have a message for you from the other side..."

The man onstage, eager and sweaty, leans forward. "Yes! I'm listening. Is it from my sister? Please, is it you, Dora?"

Madame Romanoff's voice comes out high and sweet as a girl's. "Johnny, is that you?"

A cry of joy and agony escapes the man's lips. "Yes, yes, it's me, my dear, dear sister!"

"Johnny, you mustn't weep. I'm very happy here, with all my toys to keep me company."

We take this in, slack-jawed in wonder. Onstage, the man and his little sister are enjoying a heartfelt reunion, with tears and protestations of undying love. I can barely sit still. I want it to end so that I can take my place with the medium.

The inspector behind us leans over and says, "Brilliant performance. That man is an accomplice, of course."

"How so?" Ann asks.

"They place him in the audience so that he appears to be an honest seeker, part of the crowd. But he's in on the game."

"Do you mind, sir?" Mademoiselle LeFarge fans herself with her programme.

Inspector Kent bows his head and settles back in his chair. I can't help liking him, with his wide hands and heavy moustache, and I wish Mademoiselle LeFarge would give him more of a chance. But she's loyal to her Reginald, the mysterious fiancé, as she should be – even if we've never seen him call once.

After a glass of water, Madame Romanoff takes on several more people. With some she asks questions that seem very broad, but the grieving audience members always rush in to tell her their stories. It seems almost as if she leads them on, getting them to supply the answers without her help. But

I've never seen a medium at work before and I can't say for sure.

Felicity leans over and whispers in my ear. "Are you ready?"

My stomach is turning flips. "I think so."

Mademoiselle LeFarge shushes us. Elizabeth and Cecily eye us suspiciously. Onstage, Madame Romanoff asks for one last candidate. Like a shot, Felicity is out of her seat, pulling me up by the arm.

"Oh, please, madame," she says, sounding as if she's on the verge of tears when she's really fighting back waves of laughter. "My friend is far too modest to ask for your help. Could you please help a girl reach her dear, departed mother, Mrs Sarah Rees-Toome?"

There is a chorus of murmurs and gasps. Every bit of breath has been knocked from me. "That was unnecessary," I hiss.

"You want it to be believable, don't you? Besides, you might get something in the bargain up there."

"Girls, sit down at once!" Mademoiselle LeFarge pulls hard on my skirt, trying to anchor me to my seat. But it's no use. Felicity's plea has struck a chord with Madame Romanoff. Two of her men are at my side, showing me down the aisle. I don't know whether to kill Felicity or thank her. Perhaps there is a way to contact my mother as well. My palms go sweaty with the thought that in just a few moments, I may speak with my mother again – even if I have to do it through a medium and the spirit of Sarah Rees-Toome.

As I mount the small stage, I can hear the rustle of programmes, the insect buzzing of whispers mixing with the sighs of the disappointed whose chance to contact the dead is gone, usurped by a red-haired girl whose green eyes are wild with hope.

Madame Romanoff bids me sit. There is an open pocket watch on the table showing the time to be 9:48. She reaches across the table to cradle my hand in both of hers. "Dear child, you have suffered greatly, I fear. We must all help this young lady find her beloved mother. Let us all close our eyes and concentrate for the aid of this young girl. Now, what is the name of the dearly departed?"

Virginia Doyle. Virginia Doyle. My throat is parched and tight as I say, "Sarah Rees-Toome."

Madame Romanoff swirls her fingers over the glass ball and drops her voice into a lower register. "I call now on the spirit of Sarah Rees-Toome, beloved mother. There is one who wishes to contact you. One who needs your presence here."

For a moment, I half expect to hear Sarah tell me to shove off, leave her alone, stop pretending I know her. But mostly, I'm hoping that it will be my mother's voice I hear next, laughing at my duplicity, forgiving me for everything, even this bit of trickery.

Across the table, Madame Romanoff's deep growl grows sweet as prayer song. "Darling, is that you? Oh, how I've missed you so."

It's only now that I realise how I've been holding my breath, hoping for a chance, waiting for a miracle. My heart is beating wildly in my chest, and I can't help calling out to her.

"Mother? Is that you?"

"Yes, darling, it's me, your loving mother." There are a few sniffles from the audience. My mother would never say something so coddling. I throw out a lie to see if it comes back to me.

"Mother, do you miss our home in Surrey terribly much? The rosebushes out back by the little cupid?"

I'm begging for her to say, "Gemma, have you gone a bit simple, dear?" Something. Anything. But not this.

"Oh, I can see it even now, my darling. The green of Surrey. The roses in our wonderful garden. But do not miss me too much, my child. I shall see you again one day."

The crowd sniffles and sighs in sentimental approval even as the lie turns sour in my gut. Madame Romanoff is nothing more than an actress. She's pretending to be my mother, someone named Sarah Rees-Toome who lives in a cottage with a cupid out back, when my own mother was Virginia Doyle, a woman who never once set foot in Surrey. I'd like to show Madame Romanoff a taste of what it's really like on that other side, where spirits are not happy to see you. I don't realise that I'm holding Madame Romanoff's hand with all my strength, because there's a sudden flare of light, like the world opening up, and I'm falling into that tunnel again, my rage pulling me down fast.

But this time, I'm not alone.

Somehow, I've managed to bring Madame Romanoff along, as I almost did with Pippa. I haven't the vaguest idea how it's happened, but here she is, bold as day, screaming her head off.

"Bloody 'ell! Where am I?" Madame Romanoff is Russian all right, by way of Bow's bells. "Wot kind of devil are you?"

I can't answer her. I'm struck dumb. We're in a dark, misty forest – one I recognise from my dreams. It has to be the same misty woods Mary Dowd wrote about. I've done it. I'm in the realms. And they are as real as the screaming little thief next to me.

"Wot's that, eh?" She grabs tight to my sleeve.

There's movement in the trees. The mist is crawling. They start to come out, one by one, till there are twenty or more. The dead. Hollow-eyed. Pale-lipped. Skin stretched shiny-tight over bone. A woman in rags carries a baby at her breast. She's dripping wet and strings of slick, green vegetation hang twisted in her hair. Two men stagger forward, arms outstretched. I can see the rounded knob of bone where their hands have been chopped clean off. They keep coming, their mouths all making the same hideous murmur.

"Come to us. You've come to us."

Madame Romanoff is shrieking and practically climbing up my side. "Wot the 'ell's goin' on 'ere? Sweet Jesus, get me out of 'ere. Please! I'll never con nobody no more, on me mother's grave I won't."

"Stop," I say, holding out my hand. Surprisingly, it works. "Which one of you is Sarah Rees-Toome?"

None of the spirits come forward.

"Is there one among you by that name?"

Nothing.

"Tell them to go away," Madame Romanoff says. She grabs a tree limb from the ground and swings it wildly in front of her, warding them off and grunting in fear. Through the trees, I see her. The blue silk of her dress. I hear the warm amber of her laugh.

Find me if you can, love.

I grab Madame Romanoff by the shoulders. "What's your name? Your real name."

"Sally," she says, hoarse with fear. "Sally Carny."

"Sally, listen carefully to me. I've got to leave you for a moment, but I'll be right back. You'll be all right."

"No! Don't you leave me 'ere wif them, you li'l slut, or I'll carve your creepy green eyes out when we get back! You see if I don't, now!"

She's screaming, but I'm already running through the trees, the hope of blue just ahead of me, always out of reach, and then I'm in the ruin of a temple. A Buddha sits cross-legged on an altar surrounded by candles. It's peaceful here. There's no sound save for the cooing of birds. No fear. I let my fingertips flutter against the orange-blue flame of the candles but I feel no heat or pain. A soft scent of lilies floats through the open door. I wish I could see those flowers of my childhood, of my mother and India, and then suddenly, they're everywhere. The room is filled with blooming white flowers. *I made it happen with just my thoughts.* It's so beautiful, I could stay here forever.

"Mother?" My voice comes out small and hopeful.

The room grows brighter. I can't see her, but I can hear her. "Gemma . . ."

"Mother, where are you?"

"I cannot show myself here or stay for long. These woods may not be safe. There are spies everywhere."

I don't know what she means. I still cannot grasp that I am here. That she is here.

"Mother, what's happening to me?"

"Gemma, you have great powers, my love."

Her voice reverberates in the temple. *My love, love, love . . .*

My throat tightens. "I don't understand it. I can't control any of it."

"You will, in time. But you must use your power, work with it, else it will wither on the vine, die, and then there's no getting it back. You have a great destiny, Gemma, if you choose it."

The organ-grinder's monkey appears. He sits on the Buddha's rounded shoulder, turning his head this way and that, watching me.

"There are people who don't want me to use what I have. I've been warned."

Mother's voice is calm, knowing. "The Rakshana. They're afraid of you. They are afraid of what could happen if you fail, and more afraid of the power you'll have should you succeed."

"Succeed in what?"

"Bringing back the magic of the realms. You are the link to the Order. Their magic lives in you, my love. You are the sign they've been waiting for all these years. But there is also danger. She wants your power too, and she won't stop looking till she finds you."

"Who?"

"Circe." *Circe. Circe. Circe.*

"Who is she? Where can I find her?"

"All in good time, Gemma. She is too powerful for you to face yet."

"But . . ." Tears stop me. "She murdered you."

"Do not lose yourself to revenge, Gemma. Circe has chosen her path. You must choose yours."

"How do you know all of this?"

The edges of the lilies start to turn. They brown and curl under, leaves dropping to the stone floor.

"Our time is up. It's no longer safe for you to stay. Go back now."

"No, not yet!"

"You must concentrate on the place you've left behind. The door of light will appear. Then step through."

"But when can I talk to you again?"

"You can find me in the garden. It is safe there."

"But how—"

"Choose it and the door will take you there. I must move on."

"Wait – don't go!"

But her voice fades into an icy sheet of whispers that melts into ether.

Move on. Move on. Move on.

The light goes so bright, it blinds me. I have to cover my eyes with my arm. When I open them again, the temple is a barren ruin, the dirt floor littered with shrivelled flowers. She is gone.

꘏꘏꘏꘏

The mist is thick in the trees as I make my way back to where I left Sally Carny. I can barely see, but it's not the fog. It's the tears. More than anything, I want to stay behind in that lily-scented room with my mother. A dark figure looms on the path ahead, and for a moment, I forget everything except the terror in my veins, my mother's warning that I am being hunted.

A tall, broad-shouldered man steps out. He wears the military uniform of Her Majesty's guards – not an officer, but a foot soldier. He approaches me shyly, holding his hat in his hands. There's a sweet boyishness to his face that's familiar. Except for the unearthly pallor, he could be the neighbour across the way or the loved one from a family photograph.

"Begging your pardon, but are you the one that's with my Polly tonight?"

"Polly?" I repeat. I am speaking to a ghost, so I can be forgiven any breach of manners. I am sure I've seen him before.

"Surely I saw you there with her – Miss Polly LeFarge?"

A man in a uniform. A faraway smile. A fading tintype on a tidy desk. Reginald, Mademoiselle LeFarge's beloved fiancé, is dead and buried, nothing but a memory she can't let go of.

"Do you mean Mademoiselle LeFarge? My teacher?" I ask quietly.

"Yes, miss. My Polly often talked of teaching, but I promised her I'd make a right good bit of money in the army and then I'd come home and take care of her proper, with a church wedding and a little cottage in Dover. She loves the sea, Polly does."

"But you didn't come home," I say. It's more of a question than a statement, as if I still hope that he might walk into her classroom someday.

"Influenza," Reginald says. He looks down at his hat, twirls it round in his hands like a wheel of fortune at a country carnival. "Would you give Polly a message for me, miss? Could you tell her that Reggie will always love her, and I've still got that muffler she knit for me that Christmas before I left? It held up fine, it did." He smiles at me, and though I can see the blue of his lips, it's still a good smile, a true one. "Would you do that for me, miss?"

"Yes, I will," I whisper.

"Much obliged to you for helping me cross over. And now, I think you should be getting back. They'll be looking for you here if you stay." He places his hat on his head and strolls back into the mist from whence he came, till he disappears entirely.

⌁⌁⌁⌁

When I return to Madame Romanoff, otherwise known as Sally Carny, she's singing old church hymns in a shaky voice. The dead have all gone, but she's still holding on to that tree branch for dear life. She sees me and nearly jumps into my arms. "Please take me back!"

"Why should I take you back after the cavalier way you treat people who are grieving for their loved ones?"

"I never meant no harm, miss. I swear it! You can't blame a girl fer makin' a livin', miss."

I can't, really. If she weren't doing this, Sally Carny would be on the streets, having to pay her way through far more odious, soul-crushing means. "All right. I shall take you back. But only under two conditions."

"Anything. You name it."

"First, you shall never, ever, under any circumstances – and that includes public drunkenness – tell a single soul what has happened here tonight. Because if you do . . ." I trail off, not really sure what threats I can make, but it doesn't matter. Sally's got her hand across her heart.

"As God is my witness. Not a word!"

"I shall hold you to that. As for the second condition . . ." I'm thinking now of Mademoiselle's kind face. "You will convey a message from the spirit world to someone in the audience tonight, a woman named Polly. You are to say that Reggie loves his Polly very much, that he still has the muffler she knit him at Christmas." I add this next bit on my own. "And that he wishes her to move on and be happy. Do you have it?"

The hand goes to the heart again. "Every word." Sally puts an arm about my shoulders. "But Miss . . . wot would you think a joinin' up wif me and me boys? Wot wif your gifts and me promotion, we could make a fortune. Fink on it. That's all I'm sayin'."

"Fine, stay, then."

"Forget I said anything!" Sally shrieks, and I feel reasonably sure I've scared her into keeping her mouth shut. Now, to get back. Mother said to think of the place left behind. But I've never tried it before, and I'm not sure I can do it. For all I know, Sally and I could be trapped here in the misty woods forever.

"You do know 'ow to get us back, don't you?"

"Of course I do," I say, irritated. *Dear God, please let this work.* With Sally's hand in mine, I concentrate hard on the lecture hall. Nothing happens. I open one eye and we're still in the woods, Sally in a state of complete panic beside me.

"Holy Mother of God! You can't do it, can you? Sweet Jesus, save me!"

"Will you be quiet?"

She settles into singing old hymns again. Beads of perspiration break out along my upper lip. I close my eyes, and think only of the lecture hall. My breathing grows louder and slower. There's a pulling sensation. The edges of the forest fold into mist; the mist folds back into a great hole of light, and then we are once again on the lecture hall stage. It has worked! The ticking of the pocket watch is a comfort to my ears, as is the time: 9:49. Our whole excursion into the spirit world has taken only a minute, though Sally Carny's face seems to have aged ten years in that brief time. I've been changed too.

"Madame Romanoff" is back, speaking in a shaky voice.

"I am receiving a communication now from another part of the spirit world for someone named Polly. Reggie wishes her to know he loves her with all his heart. . . ." She trails off.

"Muffler," I prompt, through clenched teeth.

"That he has the muffler from Christmas and that she must live happily without him. That is all." She makes a high moaning sound and falls slumped against her chair. Seconds later, she "awakens".

"The spirits have spoken, and now I must rest my gifts. I thank you all for coming this evening and remind you that I will be communing again in Covent Garden next month." As the audience applauds, Sally "Madame Romanoff" Carny leaps from her seat and retreats off into the wings, where her confused lackeys wait for an explanation of tonight's deviation from their plan.

‹‹‹‹‹‹

"I knew you were up to something!" Cecily whispers, taking my arm. "Was it extraordinary?"

Elizabeth cuts in. "Did you see the spirits enter Madame Romanoff's body? Did her hands go ice cold? I've heard that can happen."

I am suddenly the most popular girl at Spence.

"No. I saw no spirits. Her hands were warm and far too moist. And I'm fairly certain her rings were paste," I say, walking quickly, putting as much distance between Mademoiselle LeFarge and me as possible.

Elizabeth pouts. "But what shall I write my mother of tonight's experience?"

"Tell her to stop wasting her money on such nonsense."

"Gemma Doyle, you are an absolute horror," Cecily grouses.

"Yes," I say, ending my one-minute reign as Queen of Spence.

‹‹‹‹‹‹

"What a fake," Felicity announces as I join the throng making its way out of the lecture hall. "She believed that bit about Sarah being your mother's name. And then instead of the real Sarah Rees-Toome we get some lovesick Reggie calling for his Polly."

"Whatever is the matter with Mademoiselle LeFarge? I thought by now she'd be threatening to give us forty bad-conduct marks each," Pippa whispers.

"She's probably waiting for the ride home," Ann says, looking terrified. "She'll most likely tell Mrs Nightwing what we've done and we won't be able to attend the tea dance next month."

This makes even Felicity blanch, and I'm certain to end up in the stocks or the equivalent. Mademoiselle lags several paces behind us. She doesn't seem particularly grim. Instead, she dabs at her eyes with a handkerchief and smiles at Inspector Kent, who offers to escort us to our carriage.

"I think everything will be just fine," I say.

⁂

The crowd is a thick knot of people all trying to get to their carriages without getting wet. I'm separated from the rest of them when an older couple charges ahead of me and slows down to a near halt. I can't get around them and I can just make out Felicity's blonde head moving farther away.

"Can I help you, miss?" The familiar voice is followed by a familiar hand yanking me into a small alley beside the grand house.

"What are you doing here?" I ask Kartik.

"Watching you," he says. "Care to tell me what tonight's little stunt was all about?"

"It was just a laugh, that's all. A bit of schoolgirl fun."

My name is shouted out on the street.

"They're looking for me," I say, hoping he'll let me go.

He grips my wrist tighter. "Something happened tonight. I could sense it."

I start to explain. "It was an accident. . ."

"I don't believe it!" Kartik kicks hard at a stone on the ground, sends it flying.

"It's not what you think," I babble, trying to defend myself. "I can explain—"

"No explanations! We shall give the orders and you shall follow them. No more visions. Do you understand?" His smirk is contemptuous. He's waiting for me to tremble and agree to his terms. But something inside me has changed tonight. And I cannot go back.

I bite his hand and he yelps, dropping my wrist.

"Don't you ever speak to me that way again," I snarl. "I am no longer content to be the scared, obedient schoolgirl. Who are you, a stranger, to tell me what I can and cannot do?"

He growls at me. "I am Rakshana."

I laugh. "Ah, yes – the great and mysterious Rakshana. The powerful brotherhood who feel threatened by things they cannot understand and have to hide themselves behind a *boy*." The word hits him as if I had spit. "You're not a man. You're their *lackey*. I don't care about you, or your brother, or your ridiculous organisation. From now on, I shall do exactly as I wish and you cannot stop me. Do not follow. Do not watch. Do not even attempt to contact me or you'll be sorry indeed. Do *you* understand?"

Kartik stands, rubbing his wounded hand. He's too shocked to say anything. For the first time, he's utterly silent. And that's how I leave him.

<center>~~~~~</center>

Mademoiselle LeFarge never does reprimand us. She sits silently the whole ride back, her eyes closed, a sad smile on her face. But in her fingers is the inspector's calling card. Between the jostling of the carriage and the long evening, everyone has fallen into a twilight sleep. Everyone except me.

I'm on fire with what I've seen tonight. Everything in Mary Dowd's diary is the truth. The realms are real, and my mother is there, waiting for me. Kartik's warnings are nothing to me now. I don't know what I'll find through that door of light, and truthfully, I'm a little afraid to find out. The one thing I do know for certain is that I can no longer ignore whatever power this is inside me. The time has come.

My hand is on Felicity's shoulder, shaking her gently awake.

"Wh-what is it? Are we back?" she says, rubbing her eyes.

"No, not yet," I whisper. "I need to call a meeting of the Order."

"Yes, lovely," she says drowsily, closing her eyes again. "Tomorrow, then."

"No, it's important. Tonight. We must meet tonight."

CHAPTER
TWENTY-TWO

I AM NOT SUPPOSED TO USE MY POWERS. I AM NOT supposed to go willingly into a vision. The realms have been closed for twenty years, since whatever happened with Mary and Sarah changed it all. But if I don't travel that path, I'll never see my mother again. I'll never *know* anything. In the pit of my stomach, where intentions bloom into decisions, I know I'm ready to start down that uncertain road.

This is what swirls through my head as I sit in the darkened cave with the others. It's sticky and wet. The night's rain has done nothing to cool the air. In fact, it has only made the lingering heat stale and unbearable.

Felicity reads the latest installment from Mary's diary, but I can't take in much of it. My secret is coming out tonight, and every part of me is taut with waiting.

Felicity closes the diary. "All right, then, what's all this about?"

"Yes," Pippa says sullenly. "Why couldn't this wait till tomorrow?"

"Because it couldn't," I say. My nerves crackle. Every sound is amplified in my ears. "What if I told you the Order was real? That the realms are real?" I take a deep breath. "And that I know how to get there?"

Pippa rolls her eyes. "You pulled me out into this horrible muddy night for a joke?"

Ann snorts and nods at Pippa, showing her solidarity with her new best friend. Felicity catches my eye. She can tell that something has changed.

"I don't think Gemma is joking," she says quietly.

"I have a secret," I say at last. "There's something I need to tell you."

✳✳✳✳✳✳

I don't spare any of it – my mother's murder; my visions; what happened when I held Sally Carny's hand and ended up in the misty woods; the temple and my mother's voice. The only part I hold back is about Kartik. I'm not ready to share that yet.

When I've finished, they look at me as if I am insane. Or wonderful. I'm not entirely sure. And now I understand that truth casts a spell of its own, one I'm not sure how to hold on to, though I'm desperate to try.

"You have to take us," Felicity says.

"I'm not certain what we'll find there. I'm not certain of anything, not anymore," I answer.

Felicity holds out her hand. "I'm willing to risk it."

I catch sight of a symbol I've never noticed before at the very bottom of a cave wall. It's partially defaced, but some of it is still visible. A woman and a swan. At first glance, it seems as if she's being attacked by the great white bird, but on closer inspection, it seems as if the woman and the swan are joined together as one. A great mythical creature. A woman prepared to fly, even if she has to lose her legs to do it.

I grab Felicity's outstretched hand. Her fingers laced in mine are strong.

"Let's go," I say.

⌁⌁⌁⌁

We light candles, place them in the centre of our circle and crowd around their light, holding hands.

"What do we do now?" Felicity asks. The candlelight throws her shadow, tall and thin as a spire, on the wall.

"I've only been able to control it the one time, when I tried to get back tonight," I say in warning. I don't want to disappoint them. What if I'm unable to do it again and they think I've made up all of it?

Pippa is the first to be afraid. "Sounds a bit dodgy to me. Perhaps we shouldn't attempt this." No one answers her. "Don't you agree, Ann?"

I'm ready for Ann to join Pippa but she doesn't say a word.

"Oh, all right, then. But when it turns out to be some elaborate hoax, I shall say I told you so and not feel one bit of sympathy for you."

"Pay her no attention," Felicity says to me.

I can't help paying her attention. I have the same fear.

"My mother said that I should concentrate on the image of a door . . . ," I say, trying to gain control of my doubts.

"What kind of door?" Ann wants to know. "A red door, a wooden door, large, small . . . ?"

Pippa sighs. "Best tell her the kind, or she won't be able to concentrate. You know she needs the rules before we start anything."

"A door of light," I say. This satisfies Ann. I take a deep breath. "Close your eyes."

Should I say something to get under way? If so, what? In the past, I have slipped, fallen, been sucked down into this tunnel. But this time is different. How should I start? Instead of searching for the right words, I close my eyes and let the words find me.

"I choose this."

Whispers grow in the corners of the cave. They swell into a hum. The next second, the world drops out from under me. Felicity is holding my hand tighter. Pippa gasps. They're frightened. A tingling flows down my arms, connecting me to the others. I could stop now. Obey Kartik and reverse this. But the humming draws me in, and I have to know what's on the other side of it, no matter what. The hum stops and bends into a shudder that flows through my body like a melody, and when I open my eyes there's the glorious outline of a door of light, shimmering and beckoning as if it's been there the whole time just waiting for me to find it.

Ann's face is awed. "Criminy . . ."

"Do you see that . . . ?" Pippa asks in wonder.

Felicity tries to open it but her hand swipes clean through. The door is like a projection in a magic-lantern show. None of them can open it.

"Gemma, you try," Felicity says.

In the incandescent light of the door, my hand seems like someone else's – an angel's limb exposed for a moment. The knob feels solid and warm under my fingers. Something's bubbling up on the surface of the door. A shape. The outline glows stronger and now I can see the familiar markings of the crescent eye. My own necklace glows like the one on the door, as if they're calling to each other. Suddenly, the knob turns easily in my hand.

"You did it," Ann says.

"Yes, I did, didn't I?" I'm smiling in spite of my fear.

The door opens, and we step through into a world drenched in such vivid colours, it hurts my eyes to look at it. When I adjust, I drink it up in small gulps. There are trees dripping leaves of green-gold and red-orange. The sky is a purplish blue on top of a horizon bathed in an orange glow, like a sunset that never fades. Tiny lavender blossoms float by on a warm breeze that smells faintly of my child-hood – lilies and Father's tobacco and curry in Sarita's kitchen. A thick ribbon of river slices through, dividing our patch of dew-drenched grass from a bank on the other side.

Pippa touches a finger to a leaf. It curls in on itself, melts, re-forms as a butterfly and drifts heavenward. "Oh, it's all so beautiful."

"Extraordinary," Ann says.

Blossoms rain down, melt into our hair like fat snowflakes. They make our hair shine. We sparkle.

Felicity twirls round and round, overcome by happiness. "It's real! It's all real!" She stops. "Do you smell that?"

"Yes," I say, inhaling that comforting blend of childhood smells.

"Hot cross buns. We had them every Sunday. And sea air. I used to smell it on my father's uniforms when he returned from a voyage. When he used to come home." Her eyes glisten with tears.

Pippa's puzzled. "No, you're wrong. It's lilac. Like the sprigs I kept in my room from our garden."

The scent of rose water is strong in the air.

"What is it?" Pippa asks.

I catch a bit of song. One of my mother's lullabies. It's coming from a valley down below. I can just make out a silver arch and a path leading into a lush garden.

"Wait a minute, where are you going?" Pippa calls after me.

"I'll be right back," I say, picking up speed till I'm running towards Mother's voice. I'm through the arch and inside tall hedges broken by trees that remind me of open umbrellas. She's there in the centre of it all in her blue dress, still and smiling. Waiting for me.

My voice breaks. "Mother?"

She holds out her arms, and I'm afraid I'll end up chasing after a dream again. But it really is her arms around me this time. I can smell the rose water on her skin.

Everything goes blurry with my tears. "Oh, Mother, it's you. It's really you."

"Yes, darling."

"Why did you run from me for so long?"

"I've been here all the time. You've been the one running."

I don't understand what she means, but it doesn't matter. There's so much I want to say. So much I want to ask. "Mother, I'm so sorry."

"Shhh," she says, smoothing my hair. "That's all past. Come. Take a walk with me."

She walks me down into a grotto, past a circle of tall crystals, delicate as glass. A deer scampers through. It stops to sniff at the berries cupped in my mother's palm. The deer nibbles them, turns its sloe brown eyes to me. Unimpressed, it threads slowly through high, plush grass and lies under a tree with a wide, gnarled base. I have so many questions fighting for attention inside me that I don't know what to ask first.

"What are the realms, exactly?" I ask. The grass feels so inviting that I lie on my side in it, cupping my head in my palm.

"A world between worlds. A place where all things are possible." Mother takes a seat. She blows a dandelion. A blizzard of white fluff spreads out on the breeze. "It's where the Order came to reflect, to hone their magic and themselves, to come through the fire and be made new. Everyone comes here from time to time – in dreams, when ideas are born." She pauses. "In death."

My heart sinks. "But you're not . . ." Dead. I can't bring myself to say it. "You're here."

"For now."

"How do you know all of this?"

Mother turns away from me. She pets the deer's nose with long, steady strokes. "I didn't know anything at first. When you were five, a woman came to me. One of the Order. She told me everything. That you were special – the promised girl who could restore the magic of these realms and bring the Order back to power." She stops.

"What is it?"

"She also told me that Circe would never stop looking for you, so that the power might be hers alone. I was afraid, Gemma. I wanted to protect you."

"Is that why you wouldn't bring me to London?"

"Yes."

Magic. The Order. Me, the promised girl. My head can't hold it all.

I swallow hard. "Mother, what happened that day, in the shop? What was that . . . thing?"

"One of Circe's spies. Her tracker. Her assassin."

I can't look at her. I'm bending a blade of grass into an accordion of squares. "But why did you . . ."

"Kill myself?" I look up to see her giving me that penetrating gaze. "To keep it from claiming me. If it had taken me alive, I would be lost, a dark thing too."

"What about Amar?"

Mother's mouth goes tight. "He was my guardian. He gave his life for me. There was nothing I could do to save him."

I shudder, thinking of what could have become of Kartik's brother.

"Let's not worry about that now, shall we?" Mother says, sweeping stray strands of hair from my face. "I'll tell you what I can. As for the rest, you'll have to seek out the others to rebuild the Order."

I sit up. "There are others?"

"Oh, yes. When the realms were closed, they all went into hiding. Some have forgotten what they know. Others have turned their backs on it. But some are still faithful, waiting for the day the realms will open and the magic can be theirs again."

Rippling blades of grass tickle the tips of my fingers. It seems so unreal – the sunset sky, the raining flowers, the warm breeze, and my mother, close enough to touch. I close my eyes and open them again. She is still there.

"What is it?" Mother asks me.

"I'm afraid this isn't real. It is real, isn't it?"

Mother turns her face towards the horizon. The glow softens the sharp lines of her profile into something muted, like the fraying paper edges of a well-loved book. "Reality is a state of mind. To the banker, the money in his ledger book is all very real, though he doesn't actually see it or touch it. But to the Brahma, it simply doesn't exist the way the air and the earth, pain and loss do. To him, the banker's reality is folly. To the banker, the Brahma's ideas are as inconsequential as dust."

I shake my head. "I'm lost."

"Does it seem real to you?"

The wind blows strands of hair against my lips, tickling

them, and beneath my skirt, I can feel the dewy moisture of the grass. "Yes," I say.

"Well, then."

"If everyone comes here from time to time, why does no one speak of it?"

Mother picks dandelion fluff from her skirt. It floats up, sparkling like crushed jewels in the sun. "They don't remember it, except as fragments of a dream that they can't seem to gather into a whole no matter how they try. Only the women of the Order could walk through that door. And now you."

"I brought my friends with me."

Her eyes widen. "You were able to bring them over by yourself?"

"Yes," I say, uncertain. I'm afraid I've done something wrong, but Mother breaks into a slow, rapturous grin.

"Your power is even greater than the Order had hoped, then." She frowns suddenly. "Do you trust them?"

"Yes," I say. For some reason, her doubt irritates me, makes me feel like a small child again. "Of course I trust them. They're my friends."

"Sarah and Mary were friends. And they betrayed each other."

Far off in the distance, I can hear Felicity's shouts of joy, Ann's following after. They're calling my name.

"What happened to Sarah and Mary? I see other spirits. Why am I not able to contact them?"

A caterpillar crawls over my knuckles. I jump. Mother

gently removes it and it becomes a ruby-breasted robin, hopping about on frail legs.

"They no longer exist."

"What do you mean? What happened to them?"

"Let's not waste time discussing the past," Mother says dismissively. She gives me a smile. "I just want to look at you. My goodness, you're already becoming a lady."

"I'm learning to waltz. I'm not terribly good at it, but I am trying, and I think I should have it down fairly well by our first tea dance." I want to tell her everything. It's all coming out in a rush. She's listening to me with such attention that I never want this day to end.

A cluster of blackberries, plump and inviting, lies nestled in the ground. Before I can bring one to my mouth, Mother takes it from my hand. "You mustn't eat those, Gemma. They're not for the living." Mother sees the confusion on my face. "Those who eat the berries become part of this world. They can't go back."

She gives them a toss and they land in front of the deer, which gobbles them down greedily. Mother glances at the little girl – the one from my visions. She's hiding behind a tree.

"Who is that?" I ask.

"My helper," Mother says.

"What is her name?"

"I don't know." Mother closes her eyes tightly, as if she's fighting off pain.

"Mother, what is it?"

She opens them again, but seems pale. "Nothing. I'm a bit tired from all the excitement. It's time for you to go now."

I'm on my feet. "But there's so much I still need to know."

Mother rises, places her arms around my shoulders. "Your time has ended for today, love. The power of this place is very strong. It must be taken in small doses. Even the Order came here only when they needed to. Remember that your place is back there."

My throat aches. "I don't want to leave you."

Her fingers give the lightest of touches on my cheeks, and I can't stop the tears from coming. She kisses my forehead and bends to look me square in the face.

"I'll never leave you, Gemma."

She turns and walks up the hill, the child's hand in hers. They walk towards the sunset till they merge with it and there's nothing left but the deer and me and the lingering scent of roses on the wind.

⌐ᴧᴧᴧᴧᴧ⌐

When I find my friends again, they're frolicking like happy lunatics.

"Watch this!" Felicity says. She blows gently on a tree and its bark changes from brown to blue to red and back again.

"Look!" Ann scoops water from the river and it turns to golden dust in her hands. "Did you see that?"

Pippa is stretched out in a hammock. "Wake me when it's time to leave. On second thought, don't wake me. This is too divine a dream." She extends her arms overhead and

· 259 ·

dangles a leg over the side of the hammock, resting in her cocoon.

I am changed and spent. I want to go back to my room and sleep for a hundred years. And I want to run back down into that valley and stay here with my mother forever.

Felicity puts her arm around me. "We simply must come again tomorrow. Can you imagine if that prig Cecily could see us now? She'd be sorry she didn't want to join up."

Pippa drops an arm down to pick a handful of berries.

"Don't!" I shout, slapping them out of her hands.

"Why not?"

"If you eat them, you have to stay here forever."

"No wonder they look so tempting," she says.

I hold out my hand. Reluctantly, she drops them in my palm, and I toss them into the river.

CHAPTER
TWENTY-THREE

WE'RE SLEEPWALKING THROUGH THE DAY, RIDICULOUS smiles on our faces. The other girls rush past us in the halls like nettles blown across a lawn. We drift through them from class to class, going through the motions, absorbing nothing. We keep last night's promise alive through furtive glances and little asides spoken in code that perplex our teachers and make us all smile.

We understand each other. We share a secret.

Not a terrible secret like the one that binds me to my family and to Kartik, but a deliciously forbidden secret that bands us together. Anticipation races through our veins, stretching our skins tight to the point of bursting. It's all we can do to get through the day and wait for night to come so that we can open that door of light into the realms again. We are as one. There will be no outsiders. No intruders on our experience.

During our music lesson, Mr Grunewald drones on for the whole of the hour about the merits of a particular opera.

Elizabeth, Cecily, and Martha listen like the good girls they are, taking perfect little notes, their heads bobbing up and down in unison. Listen, write, listen, write.

We don't jot down a word of it. We're elsewhere in a land where we can be anything we choose. Mr Grunewald calls Cecily to the piano to play her Assembly Day piece for us. Her fingers plod out a careful, correct minuet.

"Ah, good, Miss Temple. Very precise." Mr Grunewald is pleased, but we know the feel of real music now, and it's difficult to feign interest in the merely pretty.

After class, Cecily pretends her playing was awful. "Oh, I simply butchered it, didn't I? Tell the truth."

Martha and Elizabeth protest, tell her she was brilliant.

"What did you think, Fee?" It's easy to see that she wants Felicity's praise.

"Very nice" is all Felicity says.

"Just nice?" Cecily forces a laugh that's meant to sound devil-may-care. "My, it must have been truly awful, then."

"It was a lovely waltz," Felicity says, getting it wrong. She can barely keep the smile from her face. I look away, trying not to break into the same ridiculous grin.

"It wasn't a waltz. It was a minuet," Cecily corrects. She's pouting openly.

Elizabeth peers at us as if she doesn't know who we are.

"Why are you looking at us that way, as if we're specimens?" Pippa asks.

"I don't quite know. There's something different about you." We exchange quick glances.

"There is something different, isn't there? Come now, if you've a secret you'd best share it."

"That would be telling, wouldn't it?" Felicity smirks. The light is shining through the hall window. It makes the dust dance in the air.

"Pippa, darling, you'll tell me, won't you?" Elizabeth puts her arm around Pippa, who twirls away from her embrace.

Cecily is quite put out. "The old Pip and Fee wouldn't have kept secrets from us."

"But those old girls are gone." Felicity gives a radiant smile. "They are dead and buried. We are new girls for a new world."

And with that we push past them, leaving them behind us in the hall like so much dust floating slowly down to earth.

⌇⌇⌇⌇⌇

Miss Moore has prepared canvases for us. There is muslin stretched taut over framing, watercolours at the ready. Can bucolic beach scenes and flower arrangements be far behind? I note the bowl of fruit placed on a table in the centre of the room. Another still life. If she wants a still life, we could just as easily paint the futures Spence is preparing us for day by day. I expect better from Miss Moore.

"A still life?" My voice drips with disdain.

Miss Moore stands by the windows. Silhouetted against the sky's grey glare, she looms like a scarecrow. "Do I sense dissatisfaction, Miss Doyle?"

"It isn't terribly challenging."

"The world's greatest artists have seen fit to paint still lifes from time to time."

She has me there, but I'm not going down without a fight. "How much challenge is there in an apple?"

"We shall find out," she says, handing me a smock.

Felicity inspects the bowl of fruit. She selects an apple, bites into it with a loud crack.

Miss Moore takes it from her hand and returns it to the bowl. "Felicity, please do not eat the exhibit or I shall be forced to use wax fruit next time and then you'll have a nasty surprise in store."

"I guess it's a still life after all," I sigh, dipping my brush into the red paint.

"It appears I am in the midst of a rebellion. You didn't seem to mind painting so much the other day."

Felicity shares one of her sly grins. "We are not the same as the other day. Indeed, we are utterly changed, Miss Moore."

Cecily exhales loudly. "Don't try to reason with them, Miss Moore. They are impossible today."

"Yes," says Elizabeth, adopting a nasty tone. "They are new girls for a new world. Isn't that right, Pippa?"

There are more furtive glances that do not go undetected by Miss Moore. "Is this true, Miss Doyle? Are we in the midst of a private revolution?"

She catches me off guard. It always feels strange to be on the other end of Miss Moore's microscope lens. It's as if she knows what I'm thinking. "We are," I say at last.

"Do you see what I mean?" Cecily huffs.

Miss Moore claps her hands together. "We could do with something new. I am overthrown. They are your canvases for the hour, ladies. Do as you will."

We erupt in cheers. The brush seems suddenly lighter in my hand. Cecily isn't happy, though.

"But Miss Moore, Assembly Day is only two weeks away, and I won't have anything decent to show my family when they arrive," she says, pouting.

"Cecily's quite right, Miss Moore," Martha joins in. "I don't care what *they* want. I can't show my family some primitive sketch of a cave wall. They would be appalled."

Miss Moore raises her chin, looking down on them. "I wouldn't want to be the cause of such distress to you and your families, Miss Temple and Miss Hawthorne. Here. The fruit bowl is yours. I'm sure your parents would enjoy a still life."

Felicity wanders over to some clay. "May I make a sculpture, Miss Moore?"

"If you wish, Miss Worthington. Ye gods, I don't know if I am holding class or the class is holding me." She hands Felicity a lump of clay for moulding.

"To make certain the afternoon is an educational one after all," Miss Moore says, glancing at Cecily, "I shall read aloud from *David Copperfield*. Chapter One: 'Whether I shall turn out to be the hero of my own life, or whether that station will be held by anybody else, these pages must show. . .'"

At the end of the hour, Miss Moore examines our paintings, murmuring both praise and correction. When she comes to my painting – a large, misshapen apple taking up the whole of the canvas – she purses her lips for what seems a long time. "How very modern, Miss Doyle."

Cecily lets out a sharp laugh when she sees it. "Is that supposed to be an apple?"

"Of course it's an apple, Cecily," Felicity snaps. "I think it's marvellous, Gem. Quite *avant-garde*."

I'm not satisfied. "It needs more light on the front to make it shiny. I keep adding white and yellow, but that only washes everything out."

"You need to add a bit of shadow back here." Miss Moore dips a brush in sepia and paints a curve along the outside edge of my apple. Immediately, the shine on the apple is apparent, and it looks much better. "The Italians call this *chiaroscuro*. It means the play of light and dark within a picture."

"Why couldn't Gemma simply add the white to make the apple shine?" Pippa asks.

"Because you don't notice the light without a bit of shadow. Everything has both dark and light. You have to play with it till you get it exactly right."

"What do you propose to call that?" Cecily's tone drips disdain.

"*The Choice*," I blurt out, surprising myself.

Miss Moore nods. "The fruit of knowledge. Most interesting, indeed."

"Do you mean as in Eve's apple? As in the Garden of

Eden?" Elizabeth asks. She's diligently trying to add sepia shadows to her painting now, and it's making her fruit look bruised and ugly. But I'm not going to tell her that.

"Let's ask the artist. Is that what you intended, Miss Doyle?"

I have no idea what I meant, really. I fumble to make sense of it. "I suppose it's any choice to know more, to see beyond what's there."

Felicity throws me a conspiratorial glance.

Cecily shakes her head. "Well, it's not a very accurate name. Eve didn't choose to eat the apple. She was tempted by the serpent."

"Yes," I argue, thoughts coming out half-formed. "But . . . she didn't have to take a bite. She chose to."

"And she lost paradise in the bargain. Not for me, thank you. I'd stay right there in the garden," Cecily says.

"That, too, is a choice," Miss Moore points out.

"A much safer one," Cecily argues.

"There are no safe choices, Miss Temple. Only other choices."

"Mama says that women were not meant to have too many choices. It overwhelms them." Pippa repeats this as if it's a lesson well taught. "That's why we're supposed to defer to our husbands."

"Every choice has consequences," Miss Moore says, sounding far away.

Felicity picks the apple from the bowl and finds her bite mark. The sweet white meat has browned in the air. She sinks her teeth in and makes a clean new mark.

"Delicious," she says, her mouth juicy full.

Miss Moore comes back to us with a laugh. "I see Felicity doesn't complicate the matter with too much deliberation. She's a hawk, diving in."

"Eat or be eaten!" Felicity takes another mouthful.

I'm thinking of Sarah and Mary, wondering what horrible choice they made. Whatever it was, it was powerful enough to shatter the Order. And that leads me to the choice I made the day I ran from my mother in the marketplace. The choice that seems to have put everything in motion.

"What happens if your choice is misguided?" I ask, softly.

Miss Moore takes a pear from the bowl and offers us the grapes to devour. "You must try to correct it."

"But what if it's too late? What if you can't?"

There's a sad sympathy in Miss Moore's catlike eyes as she regards my painting again. She paints the thinnest sliver of shadow along the bottom of the apple, bringing it fully to life.

"Then you must find a way to live with it."

CHAPTER
TWENTY-FOUR

THE AFTERNOON IS A FINE ONE, AND THE GROUNDS AND gardens of Spence are blooming with girls – on bicycles, playing pantomimes, strolling, gossiping. The four of us have taken up a game of lawn tennis. We're playing doubles, Felicity and Pippa against Ann and me. Each time my racket touches the ball, I fear I'm in danger of decapitating someone. I think it is safe to say that I may add tennis to the long list of skills I shall not acquire. By sheer luck, I manage to hit the ball to my opponents. It sails past Pippa, who watches it go by with all the enthusiasm of a cook watching water come to a boil.

Felicity throws back her head in exasperation. "Pippa!"

"It isn't my fault. That was a dreadful serve!"

"You should have reached for it," Felicity says, twirling her racket.

"It was clearly out of reach!"

"But so much is within our reach now," Felicity says, cryptically.

The girls watching us play may not know what she means, but I do. Pippa is having none of it, however.

"This is dull, and my arm aches," she complains.

Felicity rolls her eyes. "Fine, then. Let's take a walk, shall we?"

We bequeath our rackets to an eager, pink-cheeked foursome. Our game ended, we link arms and roam through the tall trees, past a group of younger girls who are playing Robin Hood. The trouble is that they all want to be Maid Marian and no one wants to be Friar Tuck.

"Will you take us into the realms again tonight?" Ann asks, when their voices have faded to a hum behind us.

"You couldn't keep me away." I smile. "There's someone I want you to meet."

"Who?" Pippa asks, bending to pick acorns.

"My mother."

Ann gapes. Pippa's head pops up. "But isn't she—"

Felicity interrupts. "Pippa, help me gather some goldenrod to bring to Mrs Nightwing. That should put her in a happy mood tonight."

Dutifully, Pippa follows Felicity on her mission and soon we're all looking for the September blooms. Down by the lake, I see Kartik leaning against the boathouse, arms crossed, watching me. His black cloak flutters in the wind. I wonder if he knows about his brother's fate. For a moment, I feel a bit sorry for him. But then I remember the threats and taunts, the smirking way he tried to order me about, and all my sympathy vanishes. I stand tall and defiant, staring straight back at him.

Pippa wanders over. "Good heavens, isn't that the Gypsy who saw me in the woods?"

"I don't recall," I lie.

"I hope he doesn't try to blackmail us."

"I doubt it," I say, trying to feign lack of interest. "Oh, look – a dandelion."

"He is rather handsome, isn't he?"

"Do you think so?" It's out of my mouth before I can stop it.

"For a heathen, that is." She tosses her head in a coy fashion. "He seems to be looking at me."

It hadn't occurred to me that Kartik could be watching Pippa and not me, and for some reason, this bothers me. As infuriating as he is, I want him to be gazing only at me.

"What are you looking at?" Ann asks. Her hands are full of drooping yellow weeds.

"That boy over there. The one who saw me in my chemise the other night."

Ann squints. "Oh. Him. Isn't he the one you kissed, Gemma?"

"You didn't!" Pippa gasps in horror.

"She did," Ann says, matter-of-factly. "But only to save us from the Gypsies."

"You were with the Gypsies? When? Why didn't you take me?"

"It's a rather long story. I'll tell you on the way back," Felicity chides. Pippa is squawking about the way we've kept vital information from her, but Felicity's eyes are on Kartik and then me with an understanding that makes me feel suddenly like running for cover. And then she has her arm around Pippa's shoulders, telling her the story of our adventures in the Gypsy camp in a way that completely exonerates me. I am a noble, self-sacrificing girl who endured his kiss only to save us. It is so convincing that I almost believe her myself.

<hr />

When we step through that door of light again, the garden realm is there to welcome us with its sweet smells and a bright sky. I'm apprehensive. I don't know how much time I shall have with my mother, and a small part of me doesn't want to share that time with my friends. But they are my friends, and perhaps it will comfort my mother to meet them.

"Follow me," I say, taking them into the grotto. She's nowhere to be seen. There are only the trees and, farther on, the circle of strange crystals.

"Where is she?" Ann asks.

"Mother?" I call out. No answer. Nothing but the chirping of birds. What if she's not really here? What if I did imagine it?

My friends avoid my eyes. Pippa whispers something low in Felicity's ear.

"Maybe you dreamed it?" Felicity suggests softly.

"She was here! I spoke with her!"

"Well, she isn't here now," Ann comments.

"Come with us," Pippa says, treating me like a child. "We'll have a jolly time. I promise."

"No!"

"Looking for me?" Mother strides into view in her blue silk dress. She's as lovely as ever. My friends are struck dumb by her presence.

"Felicity, Pippa, Ann . . . may I present Virginia Doyle, my mother."

The girls mumble their polite how-do-you-do's.

"I am so very pleased to meet you," Mother says. "What beautiful girls you all are." This has the desired effect. They blush, completely charmed. "Will you take a stroll with me?" Soon she has them regaling her with stories of Spence and themselves, the three of them competing for her attention, and I'm a bit grumpy, wanting to have my mother only to myself. But then Mother gives me a wink and takes my hand, and I'm happy again.

"Shall we sit?" Mother gestures to a blanket woven of fine silver thread, stretched out on the grass. For something so light, it is surprisingly strong and comfortable. Felicity runs her hand over the delicate threads. They give off the most striking tones.

"Dear me," she says, delighted. "Can you hear that? Pippa, you try."

We all do. It's as if we're conducting a symphony of harps through our fingers, and it sets us to laughing.

"Isn't it marvellous? I wonder what else we can do?" Felicity muses.

Mother smiles. "Anything."

"Anything?" Ann repeats.

"In this realm, what you wish can be yours. You have only to know what you want."

We take this in, not quite comprehending it. Finally, Ann stands up. "I'll give it a try." She stops. "What should I do?"

"What do you most want? No – don't tell us. Fix it in your mind. Like a wish."

Ann nods, closes her eyes. A minute passes.

"Nothing's happened," Felicity whispers. "Has it?"

"I don't know," Pippa says. "Ann? Ann, are you all right?"

Ann rocks back and forth on her heels. Her lips part. I'm afraid she's gone into some kind of trance. I look to my mother, who brings a finger to her mouth. Ann's lips open wide. What comes out is like no music I've ever heard, clear and soaring, sweet as an angel's voice. Her singing raises gooseflesh on my arms. Every note seems to change her. She's still Ann, but somehow the music makes her achingly lovely. Her hair shines. Her cheeks become smooth and bright. She's like some watery creature from the deep – a mermaid come to live on the glossy surface of the river.

"Ann, you're beautiful," Pippa gasps.

"Am I?" She runs to the river, catches sight of her reflection. "I am!" She laughs, delighted. It's startling, hearing a real laugh come from Ann. She closes her eyes and lets the music soar out of her.

"*Incroyable!*" Felicity says, showing off her French. "I want to try!"

"Me too!" Pippa cries.

They close their eyes, meditate for a moment, and open them again.

"I don't see him," Pippa says, looking around.

"Were you waiting for me, m'lady?" A beautiful young knight appears from behind a large golden oak. He sinks to one knee before Pippa. She gasps. "I have frightened you. Forgive me."

"I might have known," Felicity whispers dryly in my ear.

Pippa looks as if she's just won every prize at the carnival. Giddily she says, "You are forgiven."

He rises. He's no more than eighteen, but tall, with hair the colour of just-ripe corn and broad shoulders draped in a chain mail so light it is nearly liquid. The effect is of a lion. Powerful. Graceful. Noble.

"Where is your champion, m'lady?"

Pippa trips over her tongue, trying to be ladylike and controlled. "I have no champion."

"Then I shall ask to have that honour. If the lady would grant me her favour."

Pippa turns to us, her whisper verging on an excited squeal. "Please tell me that I'm not dreaming this."

"You are not dreaming," Felicity whispers back. "Or else we all are."

It's all Pippa can do not to shriek with happiness and jump up and down like a child. "Noble knight, I shall grant you my favour." She means to be imperious but can barely keep from giggling.

"My life for yours." He bows. Waits.

"I believe you're supposed to give him something of yours, a token of affection," I prompt.

"Oh." Pippa blushes. She removes her glove and offers it.

"M'lady," the knight says demurely. "I am yours." He

extends his arm and with a glance back at us, she takes it and lets him lead her down into the meadow.

"Any knights for you?" I ask Felicity. She shakes her head. "What did you ask for, then?"

Her smile is enigmatic. "Sheer might."

Mother regards her coolly. "Careful what you wish for."

An arrow whistles past our heads. It sticks fast in a tree just behind us. A huntress creeps into the open. Her hair is piled loosely upon her head like a goddess's. There's a full quiver of arrows strapped to her back, a bow at the ready in her hands. The quiver is all she's wearing. She's as naked as a newborn babe.

"You might have killed us," I say, catching my breath, trying not to stare at her nakedness.

She retrieves the arrow. "But I didn't." She regards Felicity, who is studying her, intrigued and undaunted. "You're not afraid, I see."

"No," Felicity says, retrieving the arrow. She runs her fingers over the sharp point. "Merely curious."

"Are you a huntress?"

Felicity hands the arrow back. "No. My father used to hunt. He said it was the sport he admired most."

"But you did not accompany him?"

Felicity's smile is bitter. "Only sons are allowed to hunt. Not daughters."

The huntress clasps a hand around Felicity's upper arm. "There is great strength in this arm. You might prove to be a very skilled huntress. Very powerful." The word *powerful* brings a smile to Felicity's face, and I know she's going to get what she's after. "Would you like to learn?"

In answer, Felicity takes the bow and arrow.

"There's a snake coiled around the limb of that tree," the huntress says.

Felicity closes one eye and pulls back on the bow with all her might. The arrow soars straight up, then bounces along the ground. Felicity's cheeks flush with disappointment.

The huntress applauds. "A solid effort. You might be a huntress yet. But first, you must observe."

Felicity, observe? Perish the thought. Huntress or not, she's got a tough road ahead of her, teaching Felicity patience. But to my surprise, Felicity doesn't scoff or argue. She follows the huntress and patiently allows her to demonstrate the proper technique over and over again.

"What did you wish for?" Mother asks me when it's just the two of us.

"I have what I want. You're here."

She strokes my cheek. "Yes. For a little while longer."

My good mood evaporates. "What do you mean?"

"Gemma, I cannot stay forever, else I could be trapped like one of those wretched lost spirits who never complete their soul's task."

"And what is yours?"

"I must set right what Mary and Sarah did so many years ago."

"What did they do?"

Before Mother can answer, Pippa runs to me, nearly

knocking me over in her gushing enthusiasm. She hugs me tightly. "Did you see him? Wasn't he the most perfect gentleman? He pledged to be my champion! He actually pledged his life for mine! Have you ever heard of anything half so romantic? Can you bear it?"

"Barely," Felicity says wryly. She's just returned from her hunt, exhausted but happy. "That's not as easy as it looks, I can tell you. My arm will ache for a week."

She moves her shoulder in small circles, wincing a bit. But I know she's grateful for that aching arm, grateful to have proof of her own hidden strengths.

Ann wanders over, her fine, lank hair curling about her shoulders in new ringlets. Even her perpetual runny nose seems to have cleared. She points to the tall, thin crystals arranged in a circle behind Mother. "What are those?"

"Those are the Runes of the Oracle, the heart of this realm," Mother says. I stand beside one. "Don't touch them," Mother warns.

"Why not?" Felicity asks.

"You must understand how the magic of the realms works first, how to control it, before you can let it live in you and use it on the other side."

"We can take this sort of power with us to our world?" Ann says.

"Yes, but not yet. Once the Order is re-established they can teach you. It's not safe until then."

"Why not?" I ask.

"It's been such a long time since the magic here has been used. There's no telling what could happen. Something could get out. Or come in."

"They're humming," Felicity says.

"Their energy is very powerful," Mother says, making a cat's cradle from a skein of golden yarn.

When I tilt my head one way, they seem almost to disappear. But when I turn my head another, I can see them rising up from the ground, more dazzling than diamonds. "How exactly does it work?" I ask.

She snakes her fingers in and out of the yarn. "When you touch the runes, it's as if you become the magic itself. It flows through your veins. And then you are able to do in the other world what you can do here in the realms."

Felicity brings her hand ever closer to a rune. "Strange. It stopped humming as I got near."

I can't resist. I hold out my hand, not touching it, but near it. I'm seized by a rush of energy. My eyes flutter. The urge to touch the rune is overwhelming.

"Gemma!" Mother barks.

I pull my hand back quickly. My amulet glows. "Wh-what was that?"

"You are the conduit," Mother explains. "The magic flows through you."

Felicity's face clouds over. But an instant later, she's wearing a ripe smile, thinking some naughty thought. She leans back on her elbows in the grass. "Can you imagine it? If we had this power at Spence?"

"We could do as we wish," Ann adds.

"I'd have a wardrobe filled with the latest fashions. And bushels of money." Pippa giggles.

"I'd be invisible for a day," Felicity adds.

"I wouldn't be," Ann says bitterly.

"I could ease Father's pain." I glance at Mother. Her eyes narrow.

"No," she says, unravelling a Jacob's ladder.

"Why not?" My cheeks are hot.

"We'd be careful," Pippa adds.

"Yes, terribly careful," Felicity chimes in, trying to charm Mother as if she were one of our impressionable teachers.

Mother crushes the yarn in her fist. Her eyes flash. "Tapping into this power is not a game. It is hard work. It takes preparation, not the wild curiosity of overeager schoolgirls."

Felicity is taken aback. I bristle at this comment, at being chided in front of my friends. "We are not overeager."

Mother places a palm on my arm, gives me a faint smile, and I feel churlish for having acted like such a child. "When it is time."

Pippa peers carefully at the base of a rune. "What are these markings?"

"It's an ancient language, older than Greek and Latin."

"But what does it say?" Ann wants to know.

"'I change the world; the world changes me.'"

Pippa shakes her head. "What does that mean?"

"Everything you do comes back to you. When you affect a situation, you are also affected."

"M'lady!" The knight has returned. He's brought out a lute. Soon, he's serenading Pippa with a song about her beauty and virtue.

"Isn't he perfection? I think I shall die from happiness. I want to dance – come with me!" Pippa pulls Ann after her towards the dashing knight, forgetting all about the runes.

Felicity brushes herself off and trails behind them. "Are you coming?"

"I'll be there in a moment," I call after her.

Mother resumes her meticulous yarn architecture. Her fingers fly, then stop. She closes her eyes and gasps, as if she's been wounded.

"Mother, what's the matter? Are you all right? Mother!"

When she opens her eyes, she's breathing hard. "It takes so much to keep it away."

"Keep what away?"

"The creature. It's still looking for us."

The dirty-faced girl peers out from behind a tree. She looks at my mother with wide eyes. Mother's face softens. Her breathing returns to normal. She's the commanding presence I remember bustling about our house, giving orders and changing place settings at the very last moment. "There is nothing to worry about. I can fool the beast for a while."

Felicity calls to me. "Gemma, you're missing out on all the sport." She and the others are twirling each other about, dancing to the lute and the song.

Mother starts to build a cup and saucer from her yarn.

Her hands tremble. "Why don't you join them? I should like to see you dance. Go on, then, darling."

Reluctantly, I amble towards my friends. Along the way, I spy the girl, still looking at my mother with her frightened eyes. There's something compelling about the child. Something I feel I should know, though I can't say what.

"It's time to dance!" Felicity takes both my hands in hers, twirling me around. Mother applauds us in our jig. The knight strums the lute faster and faster, egging us on. We're picking up speed, our hair flying, hands tight on each other's wrists.

"Whatever you do, don't let go!" Felicity shrieks, as our bodies lean back in defiance of gravity till we're nothing more than a great blur of colour on the landscape.

〰〰〰

The sky is a softer shade of night by the time we return to our rooms. Dawn is mere hours away. Tomorrow we'll have the devil to pay.

"Your mother is lovely," Ann says as she slips under her covers.

"Thank you," I whisper, running a brush through my hair. The dancing – and the subsequent fall in the grass – has left it tangled beyond hope, like my thoughts.

"I don't remember my mother at all. Do you think that's terrible?"

"No," I say.

Ann is nearly asleep, her words a low mumble. "I wonder if she remembers me..."

I start to answer but I don't know what to say to that. And anyway, it doesn't matter. She's snoring already. I give up on the brushing and slide under my own blankets, only to feel something crackle beneath me. I feel around with my hand and discover a note hidden in the covers. I have to take it to the window to read it.

Miss Doyle,

You are playing a very dangerous game. If you do not stop now, I shall be forced to take action. I am asking you to stop while you can.

There's another word scribbled hastily, then crossed out.

Please.

He hasn't signed his name, but I know this is Kartik's work. I tear the note into tiny pieces. Then I open the window and let the breeze take it.

CHAPTER
TWENTY-FIVE

FOR THREE DAYS, IT'S LIKE THIS. WE HOLD HANDS AND step into our own private paradise, where we are the mistresses of our own lives. Under the tutelage of the huntress, Felicity is becoming an accomplished archer, fleet and unstoppable. Ann's voice grows stronger every day. And Pippa isn't quite the pampered princess she was a week ago. She's kinder, less shrill. The knight listens to her as no one else does. I've always been so irritated when Pippa opens her mouth, I haven't stopped to think she may babble on because she's afraid she won't be heard. I vow to give her that chance from now on.

We're not afraid to grow close to each other here. Our friendships take root and bloom. We wear garlands in our hair, tell naughty jokes, laugh and shout, confess our fears and our hopes. We even belch without restraint. There's no one around to stifle us. No one to tell us that what we think and feel is wrong. It isn't that we do what we want. It's that we're allowed to want at all.

"Watch this!" Felicity says. She closes her eyes and in a moment, a warm rain falls from that perpetual sunset. It wets us through to the skin, and it feels delicious.

"Not fair in the least!" Pippa screams, but she's laughing.

I've never felt such lovely rain. Certainly I've never been allowed to wallow in it. I want to drink it up, lie in it.

"Aha!" Felicity shouts in triumph. "I made this! I did!"

We screech and run, slipping down into pools of mud and back up again. Coated in muck, we throw handfuls of it at each other. Each time one of us is hit with a great heaping mound of wet earth, we yelp and vow revenge. But truthfully, we're in love with how it feels to be absolutely filthy, without a care in the world.

"I'm a bit soggy," Pippa calls after we've thoroughly trounced her. She's covered in mud from head to toe.

"All right, then." I close my eyes, imagine the hot sun of India, and in seconds, the rain has gone. We're clean, dry, and pressed, ready for vespers or a social call. Beyond the silver arch, inside their wide circle, the crystal runes stand, their power locked securely inside.

"Wouldn't it be grand to show them all what we could do?" Ann muses aloud.

I take her hand, and when I do, I notice her wrist has no new marks, only the fading scars of past injuries.

"Yes, it would."

We sprawl out in the grass, heads together, like a great windmill. And we lie like this for a very long time, I think, holding each other's hands, feeling our friendship in thumbs and fingers, in the sure, solid warmth of skin, until someone gets the bright idea to make it rain again.

⌁⌁⌁⌁

"Tell me again how the magic of the runes works." I'm lying in the grass next to Mother, watching the clouds in their metamorphoses. A fat, puffy duck is losing the good fight, stretching into something else.

"It works through months and years of training," Mother responds.

"I know that. But what happens? Do they chant? Speak in tongues? Do the runes sing 'God Save the Queen' first?" I'm being cheeky, but she's provoked me.

"Yes. In E flat."

"Mother!"

"I believe I explained that part."

"Tell me again."

"You touch your hands to the runes and the power enters you. It lives inside you for a while."

"That's it?"

"The gist, yes. But you first have to know how to control it. It's influenced by your state of mind, your purpose, your strength. It's powerful magic. Not to be toyed with. Oh, look, I see an elephant."

Overhead, the duck blob has become something resembling a blob with a trunk.

"It has only three legs."

"No, there's a fourth."

"Where?"

"It's right there. You're just not looking."

"I am so!" I say, indignant. But it doesn't matter. The cloud is moving, changing into something else. "How long does the magic last?"

"Depends. For a day. Sometimes less." She sits up and peers down at me. "But Gemma, you are—"

"Not to use the magic yet. Yes, I believe you mentioned that once or twice."

Mother is quiet for a moment. "Do you really believe you're ready?"

"Yes!" I practically shout.

"Take a look at that cloud up there. The one just above us. What do you see?"

I see the outline of ears and a tail. "A kitten."

"You're certain?"

She is taxing me. "I do know a kitten when I see one. That doesn't require any magical powers."

"Look again," Mother says.

Above us, the sky is in turmoil. The clouds swirl and crackle with lightning. The kitten is gone and what emerges in its place is a menacing face from a nightmare. It shrieks down towards us till I have to bury my eyes behind my arm.

"Gemma!"

I take my arm away. The sky is calm. The kitten is now a large cat.

"What was that?" I whisper.

"A demonstration," Mother says. "You have to be able to

see what's really there. Circe will try to make you see a monster when there is only a kitten, and vice versa."

I'm still shaking. "But it seemed so real."

She takes my hand in hers and we lie there, not moving. In the distance, Ann is singing an old folk song, something about a lady selling cockles and mussels. It's a sad song and it makes me feel strange inside. As if I'm losing something but I don't know what.

"Mother, what if I can't do this? What if it turns out all wrong?"

The clouds bunch together and thin out. Nothing's taking shape yet.

"That's a chance we have to take. Look."

Above us, the clouds have spread themselves into a wispy ring with no beginning, no end, and in the centre is a perfect circle of absolute blue.

❧❦❧❦

On Friday, I receive a surprise visit. My brother is waiting for me in the parlour. A gaggle of girls is inventing reasons to walk past so that they can peek in at him. I close the doors behind me, cutting Tom off from his admiring flock before my nausea overtakes me.

"Well, if it isn't my lady Dour!" Tom says, standing. "Have you managed to find me a suitable wife yet? I'm not picky – just someone pretty, quiet, with a small fortune and her own teeth. Actually, I am flexible on all points but the small fortune. Unless, of course, it's a large one."

For some reason, the sight of Tom, reliable, snobby, shallow Tom, fills me with good cheer. I hadn't realised how much I'd missed him. I throw my arms around him. He stiffens for a second, then hugs me back.

"Yes, well, they must be treating you like a dog if you're glad to see me. I must say you're looking well."

"I feel well, Tom. Truly." I want so much to tell him about Mother, but I know I can't. Not yet. "Have you heard from Grandmother? How's Father?"

Tom's smile slips. "Oh, yes. They're doing well."

"Will he come for Assembly Day? I can't wait to see him again, and introduce him to all my friends here."

"Well, I wouldn't get my hopes up yet, Gemma. He might not be able to get away just now." Tom adjusts his cuffs. It's a nervous habit. Something I've begun to realise he does only when he lies.

"I see," I say quietly.

There's a knock at the door and Ann pushes through, eyes wide. She's shocked that I'm in the parlour alone with a man. She covers her eyes with her hand to block her view of us. "Oh, I'm terribly sorry. I only wanted to let Gemma, Miss Doyle, know that we're ready to practice our waltzing."

"I can't just now. I have a visitor."

Tom stands, relieved. "Don't neglect your waltzing on my account. I say, are you all right?" He's squinting at Ann, who is still averting her eyes.

"Oh, for heaven's sakes," I mutter under my breath. I make the necessary introductions. "Miss Ann Bradshaw, may I present Mr Thomas Doyle? My *brother*. I'll just show him out and then we can get to our infernal waltzing."

"That was your brother?" Ann asks shyly while I'm gliding her around the ballroom.

"Yes. The beast himself." I'm still a bit ruffled by the news about Father. I'd hoped by now he'd be on the mend.

"He seems very kind." Ann steps on both my feet and I wince in pain.

"Tom? Ha! He never opens his mouth except to put on airs. He's insufferably impressed with himself. Pity the girl who gets him."

"Still, I think he seems very nice. A true gentleman."

God in heaven. She likes my brother. It's so laughable that it's somewhere beyond comedy and right into tragedy again.

"Is he . . . engaged to anyone?"

"No. No one seems to measure up to his first love."

Ann's face falls. She stops without warning and I twist uncomfortably before springing back to her side. "Oh?"

"Himself."

It takes her a minute to get the joke, but then she laughs and blushes some more. I haven't the heart to tell her that Tom's looking for a rich wife, probably a pretty one, too, and that she will never be able to compete. If only he could see and hear her as she is in the realms. It's infuriating that the things we can do there – all that power – must remain there for the time being.

"I cannot dance another step with you or I shall be bruised for a week."

"You're the one who can't remember the rhythm," Ann chides, following me into the hall.

"And you can't remember that my feet and the floor are not one and the same."

Ann starts to retort, but we're interrupted by the sight of Felicity barrelling down the hall. She waves a sheet of paper over her head.

"He's coming! He's coming!"

"Who's coming?" I say.

She grabs our hands and twirls us around in a circle. "My father! I've just had a note. He's coming for Assembly Day! Oh, isn't it marvellous?" She stops. "Gracious, I've got to get ready. I've got to prepare. Well, come on – don't just stand here! If I don't learn how to waltz like a proper lady by Sunday, I'm doomed!"

※

Paradise has turned sour. Mother and I are fighting.

"But why can't we take the magic out of the realms where it could do some real good?"

"I've told you – it isn't safe yet. Once you do that, once you bring magic back through the portal, it's fully open. Anyone who knows how could get in." She pauses, tries to get herself under control. I remember these fights now – the ones that used to make me hate her.

I pull up a clump of berries, twirl them in my hands. "You could help me do it. Then I'd be safe."

Mother takes the berries away. "No, I can't. I can't go back, Gemma."

"You don't want to help Father." It's a hurtful thing to say, and I know it.

She takes a deep breath. "That's unfair."

"You don't trust me. You don't think I'm capable!"

"Oh, for heaven's sake, Gemma." Her eyes flash. "Just yesterday you weren't able to tell the difference between a cloud and an illusion. The dark spirit under Circe's control is much more cunning than that. How do you propose to banish it?"

"Why can't *you* tell me how?" I snap.

"Because I don't know! There is no hard rule, do you understand? It's a matter of knowing the spirit in question, knowing its vulnerability. It's a matter of not allowing it to use your weaknesses against you."

"What if I just used a bit of magic, just enough to help Father and my friends with it – nothing else?"

She takes me by the shoulders like a child. "Gemma, you must listen to me. Do not take the magic out of the realms. Promise me."

"Yes, fine!" I say, tearing out of her grasp. I can't believe we're fighting again. My eyes are hot with tears. "I'm sorry. Assembly Day is tomorrow. I need sleep."

She nods. "See you tomorrow?"

I'm too angry to answer her. I march off to join my friends. Felicity is poised on the crest of the hill, pulling back on her bow. She looks like the bas-relief of a goddess. With a sharp snap, she lets it fly and it splits a piece of wood cleanly in two. The huntress commends her, and the two of them huddle together in conference. I can't help wondering what it is they talk about on their hunts or why Felicity tells me less and less. Perhaps I've been too engrossed in my own questions to ask any of her.

Pippa is lying in the hammock while her knight regales her with some tale of chivalrous deeds done on her behalf. He gazes at her as if she's the only girl in the world. And she drinks it in like ambrosia. Ann is busy singing, gazing into the river, where she has assembled a make-believe audience of hundreds who clap and sigh and adore her. I'm the only one chafing here, feeling discontented and powerless. The thrill of our adventures has begun to wear off. What good is it to have this supposed power if I can't use it?

Pippa finally strides over, twirling a rose in her hands. "I wish I could stay here forever."

"Well, you can't," I tell her.

"Why not?" Ann asks, coming up behind me. Her hair is loose and wavy across her shoulders.

"Because this is not a place to stay," I answer, defensively. "It's a place of dreams."

"What if I choose the dream instead?" Pippa says. It's such a Pippa thing to say – foolish and taunting.

"What if I refuse to bring you here the next time?"

Felicity has managed to pierce a small rabbit. It hangs limp and lifeless from her arrow. "What is the matter?"

Pippa pouts. "It's Gemma. She doesn't want to bring us back."

Felicity is still holding the bloody arrow in one hand. "What's all this, Gemma?" Her face is grim and determined and I find myself breaking the staring contest by looking away.

"I didn't say that."

"Well, you implied it," Pippa sniffs.

"Can we just forget this whole silly argument?" I snap.

"Gemma." Pippa sticks her bottom lip out in an exaggerated pout. "Don't be cross."

Felicity adopts the same ridiculous face. "Gemma, please stop. It's very hard to talk with my mouth like this."

Ann is on it now. "I won't smile until Gemma does. You can't make me."

"Yes." Felicity is giggling through her bulldog face. "And everywhere people will say, 'They use to be so attractive. Pity about that lip problem.'"

I can't help it. I start to laugh. They roll on the ground with me then, the four of us screaming and making the most asinine faces imaginable till we're exhausted and it's time to go.

❧❧❧❧

The door appears, and we slip one by one through the portal. I'm the last to go. My skin is beginning to tingle with the door's breath-stopping energy when I catch sight of Mother holding the little girl's hand. Beneath the large white pinafore, the girl's dress is colourful and unusual. Not something one would see at an English girls' school. Interesting that I've never noticed it.

The two of them are looking at me, hopeful and wary. As if I can change things for them. But how can I help them when I don't even know how to help myself?

CHAPTER
TWENTY-SIX

TODAY IS ASSEMBLY DAY. MY DICTIONARY HAS NO formal entry for this occasion, but if it did, it might go something like this:

Assembly Day (*n.*) A boarding school tradition in which the family of the schoolgirl is allowed a visit, resulting in the mortification of all and the enjoyment of none.

I've coiffed my hair, buttoned, laced, and pinned myself into ladylike perfection – or as close as I can get to it. But inside, I'm still reeling from my visit with Mother and our argument. I behaved terribly. Tonight I'll go to her and apologise, feel her warm arms around me again.

Still, I wish I could tell my family – Father especially – that I've seen Mother. That somewhere beyond here in another world, she is alive and loving and beautiful as we all remember her to be. I have no idea what I'll find when I go downstairs, and I'm torn up with hoping and wishing. Father might walk in, looking well fed and well groomed in his fine black suit. He might hold out a gift for me, something wrapped in gold paper. He might call me his jewel, might even get sour-faced Brigid to laugh at his tales, might hold me close. *He might. He might. Might. Is there any opiate more powerful than that word?*

"Perhaps I could come along with you," Ann says as I try to tame my hair for the hundredth time. It doesn't want to stay neatly coiled atop my head as a lady's should.

"You'd be dreadfully bored within five minutes," I say, pinching roses into my cheeks that flare and fade straightaway. I don't want Ann along when I'm not sure of what I'll find.

"Will your brother be coming today?" Ann asks.

"Yes, God help us all," I mutter. I don't want to encourage Ann where Tom is concerned. Two springy curls flop down low on my forehead. I've got to do something with this hair.

"At least you have a brother to annoy you."

In the washstand mirror, I catch a glimpse of Ann sitting forlornly on her bed, dressed in her best with nowhere to go, no one to see. I'm going on and on about the trials of seeing my family, while she'll spend the entire day alone. Assembly Day must be excruciating for her.

"All right," I sigh. "If you're up for the torture, you can come along."

She doesn't say thank you. We both know it's a mission of mercy, but for which one of us, I can't say yet. I take in the sight of her. White dress straining at the seams over her chubby body. Wisps of lank hair already escaping from her chignon, hanging in her watery eyes. She's not the beauty I saw last night in the garden.

"Let's do something with that hair of yours."

She tries to see around me in the mirror. "What's wrong with my hair?"

"Nothing a good brushing and several pins can't cure. Hold still."

I take down her hair. The brush yanks through a knotty snarl at the base of her scalp. "Ouch!"

"The price of beauty," I say by way of apologising without really apologising. After all, she said she wanted to come along.

"The price of baldness, you mean."

"If you'd hold still, this wouldn't be so difficult."

She's suddenly so still she could be mistaken for a stone. Pain is underrated as a tool of motivation. I put what seems like a thousand pins in to hold her hair in place. It's not half bad. At least it's an improvement, and I'm feeling a little impressed with myself, actually. Ann positions herself in front of the mirror.

"What do you think?" I ask.

She turns her head left and right. "I liked it the other way."

"There's gratitude for you. You're not going to be this sullen all day, are you? Because if you are—"

Felicity pushes open the door and leans provocatively against the frame, playing the coquette. "*Bonjour, mesdemoiselles.* 'Tis I, the Queen of Sheba. You may save your genuflecting for later." The laces of her corset have been cinched so tight that her breasts are pushed forward noticeably. "What do you think, darlings? Am I not irresistible?"

"Beautiful," I answer. When Ann hesitates, I nudge her foot with mine.

"Yes, beautiful," she echoes.

Felicity smiles as if she's only just discovering the world. "He's coming. I can't wait for him to see what a lady I've become these past two years. Can you believe it's been two long years since I last saw my father?" She twirls around the room. "Of course, you must meet him. He'll adore you all, I'm sure of it. I want him to see that I'm getting on well here. Does either of you have any scent?"

Ann and I shake our heads.

"No perfume at all? I can't go without smelling lovely!" Felicity's mood is dropping fast.

"Here," I say, pulling a rose from a vase on the window-sill. The petals crush easily, leaving a sweet, sticky juice on my fingers. I dab it behind Felicity's ears and onto her wrists.

She brings her wrist to her nose and inhales. "Perfect! Gemma, you are a genius!" She throws her arms around me, gives me a little kiss. It's a bit disconcerting, this side of Felicity, like having a pet shark that thinks itself a goldfish.

"Where's Pip?" Ann asks.

"Downstairs. Her parents came with Mr Bumble. Can you imagine? Let's hope she sends him packing today. Well," Felicity says, breaking away. "*Adieu, les filles.* I shall see you anon." With a low bow, she is gone in a haze of roses and hope.

"Come on, then," I say to Ann, wiping the last traces of flower from my fingers. "Let's get this over with, shall we?"

~~~~~~~~

The front parlour is crowded with girls and their various family members when we arrive downstairs. I've seen better organisation on India's infamous trains. My family is nowhere to be seen.

Pippa comes over to us, head bowed. A woman in a ludicrous hat complete with feathers trails behind her. She is outfitted in a dress better suited for a younger woman and for evening wear at that. A fur stole hangs from her shoulders. There are two men with her. I recognise the bushy-whiskered Mr Bumble straightaway. The other I take to be Pippa's father. He has her dark colouring.

"Mother, Father, may I present Miss Gemma Doyle and Miss Ann Bradshaw?" she says, her voice almost a whisper.

"How do you do? It's so charming to meet Pippa's little friends." Pip's mother is as beautiful as her daughter, but her face is harder, a fact she's tried to hide with plenty of jewels.

Ann and I make our polite hellos. After a silence, Mr Bumble clears his throat.

Mrs Cross's mouth is a tight line of a smile. "Pippa, aren't you forgetting someone?"

Pippa swallows hard. "May I also present Mr Bartleby Bumble, Esquire?" The next part comes out like a quiet cry. "My fiancé."

Ann and I are too astonished to speak.

"A pleasure to make your acquaintances." He looks down

his nose at us. "I do hope they serve tea soon," he says, glancing at his pocket watch with impatience.

This rude old man with the fat face is going to be lovely Pippa's husband? Pippa, whose every waking moment is consumed by thoughts of a pure, undying, romantic love, has been sold to the highest bidder, a man she does not know, does not care about. She stares at the Persian carpet as if it might open up and swallow her down whole, save her.

Ann and I extend our hands and make our subdued greetings.

"It's good to see that my fiancée is acquainted with the right sort of girls," Mr Bumble sniffs. "There's so much that can taint the young and impressionable. Wouldn't you agree, Mrs Cross?"

"Oh, absolutely, Mr Bumble."

He deserves to have his head on a spike for all to see. Warning: If you are insufferable, do not walk here. We shall eat you down to the marrow.

"Oh, there is Mrs Nightwing. She will need to know our news. She might even want to announce it today." Mrs Cross swans across the room with her husband in tow. Mr Bumble smiles at the back of Pippa's head as if she were the biggest prize on display at this carnival.

"Shall we?" he says, offering his arm.

"May I have a moment with my friends, please? To share my news?" Pippa asks in a sad, quiet way. The idiot thinks he's being flattered.

"Of course, my dear. But don't be too long about it."

When he's gone, I reach out for Pippa's hands. "Please don't," she says. Tears pool in her violet eyes. I can't think of anything to say.

"He seems quite distinguished," Ann offers after a moment of silence.

Pippa gives a short, sharp laugh. "Yes. Nothing like a wealthy barrister to wipe away Father's gambling debts and save us from ruin. I'm nothing more than a marker, really." She doesn't say it bitterly. That's what hurts. She's accepted her fate without fighting it.

Behind her, Bartleby Bumble, Esquire, is anxiously waiting for his future bride. "I've got to go," Pippa says with all the enthusiasm of a woman meeting her executioner.

"Her ring is lovely," Ann says, after a moment. Above the crowd, we can hear Mrs Nightwing offering her loud congratulations and others chiming in.

"Yes. Very lovely," I agree. We're both trying to put a good face on it. Neither of us wants to admit the enraging hopelessness of the situation – or the guilt at not having drawn that short straw ourselves. Not yet, at least. I can only hope that when my time comes, I'm not foisted off on the first man who dazzles my family.

Felicity breezes by. She's got a handkerchief in her hand that she's twisting into a messy lump.

"What is the matter? You look as if the world has ended."

"Pippa is engaged to Mr Bumble," I explain.

"What? Oh, poor Pip," she says, shaking her head.

"Has your father come?" I ask, hoping for happier news.

"Not yet. Forgive me, but I'm far too nervous to wait

around here. I'm going to stay out in the garden till he comes. Are you certain I look presentable?"

"For the last time, yes," I say, rolling my eyes.

Felicity is so anxious she doesn't come back with a snappy reply. Instead, she nods gratefully and, looking as if she might be unable to hold her breakfast a moment longer, dashes off towards the lawn.

⁂

"Well, if it isn't the lady Doyle."

With a great flourish and an exaggerated bow, Tom announces his arrival. Grandmama is beside him in her best black crepe mourning clothes.

"Is Father here? Did he come?" I'm nervously craning my neck, searching for him.

"Yes," Tom starts. "Gemma . . ."

"Well, where is he?"

"Hello, Gemma."

At first I don't see Father. But there he is, hidden away behind Tom, a ghost in his ill-fitting black suit. There are deep circles under his eyes. Grandmama takes his arm in an effort to hide how badly he shakes. I'm sure she's given him only a touch of his usual dose to get him through, with a promise of more after. It's all I can do not to cry.

I'm ashamed for my friends to see him this way.

And I'm ashamed of being ashamed.

"Hello, Father," I manage, kissing his hollow cheeks.

"Did anyone know we'd be seeing a queen today?" he

jokes. The laugh makes him cough hard and Tom has to hold him steady. I can't look at Ann.

"They're serving tea in the ballroom," I say, steering them upstairs to a quiet, out-of-the-way table, away from the crowd and the gossips. Once we're seated, I introduce Ann.

"Charming to see you again, Miss Bradshaw," Tom says. Ann blushes.

"And where is your family today?" my grandmother asks, looking around for someone more interesting to talk to than the two of us. She would have to ask that question, and it will have to be answered, and then we'll all sit in awkward silence or my grandmother will say something unkind under the guise of being kind.

"They're abroad," I lie.

Happily, Ann doesn't try to correct me. I think she's grateful not to have to explain that she's an orphan and endure everyone's polite, silent pity. Sudden interest overtakes my grandmother, who, I'm sure, is wondering at this very moment whether Ann's relatives are rich or titled or both.

"How very exciting. Where are they travelling?"

"Switzerland," I say, just as Ann barks out, "Austria."

"Austria and Switzerland," I say. "It's an extensive trip."

"Austria," my father starts. "There's a rather funny joke about Austrians . . ." He trails off, his fingers shaking.

"Yes, Father?"

"Hmmm?"

"You were saying something about the Austrians," I remind him.

He knits his brows together. "Was I?"

There's a lump in my throat that will not go away. I offer the sugar bowl to Tom. Ann is watching his every move with fascination, though he's hardly noticed her.

"So," Tom says, dropping three lumps of sugar into his tea. "Miss Bradshaw, has my sister driven you out of your wits yet with her forthright manner?"

Ann blushes. "She's a most genial girl."

"Genial? We are speaking of the same Gemma Doyle? Grandmama, it seems Spence is more than a school. It's a house of miracles."

Everyone has a polite laugh at my expense, and truly, I don't mind. It's so nice to hear them laugh, I wouldn't care if they poked fun at me all afternoon. Father fumbles with his spoon as if he's not quite sure what to do with it.

"Father," I say gently. "Could I pour you some tea?"

He gives me a weak smile. "Yes, thank you, Virginia."

Virginia. At my mother's name, an embarrassed quiet descends. Tom stirs his tea around and around, chasing it with his spoon.

"It's me, Father. It's Gemma," I say quietly.

He squints, turns his head to one side, studying me. Slowly he nods. "Oh, yes. So it is." He goes back to playing with his spoon.

My heart's a stone, sinking fast. We make polite conversation. Grandmama tells us of her garden and her visiting and all about who is not speaking to whom these days. Tom prattles on about his studies while Ann hangs on his every word as if he were a god. Father is lost to himself. No one asks how I am or what I am doing. They could not care less. We're all looking glasses, we girls, existing only to reflect their images back to them as they'd like to be seen. Hollow vessels of girls to be rinsed of our own ambitions, wants, and opinions, just waiting to be filled with the cool, tepid water of gracious compliance.

A fissure forms in the vessel. I'm cracking open. "Is there any news about Mother? Have the police found anything new?"

Tom sputters. "Ho-ho! At it again, are we? Miss Bradshaw, you'll have to excuse my sister. She has a keen sense of the dramatic. Our mother died of cholera."

"She knows. I told her," I say, watching for their reactions.

"I'm sorry that my sister has had such a poor joke at your expense, Miss Bradshaw." His words to me through gritted teeth are a warning. "Gemma, you know that cholera took poor Mother."

"Yes, her cholera. Amazing that her cholera didn't kill us all. Or perhaps it is. Perhaps it's coiled in our blood, suffocating us all slowly with its poison each day," I spit back with an equally venomous smile.

"I think we'd best change the topic. Miss Bradshaw certainly does not need to be subjected to such histrionics." Grandmama dismisses me with a sip of her tea.

"I think my poor mother is an excellent topic of conversation. What do you think, Father?"

Come on, Father. Stop me. Tell me to behave, to go to hell, something, anything. Let's see some of that old fighting spirit. There's nothing but the syrupy whistle of wet air going in and out of his slack mouth. He's not listening. He's lost in his own reflection, the one staring back at him, bloated and distorted, in the shiny hollow of the teaspoon he's twirling between skeletal fingers.

I can't stand the sight of them huddled together against the truth, deaf and dumb to anything remotely real. "Thank you for coming. As you can see, I'm getting along quite well here. You've done your duty, and now you're free to go back to whatever it is you all do."

Tom laughs. "Well, that's a fine thank-you. I'm missing a cricket match for this. Weren't they supposed to civilise you here?"

"You're being childish and rude, Gemma. And in front of your guest. Miss Bradshaw, please excuse my granddaughter. Would you care for more tea?" Grandmama pours it without waiting for a response. Ann stares at the cup, grateful for something to focus on. I'm embarrassing her. I'm embarrassing everyone.

I rise. "I have no desire to ruin everyone's pleasant afternoon, so I shall say goodbye. Are you coming, Ann?"

She glances shyly at Tom. "I haven't finished my tea," she says.

"Ah, at last a real lady among us." Tom applauds lightly. "Bravo, Miss Bradshaw."

She smiles into her lap. Tom offers cakes and Ann, who has never refused a morsel of food in her life, declines as a well-born, properly bred lady should, lest she seem a glutton. I've created a monster.

"As you wish," I grumble. I bend at Father's knees, take

hold of his hands, and pull him away from the table. His hands shake. Perspiration beads on his forehead. "Father, I'm going now. Why don't you walk with me?"

"Yes, all right, darling. See the grounds, eh?" He attempts a half-smile that fades into a grimace of pain. Whatever Grandmama has given him isn't enough. He'll need more soon, and then he'll be lost to us all. We take a few steps, but he stumbles and has to right himself on a chair. Everyone looks up and Tom is quickly by my side, ushering him back to the table.

"There now, Father," he says a bit too loudly, so that it can be overheard. "You know Dr. Price said you mustn't walk on that ankle yet. That polo injury must heal." Satisfied, the heads go down in the room, save for one. Cecily Temple has spotted us. With her parents in tow, she's headed to our table.

"Hello, Gemma. Ann." Ann's face is the picture of panic. Cecily sizes up the situation. "Ann, will you be singing for us later? Ann has the sweetest voice. She's the one I told you about – the scholarship student."

Ann shrinks down low in her chair.

Grandmama's confused. "I thought you said your parents were abroad. . ."

Ann's face contorts and I know she's going to cry. She bolts from the table, knocking over a chair on the way.

Cecily pretends to be embarrassed. "Oh, my, I hope I haven't said the wrong thing."

"Every time you open your mouth and speak it's the wrong thing," I snap.

Grandmama barks, "Gemma, whatever is the matter with you today? Are you ill?"

"Yes, forgive me, everyone," I say, tossing my wadded napkin onto the table in a heap. "My cholera is acting up again."

Later, there will need to be an apology – *sorry, so sorry, can't explain myself, sorry*. But for now, I'm free from the tyranny of their need masquerading as concern. Gliding through the ballroom and down the stairs, I have to put a hand to my stomach to keep from breathing too fast and fainting. Thankfully, the French doors are open to allow a breeze and I walk out onto the lawn, where a game of croquet has sprung up. Fashionable mothers in large-brimmed hats knock brightly coloured wooden balls through narrow hoops with their mallets while their husbands shake their heads and gently correct them with an arm here, an embrace there. The mothers laugh and miss again, deliberately, it would seem, so as to have their husbands stand close again.

I pass unnoticed through them, down the hill to where Felicity sits alone on a stone bench.

"I don't know about you, but I've had quite enough of this absurd show," I say, forcing a surly camaraderie into my tone that I don't feel at all. One hot tear trickles down my cheek. I wipe it away, look off at the croquet game. "Has your father come yet? Did I miss him?"

Felicity says nothing, just sits.

"Fee? What's the matter?"

She passes me the note in her hand, on a fine white card stock.

My dearest daughter,

I am sorry to tell you on such short notice but duty calls me else-where, and duty to the Crown is of the utmost importance, as I'm sure you would agree. Have a jolly day, and perhaps we shall see each other again at Christmastime.

Fondly,
Your father

I cannot think of anything to say.

"It's not even his handwriting," she says at last, her voice flat. "He couldn't even be bothered to pen his own goodbye."

Out on the lawn, some of the younger girls play happily in a circle, ducking under each other's arms, falling to the ground in fits of laughter while their mothers hover nearby, fretting over soiled dresses and hair shaken free of ribbons and bonnets. Two girls skip past us, arm in arm, reciting the poetry they've learned for today's occasion, something to show how much they've become small buds of ladies.

> *"She left the web, she left the loom,*
> *She made three paces thro' the room,*
> *She saw the water-lily bloom,*
> *She saw the helmet and the plume,*
> *She look'd down to Camelot."*

Overhead, the clouds are losing their fight to keep the sun. Patches of blue peek out from behind larger clumps of threatening grey, holding on to the sun with slipping fingertips.

> *"Out flew the web and floated wide;*
> *The mirror crack'd from side to side;*
> *'The curse is come upon me,' cried*
> *The Lady of Shalott."*

The girls throw back their carefree heads and laugh riotously at their dramatic reading. The wind has shifted to the east. A storm isn't far off. I can smell the moisture in the air, a fetid, living thing. Isolated drops fall, licking at my hands, my face, my dress. The guests squawk in surprise, turn their palms up to the sky as if questioning it, and dash for cover.

"It's starting to rain."

Felicity stares straight ahead, says nothing.

"You'll get wet," I say, jumping up, angling towards the shelter of the school. Felicity makes no move to come inside. So I go on, leave her there, even though I don't feel right about it. When I reach the door, I can still see her, sitting on the wet bench, getting drenched. She's opened up her father's note to the wet, watching it erase every pen mark on the soggy page, letting the rain wash them both clean as new skin.

CHAPTER TWENTY-SEVEN

THE EVENING IS THE MOST DISMAL YET. COLD, HARD
rain falls in sheets from the sky, letting us know that summer is over for good now. A clammy chill seeps into our
bones, makes fingers, backs, and hearts ache. Thunder rumbles closer and closer, competing with the steady drum of
the rain. The occasional flash of lightning streaks the sky,
light spreading down and out in a smoky crackle. It bounces
around the mouth of the cave.

We are all here. Wet. Cold. Silent. Miserable. Felicity sits
on the flattened boulder, braiding the same section of hair,
unbraiding, braiding it again. Every bit of her fire is gone,
washed out to wherever the rain takes things.

Pippa wraps the ends of her cape about her, paces, moaning. "He's fifty! Older than my own father! It's too horrible
to contemplate."

"At least someone wants to marry you. You're not a pa-
riah." It's Ann, taking a break from holding the palm of one
hand over the candle flame. She dips it lower and lower till

she's forced to pull back fast. But her wince lets me know she's burned herself on purpose – testing once again to make sure she can still feel something.

"Why does everyone want to own me?" Pippa mumbles. She's got her head in her hands. "Why do they all want to control my life – how I look, whom I see, what I do or don't do? Why can't they just let me alone?"

"Because you're beautiful," Ann answers, watching the fire lick at her palm. "People always think they can own beautiful things."

Pippa's laugh is bitter, tinged with tears. "Ha! Why do girls think that being beautiful will solve every problem? Being beautiful creates problems. It's a misery. I wish I were someone else."

It's a luxury of a comment – one that only pretty girls can make. Ann answers this with a sharp snort of disbelief.

"I do! I wish I were . . . I wish I were you, Ann."

Ann is so stunned, she holds her hand to the flame a second too long, pulling it back with an audible gasp. "Why on earth would you want to be me?"

"Because," Pippa sighs, "you don't have to worry about these things. You're not the sort of girl people are constantly fussing over so there's no room to breathe. No one wants you."

"Pippa!" I bark.

"What? What did I say now?" Pippa moans. She's completely unaware of her stupid cruelty.

Ann's face clouds over, her eyes narrow, but she's too beaten down by her life to say anything and Pippa is too selfish to notice. "You mean I don't stand out," Ann says flatly.

"Exactly," Pippa says, looking at me with triumph that someone in the cave understands her misfortune. A second passes and now it dawns on Pippa. "Oh. Oh, Ann, I didn't mean it like that."

Ann switches hands, puts the left one to the candle.

"Ann, darling Ann. You must forgive me. I'm not clever like you are. I don't mean half of what I say." Pip throws her arms around Ann, who can't resist having someone, anyone, pay attention to her, even a girl who sees her as just a convenience, like the right necklace or hair ribbon. "Come on, tell us a story. Let's read from Mary Dowd's diary."

"Why should we bother when we know how it all ends?" Ann says, going back to her candle. "They die in the fire."

"Well, I want to read from the diary!"

"Pippa, can't you let it alone tonight?" I sigh. "We're not in the mood."

"That's fine for you to say. You're not the one being married against your will!"

The sky rumbles while we sit in our separate corners, alone in our togetherness.

"Shall I tell you a story? A new and terrible one? A ghost story?"

The voice, a faint echo in the great cave, belongs to Felicity. She turns around on the rock, faces us, wraps her arms across bent knees, hugging them close. "Are you ready? Shall I begin? Once upon a time there were four girls. One was pretty. One was clever. One charming, and one . . ." She glances at me. "One was mysterious. But they were all damaged, you see. Something not right about the lot of them. Bad blood. Big dreams. Oh, I left that part out. Sorry, that should have come before. They were all dreamers, these girls."

"Felicity . . . ," I start, because it's her and not the story that's beginning to frighten me.

"You wanted a story, and I'm going to give you one." Lightning shoots across the cave walls, bathing half her face in light, the other in shadows. "One by one, night after night, the girls came together. And they sinned. Do you know what that sin was? No one? Pippa? Ann?"

"Felicity." Pippa sounds anxious. "Let's go back and have a nice cup of tea. It's too cold out here."

Felicity's voice expands, fills the space around us, a bell tolling. "Their sin was that they believed. Believed they could be different. Special. They believed they could change what they were – damaged, unloved. Cast-off things. They would be alive, adored, needed. Necessary. But it wasn't true. This is a ghost story, remember? A tragedy."

The lightning's back, a big one, two, three of light that lets me see Felicity's face, slick with tears, nose running. "They were misled. Betrayed by their own stupid hopes. Things couldn't be different for them, because they weren't special after all. So life took them, led them, and they went along, you see? They faded before their own eyes, till they were nothing more than living ghosts, haunting each other with what could be. What can't be." Felicity's voice goes feathery thin. "There, now. Isn't that the scariest story you've ever heard?"

The rain beats down relentlessly, mixing with the strangled sounds of Felicity's sobbing. Ann has stopped torturing her hands. Now she stares through the flame at cave walls that show her history, promise nothing. Pippa twirls her engagement ring round her finger till I fear she'll break it off.

Maybe it's the steady downpour driving me mad. Maybe it's the thought of lovely Pippa, married off to a man she doesn't love, who doesn't love her, only wants to acquire her. Maybe it's imagining Ann squelching her voice to work for pompous aristocrats and their hateful children. Or Felicity trying to hold back her tears. Maybe it's that every word she's said is true.

Whatever the reason, I'm thinking now of a way out, of bringing the magic back from the realms. I'm thinking of those mothers today in their ornate dresses and their vacant lives. And I'm thinking of my mother's warning that I'm not ready to use my full powers yet.

Oh, but I am, Mother. I am.

Outside, there's a fresh wave of thunder rumbling a warning, a prayer. All around me in the semidarkness are the symbols etched into rock with the sweat and blood of women who've gone before us. Their whispers urge me on in a single word.

Believe.

I can see the glint off Pippa's unwanted ring. Hear the

laboured struggle of Ann's mouth-breathing. Feel the desperation meeting the silence with its unasked wish.

There's got to be something better than this.

My voice rises to the unseen top of the cave, a bird taking flight.

"There is a way to change things. . ."

CHAPTER
TWENTY-EIGHT

"ARE YOU SURE YOU KNOW HOW TO USE THESE RUNES?"
Ann asks as we place the candles in the centre of our circle.

"Of course she does! Stop trying to frighten her," Pippa
snaps. "You do know, don't you?"

"No. But Mary and Sarah did it. It can't be that difficult.
Mother said I simply place my hands against the runes
and . . . and then . . ." Then what? The magic enters me. It's
precious little to go on.

Felicity is beside me. She's stopped crying.

"We'll just try it and see. That's all. Just a trial run," I say, as
if to convince myself.

※※※

We enter the realms through our door of light and make
our way to the grotto as quickly as possible. The runes rise
before us, tall and imposing. They're guards protecting the
sky's secrets.

"I didn't see anyone," Felicity pants.

"Then I don't think anyone saw us," Pippa says.

Promise me you won't take the magic out of the realms, Gemma...

I've promised her. And yet I can't abandon my friends to these empty lives.

It's been such a long time since the magic here has been used. There's no telling what could happen.

That doesn't mean something terrible *will* happen. Perhaps Mother is worrying about nothing. We'll be so very careful. Nothing will find its way in.

The huntress appears. "What are you doing?"

Pippa yelps in surprise.

"Nothing," I say, too quickly.

She's silent, watching us. "Will you hunt today?" she asks Felicity at last.

"Not today. Tomorrow," Felicity answers.

"Tomorrow," the huntress repeats. She turns and walks towards the silver arch, glancing back once with a curious expression. And then she's gone.

"That was a close call," Ann says, letting her breath out.

"Yes. I think we'd best act quickly," I say.

"What do you think will happen to us?" Pippa's voice is filled with apprehension.

"There's only one way to find out," I say, moving closer to the runes. I can feel their energy calling me. I'll touch them only for a second or two, no more. What can possibly happen in an instant?

The girls place their hands on me. We're connected, like

some newfangled apparatus that gives off electric light. Slowly, I place my palms against the warm strength of the crystalline shapes. They hum against my skin. The hum bends into a shudder. It's more powerful than I could have dreamed. They glow, faintly at first, then more strongly, the light spreading quickly into a swirling pillar that spins out, around and through me. I can sense my friends within me – the quick pulse of blood in their veins. The rhythm of our hearts beating in unison, like the thundering of horses trampling across winter-bleached fields, hope thumping freedom inside us. A locomotive scream of thoughts flies by. Different voices, different languages overlap, merging into one flickering murmur. It's too fast. I can't absorb it. It could break me. I need to tear away but I can't.

And then the world falls away.

The vast night sky wraps us in its blanket. We're standing at the top of a mountain. Clouds rush overhead at impossible speed, coiling and uncoiling. The strong wind is a roar as it whips our hair out behind us. And yet there's no fear. Nothing about me feels the same. Every cell in my body is acutely aware, every sense heightened. We don't need to speak. We can each sense what the others are feeling.

I'm suddenly aware of Felicity's face; the grey of her eyes looms larger. The black heart in the centre of her gaze moves and swirls till I'm drawn inside, where I'm floating over an open sea, icebergs poking through the waves, the cry of whales nearby. Like liquid, I'm poured into that sea, swallowed whole, and then I fall through the bottom of it into a London twilight. Below me is the Thames, dappled with street light. I'm flying. I'm flying! We all are, rising so high that the chimneys and rooftops are no more significant than coins thrown into a gutter. *Close your eyes; close your eyes, Gemma.* I'm awake in a desert under a full moon. Dunes rise and fall like breath. My foot sinks in. I'm melting into the warm brown sand. Under my touch, the fine sandy grit changes into the softness of skin. His body rolls out underneath me like a plain. Kartik feels like a country I want to travel – vast, dangerous, and unknown. When we kiss, I'm falling again, back onto that mountaintop where Felicity, Pippa, and Ann are standing, back from their own journeys, and yet it feels as if we've never left this place. We smile at each other. Our fingertips graze; our hands clasp. There is a searing white light. And then nothing.

~~~~~~

"Gemma, wake up." Ann gives me a little shake. My room comes into focus by degrees – the ceiling, the grey light at the window, the worn wooden floor. Vague recollections of last night come to me – the realms, the runes, the huntress's strange expression, the four of us stumbling home from the caves afterwards – but it's mostly a fog in my head. I've lost all sense of time and direction.

"What time is it?" I mumble.

"Time for breakfast."

It can't be, I think, rubbing my head.

"Well, it is," she answers.

That's odd. "How did you know what I was thinking?" I ask.

"I don't know," she says, wide-eyed. "I heard it in my head."

"The magic . . . ," I say, sitting straight up.

Felicity and Pippa burst into the room.

"Look at my dress," Pippa says, beaming. There's a large grass stain on the hem.

"Bad luck, Pip," I say.

She's still smiling like an idiot. She closes her eyes and in seconds the stain is gone.

"You made it disappear," Ann says in wonder.

Pippa's smile shines. She twirls her skirt this way and that, letting it catch the light.

"So we've done it," I say. "We've taken the magic out of the realms." *And everything is fine.*

⊰⊰⊰⊰

I am dressed in record-setting time. We trip down the hall and the stairs like a breeze, whispering to each other in half-spoken sentences that somehow are finished inside our heads. We're so alive with our discovery that we can't stop giggling.

A figurine of a little cupid sits inside an alcove under the stairs.

"I want to have a bit of fun," Pippa says, pulling us to a stop. She closes her eyes, waves her hands over the cherubic plaster boy, and then he's sporting rather large breasts.

"Oh, that's awful, Pip!" Felicity says. We dissolve in laughter.

"Think of the redecorating possibilities!" Pippa says, in hysterics.

Brigid is bustling down the hall towards us.

"Great heavens, fix it quick!" I whisper.

We're falling all over ourselves trying to hide the thing.

"I can't do it under pressure!" Pippa says in a panic.

"Here now, wot's all this fuss about?" Brigid puts her hands on her hips. "Wot you got there? Move aside and lemme see."

Reluctantly, we obey.

"Wot on earth is this?" Brigid holds up a statuette of the world's ugliest cancan dancer, formerly a cupid with breasts.

"It's the latest from Paris," Felicity says coolly.

Brigid puts it back in the alcove. "Belongs on the rubbish heap, if you ask me."

She moves on and we're all giggles again.

"It was the best I could manage," Pippa says. "Under the circumstances."

❧❧❧❧

Every head turns when we arrive for breakfast and take our places at the long table. Cecily can't stop staring at Ann.

"Ann, is that a new dress?" she asks between bites of her bacon. We've come late so there's only porridge.

"No," Ann answers.

"Did you change your hair, then?"

Ann shakes her head.

"Well, it's an improvement, whatever it is." This makes the rest of the girls titter. Cecily goes right back to her bacon.

Felicity puts her spoon down hard. "You're very rude, Cecily. Did you know that? I think it would be best if you just didn't say anything else today."

Cecily opens her mouth to reprimand Felicity, but no words come. She can barely speak above a whisper. Her hands fly to her throat.

"Cecily, what's the matter?" Elizabeth hands her some water.

"Cat's got her tongue," Felicity says, smirking.

"Fee, you have to give Cecily her voice back at some point," Pippa chides as we make our way to French.

Felicity nods. "I know. But you must admit – it is an improvement."

※※※※

Mademoiselle LeFarge has a particularly sadistic smile on her face when we arrive. It doesn't bode well.

"*Bonjour, mes filles.* Today we will have a conversation to test your French."

A conversation class. I am the absolute worst at this, and I wonder how long I can make myself unnoticeable.

Elizabeth raises a hand. "Mademoiselle, our Cecily has lost her voice."

"Has she? That was very sudden, Mademoiselle Temple."

Cecily tries again to speak but it's useless. Ann gives her a small smile and Cecily looks positively terrified. She buries her nose in her book.

"Very well," Mademoiselle LeFarge says. "Mademoiselle Doyle, you shall go first."

I'm in for it now. *Please, please, please let me keep up.* My stomach is aflutter. This may be the day that Mademoiselle LeFarge gives me the boot down to the lower classes. She bats a question about the Seine into my court, waits for my response. When I open my mouth, we are all astonished. I'm speaking French like a Parisian, and I find I know a great deal about the Seine. And France's geography. Its monarchy. The Revolution. I'm feeling so clever that I want to go on for the whole of the period, but finally Mademoiselle LeFarge recovers from her shock, breaking her own rules in the process.

"That was remarkable, Mademoiselle Doyle! Truly remarkable," she gasps in English. "As you can see, ladies, when you are willing to apply yourselves, the results speak for themselves! Mademoiselle Doyle, today you shall receive thirty good-conduct marks – a record for my class!"

Someone should probably close Martha's, Cecily's, and Elizabeth's mouths before the rains come and drown them like turkeys.

~~~~~

"What do we do now?" Pippa whispers as we take our seats for Grunewald's instruction.

"I think it's Ann's turn," I say.

Ann's face falls. "M-me? I d-d-don't know. . ."

"Come on, then. Don't you want everybody to know what you can do?"

She furrows her brow. "But it won't be me, will it? It will be the magic. Like your French."

This brings a blush to my cheeks. "I did get a bit carried away. But you can truly sing, Ann. It will be you at your very best."

Ann is skeptical. She chews nervously on her lips. "I don't think I can."

We're interrupted by the arrival of the short, squat Austrian. Mr Grunewald in usually in one of two tempers – foul and fouler. Today, he surpasses himself, sliding right into foulest.

"Cease the incessant chatter!" he barks, raking a hand through his thinning white hair. One by one, we're called to the front of the class to practice the same hymn. One by one, he criticises us nearly to death. Our vowels are too flat. Our mouths are not open sufficiently. I crack on a high note and he lets out with a sharp "Ack!" as if he's being tortured. Finally, it's Ann's turn.

She's timid at first. Mr Grunewald shouts and grumbles, which doesn't help. I'm practically willing Ann to let her voice fly. *Sing, Ann. Come on!* And then, she does. It's like a bird leaving the nest, soaring high and free. We're all quiet and awed. Even Mr Grunewald has stopped counting. He stares with a look of utter joy on his face.

I'm so proud of her. How could my mother not want us to use this magic? How could she think we weren't ready for it?

When she finishes, Mr Grunewald applauds. The man whose hands have never joined together to make a clapping sound is applauding Ann. Every girl joins in. They see her differently now, as somebody. And isn't that what everyone wants? To be seen?

<center>~~~~</center>

We bask in the glory of our day until evening comes. That's when we can feel the last of the magic draining from our bodies, leaving us all a bit worn out. Mrs Nightwing appraises Pippa during our free time.

"Miss Cross, you're looking a bit tired this evening."

"I am rather tired, Mrs Nightwing." Pippa blushes. Mrs Nightwing has no idea what's going on while she sleeps off her sherry.

"Best get to bed straightaway for your beauty sleep. You want to look your best when Mr Bumble comes to call tomorrow."

"Ugh, I'd forgotten he's coming to call," Pippa laments as we trudge up to bed.

Ann stretches her arms overhead in a catlike movement. "Why couldn't you dispense with him? Just tell him you're not interested."

"That should go over very well with my mother," Pippa scoffs.

"We could go back into the realms and make you hideously ugly," Felicity says.

"I think not!"

We've reached the landing. The ceiling is smudged where the gaslights have deposited their grime. Funny how I've never noticed that before.

"All right, then. Say goodbye to Sir Perfection and become a barrister's wife," Felicity says, sneering.

Pippa's lovely face is all worry, but the frown lines smooth. There's a new determination to her brow. "I could simply tell him the truth. About my epilepsy."

The walls are sooty too. So much I haven't noticed.

"He's to come for a visit tomorrow at eleven o'clock," Pippa says.

Felicity nods. "Then let's send him packing, shall we?"

With a yawn, I pass the all-too-familiar photographs, those half-erased women. But it's a night for seeing things for the first time. In its severe black frame, one of the photographs has begun to buckle and ripple behind the glass. Probably the damp. It's sliding towards ruin. But there's something else. When I look closer I can see the smudgy outline on the wall where a fifth portrait once hung.

"That's odd," I say to Ann.

"What?" She yawns.

"Look here on the wall. See the mark. There *was* another photograph."

"So there was. What of it? Perhaps they got tired of it."

"Or perhaps it's the missing class of 1871 – Sarah and Mary," I say.

Ann drifts off to our room, stretching and yawning. "Fine. You look for it, then."

Yes, I think. *Perhaps I will at that.* I don't believe there was no photograph.

I think it was removed.

⚡⚡⚡

My sleep is fitful, filled with dreams. I see my mother's face in the clouds, soft and fair. The clouds blow apart. The sky changes. It swells into a grey beast with holes for eyes. Everything goes dark. The little girl appears. The white of her pinafore, the exotic dress underneath it, stand out in the darkness. She turns around slowly and it starts to rain. Cards. It's raining tarot cards. They catch fire as they fall.

No. I don't want this dream.

It's gone. I'm dreaming of Kartik again. A hungry dream. Our mouths are everywhere at once. The kissing is feverish and hard. His hands rip at the fabric of my nightgown, exposing the skin of my neck. His lips rake the curve there, taking small nips that almost hurt but mostly inflame. We're rolling together, a wheel of hands and tongues, fingers and lips. A pressure builds inside me till I think I might come apart from it. And when I feel I can't take another moment of it, I wake with a start. My nightgown is damp against my body. My breath is shallow. I place my hands rigidly beside me and do not move for a very long time, until at last I sleep and do not dream.

CHAPTER
TWENTY-NINE

MR BUMBLE COMES TO CALL FOR PIPPA AT ELEVEN o'clock sharp. He's well turned out in his handsome black coat, crisp shirt, and cravat, clean white spats protecting his shoes, and a brushed bowler in his hand. If I didn't know better, I'd suspect that he was a doting father come to call on his young daughter, not his future wife.

Mrs Nightwing has readied a small sitting room. She's got her knitting so that she can sit in a corner as the silent chaperone. But we've thought of this, too. Felicity is having a sudden, all-consuming attack of stomach pains. She's upstairs writhing in agony on her bed. Appendicitis is feared, and Mrs Nightwing has no choice but to rush to her bedside at once. Which leaves me to act as chaperone in the interim. And so I find myself sitting quietly with a book as a rose-coloured teacup trembles in Pippa's hands.

Mr Bumble watches her as if he's appraising a piece of land he might buy. "I take it your ring is most satisfactory?"

It's not a question but a chance to be complimented on his taste.

"Oh yes," Pippa says, distracted.

"And your family? They're well?"

"Yes, thank you."

I cough, flash Pippa an urging look. *Go ahead – get on with it.* Upon hearing my cough, Mr Bumble gives me a weak smile. I cough again and dive into my book.

"And I trust you are well?" he presses.

"Oh, yes," Pippa says. "Well, no."

Here we go.

His teacup stops mid-sip. "Oh? Nothing serious, I trust, my dear."

Pippa brings her handkerchief to her mouth as if overcome. I could swear she's worked up real tears. She's very good and I must say that I am quite impressed.

"What is it, my dear? You must unburden yourself to me, your fiancé."

"How can I when I've worked to deceive you!"

He draws back a bit, his voice suddenly cool. "Go on. How is it that you have deceived me?"

"It's my affliction, you see. I have terrible seizures that could come on at any time."

Mr Bumble stiffens. "How – how long have you had this . . . affliction?" His well-bred lips can scarcely say it.

"All my life, I'm afraid. My poor mother and father have suffered so. But as you are such an honourable man, I find that my heart will not permit me to continue this deceit."

Bravo. The stage is missing a fine actress in Pippa. She gives me a sideways glance. I smile in approval.

Mr Bumble looks exactly like a man who has bought a fine piece of china, only to bring it home and discover the crack. "I am an honourable man. One who honours his commitments. I shall speak to your parents at once."

Pippa grabs hold of his hand. "Oh, no. Please! They would never forgive me for telling you the truth. Please understand that I'm only looking out for your welfare."

She's giving him her large, pleading eyes. Her charms have the desired effect.

"You do understand that if I were to break this engagement, your reputation – your very virtue – would be called into question."

Ah, yes. Wouldn't want us if the old virtue were questionable. Heaven forbid.

"Yes," Pippa says, eyes downcast. "That is why I think it would be best for *me* to refuse *you*." She slides the ring from her finger and drops it into his palm. I wait to see if he will beg her to reconsider, if he will pledge his love in spite of her ailment. But he seems relieved, his tone imperious.

"What shall I say to your parents, then?"

"Say that I am too young and foolish to take as a wife and that you have been noble enough to allow me to end things and save my reputation. They will not press you."

Pippa has never been lovelier than she is at this moment, with her head held high, her eyes shining in triumph. For once, she's not flowing with the current but swimming against it.

"Very well, then."

Mrs Nightwing enters. "Oh, Mr Bumble, I'm sorry to have kept you waiting. One of our girls had a bit of the hysterics, but she seems to be fine now."

"It's no matter, Mrs Nightwing. I was just leaving."

"Already?" Mrs Nightwing is quite flummoxed.

"Yes. I'm afraid I have a pressing matter that needs my attention. Ladies, good day to you."

Confused but duty-bound, Mrs Nightwing sees him out.

"How was I?" Pippa asks, sinking into the chair like lead.

"Brilliant. Miss Lily Trimble herself couldn't have done better."

Pippa surveys her bare finger. "Pity about the ring, though."

"You could have waited till he asked to have it back!"

"He wouldn't have, though."

"Exactly my point!"

We're laughing when Mrs Nightwing enters, suspicious and predatory. "Pippa, is all as it was between you and Mr Bumble?"

Pippa swallows hard. "Yes, Mrs Nightwing."

"Then where, pray tell, has your ring gone to?"

We hadn't got this far in our planning – how to explain the loss of the ring to everyone. Now we're stuck, I fear. But Pippa lifts her chin, the faintest hint of a smile beginning to show.

"Oh, that. He noticed a flaw."

∼∼∼∼

We sit, sheltered by the colourful scarves of Felicity's private salon. Pippa and I are giving an account of the morning's adventure with Mr Bumble in rapid, sometimes overlapping detail.

"And then Pippa said . . ."

". . . he found a flaw!"

We laugh till no sound comes out of our mouths, till our sides ache from it.

"Oh, that's sublime," Felicity says, wiping a tear from her eye. "Let us hope that is the last we shall see of the unfortunate Mr Bumble."

"Mrs Bartleby Bumble." Pip spits out the hard Bs. "Can you imagine the horror of that?"

We laugh again and our laughter drifts down into sighs.

"Gemma, I want to go again," Felicity says when it's quiet.

Ann nods. "Me too."

"It might be pressing our luck to do it again so soon," I say.

"Do be a sport," Ann pleads.

Felicity nods. "Yes, after all, nothing terrible happened. And think of how marvellous it's been having all that power at our fingertips. Perhaps your mother was simply doing what mothers do best – worrying needlessly."

"Perhaps," I say. I must admit that I'm in love with the feeling the magic of the runes provides. One more visit to them can't hurt. And then I promise I'll stop and do as my mother says. "All right, then," I say. "The caves it is."

"Oh, honestly, I'm too tired to run off to the woods tonight," Pippa groans.

"We could do it right now. Right here," Felicity says.

Pippa's eyes widen. "Are you mad? With Mrs Nightwing and all the others around us?"

Felicity lifts a section of scarf with her finger. Crowded around the warm fire in clumps of threes and fours, the others are oblivious to us. "They'll never know we were gone."

~~~~~~

We take that ride on the mountaintop, falling into ourselves without trying to stop. I have only one rough moment. I'm a mermaid, rising from the sparkling sea, but when I look down, the water is my mother's face, tight and fearful. I'm suddenly afraid and wish I could stop. But in the next moment we're swept away to Felicity's tent. Our eyes are shining, our skin is rosy, our all-knowing smiles are back. Our bodies feel like luxurious sighs as we stand in the great hall, completely invisible.

Oh, God, the great and terrible beauty of it. Around us, the motion of the room has slowed to the lethargic tempo of a music box coming unwound. Their voices are deep and every word seems to take a lifetime to say. Mrs Nightwing sits in her chair, reading *David Copperfield* aloud to the younger girls. The temptation is too much for me. I touch her arm, ever so slightly. She doesn't stop reading, but slowly, slowly, her free hand lifts and comes to rest on the spot I've touched. She scratches at the place where my hand has been, an irritation like an insect bite she's reacted to and forgotten again. It's extraordinary.

Pippa lets out with a tiny whelp of joy. "They can't see us! It's as if we're not really here! Oh, the things I'd like to do . . ."

"Why not do them?" Felicity says, arching a brow. With

that, she reaches over and flips the book in Mrs Nightwing's hands so that it is upside down. It takes Mrs Nightwing a moment to register what has happened, but when she does, she's completely perplexed. The girls at her feet cover their mouths with their hands to suppress their giggles.

"Why is everything so slow?" I say, leaning my hand against a marble column. It wriggles beneath my hand and I pull it back fast.

The column is alive.

Hundreds of tiny marble fairies and satyrs move on the surface. An odious little gargoyle unfurls his wings, cocks his head to one side. "You see things the way they really are now," he says. "The others think this is only dreaming. But they live in the dream, not us." He spits and wipes his nose on his wing.

"Ugh," Felicity says. "Disgusting. I'm tempted to squash him."

With a screech, the gargoyle is off, flying higher on the column.

A glimmering fairy boy with yellow eyes smiles up at me. "Why don't you free us, then?" His voice is a soft murmur.

"Free you?"

"We're trapped here. Free us – just for a moment, long enough to stretch our wings."

"All right," I say. It seems a reasonable request, after all. "You are free."

With screeches and yelps, the fairies and nymphs run down the column like water till they're scurrying about the floor, scavenging bits of cheese, hunks of bread, the odd checker piece. It's madness with all these creatures running and flying about.

"Gracious!" Pippa squeals.

A satyr the size of my thumb strides to a girl seated on the rug. He peeks under the hem of her dress, lets loose with a lascivious howl.

"So sweet and plump," he growls.

"What filthy creatures," Felicity says, laughing. "The ladies of Spence are in for a very naughty treat."

"We can't let them do this," I say, half-laughing myself at their pranks. As the satyr climbs the girl's calf, I pick him up with my fingers. "Oh, no you don't," I chide merrily.

He writhes and curses in protest. In an instant, his face transforms into a demonic mask and he sinks his sharp teeth into the tender skin of my wrist. With a cry of pain, I drop him. Is it my imagination, or is he suddenly larger? Felicity gasps beside me, and now I know it's true – the beast is growing. He looms over us, his horned head touching the ceiling.

"Let's see how you taste, sweet or sour," he hisses in a deep, gravelly voice.

"What's happening?" Pippa shrieks. "Make it stop!"

"Stop, this instant!" I shout. The satyr only laughs to see us so frightened.

Pippa is pawing at me in her fright. "It isn't working! Why isn't it working?"

"I don't know!" I shout back. Using the magic is more complicated than I thought.

"I knew this was a bad idea," Pippa chides. Wasn't she the one begging to do it only moments earlier?

"We've got to get them back on the columns," Felicity screeches.

A gargoyle hops onto my leg. In one quick motion, I grab him by the wings and rush to the fireplace, where I hold the naughty beast over the fire. He screams in terror.

"Tell me how to undo it." He curses at me, and I lower him just a bit, till the flames lick at his legs. "Tell me or I shall drop you in!"

The gargoyle calls out to his friends for help, but the satyr only laughs. "Proceed. What's one less gargoyle in the world? It should prove most amusing."

I lower the creature another inch. "Tell me!"

He screams. "Yes, yes! I shall tell you! Repeat after me: *For your lies in marble shall you lie . . .*"

A bare-breasted nymph hops onto the mantel. "You bastard! Don't tell her any more!"

"*For a thousand years and never die . . .*"

The nymph tries to swipe at him, misses and falls into the fire, which accepts her with a crackle and hiss.

Wide-eyed, the gargoyle yells, "That's it. That's the phrase!"

"Go on, then! Say it!" Felicity shouts. The satyr has them cornered.

Dry-mouthed, I start. "For your lies in marble shall you lie . . ."

The most hideous screeches fill the room. The beasties like their freedom. My heart is beating as fast as their wings, and the next part comes out in a rush. "For a thousand years and never die!"

Inches from me, the satyr shrinks till he's no more than thimble-sized again. Fairies, nymphs, gargoyles, and satyrs whoosh past us, flying backwards through the air, till they stick fast to the columns, shrieking the entire way. They spit and curse us. Slowly, the marble freezes them into silence, their angry faces and open mouths the only testament to what has just happened.

I'm shaking and sweat-drenched. We all look a fright.

Pippa shudders. "I never did like this room. Now I know why."

"I think I've had enough magic for one night," Felicity says, wiping her brow with the back of her hand.

Only Ann disagrees. She lingers near Cecily and Elizabeth. "One last bit of fun."

"What are you going to do?" Pippa asks.

Ann smiles. "Nothing they don't deserve."

CHAPTER
THIRTY

"SHOULD BE RIGHT . . . ABOUT . . . NOW," FELICITY SAYS, opening the curtain of scarves just in time for us to hear Cecily's and Elizabeth's ear-piercing screams, followed by Mrs Nightwing's screeching, "Merciful heavens!"

They're completely naked, their clothes strewn about the room – a stocking thrown across an ottoman, a chemise wadded upon the floor. When they realise their state, the two of them squeal and try to cover themselves with their arms. Cecily actually attempts to use Elizabeth as a human shield, while Elizabeth cries and pulls Cecily's hair.

"What is the meaning of this!" Mrs Nightwing booms. The room erupts in shocked giggles, gasps, and a round of pointing. Finally, Miss Moore covers their nakedness with a blanket, and Mrs Nightwing pulls them into the hall, where we can hear her voice rising into a tone that's nearly operatic.

"Now, that was brilliant," Felicity says, sniggering. Ann beams. Her revenge has been sweet indeed. I've got that twisted feeling inside that comes from enjoying something I know I'll regret later. I try not to think about it. My gaze falls on Miss Moore. It's probably my guilty conscience coming to call, but the penetrating way she looks at me, I could almost swear she knows what we've done.

Something Pippa has just said starts a fresh round of hysterics. I've missed it. I've been watching Miss Moore stride towards us.

"Have we been set upon by hyenas?" she asks, poking her head inside the tent.

We try to compose ourselves.

"Forgive us, Miss Moore. We shouldn't laugh. That display was most shocking," Felicity says, struggling to keep the giggle out of her voice.

"Yes. Shocking. And very strange," Miss Moore says. Her gaze falls on me again. I stare at the floor. "May I come in?"

"Yes, please do," Pippa answers, making room inside.

"I've never been inside the inner sanctum before, Felicity. It's quite nice."

"I know another place that's far lovelier," Felicity answers. I flash her a warning glance.

"Really? Any place I might've been?"

"Oh, I don't think so. It's a secret place. A sort of private paradise." Felicity smiles dreamily.

"Best not tell me, then. I don't know if I could be trusted in paradise."

She gives an almost girlish laugh. I try to imagine what Miss Moore must have been like as a girl. Was she obedient?

Cruel? Rebellious? Shy? Did she have a good friend and a secret place where she found a retreat from the world? Was she ever like us?

"What is this you're reading?" The diary is sitting out in plain view. Ann goes to snatch it but Miss Moore is quicker. My heart is in my throat as Miss Moore turns the diary over in her hands, examining it.

Felicity is quick. "It's just some silly romance. We found it in the library. After your suggestion."

"Was this my suggestion?"

"Going to the library, I mean."

Miss Moore opens the book. We don't dare look at each other.

"'The Secret Diary of Mary Dowd.' My . . ." A page falls to the floor. "What's this?"

Dear God! The illustration! Felicity and I nearly knock each other down in our mad rush to reach the forbidden image before she does.

"Nothing," Felicity says. "Just some doodling."

"I see." Miss Moore turns a page and then another.

"We take turns reading it aloud," Ann offers. We're squirming in our seats.

Miss Moore's eyes never leave the pages as she says, "Perhaps tonight I shall join you. Would you indulge me?"

It's not as if we can say no.

"Of course," Felicity croaks. "I'll show you where we left off. We're almost to the end, I believe."

Miss Moore's eyes scan the page in her hands. The waiting is interminable. I'm sure she's going to march us off to Mrs

Nightwing at any moment. But at last, her deep, warm voice fills the tent.

"April 6, 1871

"*What we have done cannot be undone. Tonight, I went into the woods with Sarah. Night bloomed, and the moon grew fat in the sky. It wasn't long before Mother Elena's child, Carolina, came tripping along to us. We had promised her a dolly.*

"'*Have you brought my dolly back?'*

"'*Yes,' Sarah told her. 'She's clean and new and waiting for you just beyond these trees. Come, Carolina, and we'll take you to her.'*

"*It was a most egregious lie and one that hid the dreadful purpose of our hearts.*

"*But the child believed us. She took our hands and wandered off happily with us, singing a bit of an old tune.*

"*When we reached the school, she asked, 'Where is my dolly?'*"

"'*Inside,' I said, my heart turning to stone.*

"*But the child was afraid and refused to go.*

"'*Your pretty dolly is missing you. And we've got lovely toffees, besides,' Sarah said.*

"'*And I shall let you wear my pretty white pinafore,' I said, lacing her arms through and tightening the ribbons at the back. 'My, how pretty you look.' This cheered her considerably and she followed us into the cupola of the East Wing, where we set our candles to burning.*"

Miss Moore pauses. The room falls silent. This is it. All that's left is for her to snap the book shut and throw it on the fire. But she has only stopped to clear her throat, and in a few seconds, she starts anew.

"'Where is my dolly?' the child whimpered, and Sarah threw the old rag doll to her. It wasn't what she expected and she cried.

"'Shhh, shhh,' I said, trying to comfort her.

"'Leave her,' Sarah snapped. 'And let's to our purpose, Mary.'

"There is a time in every life when paths are chosen, character is forged. I could have chosen a different path. But I didn't. I failed myself. While I held the child down, my hand covering her mouth to silence those cries, Sarah called the beast from its hiding place in the dark heart of the Winterlands. 'Come to us,' she cried, her arms lifted high. 'Come and grant me the power that should be mine.'

"And then, such a fearful thing. We were pulled into a vision then, into that twilight world between this one and the next. A great black void approached, taking shape into the beast. Oh, I would have run then if I'd only had legs to do so. The cries of the damned near to stilled my heart. But Sarah smiled, lost to the pull of it. The child struggled hard against me, terrified as she was, and I pressed my hand more firmly against her small face, trying to shush her, to block out my own fear. Then slowly I raised my hand and covered the small nose there as well. She knew what I intended then and she fought me. But it was her life for ours, or so I saw it. I held fast to the child till her struggling ceased and she lay still on the floor of the East Wing, her eyes wide open, dead to the world. A terrible realisation came over me at what I had done.

"The creature shrieked in anger. 'I needed her whole! Your sacrifice is worthless to me now.'

"'But you promised . . . ,' I whispered.

"Sarah's eyes blazed. 'Mary, you have ruined everything! You never wanted me to have the power, to be my sister! I should have known.'

"'I will have payment,' the creature cried, grabbing fast to Sarah's arm. She screamed and then I did find my legs, oh, diary, found them and ran as the wind to Eugenia, told her all as she grabbed her robe and candle. When we returned, the child lay there, a reminder of my sin, but Sarah was gone.

"Eugenia's mouth tightened. 'We must hie to the Winterlands.'

"We found ourselves in that land of ice and fire, of thick, barren trees and perpetual night. The creature had begun its work, Sarah's eyes turning black as stones. Eugenia stood tall.

"'Sarah Rees-Toome, you will not be lost to the Winterlands. Come back with me. Come back.'

"The creature turned on her. 'She has invited me. She must pay, or the balance of the realms is forfeit.'

"'I shall go in her place.'

"'No!' I shouted, even as the creature's mouth twisted from surprise into a hideous grin.

"'So be it. There is much we could do with one so powerful. We could breach the other world in time.'

"Sarah moaned then. Eugenia threw to me her amulet of the crescent eye. 'Mary, run! Take Sarah with you through the door, and I shall close the realms!'

"The thing howled in fury. 'Never!'

"I could not move, could not think at all. 'No! You mustn't!' I cried. 'We cannot lose the realms!'

"The thing caused her to cry out in pain then. Her eyes were filled with a pleading that took my breath away, for I had never seen Eugenia frightened before. 'The realms must stay closed until we can find our way again. Now – run!' she screamed. And oh, diary, I did, pulling Sarah with me. Eugenia made the door appear for us, we jumped through to safety, and the last I saw of Eugenia, she was shouting the spell to close the realms, even as she was swallowed by the dark without a trace. The thing raced for us then. I placed the amulet against the shape in the door, locking it fast.

"'Open the door again, Mary.' Sarah was on her feet. She'd been changed by the creature, the two of them linked.

"'No, Sarah. The magic is gone now. We have ended it. Look.' The door of light began to fade before us.

"She ran for me, turning the candle over. Within seconds, the room was ablaze. I cannot say what happened next, for I ran from the East Wing, ran hard for the woods and watched as a strange light filled the sky over it, watched the flames burn and my dearest friend with it. So the magic of the Order and the realms is gone now. I can feel all traces of it slipping from the world with the harsh first light of morning. It is gone and so is Mary Dowd. She no longer exists.

"Tonight, she went into the woods, and I fear she shall live in the woods of my soul for the rest of my days."

Miss Moore closes the book. We're speechless.

"Please go on," Pippa says, her voice a mere whisper.

Miss Moore riffles through the pages. "I can't. There is no more. That is where our story ends, it would seem, in a dark wood." She stands and straightens her skirt. "Thank you for sharing that with me, ladies. It was most interesting."

"I can't believe Mary killed that poor little girl," Ann says when we're alone again.

"Yes," Felicity says. "Who would do such a thing?"

"A monster," I say. *She no longer exists.* It's what my mother said. Something about that creeps inside me and won't leave. I don't know why.

～～～～

I can't sleep. There's still too much magic running in my veins, and the story of Mary and Sarah has me feeling uneasy, as if I need to prove that what we're doing is different. Good. I dress quickly and walk in the woods till I find myself just outside Kartik's tent, where he sits reading.

I step from behind a tree, startling him. "What are you doing?" he asks.

"I couldn't sleep."

He goes back to his book. I want him to know that I am good, not like Mary and Sarah. I would never do the horrible things they did. For some reason, I desperately want him to like me. I want him to wake from dreams of me, sweating and alive. I can't say why. But I do. "Kartik, what if I could show you that the Rakshana is wrong? What if I could prove to you that my power, the magic of the Order, is wonderful?"

His eyes widen. "Tell me you haven't done what I think you've done."

I step forward. I don't recognise my voice, it is so desperate and near tears. "There's nothing wrong with it. It's beautiful. I'm . . ." I want to say "beautiful", but I don't because I'm on the verge of crying.

· 346 ·

He shakes his head, backs away. I'm losing him. I should let it alone. Go away. Stop. But I can't.

"Let me show you. I'll take you with me. We could look for your brother!"

I reach for his hand but he practically leaps to the other side of the tent. "No. It's not for me to see. Not for me to know."

"Just take my hand. Please!"

"No!"

Why did I think I could win him over? Why did I think I could make him see me differently? Worse, what if the way he sees me is the way I really am – someone to be wary of, not loved? A sideshow abomination. A monster.

I turn and run as fast as I can, and he doesn't chase me.

～～～

I'm making that long, miserable climb up to my room when Brigid stops me, candle in hand, nightcap on head. "Who goes there?"

"It's only me, Brigid," I say, hoping she doesn't get any closer and notice I'm fully dressed.

"Wot are you doin' skulkin' round in the dead o' night?"

"Please don't tell Mrs Nightwing. It's just that I couldn't sleep."

"Thinkin' about your mum, then?"

I nod, feeling craven for the lie.

"All right. It's just between you and me. But get yourself to bed."

It breaks me, this sudden kindness from Brigid. I can feel

my borders unravelling. "Goodnight," I whisper, passing her on my way up.

"Oh, by the way, I thought of that fancy name. The one Sarah started callin' herself. Came to me clear as day as I was doin' the washing up tonight. I remembered Missus Spence tellin' me, 'Oh, our Sarah thinks she's a goddess of old, just like the Greeks.' That's when it come to me, when I was washin' up the china cups with the Greek key pattern."

"Yes?" I ask. I'm suddenly very tired and not in the mood for one of Brigid's long-winded stories.

"Circe," she says, descending the stairs, her shadow just ahead of her. "That were the name she used to call herself – Circe."

ᚾᚾᚾᚾ

Circe is Sarah Rees-Toome.

Sarah Rees-Toome, who did not die in a fire twenty years ago, but who is alive and well and waiting for me. She is no longer a shadowy enemy but flesh and blood. Someone I could get to before she gets to me. If only I had some idea where she could be or what she must look like.

But I don't. I am completely at her mercy.

Or am I?

Circe, Sarah Rees-Toome, was once a Spence girl, class of 1871. A girl in a photograph that has been removed but still exists somewhere. Finding that photograph is no longer a matter of curiosity. It is a necessity, my only means of finding her before she finds me.

CHAPTER
THIRTY-ONE

BY THE NEXT MORNING, OUR NIGHTTIME EXPERIMENTS
in power and magic have begun to take their toll. Our
faces are pasty and pale, our lips cracked. My mind's in a
fog, and I'm so tired that I can barely speak in English, let
alone French, which presents problems in Mademoiselle
LeFarge's class. It doesn't help that I've stumbled in, nearly
late.

Mademoiselle LeFarge chooses to make a game of my tar-
diness. Now that I am her prize student, a shining example
of her superior teaching skills, she's inclined to be playful
with me. "*Bonjour, Mademoiselle Doyle. Quelle heure est-il?*"

I know the answer. It's on the tip of my tongue.
Something about the weather, I think. If only I had enough
magic left over to help me make it through her class. But
sadly, I'm going to have to sail through under my own paltry
steam.

"Er . . . the weather is . . ." Bloody hell. What is the French
word for rain? Le rain? La rain? Is the rain masculine or

feminine? It's such a bother that it must be masculine. "Le weather est le rainy," I say, mangling the last bit, though the *le* makes it sound more French.

The girls giggle, which only convinces Mademoiselle LeFarge that I'm making fun of her. "Mademoiselle Doyle, this is a disgrace. Just two days ago, you proved yourself an exemplary student. Now, you have the audacity to mock me. Perhaps you'll fare better in a room of eight-year-olds." She turns her back on me, and for the remainder of the class, it's as if I don't exist.

⌇⌇⌇

Mrs Nightwing has noticed our pallor. She forces us to take a walk in the gardens, thinking the cool air will put roses in our cheeks. I take the opportunity to tell my friends about my run-in with Brigid last night.

"So Circe is Sarah Rees-Toome. And she's alive." Felicity shakes her head, incredulous.

"We've got to find that photograph," I say.

"We tell Mrs Nightwing we're searching for a lost glove. She lets us search high and low. We scour the rooms one by one," Ann suggests.

Pippa groans. "It will take us a year."

"Let's each take a floor, shall we?" I say.

Pippa gives me her large doe eyes. "Must we?"

I push her towards the school. "Yes."

After an hour of searching, I still haven't found it. I've paced the third floor so many times, I'm sure I've worn the carpets thin. With a sigh, I stand in front of the existing class photographs, willing them to talk, to tell me something about where I might find what's missing. The ladies do not oblige me.

I'm drawn to the photograph from 1872, with its rippled surface. Gently, I remove it from the wall and turn it over. The back of the photograph is smooth, not ruined at all. Turn it back over and there's the wavy front. How can that be? Unless it's not the same photograph at all.

Hurriedly, I tug at the corners of the photograph, as if I'm pulling back a carpet. There is another photograph behind the one in the frame. A buzzing starts in my ears. Eight graduating girls sit grouped on the lawn. In the background is the unmistakable outline of Spence. At the bottom, in fine print, it reads *Class of 1871*. I've found it! Names are written along the bottom in a cramped hand.

Left to right – Millicent Jenkins, Susanna Meriwether, Anna Nelson, Sarah Rees-Toome . . .

My head bobs. My finger traces up to Sarah. She turned her head at the moment the picture was snapped, leaving a blurred profile that's hard to read. I squint but can't really make out much.

My finger moves on to the girl next to her. My mouth goes dry. She's looking directly into the camera with her wise, penetrating eyes – eyes I've known my whole life. I look for her name, though I already know the one I'll find, the one she abandoned and left to die in a fire years before I was even born. Mary Dowd.

The girl staring back at me from that class of 1871 is Mary Dowd – my mother.

CHAPTER THIRTY-TWO

I WAIT UNTIL THE OTHERS ARE SETTLED AT DINNER, then slip away to my room. In the gathering darkness, it fades by degrees. Shapes fade into impressions of things. Everything is stripped down to its essence. I am ready. Eyes closed, I summon the door. The familiar pulsing travels through my veins, and I step through, alone, into the other world, the garden, where sweet-smelling flowers fall around me like ash.

"Mother," I say, and my voice sounds strange and hard in my ears.

A soft wind blows. Behind it, like rain, is the smell of rose water. She is coming.

"Find me if you can," she says with a smile. I won't return it. I won't even look at her. "What is it?"

My mother is not at all the woman I thought she was. I've never really known her. She is Mary Dowd. A liar and a sorceress. A killer.

"You're Mary Dowd."

Her smile falls. "You know."

Some part of me has been holding out hope that I'm mistaken and that she'll laugh, tell me it's a silly mistake, explain it all away. The truth is a blow.

"No one came to you, told you all those things about me. You knew. You were a member of the Order all along. Everything you've told me is a fabrication."

Her voice is surprisingly soft. "No. Not everything."

I'm blinking back tears. "You lied to me."

"Only to protect you."

"That's another lie." I feel such hate; I'm nearly sick with it. "How could you?"

"It was all so very long ago, Gemma."

"And that excuses everything? You led that little girl into the East Wing. You killed her!"

"Yes. And I spent every day of my life atoning for it." A bird sings a hollow evening song from a branch. "Everyone assumed I had died, and in a way, I had. Mary Dowd was gone and in her place was Virginia. I made a new life for myself, with your father, and then Tom and you."

The tears fall hot and wet on my cheeks. She tries to take my hand, but I step away.

"Oh, Gemma, how could I tell you what I'd done? That's the curse of mothers, you know. We're never prepared for how much we love our children, for how much we wish we could protect them by being perfect." She blinks fast, trying not to cry. "I thought I could start again. That it was all forgotten and I was free. But I wasn't." Her voice is tinged with bitterness. "Slowly, I began to realise that you were different. That the long-dead power of the Order and the realms was starting again in you. I was afraid of that. I didn't want you to have that burden. I thought by saying nothing I could protect you until perhaps it would pass and fade into legend again. No more. But I was wrong, of course. We can't escape destiny. And then it was too late, and Circe found me before I'd had a chance to tell you everything."

"She didn't die in the fire."

"No. I thought she had until a year ago, when Amar came to me, told me she was using her link to the creature to find us all. She'd heard that one of us was a portal to the realms again. She just didn't know who." She smiles at me, but her smile is pained.

My tears stop. Anger rises like a new building, shiny-hard and attractive, a place I want to live in forever.

"Fine. You've completed your soul's task. You've told me the truth," I say, spitting out the last word. "Why don't you go on and leave me alone, then?"

"My soul's task is in your hands," she says softly in that voice that once sang me to sleep, told me I was lovely when I wasn't. "It's your choice."

"What could I possibly do for you now?"

"Forgive me."

The sobs I've been holding in check come spilling out. "You want me to forgive you?"

"It's the only way I can be at rest."

"What about me? Do you think I'll ever be at rest again with what I know?"

Her hand touches my cheek. I recoil. "I'm sorry, Gemma. But we can't live in the light all of the time. You have to take whatever light you can hold into the dark with you."

I can't think of anything to say. I never asked for any of this, and I've never felt more alone in my life. I want to hurt her.

"You were wrong about the runes. We've used the magic twice and nothing has happened."

Her eyes blaze. "You what? I told you not to. It isn't safe, Gemma."

"How do I know that isn't another one of your lies? Why should I believe anything you say?"

She puts a hand to her mouth, paces. "Then the realms have been left unguarded. Circe's creature could already have been here and corrupted one of us. Gemma, how could you?"

"I might ask you the same," I say, walking away.

"Where are you going?" she asks me.

"Back," I say.

"Gemma. Gemma!"

I pass out of the garden. The huntress surprises me. I hadn't even heard her coming up behind me, her bow and arrow at the ready.

"The deer is close. Will you hunt with me?"

"Another time," I mumble through lips still thick with crying.

She bends to pick some berries, pops one in her mouth. She dangles them before me like a pendulum. "Care for a berry?"

She knows I can't eat the fruit. So why is she offering it to me?

"No, thank you," I say, walking on a bit more quickly.

As if I haven't moved, she is in front of me, the berries in her outstretched hand. "Are you certain? They are delicious."

The hair on the back of my neck stands up. Something isn't right.

"I'm sorry, but I have to go now," I say, but I can hear the thin scraping of a voice behind me as I'm hurrying through the green velvet of the grass by the river.

"At last . . . at last . . ."

✛✛✛✛

Ann stands over my bed in the dark. "Gemma? Are you awake?"

I keep my eyes closed and hope she can't tell that I'm still crying.

Felicity and Pippa shake me till I'm forced to turn over and face them.

"Let's go," Felicity whispers. "The caves await, fair lady."

"I don't feel well." I roll over and study the tiny cracks in the wall again.

"Don't be such a spoilsport," Pippa says, nudging me with her boot.

I say nothing, just focus on my spot on the wall.

"Whatever's the matter with her?" Pippa sniffs.

"I told you not to eat the liver," Ann says.

"Well," Felicity sighs after a while, "I hope you recover. But don't expect to get off quite so easily tomorrow night."

I have no intention of stepping through into the realms. Not tomorrow. Not ever. The door of my room closes, taking the last of the light with it, and the cracks all fade into nothing.

CHAPTER
THIRTY-THREE

MR BUMBLE IS NOT QUITE THE EASY MARK WE'VE MADE him out to be. He's gone to the Crosses, told them everything. The Crosses are horrified that they've lost control over the one thing that should always be in their control – their daughter. Their collateral. They've assured Mr Bumble that it's all some youthful folly invented by a girl nervous about her wedding day. After all, how could a girl as lovely as Pippa be anything other than the very picture of health? Mr Bumble accepts their explanation in full, for they are the parents and we are merely silly girls. The whole episode has caused a scene at Spence, however. And so the four of us are assembled in Mrs Nightwing's office, under the reproachful eyes of the peacock-tail wallpaper, listening to accusations and blame, watching helplessly as our freedom unravels thread by thread.

Tomorrow, Pippa will leave with her parents, and she will be married to Mr Bumble by the week's end. Hasty preparations have begun. Order will be restored. Pride upheld.

Who cares about one girl's lifelong happiness in the face of such important matters as maintaining appearances?

She stares into her lap, biting hard at her bottom lip, completely beaten, while Mrs Nightwing works to soothe her parents and fiancé. Mrs Nightwing rings a bell on a long rope – the one that leads to the kitchen – and moments later, Brigid appears, huffing and puffing from the race up the stairs.

"Brigid, please show Mr Cross and Mr Bumble to the library and offer them a glass of our best port."

This pleases the men. They're all smug smiles and puffed chests.

"I do hope you'll accept this with a full apology and my assurance that there'll be no further unpleasantness." Mrs Nightwing gives Mr Bumble a sideways glance.

Mr Cross waves the idea away. "No great harm done, fortunately."

Mr Bumble crinkles his moustache as if choosing a cigar. "I'm a reasonable man. But you should keep a much tighter rein on these girls. They shouldn't be left to their own decisions. It's not healthy."

I close my eyes and imagine Mr Bumble careening head-first down the long staircase and snapping his neck before he can sip that port. The great irony is that we told him the truth. And now we'll be punished for it.

"You're quite right. I shall follow your advice to the letter, Mr Bumble," Mrs Nightwing says in a rare capitulation. She's appeasing him, but he's far too pompous to realise that.

The men leave with Brigid. Mrs Cross stands and adjusts

her gloves, pulling them tighter on her hands, smoothing out the wrinkles. "Come along, Pippa. We must have you measured for your wedding dress. I think a duchesse satin will be nice."

Pippa's quivering lip gives way to a quiet, desperate wail. "Please, Mother! Please don't make me marry him."

Mrs Cross's mouth tightens into an ugly, flat line that lets the words escape in a hiss. "You are shaming this family."

"Pippa," Mrs Nightwing says, stepping between them. "You shall be a beautiful bride. The talk of London. And after your honeymoon, when you are blissfully happy and this has all been forgotten, you will come to visit us."

Mrs Cross's mouth has relaxed and there are actually tears pooling in her eyes. She cups Pippa's chin tenderly. "I know you despise me now. But I promise, someday you will thank me. There's an independence in marriage. Truly. If you're clever, you can have whatever you want. Now, let's see about a dress, shall we?"

Pippa follows her mother out, but as she does, she turns to us with such a look of despair that I feel as if I'm the one being forced to marry against my will.

It's just the three of us across from Mrs Nightwing and her equally imposing desk. A drawer is opened. Mary Dowd's diary drops with a thud onto the desk's gleaming mahogany surface. Fear turns my insides. We are all marked for death now.

"Who can tell me about this?"

Seconds, loud as cannon fire, tick by on the mantel clock. "Ann?"

Ann is on the verge of tears. "It's-s-s a b-b-book."

"I can see that it is a book. I have examined every page." Mrs Nightwing glowers at us over the tops of her spectacles. "Every page."

We know the one she means, and we tremble in our seats.

"Miss Worthington, would you care to tell me what you were doing in possession of this diary?"

Felicity's head shoots up. "You searched my room?"

"I'm waiting for an answer. Or will I need to contact your father about this matter?"

Felicity looks as if she's going to burst into tears.

I swallow hard. "It's mine," I say.

Mrs Nightwing whips her head around suddenly and blinks. The effect is of an owl spotting prey. "Yours, Miss Doyle?"

My stomach goes fluttery. "Yes." Fine, let them expel me. Let this all be over.

"And where, pray tell, did you come upon such filth?"

"I found it."

"You found it?" She repeats my words slowly, showing just how much she believes me. "Where?"

"In the woods."

Mrs Nightwing glares at me but I'm too numb to be afraid. "It seems a great many things have been going on in the woods. Pippa has confessed to me."

Beside me I can hear Ann starting to cry, Felicity squirming in her chair. But I'm hollowed out, waiting for the inevitable.

"She told me that Miss Moore gave you the book."

It's not what I expected. I'm pulled back into the room by it.

"Is this true?"

My mouth opens, ready to say no, it's all my fault, but Felicity is quicker.

"Yes," she says so calmly that I can scarcely believe it. "It was Miss Moore."

"I'm sorry to hear it. But you'll need to tell me everything, Miss Worthington."

"No. That's not true," I say, finding my voice at last.

"You said yourself that you got it at the library." Felicity has a hard, desperate look in her eyes. "And Miss Moore did tell us that if we wanted to know more about the Order, we should go to the library."

"The Order? Why on earth was Miss Moore filling your heads with such poppycock?"

"She took us to the caves to see their drawings."

"Some of them are in blood," Ann adds. They're joined in this.

"I never gave Miss Moore leave to take you to any caves," Mrs Nightwing says.

"She took us all the same, Mrs Nightwing." Felicity widens her eyes, trying for an innocent look.

"That's not the way it happened. I found the diary—"

Felicity puts her hand on my arm. It looks as if it's just resting there, but she's giving it a sharp squeeze. "Mrs Nightwing already knows what happened, Gemma. We've got to tell the truth now." To Mrs Nightwing, she says, "She even read part of it to us in my sitting area."

I'm on my feet. "Because we asked her!"

"Miss Doyle, sit down at once!"

I drop into my seat. I can't look at Felicity.

"These are very serious charges against Miss Moore." Mrs Nightwing has already taken the idea and shaped it into exoneration for us, for Spence, and for herself. She needs someone to blame. She needs to believe anything but the truth – that we are capable of all of it, all on our own. And that we did it all right under her very nose. "Is this true, Ann?"

"Yes," Ann says, without stammering once.

"Mrs Nightwing," I plead. "It's all my fault. You can punish me as you see fit, but please don't blame Miss Moore."

"Miss Doyle. I know your heart is in the right place, but there is nothing to be gained by protecting Miss Moore."

"But I'm not protecting her!"

Mrs Nightwing softens. "Did Miss Moore read to you from this book?"

"Yes, but—"

"And did she take you to the caves?"

"Just to see the pictographs . . ."

"Did she tell you stories about the occult?"

I can't make a sound. I only nod. I've heard it said that God is in the details. It's the same with the truth. Leave out the details, the crucial heart, and you can damn someone with the bare bones of it. Mrs Nightwing settles against the great wingback chair. It creaks and sighs under her weight.

"I know how impressionable young girls are. I was a girl once myself," she says, though I can only see her behind the bars of what she is now. "I know how much girls wish to please and how powerful a teacher's influence can be. I shall deal with Miss Moore at once. And so that this sort of behaviour does not occur again, I shall see that all the doors are locked each evening and that the keys are in my keeping until such time as you have earned my trust again."

"What will happen to Miss Moore?" I ask. It's barely a whisper.

"I will not tolerate a reckless disregard for my authority in my teachers. Miss Moore will be dismissed."

This can't be happening. She's going to sack our beloved Miss Moore. What have we done?

A bloodcurdling scream rips the quiet of the room. It comes from downstairs. Mrs Nightwing is up and flying down the stairs with us right behind her. Brigid is standing on the diamond-patterned floor of the foyer, clutching something in her hand.

"May all the saints protect me! It's her – she's come for me."

Mrs Nightwing has her by the shoulders. Brigid's eyes are wild with fear. She drops the thing in her hand onto the floor as if it were a snake. It's a Gypsy poppet, slightly burned, with a lock of hair wrapped tightly about its throat.

Circe.

"She's come back," Brigid whimpers. "Sweet Jesus, she's come back!"

CHAPTER
THIRTY-FOUR

Reverend Waite has us standing, Bibles in hand, reading in unison from Judges, chapter eleven, verses one through forty. Our voices fill the chapel like a dirge.

"And Jephthah vowed a vow unto the Lord, and said, If thou shalt without fail deliver the children of Ammon into mine hands, Then it shall be, that whatsoever cometh forth of the doors of my house to meet me, when I return . . . I will offer it up for a burnt offering."

"I had to tell her about Miss Moore," Pippa whispers low in my ear. "It was the only way to keep us together for one last night."

At the front of the church is a stained-glass window of an angel. There's a large chip of glass gone from the angel's eye like a gaping wound. I stare at the hole and say nothing, mouthing along to my Bible verse, listening to words swirl around me.

". . . and the Lord delivered them into his hands . . ."

"It's not as if she was entirely blameless, you know."

"And Jephthah came . . . unto his house, and behold, his daughter came out to meet him . . . and she was his only child . . ."

"Please, Gemma. I have to see him again. Do you know what it is to lose someone without saying goodbye?"

If I stare hard, the hole grows and the angel disappears. But if I blink, I see the angel, not the hole, and I have to start all over again.

". . . when he saw her, . . . he rent his clothes and said, Alas, my daughter! thou hast brought me very low . . . for I have opened my mouth unto the Lord, and I cannot go back . . ."

Pippa starts to plead with me again, but Mrs Nightwing turns around to inspect us from her pew. Pippa buries her face in her Bible and reads along with renewed fervour.

". . . And she said unto her father, Let this thing be done for me: let me alone two months, that I may go up and down upon the mountains, and bewail my virginity . . ."

Some of the younger girls snigger at this. It's followed by a loud chorus of shushing from the teachers – all of them except Miss Moore, who isn't here. She's back at the school, packing to leave.

". . . And he sent her away . . . and she went with her companions . . . upon the mountains."

Reverend Waite closes his Bible. "Thus sayeth the Lord. Let us pray."

There is a wave of shuffling and thumping as we sit and pass our Bibles down, girl to girl, till they're stacked neatly on the ends of the pews. I pass mine to Pippa, who holds it tight.

"Just one last night. Before I'm gone forever. That's all I'm asking."

I let go, and the Bible crashes into her lap. Freed, I go back to staring at the angel. I stare so long and hard that the angel seems to move. It's the dark coming in, making everything hazy. But for a moment, I could swear I see the angel's wings fluttering, the hands tightening on the sword, the sword cleaving through the lamb quick as a scythe. I look away, and it's gone. A trick of the light.

〰〰〰〰

I don't join the others in the great hall after dinner. I hear them calling for me. I don't answer. Instead, I'm sitting alone in the parlour with an open French book on my lap, pretending to pay attention to conjugations and tenses that make my eyes hurt. But really, I'm waiting for her footsteps in the hall. I'm not certain what to say, but I know I can't let Miss Moore leave without trying to explain or apologise.

Just after dinner, she passes by in a smart travelling outfit. On her head is a broad-brimmed hat trimmed with cabbage roses. She looks as if she could be heading to sea for a holiday – not leaving Spence in a cloud of half-lies and shame.

I follow her to the front door.

"Miss Moore?"

She buttons a glove at the wrist, stretches her fingers into it. "Miss Doyle, what brings you here? Aren't you missing out on valuable socialising?"

"Miss Moore," I say, my voice catching in my throat. "I'm so sorry."

She gives a wan smile. "Yes, I believe you are."

"I wish . . ." I stop, trying not to cry.

"I'd give you my handkerchief, but I believe you're already in possession of it."

"I'm sorry," I gasp, remembering the one she loaned me after Pippa's seizure. "Forgive me."

"Only if you forgive yourself."

I nod. There's a knock at the door. Miss Moore doesn't wait for Brigid. She opens the door wide, directs the driver to her trunk, and watches as he loads it onto the carriage.

"Miss Moore . . ."

"Hester."

"Hester," I say, feeling guilty for the luxury of her first name. "Where will you go?"

"I should like to travel for a bit, I think. Then I shall take a flat somewhere in London and offer my services as a tutor."

The driver is ready. Miss Moore nods to him. When she turns to me, her voice is halting, but her grip on my hands is sure.

"Gemma . . . should you ever need anything . . ." She stops, searching for words, it seems. "What I mean to say is, you seem a breed apart from the other girls. I think perhaps your destiny does not lie in tea dances and proper place settings. Whatever path you should decide to follow in life, I do hope I shall continue to be a part of it, and that you shall feel free to call on me."

A shiver travels up my arm. I am so very grateful for Miss Moore. I do not deserve her kindness.

"Will you do that?" she asks.

"Yes." I hear myself agreeing.

Head held high, she releases my hands and sails through the door towards the carriage. Halfway there, she calls back. "You'll have to find a way to make those still lifes interesting."

With that, she steps into the carriage and raps twice. The horses whinny into action, trotting towards the gate, kicking up dirt as they go. I watch the carriage getting smaller in the distance till it turns a corner and folds quickly into the night and Miss Moore is gone.

CHAPTER
THIRTY-FIVE

AT HALF-PAST TEN, MRS NIGHTWING MAKES HER rounds to ensure that all her tender chickens are accounted for – lying safely in bed, far away from any wolves. When the downstairs clock gongs midnight, there's a scratching at our door by Pippa and Felicity, letting us know that it's safe to come out for one last evening together.

"How will we get out?" I ask. "She's locked the doors."

Felicity dangles a key. "It seems that Molly the upstairs maid owed me a favour after I caught her with the stable boy. Now, get dressed."

<hr style="width:20%" />

The caves welcome us one last time. The nights have grown colder, and we huddle together for warmth over the last of our candles. When they realise that I won't take them into the realms, they're furious with me.

"But why won't you take us?" Pippa cries.

"I've told you. I don't feel well."

I have no intention of going back through the shimmering door. Instead, I shall master French. Perfect my posture. Learn how to curtsy and draw clever pictures. I shall be what they want me to be – safe. And nothing bad will ever happen again. It's possible to pretend I'm someone other than who I am, and if I pretend long enough, I can believe it. My mother did.

Pippa kneels at my feet and puts her head in my lap like a child. "Please, Gemma? Darling, darling Gemma. I'll let you wear my lace gloves. I'll let you keep them!"

"No!" My shout slaps at the cave's walls.

Pippa plops onto the ground to sulk. "Fee, you talk to her. I'm doing no good."

Felicity is surprisingly cool. "It would seem Gemma won't be moved this evening."

"Now what shall we do?" Pippa whines.

"There's still some whiskey left. Here, have a little." Felicity pulls the half-empty bottle from its hiding place inside a rocky crevice. "This will change your mind." After two quick swallows, she dangles the bottle in front of me. I get up and move to another rock. "Are you still cross about Miss Moore?"

"Among other things." I'm cross that we let her down so terribly. I'm cross that my mother is a liar and a murderer. That my father is an addict. That Kartik despises me. That everything I touch seems to go wrong.

"Fine," Felicity says. "Go off and sulk, then. Who wants a drink?"

How can I tell them what I know? I don't even want to

know it. I wish I could make it all go away, just go back to that first day in the realms when everything seemed possible again. Felicity keeps passing the bottle, and soon, they're all flushed and glassy-eyed, noses running a bit from the sudden warmth of the whiskey in their blood. Felicity twirls around the cave, reciting poetry.

> "But in her web she still delights
> To weave the mirror's magic sights,
> For often thro' the silent nights
> A funeral, with plumes and lights
> And music, went to Camelot . . ."

"Oh, not this again," Ann snarls, leaning her head against the boulder.

Felicity is taunting me with the poem. She knows it reminds me of Miss Moore. Like a whirling dervish, she throws out her arms, spiralling faster into ecstasy.

> "Or when the Moon was overhead,
> Came two young lovers lately wed.
> 'I am half sick of shadows,' said
> The Lady of Shalott."

Her hands fly out against the cave wall to stop her fall. She rolls her body against the craggy surface till she's facing us again. Strands of hair, wet with perspiration, stick to her forehead and cheeks. She's got a strange look on her face.

"Pip, darling, do you really want to see your knight?"

"More than anything!"

Felicity grabs Pip's hand and runs towards the cave's mouth.

"Wait for me," Ann yells, following after.

They spill out into the night like Bedouins, with me trailing in their wake. The cold air is a shock to our damp skin.

"Felicity, what are you up to?" I ask.

"Something new," she teases.

The sky, indifferent earlier, pulses with the light of a million stars. There's an early-autumn moon, buttery golden, riding high over spun-thin wisps of cloud that tell us all it will soon be the time for harvest, the time when the farmers raise a pint to the legendary murder of John Barleycorn.

Felicity howls at the globe in the sky.

"Shhh," Pippa says. "You'll wake the entire school."

"No one will hear us. Mrs Nightwing had two sherries tonight. We couldn't wake her if we placed her in the centre of Trafalgar Square with a pigeon in each hand." She lets loose with another howl.

"I want to see my knight." Pippa pouts.

"And you will."

"Not if Gemma won't take us."

"We all know there's another way," Felicity says. In the moonlight, her pale skin glows white as bone. A chill works its way up my spine.

"What do you mean?" Pippa asks.

Something stirs in the trees. There's the sound of twigs breaking and movement, quick and furtive. We jump. A deer wanders closer to the clearing. It has its nose to the ground, sniffing for food.

"It's only a deer." Ann exhales in a whoosh.

"No," Felicity says. "It's our sacrifice."

The moon dips behind clouds for an instant and our faces are mottled with light.

"You aren't serious," I say, coming out of my sullen stupor.

"Why not? We know they did it. But we'll be smarter." She's like a carnival barker trying to entice a crowd into a sideshow tent.

"But they couldn't control it—" I start. Felicity cuts me off.

"We're stronger than they are. We won't make the same mistakes. The huntress told me . . ."

The huntress offering me the berries, whispering to Felicity on their hunts. Something's fighting to take shape in my mind, but it won't come. Only the fear remains, bold and undeniable.

"What about the huntress?"

"She tells me things. Things you are not privy to. She's the one who told me I could have the power if I offer her a token."

"No . . . that's not—"

"She told me you'd react this way. That you couldn't be trusted because you want the power of the realms all to yourself."

Pippa and Ann look from Felicity to me and back again, waiting.

"You can't do this," I say. "I won't let you."

Felicity creeps forward, knocks me backwards into the dirt. "You. Can't. Stop. Us."

"Felicity . . ." Ann looks as if she doesn't know whether to help me or run away.

"Don't you see? Gemma wants the power all to herself! She wants power over us."

"That's not true!" I struggle to my feet and take a step backwards, away from them.

Pippa comes up behind me. I can feel her breath on my neck. "Then why won't you take us?"

I'm caught. "I can't tell you."

"She doesn't trust us," Felicity says. Suspicion spreads like a disease. She crosses her arms in triumph, lets the damage sink in.

The deer is just beyond us in the thicket. Pippa watches it. She shifts her weight from one foot to the other. "I wouldn't have to marry him. Would I?"

Felicity takes her hands. "We could change everything."

"Everything," Ann says, joining them.

✳✳✳✳

I saw a fire start once in India. One second, it was only a spark lost from a beggar's fire, caught on a high wind. Within minutes, everything in sight was ablaze, thatched roofs crackling like so much dry kindling, mothers scurrying into the streets, carrying crying children.

That is how fires start. With a spark. And I see the spark catching the wind.

"All right," I say, desperate to keep them from going it alone. "All right, I'll take you. Let's go back to the cave and join hands."

"That time has passed," Felicity says, crossing her arms over her chest.

"What do you mean?"

"I mean that we are no longer content to ride on your coat-tails, Gemma. We'll enter the realms by ourselves, thank you."

"But I'll take—"

Pippa turns her back to me. "How do we catch it?"

"We chase it to the ravine. Trap it there." Felicity unbuttons her sleeves, shimmies out of her blouse.

"What are you doing?" I ask, alarmed.

Felicity explains to the others, ignoring me. "Take them off. We can't catch a deer in corsets and petticoats. We'll never stand a chance. We've got to be naked, like the huntress."

This whole situation is veering wildly out of control. I feel as if I'm watching a building collapse, with no way to stop it.

Ann folds her arms protectively across her plump middle. "Is it absolutely necessary? Can't we catch the deer as we are?"

"How exactly will you explain the stains to Mrs Nightwing?" Felicity is naked now. Pale, like bark whittled raw. Her voice, hard and aching, cuts through the rustle of dry leaves. "Stay if you like. But I won't go back to the way it was. I can't."

Pippa sits on the grass and pulls off her boots, starts removing her petticoats. Ann follows suit.

"Ann, Pippa, listen to me. This isn't right. You can't do this. Please listen to me!" They're paying me no mind, peeling off their garments with frantic fingers. The deer's head darts up. They crouch low on the forest floor. Felicity holds up a finger for silence. The deer senses danger, bolts for the cover of trees.

With a grunt, they're up, naked and shining, running towards the woods till they're nothing but a flurry of white, a flapping of angel's wings in the moss-covered night.

I chase them as they chase the deer. It slips in and out of trees. Felicity is in the lead, her skin a beacon. I hear the sharp cracking sound of twigs trampled, hear the heavy panting of my own breath in my ears. And then something that sounds like a great crash up ahead where I can't see.

When I reach the ravine, Ann and Pippa are poised on the edge, breathing hard. The deer is nowhere to be seen. A great chunk of earth wall has been torn away. Carefully, I scoot to the edge. My boot sends showers of dirt and rocks into the ravine, and I have to grab hold of a low-lying root to keep from falling in.

The deer lies wounded at the bottom, struggling to lift its head, making the most awful sounds. Felicity crouches low, creeps closer. She leans over it, stroking the brown fur, making comforting shushing noises. *She's not going to do it.* A feeling of relief floods through me as I wait for her to scramble up the embankment.

The clouds shift, stretch out thin as a scream. The moon

is dazzling us with its hard fair light. It bathes Felicity in a white like plaster, turns her into a statue frozen in time.

She's fumbling with something down there in the dark. In an instant, her hand flies up. She brings the rock down with a sickening thud. And again. Again till there's nothing moving in the ravine but her and creatures too small to detect from where we stand above her. Slowly, Ann and Pippa scuttle down the slope in crablike movements and each take their turns with the rock. Their bare backs, arched and taut, shine in the night. When they move away, the thing at the bottom of the ravine no longer resembles a deer above the neck. The head is pulpy, an overripe melon fallen on the ground and split open in surprised outrage. I turn and vomit into a sparse bush.

When I stagger over again, they're crawling back up the steep slope on hands and knees. In the dark, the splattered blood looks black as ink on their alabaster skin. Felicity climbs up last. She still grips the blood-slick rock in her hand.

"It's done," she says, her voice ripping the still of the night.

This is how the fire starts.

This is how we burn.

Everything is slipping out of my control.

She places the rock in my hand. The weight of it pulls me forward and I stumble. It's sticky in my hand.

"What happens now?" Ann asks. In the dark, there is no answer, just a slight breeze rustling through the dry leaves over our heads.

"We hold hands and make the door of light appear," Felicity says.

They join hands and close their eyes but nothing happens.

"Where is it?" Pippa asks. "Why don't I see it?"

For the first time this evening, Felicity seems lost. "She promised me . . ."

It hasn't worked. They've been tricked. I would feel sorry for them if I weren't both relieved and appalled.

"She promised . . . ," Felicity whispers.

Kartik steps into the clearing, stops when he takes us in, bloodstained and half wild. He takes a step back, ready to retreat, but not before Felicity sees him.

"What are you doing here?" she screams.

Kartik doesn't answer. Instead, his eyes flit to the rock in my hand. I drop it fast, and it hits the earth with a thud.

In that one instant of distraction, Felicity seizes her chance. Grabbing a sharp stick, she charges Kartik, scraping him across the chest. Blood seeps up through the torn shirt, and he doubles over from the surprise of the gash. Her new skill as an archer is on display. She's got the stick poised, ready to run him through.

"I told you we'd carve your eyes out the next time," she growls.

I had thought Felicity dangerous a moment ago, when she felt powerful. I was wrong. Wounded and powerless, she is more dangerous than I could imagine.

Injured, Kartik is unable to defend himself for the moment.

"Stop!" I shout. "Let him go and I'll take you into the realms."

Felicity is panting, the stick still raised above his eyes.

"Fee," Pippa whines, sounding a bit scared herself. "She's going to take us."

Slowly, Felicity releases him, saunters back to join us.

"She'll give us the power once we're there," she says, trying to save face. "I'm sure of it."

On the ground behind her, Kartik is worried. I give him a small nod to let him know it's going to be all right, though I don't know that. I have no idea what will greet us on the other side of that door now. I don't know what they've started, if anything. I only know that I've got to do it.

Felicity gives me a hard look. Things have changed forever. There's no going back. I follow them into the woods so that they can dress again. Soon, they are ready.

"Take my hands," I say, hoping for the best, fearing the worst.

CHAPTER
THIRTY-SIX

THE DOOR PULSES WITH LIGHT. WHEN WE STUMBLE through, everything seems as it was. The river sings sweetly on. The sunset is still a gorgeous spill of colours. Flowers float by.

"You see?" Felicity says, eyes shining in triumph. "There's nothing amiss. I told you she only wanted the power for herself."

I ignore her, listening for anything out of place.

They glide down into the meadow ahead of me, walking towards the garden, hand in hand like a trio of paper-doll cutouts from a doily.

The wind shifts, bringing the scent of roses and that other, unfamiliar stench, which sends me running after them.

"Wait! Felicity, please listen, I think we should go back."

"Go back? We just got here," she says, mocking me.

Ann's face is a stone. "We're not going back without the power to cross over by ourselves."

The huntress is suddenly by our sides. It startles me. Odd that I never heard her approach. I can't help thinking of her offering me the berries. It makes me cold all over. She wipes a finger across Felicity's bloody face, rubs the stain with her thumb. She brings the finger to her mouth, tastes it and smiles.

"You've made a sacrifice, I see."

"Yes," Felicity says. "Will you grant us the power to enter the realms?"

"Didn't I promise that I would?" She smiles but there's no warmth in it. "Follow me."

I grab Felicity by the arm. "This is wrong. We shouldn't go," I whisper.

"No, something's finally right," she says, breaking away and running after the others.

I follow them under the silver arch, into the grotto. My mother is nowhere to be seen. The smells of my childhood waft by. Curry. Pipe smoke. And something else. There it is again. That unpleasant stench.

We've reached the Runes of the Oracle, the heart of everything.

~~~~~~

The breeze shifts. The smell is back. Underneath the memories is something pungent, like meat rotting in the sun. Does no one else smell it?

"What do we do now?" Pippa asks.

"Use the magic to take me through to the other side," the huntress says.

"If we join hands and take you through, you'll give us the power we need, to come and go as we please?"

"Not me. My mistress. She will give you what you deserve."

Wariness steals inside me and takes its perch.

"Your mistress?" Felicity is confused.

Everything in me is screaming to run. I've got my hand on Felicity's arm, and as if she can feel my terror, she backs slowly away from the circle. The huntress seems to grow taller. Her eyes go black; her voice becomes a hiss.

"Come to me, my pretty ones."

The sky opens into a churning sea of dark clouds. Quick as rain, she rises before us, a towering, screeching wraith, carrying the souls of the damned inside her unfurling black cape. Felicity can't break away, can't stop staring at that skeletal face, the eyes rimmed in red with swirling black ovals for centres, the sharp, jagged teeth. The thing clamps a hand onto her arm. Felicity's mouth stretches into a ghastly O. Like ink, the black floats across her eyes, till they're bottomless.

"No!" I scream, barrelling headlong into Felicity, the two of us sprawled on the ground. She's shaking all over, her eyes still black. Screaming, Pippa falls to the ground, scrambles down the hill, towards the river.

"Ann! Help me! We've got to get her back now!"

We're on either side of Felicity, running for the river. We have to find Pippa. We have to leave. A storm wind is blowing. It rips blossoms, leaves, and branches from trees, sends them flying over us. A branch narrowly misses my head and scrapes the side of my cheek, drawing blood.

The dark wraith grows another pair of arms and another. She slinks towards us, ready to crush us in her embrace. Felicity is coming out of it now, stumbling, then running. We've reached the river, but where is Pippa?

Ann's scream rips the air apart. "Help me!"

She's staring into the river, tearing at her hair. Her reflection has turned. She's covered in hideous boils. Her hair falls out in thick clumps and sores bubble up on her scalp. It's as if her skin is melting from her bones.

"Stop looking at yourself, Ann! Stop!" I scream.

"I can't! I can't!"

She's leaning closer to the water's edge. I slip my arms around her chest, but she's heavy and won't budge, and then she's free, falling back in the grass, thanks to a hard tug from Felicity. The grey of Ann's eyes has returned.

"Where's Pippa?" she screams over the wind.

"I don't know," I shout.

Something slithers over my hand. Snakes wind through the tall grass as it shrivels and dries up. We jump onto a rock. Pears fall from a tree and rot at our feet. Ann is whimpering, watching her skin dissolve into ugliness.

"Help me!" Pippa's scream tears through us. When we stumble across the brittle grass, we see her. She has taken a large boat, a bier, onto the river, where the wind has pushed her out into the wide deep of it. The wraith paces the bank, forcing us to keep our distance.

"*Yes, that's it . . . come for her . . . ,*" it laughs.

"Please! Help me!" Pippa cries. But there's nothing we can

do. She's cut off from us. We can't let it capture us. I'm so afraid, I can think only one thing – I've got to get us out.

"Through the door – quickly!" I shout.

The wind whips Felicity's hair across her pale face. "We can't leave Pip!"

"We'll come back for her!" I scream, pulling her hand.

"No!"

"Don't leave me!" Pippa moves onto the bow of the boat. It tips under her weight.

"Pippa – no!" I scream, but it's too late. She jumps into the river and it closes over her grasping hands like ice, entombing everything but her watery, strangled cry. I remember my vision the day of Pippa's seizure, of her pulled down into the water. And now, with great horror, I understand at last.

Outraged, the thing howls and the dark races towards us, shrieking.

"Pippa! Pippa!" Felicity shrieks till she's hoarse.

"Felicity, we've got to go – now!"

The wraith is nearly upon us. There's no time to think. I can only react. I reach the door and pull us through into the caves as the candles flicker and cough with the last of their light. We're all here, safe and accounted for, it seems. But on the floor, Pippa's body has gone rigid. It seizes uncontrollably.

Ann's voice is fluttery. "Pippa? Pippa?"

Felicity is sobbing. "You left her there! You did it!"

The last candle splutters and dies.

CHAPTER
THIRTY-SEVEN

"YOU'VE GOT TO HELP ME!"

I'm a wild-eyed thing standing outside Kartik's tent. He doesn't argue with me, doesn't say a word, not even when I tell him what's happened. He hoists Pippa over his shoulder and carries her through the woods all the way to Spence. The only time he stops is when we pass the ravine and the corpse of the deer we've left there. He helps us get Pippa to her room, and then I'm racing for Mrs Nightwing's door. I bang furiously, calling her name with a desperation I can't hold back.

Our headmistress throws open the door. Her nightcap is sliding down her long, greying braids. "What on earth? Miss Doyle, what are you doing in your clothes? Why aren't you in bed?"

"It's Pippa," I gasp. "She . . ." I can't finish, but it doesn't matter. Mrs Nightwing has caught the alarm in my voice. She springs into action with that immovable firmness of hers, a quality I've never truly appreciated until this moment.

"Tell Brigid to call for Dr. Thomas at once."

The lights burn through the night. I sit at the window in the library, hugging my knees in my arms, making myself as small as possible. At the edges of sleep, I see her. Wet. Hollow-eyed. Slipping under the smooth surface with a scream for help. I dig my fingernails into my palm to stay awake. Felicity paces past me. She avoids looking at me, but her silence speaks for her.

You left her there, Gemma. Alone in that watery grave.

A lantern moves across the lawn. Kartik. The light bobs and shakes in its metal cage. I have to strain to see him. He's carrying a shovel, and I know that he's going back to what he couldn't ignore in the ravine. He's going to bury the deer.

But whether he's doing it to protect me or himself, I cannot know.

I sit for a long time and watch the night bruise towards morning, the purple turning yellow, the yellow fading till it's as if the dark has never marked the skin of the sky at all. By the time the sun peeks over the trees, I'm ready to take one last journey.

❦❦❦❦

"Keep this," I say, crumpling the crescent eye amulet into Felicity's hands.

"But why?"

"If I don't come back . . ." I stop. "If something should go wrong, you'll need to find the others. They'll need to know you're one of them."

She stares at the silver amulet.

"It will be up to you to come after me." I pause. "Or close the realms for good. Do you understand?"

"Yes," she whispers. "Promise you'll come back."

The scrap of silk from my mother's dress is soft in my tight fist. "I'm going to try."

THERE ARE NO BIRDS. NO FLOWERS. NO SUNSET. THERE'S an eerie greyness to everything beyond the bright door. The empty boat is still on the river, stuck fast in a thin sheet of ice.

"If you want me, here I am," I shout. It echoes all around me. *I am, I am, I am.*

"Gemma? Gemma!" My mother emerges from behind a tree. Her voice, sure and strong, draws me in.

"Mother?"

Tears spring to her eyes. "Gemma, I was afraid . . . but you're all right." She smiles, and everything inside me bends to her. I'm tired and uncertain but she's here now. She'll help me set things right.

"Mother, I'm sorry. I've made a mess of things. You told me not to use the magic yet, and I did, and now it's all ruined and Pippa's . . ." I can't bring myself to say anything more, can't even think it.

"Shhh, Gemma, no time for tears. You're here to bring Pippa back, aren't you?"

I nod.

"There's no time to lose, then. Quickly, before the creature returns."

I follow her past the silver arch, deep into the garden, to the centre of those tall crystals that hold so much power.

"Put your hands on the runes."

I hesitate. I don't know why.

"Gemma," she says, green eyes narrowing. "You have to trust me or your friend will be lost forever. Do you want that on your conscience?"

I think of Pippa struggling in the icy water where she fell. Where I left her. My hands hover over the runes.

"That's it, my darling. Everything's forgotten now. Soon, we'll be together again."

I put my left hand to the rune. The vibration travels through me. I'm weakened from our other trips, and the magic starts to pull me under with its power. It's too much for me. Mother opens her hand to me. There it is, pink and alive and open. I have only to take hold of it. My arm rises. My fingers reach towards hers, till my skin vibrates with the nearness of her. Our fingers touch.

"At last . . ."

Instantly, the thing that hides in my mother's shape emerges, rising high as the stones themselves. With a great yell, the creature grabs hold of my arm. I can feel the coldness of it sliding through my arm, into my veins, creeping towards my heart. The heat leaving me. I'm no match for it.

Everything falls away. We're falling fast together, past the mountain and the churning sky, through the veil that separates the realms from the mortal world. The thing cackles in delight.

"At last . . . at last . . ."

This new magic takes me by surprise as it surges through me, joining to my will. It is overwhelming, the raw nakedness of this power. I never want to let it go. I could use it to control, to wound, to win.

The creature cackles. "Yes . . . it's intoxicating, isn't it?"

Yes, oh, yes. Is this what my mother and Circe felt, what they were afraid of losing – a power they could not have in their own world? Anger. Joy. Ecstasy. Rage. All theirs. All mine.

"We're almost there," the thing whispers.

Below me London spreads out like a lady's fan, ornate and delicate. A city I wanted to see when I lived in India. A city I still want to see. On my own.

The thing senses my discomfort. "You could rule it," it says, nearly licking my ear.

Yes, yes, yes.

No. Not really. Not attached to this creature. The power would never be mine. It would control me. *No, no, no. Let it win.* Be joined. I'm weary with choice. It makes me heavy. So heavy I could sleep forever. Let Circe win. Abandon my family and friends. Float downstream.

No.

At this the thing seems to grow weaker. You have to know yourself, know what you want. That's what Mother told me. What I want . . . what I want . . .

I want to go back. And it's coming with me. Suddenly, London shrinks to a pinpoint, out of reach. I'm pulling the thing back from the world with me, back to the mountain-top, back to the grotto and the runes.

Shrieks and howls, the hideous cries of the damned lash at me. "You tricked us!"

It expands into a ghastly, churning wall that reaches up to the sky. I've never seen anything more terrifying, and for a moment, I can't feel anything but a fear so real I'm frozen there. Those skeletal hands grip tightly around my neck, squeezing. Panicked, I fight back, using the magic to wound it as much as possible. Each time it comes back, taking more and more of my energy.

The hands come around my neck again, but I've got very little fight left.

"Yes, that's it. Give yourself over to me."

I can't think. Can barely breathe. Overhead, the sky roils grey and black. We sat here and counted clouds in the blue. Blue as my mother's silk dress. Blue as a promise. A hope. She came back for me. I can't leave her to this.

Those black, swirling orbs lean closer. The smell of rot fills my nostrils. Tears sting at my eyes. I have nothing left but that hope and a whisper.

"Mother . . . I forgive you."

The grip loosens. The thing's eyes widen, the hideous mouth opens. Its power shrinks. "No!"

I feel my strength returning. My voice grows, the words take on a life of their own. "I forgive you, Mother. I forgive you, Mary Dowd."

The creature writhes and screams. I roll from its grasp. It is losing the fight, diminishing. It howls at me in pain, but I don't stop. I repeat it like a mantra as I grab a rock and smash the first rune. It crumbles in a shower of crystal rain, and I smash the second.

"*Stop! What are you doing?*" it shrieks.

I smash the third and fourth runes. For a moment, the thing changes shape, becomes my mother, trembling and weak on a patch of strawlike grass.

"Gemma, please stop. You're killing me."

I hesitate. She turns her face to me, soft and tear-stained. "Gemma, it is me. It's Mother."

"No. My mother is dead."

I smash the fifth rune, falling back against the hard earth. With a great gasp, the thing loses its grip on my mother's spirit. It shrinks in on itself, becomes a thin column of twisting moans, until it is sucked up into the sky and all is silent.

I lie still.

"Mother?" I say. I'm not really expecting an answer, and I don't get one. She's truly gone now. I am alone. And somehow, this is as it should be.

In some ways, the mother I remember was as much an illusion as the leaves we turned into butterflies on our first trip to the realms. I'm going to have to let her go to accept the mother I'm only just discovering. One who was capable of murder, but who fought the dark to come back to help me. A scared, vain woman, and a powerful member of an ancient Order. Even now, I don't really want to know this. It would be so very easy to escape into the safety of those illusions and hold fast there. But I won't. I want to try to make room for what is real, for the things I can touch and smell, taste and feel – arms around my shoulders, tears and anger, disappointment and love, the strange way I felt when Kartik smiled at me by his tent and my friends held my hands and said, yes, we'll follow you . . .

What is most real is that I am Gemma Doyle. I am still here. And for the first time in a long time, I am very grateful for that.

❧❧❧❧

It's a lot to think about, but I'm at the river's edge now. Pippa's pale face pushes up against the ice, her loose, dark curls spreading out underneath the surface. I use a rock to break through. Water rushes up through the cracks.

To pull her out, I have to plunge my hand into that murky, forbidden river. It's warm as a bath. Inviting and calm. I'm tempted to submerge myself in that water, but not yet. I've got hold of Pippa's hand and I'm pulling with all my might, yanking her free of the weight of water, till she's on the bank. She splutters and coughs, vomits river water onto the grass.

"Pippa? Pippa!" She's so pale and cold. There are great

dark circles beneath her eyes. "Pip, I've come to take you back."

Those violet eyes open.

"Back." She turns the word over softly, glances longingly at the river, whose secrets I both want to know and want to keep far from me, for now. "What will happen to me?"

I have no more magic left for lies. "I don't know."

"Mrs. Bartleby Bumble, then?"

I say nothing. She strokes the side of my face with her cold, wet hand and I already know what she's thinking, not because it's magic but because she is my friend and I love her. "Please, Pip," I say, and stop because I'm starting to cry a little. "You have to come back. You just have to."

"Have to . . . my whole life has been that."

"It could change . . ."

She shakes her head. "I'm not a fighter. Not like you." In the winter-brittle grass, she finds a small handful of shrivelled berries, no bigger than seeds. They rest in her palm like coins.

My throat aches. "But if you eat them . . ."

"What was it Miss Moore said? There are no safe choices. Only different ones." She takes a last look at the river, and her hand flies to her mouth. There's a moment when it's so quiet that I can hear the ragged edges of my breathing. And then colour flows beneath her skin, the hair curling into ringlets, the cheeks a vibrant rose. She's radiant. All around me, the land is coming alive again in a ripple of blooms and golden leaves. On the horizon, a new pink sky is born. And the knight stands waiting, her glove in his hand.

The warm breeze has pushed the boat to our shore.

This is a time for goodbyes. But I've had too many good-byes of late, a lifetime of them to come, so I say nothing. She smiles. I return the smile. That's all that's needed. She steps into the boat and lets it carry her across the river. When she reaches the other side, the knight helps her out, into the sweet green grass. Beneath the silver arch of the garden's gate, Mother Elena's little girl, Carolina, watches too. But soon she realises this is not the one she's waiting for and she drifts out of sight, cradling her doll in her arms.

～～～～

When I return, I find Felicity perched outside Pippa's room, her back pressed up against the wall. She throws her arms around me, sobbing. Down the hall, Brigid sniffles as she places a sheet over a mirror. Ann comes from Pippa's room, red-eyed, nose running.

"Pippa . . ." She breaks down. But she doesn't have to finish it.

I already know that Pippa is gone.

～～～～

The morning we bury Pippa, it rains. A cold October rain that turns the clump of dirt in my hand into mud. When it's my turn at the graveside, the dirt slips through my fingers onto Pippa's burnished coffin, where it makes the lightest of sounds.

All morning, Spence has been a well-oiled machine of activity. Everyone doing her bit, quietly and efficiently. It's strange how deliberate people are after a death. All the indecision suddenly vanishes into clear, defined moments – changing the linens, choosing a dress or a hymn, the washing up, the muttering of prayers. All the small, simple, conscious acts of living a sudden defense against the dying we do every day.

The girls of first class have been allowed to travel the thirty miles to the Crosses' country home for the funeral. Mrs Cross has insisted that Pippa be buried with her sapphire engagement ring, which, no doubt, pains Mr Bumble greatly. He spends the entire funeral checking his pocket watch and grimacing. In deep, resonant tones, the vicar tells us of Pippa's beauty and her unfailing goodness. I don't know this flat placard of a girl. I wish I could stand and give a full account of her – the Pippa who could be vain and selfish and in love with her romantic illusions; the Pippa who was also brave and determined and generous. And even if I told them all this, it still wouldn't be a full measure of her. You can never really know someone completely. That's why it's the most terrifying thing in the world, really – taking someone on faith, hoping they'll take you on faith too. It's such a precarious balance, it's a wonder we do it at all. And yet . . .

The vicar gives a final blessing. There's nothing left but for the gravediggers to begin their work. They fix their caps on their heads and bite into the mud with their shovels, burying a girl who was my friend. All the while, I can feel him watching me from the trees. When I turn to look, he's there, his black cloak peeking out. As soon as Mrs Nightwing is occupied with comforting the Crosses, I sneak away to Kartik in his hiding spot behind a large marble seraph.

"I'm sorry," he says. It's simple and direct, with none of the nonsense about God calling home an angel too young and who are we to question his mysterious ways. Rain beats against my umbrella in a steady rhythm.

"I let her go," I say, haltingly, glad at last of the chance to make a confession of sorts. "I suppose I could have tried harder to stop her. But I didn't." Kartik lets me get it out.

Will he tell the Rakshana what I have done? Not that it matters. I've already made my decision. The realms are my responsibility now. Somewhere out there, Circe waits, and I've got an Order to put together again, mistakes to remedy, many things to master in time.

Kartik is silent. There's nothing but the constancy of the rain in answer. Finally, he turns to me. "You've got dirt on your face."

I swipe haphazardly at my cheeks with the back of my hand. He shakes his head to let me know that I haven't removed it. "Where?" I ask.

"Here." It's only his thumb brushing slowly across the lower edge of my lip, but it's as if time slows and the sweep of that thumb below my mouth takes forever. It is no spell that I know of, but it holds such magic, I can scarcely breathe. He pulls his hand away fast, aware of what he's done. But his touch lingers.

"My condolences," he mumbles, turning to go.

"Kartik?" He stops. He's soaked to the bone, black curls matted to his head. "There's no going back. You can tell them that."

He cocks his head to one side quizzically, and I realise he's not certain whether I mean there's no backing away from my powers or from his touch. I start to clarify but I realise I'm not certain either. And anyway, he's gone, running on strong legs to the safety of the cart I can see down the road.

When I join the others again, Felicity is staring at the new grave, crying in the rain. "She's really gone, isn't she?"

"Yes," I say, surprised at how sure I sound.

"What happened to me on the other side, with that thing?"

"I don't know."

We look down at the mourners, blotches of black in a sea of grey rain. Felicity can't bring herself to look at me. "Sometimes I see things, I think. Out of the corner of my eye, taunting me, and then it's gone. And dreams. Such horrible dreams. What if something terrible happened to me, Gemma? What if I am damaged?"

The rain is a cool kiss on my sleeve as I link my arm through hers. "We're all damaged somehow."

CHAPTER
THIRTY-NINE

WE'VE BEEN GIVEN THE DAY TO REST AND REFLECT, and so Mademoiselle LeFarge is surprised to see me at her classroom door. She's positively flummoxed when I hand her five neat, orderly pages of French translation.

"This is all quite good," she announces after careful inspection of my work. There's a smart new vase of flowers on her desk where the tintype of Reginald used to sit. She stacks the papers and offers them to me with her corrections noted in ink.

"Good work, Mademoiselle Doyle. I believe there's hope for you yet. *Dans chaque fin, il y a un début.*"

My translation skills aren't quite up to this one. "In the end, also, is a debutante?"

Mademoiselle LeFarge shakes her head. "In every end, there is also a beginning."

<hr style="width:20%" />

The rain has stopped but it has ushered in a bracing autumn wind that pinkens my cheeks till they look freshly slapped.

October blooms in bursts of red and gold. Soon the trees will lose their cover and the world will be laid bare.

Miles from here, Pippa lies in her coffin, fading into memory, a bit of Spence legend to be whispered late at night. *Did you hear about the girl who died in that very room down the hall?* I do not know if she regrets her choice. I like to think of her as I saw her last, walking confidently towards something I shan't see, I hope, for a very long time.

In a world beyond this one, that river goes on singing sweetly, enchanting us with what we want to hear, shaping what we need to see in order to keep going. In those waters, all disappointments are forgotten, our mistakes forgiven. Gazing into them, we see a strong father. A loving mother. Warm rooms where we are sheltered, adored, wanted. And the uncertainty of our futures is nothing more than the fog of breath on a windowpane.

⌇⌇⌇⌇⌇

The ground is still wet. The heels of my boots sink in, making it a rough walk, but I see the wagons of the Gypsy camp just through the trees ahead. I'm on my way to deliver a gift. Or a bribe. I'm not entirely certain of my motives just yet. The point is that I am on my way.

The package is wrapped in today's newspaper. I leave it outside Kartik's tent and slip back into the trees to wait. He comes soon enough, carrying some squab on a string. He notices the package and spins around to see who might have left it. Seeing no one, he opens it and finds my father's gleaming cricket bat. I don't know if he'll accept it or find it insulting.

His hands run along the wood in a caress. A hint of a smile tugs at the corners of what I have come to realise is a most beautiful mouth. He picks a crab apple from the ground and tosses it into the air. The bat makes a gratifying crack as it sends the apple soaring, flying high on a lucky combination of direction and possibility. Kartik lets out a small yelp of satisfaction, and swats at the sky. I sit and watch him hit the apples, again and again, until I'm left with two thoughts: *Cricket is a wonderfully forgiving game*, and *Next time, I must get him a ball*.

Forgiveness. The frail beauty of the word takes root in me as I make my way back through the woods, past the caves and the ravine, where the earth has accepted the flesh of the deer, leaving nothing but a bone or two, peeking above Kartik's makeshift grave, to prove that any of this ever happened. Soon, they'll be gone too.

But forgiveness . . . I'll hold on to that fragile slice of hope and keep it close, remembering that in each of us lie good and bad, light and dark, art and pain, choice and regret, cruelty and sacrifice. We're each of us our own *chiaroscuro*, our own bit of illusion fighting to emerge into something solid, something real. We've got to forgive ourselves that. I must remember to forgive myself. Because there's an awful lot of grey to work with. No one can live in the light all the time.

The wind shifts, bringing with it the smell of roses, strong and sweet. Across the ravine, I see her in the dry crackle of leaves. A deer. She spies me and bolts through the trees. I run after her, not really giving chase. I'm running because I can, because I must.

Because I want to see how far I can go before I have to stop.

ABOUT THE AUTHOR

LIBBA BRAY is the author of five and a half plays, a few short stories and essays, and lots of things that, in her words, "should never see the light of day". She has worked as a waitress, a nanny, a burrito roller, a publishing plebe, and an advertising copywriter. Raised in Texas on a steady diet of British humour, underground bands, suburban dysfunction, and bad TV, she somehow managed to escape with only a few seriously deranged haircuts. She lives in Brooklyn, New York, with her husband and son.